PRAISE
CLIVE BARKER

BOOKS BY CLIVE BARKER

CLIVE BARKER

CABAL

POCKET BOOKS
NEW YORK LONDON TORONTO SYDNEY

Some of the stories in this volume have been previously published in Great Britain by Sphere Books, Ltd.

 POCKET BOOKS, a division of Simon and Schuster, Inc. 1230 Avenue of the Americas, New York, NY 10020

ISBN: 0-7434-1732-1

First Pocket Books trade paperback printing January 2001

10 9 8 7 6 5

POCKET and colophon are registered trademarks of Simon & Schuster, Inc.

Cover design by Brigid Pearson
Front cover photo by Pinakothek Museum, Munich/SuperStock

Printed in the U.S.A.

FOR ANNIE

contents

CABAL

PART ONE

LOCO

"I was born alive.
Isn't that punishment enough?"
—MARY HENDRICKSON,
AT HER TRIAL FOR PATRICIDE

1
THE TRUTH

Of all the rash and midnight promises made in the name of love, none, Boone now knew, was more certain to be broken than *"I'll never leave you."*

What time didn't steal from under your nose, circumstance did. It was useless to hope otherwise, useless to dream that the world somehow meant you good. Everything of value, everything you clung to for your sanity, would rot or be snatched in the long run, and the abyss would gape beneath you, as it gaped for Boone now, and suddenly, without so much as a breath of explanation, you were gone. Gone to hell or worse, professions of love and all.

His outlook hadn't always been so pessimistic. There'd been a time—not all that long ago—when he'd felt the burden of his mental anguish lifting. There'd been fewer psychotic episodes, fewer days when he felt like slitting his wrists rather than enduring the hours till his next medication. There'd seemed to be a chance for happiness.

It was that prospect that had won the declaration of love from him, that *"I'll never leave you,"* whispered in Lori's ear as they lay in the narrow bed he'd never dared hope would hold two. The words had not come in the throes of high passion. Their love life, like so much else between them, was fraught with problems. But where other women had given up on him, unforgiving of his failure, she'd persevered, told him there was plenty of time to get it right, all the time in the world. I'm with you for as long as you want me to be, her patience had seemed to say.

Nobody had ever offered such a commitment, and he wanted to

offer one in return. Those words—"I'll never leave you"—were it.

The memory of them, and of her skin almost luminous in the murk of his room, and of the sound of her breathing when she finally fell asleep beside him—all of it still had the power to catch his heart, and squeeze it till it hurt.

He longed to be free of both the memory and the words, now that circumstance had taken away any hope of their fulfillment. But they wouldn't be forgotten. They lingered on to torment him with his frailty. His meager comfort was that *she*—knowing what she must now know about him—would be working to erase her memory; and that with time she'd succeed. He only hoped she'd understand his ignorance of himself when he'd voiced that promise. He'd never have risked this pain if he'd doubted health was finally within his grasp.

Dream on!

Decker had brought an abrupt end to those delusions, the day he'd locked the office door, drawn the blinds on the Alberta spring sunshine, and said, in a voice barely louder than a whisper:

"Boone, I think we're in terrible trouble, you and I."

He was trembling, Boone saw, a fact not easily concealed in a body so big. Decker had the physique of a man who sweated out the day's angst in a gym. Even his tailored suits, always charcoal, couldn't tame his bulk. It had made Boone edgy at the start of their work together; he'd felt intimidated by the doctor's physical and mental authority. Now it was the fallibility of that strength he feared. Decker was a Rock; he was Reason; he was Calm. This anxiety ran counter to all he knew about the man.

"What's wrong?" Boone asked.

"Sit, will you? Sit and I'll tell you."

Boone did as he was told. In this office, Decker was lord. The doctor leaned back in the leather chair and inhaled through his nose, his mouth sealed in a downward curve.

"Tell me . . ." Boone said.

"Where to start."

"Anywhere."

"I thought you were getting better," Decker said, "I really did. We *both* did."

"I still am," Boone said.

Decker made a small shake of his head. He was a man of considerable intellect, but little of it showed on his tightly packed features, except perhaps in his eyes, which at the moment were not watching the patient, but were fixed on the table between them.

"You've started to talk in your sessions," Decker said, "about crimes you think you've committed. Do you remember any of that?"

"You know I don't." The trances Decker put him in were too profound. "I only remember when you play the tape back."

"I won't be playing any of these," Decker said. "I erased them."

"Why?"

"Because . . . I'm afraid, Boone. For you." He paused. "Maybe for both of us."

The crack in the Rock was opening and there was nothing Decker could do to conceal it.

"What *are* these crimes?" Boone asked, his words tentative.

"Murders. You talk about them obsessively. At first I thought they were dream crimes. You always had a violent streak in you."

"And now?"

"Now I'm afraid you may have actually committed them."

There was a long silence while Boone studied Decker, more in puzzlement than anger. The blinds had not been pulled all the way down. A slice of sunlight fell across him, and onto the table between them. On the glass surface was a bottle of still water, two tumblers, and a large envelope. Decker leaned forward and picked it up.

"What I'm doing now is probably a crime in itself," he told Boone. "Patient confidentiality is one thing, protecting a killer is another. But part of me is still hoping to God it isn't true. I want to believe I've succeeded. *We've* succeeded. Together. I want to believe you're well."

"I *am* well."

In lieu of reply Decker tore open the envelope.

"I'd like you to look at these for me," he said, sliding his hand inside and bringing out a sheaf of photographs to meet the light.

"I warn you, they're not pleasant."

He laid them on his reflection, turned for Boone's perusal. His warning had been well advised. The picture on the top of the pile was like a physical assault. Faced with it a fear rose in him he'd not felt since being in Decker's care: that the image might *possess* him. He'd built walls against that superstition, brick by brick, but they shook now, and threatened to fall.

"It's just a picture."

"That's right," Decker replied, "it's just a picture. What do you see?"

"A dead man."

"A murdered man."

"Yes. A murdered man."

Not simply murdered: butchered. The life slashed from him in a fury of slices and stabs, his blood flung on the blade that had taken out his neck, taken off his face, onto the wall behind him. He wore only his shorts, so the wounds on his body could be easily counted, despite the blood. Boone did just that now, to keep the horror from overcoming him. Even here, in this room where the doctor had chiseled another self from the block of his patient's condition, Boone had never choked on terror as he choked now. He tasted his breakfast in the back of his throat, or the meal the night before, rising from his bowels against nature. Shit in his mouth, like the dirt of his deed.

Count the wounds, he told himself, pretend they're beads on an abacus. Three, four, five in the abdomen and chest: one in particular ragged, more like a tear than a wound, gaping so wide the man's innards poked out. On the shoulder, two more. And then the face, unmade with cuts. So many their numbers could not be calculated, even by the most detached of observers. They left the victim beyond recognition: eyes dug out, lips slit off, nose in ribbons.

"Enough?" Decker said, as if the question needed asking.

"Yes."

"There's a lot more to see."

He uncovered the second, laying the first beside the pile. This one was of a woman, sprawled on a sofa, her upper and lower body twisted in a fashion life would have forbidden. Though she was presumably not a relation of the first victim, the butcher had created a vile resemblance. Here was the same liplessness, the same eyelessness. Born from different parents, they were siblings in death, destroyed by the same hand.

And am I their father? Boone found himself thinking.

"No," was his gut's response. *"I didn't do this."*

But two things prevented him from voicing his denial. First, he knew that Decker would not be endangering his patient's equilibrium this way unless he had good reason to do so. Second, denial was valueless when both of them knew how easily Boone's mind had deceived itself in the past. If he was responsible for these atrocities, there was no certainty he'd know it.

Instead he kept his silence, not daring to look up at Decker for fear he'd see the Rock shattered.

"Another?" Decker said.

"If we must."

"We must."

He uncovered a third photograph, and a fourth, laying the pictures out on the table like cards at a tarot reading, except that every one was Death. In the kitchen, lying at the open door of the refrigerator. In the bedroom, beside the lamp and the alarm. At the top of the stairs, at the window. The victims were of every age and color: men, women, and children. Whatever fiend was responsible, he cared to make no distinction. He simply erased life wherever he found it. Not quickly, not efficiently. The rooms in which these people had died bore plain testament to how the killer, in his humor, had toyed with them. Furniture had been overturned as they stumbled to avoid the coup de grace, blood prints left on walls and paintwork. One had lost his fingers to the blade, snatching at it perhaps; most had lost their eyes. But none had escaped, however brave their resistance. They'd all fallen at last, tangled in their underwear, or seeking refuge behind a curtain. Fallen sobbing, fallen retching.

There were eleven photographs in all. Every one was different, but also the same: all pictures of a madness performed, taken with the actor already departed.

God almighty, was *he* that man?

Not having an answer for himself, he asked the question of the Rock, speaking without looking up from the shining cards.

"Did I do this?" he said.

He heard Decker sigh, but there was no answer forthcoming, so he chanced a glance at his accuser. As the photographs had been laid out before him, he'd felt the man's scrutiny like a crawling ache in his scalp. But now he once more found that gaze averted.

"Please tell me," he said. "Did I do this?"

Decker wiped the moist purses of skin beneath his gray eyes. He was not trembling any longer.

"I hope not," he said.

The response seemed ludicrously mild. This was not some minor infringement of the law they were debating. It was death times eleven, and how many more might there be, out of sight, out of mind?

"Tell me what I talked about," Boone said. "Tell me the words—"

"It was ramblings mostly."

"So what makes you think I'm responsible? You must have reasons."

"It took time," Decker said, "for me to piece the whole thing together." He looked down at the mortuary on the table, aligning a photograph that was a little askew with his middle finger.

"I have to make a quarterly report on our progress. You know that. So I play all the tapes of our previous sessions sequentially, to get some sense of how we're doing . . ." He spoke slowly, wearily. ". . . and I noticed the same phrases coming up in your responses. Buried most of the time, in other material, but *there*. It was as if you were confessing to something, but something so abhorrent to you even in a trance state you couldn't quite bring yourself to say it. Instead it was coming out in this . . . *code*."

Boone knew codes. He'd heard them everywhere during the bad times. Messages from the imagined enemy in the noise between stations on the radio, or in the murmur of traffic before dawn. That he might have learned the art himself came as no surprise.

"I made a few casual inquiries," Decker continued, "among police officers I've treated. Nothing specific. And they told me about the killings. I'd heard some of the details, of course, from the press. Seems they've been going on for two and a half years. Several here in Calgary, the rest within an hour's drive. The work of one man."

"Me."

"I don't know," Decker said, finally looking up at Boone. "If I was certain, I'd have reported it all—"

"But you're not."

"I don't want to believe this any more than you do. It doesn't cover me in glory if this turns out to be true." There was anger in him, not well concealed. "That's why I waited. Hoping you'd be with me when the next one happened."

"You mean some of these people died while you knew?"

"Yes," Decker said flatly.

"Jesus!"

The thought propelled Boone from the chair, his leg catching the table. The murder scenes flew.

"Keep your voice down," Decker demanded.

"People died, and you *waited*?"

"I took that risk for *you*, Boone. You'll respect that."

Boone turned from the man. There was a chill of sweat on his spine.

"Sit down," said Decker. "Please sit down and tell me what these photographs mean to you."

Involuntarily Boone had put his hand over the lower half of his face. He knew from Decker's instruction what that particular piece of body language signified. His mind was using his body to muffle some disclosure, or to silence it completely.

"Boone, I need answers."

"They mean nothing," Boone said, not turning.

"At all?"

"At all."

"Look at them again."

"No," Boone insisted, "I can't."

He heard the doctor inhale, and half expected a demand that he face the horrors afresh. But instead Decker's tone was placatory.

"It's all right, Aaron," he said, "it's all right. I'll put them away."

Boone pressed the heels of his hands against his closed eyes. His sockets were hot and wet.

"They're gone, Aaron," Decker said.

"No, they're not."

They were with him still, perfectly remembered. Eleven rooms and eleven bodies, fixed in his mind's eye. The wall Decker had taken five years to build had been brought down in as many minutes, and by its architect. Boone was at the mercy of his madness again. He heard it whine in his head, coming from eleven slit windpipes, from eleven punctured bellies. Breath and bowel gas, singing the old mad songs.

Why had his defenses tumbled so easily after so much labor? His eyes knew the answer, spilling tears to admit what his tongue couldn't. He was guilty. Why else? Hands he was even now wiping dry on his trousers had tortured and slaughtered. If he pretended otherwise he'd only tempt them to further crime. Better that he confessed, though he remembered nothing, than offer them another unguarded moment.

He turned and faced Decker. The photographs had been gathered up and laid facedown on the table.

"You remember something?" the doctor said, reading the change on Boone's face.

"Yes," he replied.

"What?"

"I did it," Boone said simply, "I did it all."

2

ACADEMY

I

Decker was the most benign prosecutor any accused man could ask for. The hours he spent with Boone after that first day were filled with carefully plied questions as—murder by murder—they examined together the evidence for Boone's secret life. Despite the patient's insistence that the crimes were his, Decker counseled caution. Admissions of culpability were not hard evidence. They had to be certain that confession wasn't simply Boone's self-destructive tendencies at work, admitting to the crime out of hunger for the punishment.

Boone was in no position to argue. Decker knew him better than he knew himself. Nor had he forgotten Decker's observation that if the worst was proved true, the doctor's reputation as a healer would be thrown to the dogs: they could neither of them afford to be wrong. The only way to be sure was to run through the details of the killings—dates, names, and locations—in the hope that Boone would be prompted into remembering. Or else that they'd discover a killing that had occurred when he was indisputably in the company of others.

The only part of the process Boone balked at was reexamining the photographs. He resisted Decker's gentle pressure for forty-eight hours, only conceding when Decker rounded on him, accusing him of cowardice and deceit. Was all this just a game, Decker demanded, an exercise in self-mortification that would end with them both none the wiser?

12

If so, Boone could get the hell out of his office now and bleed on somebody else's time.

Boone agreed to study the photographs.

There was nothing in them that jogged his memory. Much of the detail of the rooms had been washed out by the flash of the camera; what remained was commonplace. The only sight that might have won a response from him—the faces of the victims—had been hacked beyond recognition; the most expert of morticians would not be able to piece those shattered facades together again. So it was all down to the petty details of where Boone had been on this night or that, with whom, doing what. He had never kept a diary, so verifying the facts was difficult, but most of the time—barring the hours he spent with Lori or Decker, none of which seemed to coincide with murder nights—he was alone, and without alibi. By the end of the fourth day the case against him began to look very persuasive.

"Enough," he told Decker, "we've done enough."

"I'd like to go over it all one more time."

"What's the use?" Boone said. "I want to get it all finished with."

In the past days—and nights—many of the old symptoms, the signs of the sickness he thought he'd been so close to throwing off forever, had returned. He could sleep for no more than minutes at a time before appalling visions threw him into befuddled wakefulness; he couldn't eat properly; he was trembling from his gut outward, every minute of the day. He wanted an end to this, wanted to spill the story and to be punished.

"Give me a little more time," Decker said. "If we go to the police now they'll take you out of my hands. They probably won't even allow me access to you. You'll be alone."

"I already am," Boone replied. Since he'd first seen the photographs, he'd cut himself off from every contact, even with Lori, fearing his capacity to do harm.

"I'm a monster," he said. "We both of us know that. We've got all the evidence we need."

"It's not just a question of evidence."

"What, then?"

Decker leaned against the window frame, his bulk a burden to him of late.

"I don't understand you, Boone," he said.

Boone's gaze moved off from man to sky. There was a wind from the southeast today; scraps of cloud hurried before it. A good life, Boone thought, to be up there, lighter than air. Here everything was heavy, flesh and guilt cracking your spine.

"I've spent five years trying to understand your illness, hoping I could cure it. And I thought I was succeeding. Thought there was a chance it would all come clear . . ."

He fell silent, in the pit of his failure. Boone was not so immersed in his own agonies he couldn't see how profoundly the man suffered. But he could do nothing to mitigate that hurt. He just watched the clouds pass, up there in the light, and knew there were only dark times ahead.

"When the police take you . . ." Decker murmured, "it won't just be you who's alone, Boone, I'll be alone too. You'll be somebody else's patient, some criminal psychologist. I won't have access to you any longer. That's why I'm, asking . . . give me a little more time. Let me understand as much as I can before it's over between us."

He's talking like a lover, Boone vaguely thought, like what's between us is his life.

"I know you're in pain," Decker went on, "so I've got medication for you. Pills, to keep the worst of it at bay. Just till we've finished—"

"I don't trust myself," Boone said. "I could hurt somebody."

"You won't," Decker replied, with welcome certainty. "The drugs'll keep you subdued through the night. The rest of the time you'll be with me. You'll be safe with me."

"How much longer do you want?"

"A few days at the most. That's not so much to ask, is it? I need to know why we failed."

The thought of retreading that bloodied ground was abhorrent, but there was a debt here to be paid. With Decker's help he'd had a glimpse of new possibilities; he owed the doctor the chance to snatch something from the ruins of that vision.

"Make it quick," he said.

"Thank you," Decker said. "This means a lot to me."

"And I'll need the pills."

2

The pills he had. Decker made sure of that. Pills so strong he wasn't sure he could have named himself correctly once he'd taken them. Pills that made sleep easy, and waking a visit to a half-life he was happy to escape again. Pills that, within twenty-four hours, he was addicted to.

Decker's word was good. When he asked for more, they were supplied, and under their soporific influence they went back to the business of the evidence, as the doctor went over, and over again, the details of Boone's crimes in the hope of comprehending them. But nothing came clear. All Boone's increasingly passive mind could recover from these sessions were slurred images of doors he'd slipped through and stairs he'd climbed in the performance of murder. He was less and less aware of Decker, still fighting to salvage something of worth from his patient's closed mind. All Boone knew now was sleep and guilt and the hope, increasingly cherished, of an end to both.

Only Lori, or rather memories of her, penetrated the drugs' regime. He could hear her voice sometimes in his inner ear, clear as a bell, repeating words she'd spoken to him in some casual conversation, which he was dredging up from the past. There was nothing of consequence in these phrases; they were perhaps associated with a look he'd treasured, or a touch. Now he could remember neither look nor touch—the drugs had removed so much of his capacity to *imagine*. All he was left with were these dislocated lines, distressing him not simply because they were spoken as if by somebody at his shoulder, but because they had no context that he could recall. And worse than either, their sound reminded him of the woman he'd loved and would not see again, unless across a courtroom. A woman to whom he had made a promise he'd broken within weeks of his making it. In his wretchedness, his thoughts barely cogent, that broken promise was as monstrous as the crimes in the photographs. It fitted him for hell.

Or death. Better death. He was not entirely sure how long had passed since he'd done the deal with Decker, exchanging this stupor for a few more days of investigation, but he was certain he had kept his side of the bargain. He was talked out. There was nothing left to say or hear. All that remained was to take himself to the law and confess his crimes, or to do what the state no longer had the power to do, and kill the monster.

He didn't dare alert Decker to this plan; he knew the doctor would do all in his power to prevent his patient's suicide. So he went on playing the quiescent subject one day more. Then, promising Decker he'd be at the office the following morning, he returned home and prepared to kill himself.

There was another letter from Lori awaiting him, the fourth since he'd absented himself, demanding to know what was wrong. He read it as best his befuddled thoughts would allow, and attempted a reply, but couldn't make sense of the words he was trying to write. Instead, pocketing the appeal she'd sent to him, he went out into the dusk to look for death.

3

The truck he threw himself in front of was unkind. It knocked the breath from him but not the life. Bruised and bleeding from scrapes and cuts, he was scooped up and taken to the hospital. Later, he'd come to understand how all of this was in the scheme of things, and that he'd been denied his death beneath the truck wheels for a purpose. but sitting in the hospital, waiting in a white room till people worse off than he had been attended to, all he could do was curse his bad fortune. Other lives he could take with terrible ease; his own resisted him. Even in this he was divided against himself.

But that room—though he didn't' know it when he was ushered in— held a promise its plain walls belied. In it he'd hear a name that would with time make a new man of him. At its call he'd go like the monster he was, by night, and meet with the miraculous.

That name was Midian.

It and he had much in common, not least that they shared the power to make promises. But while his avowals of eternal love had proved hollow in a matter of weeks, Midian made promises—midnight, like his own, deepest midnight—that even death could not break.

3
THE RHAPSODIST

In the years of his illness, in and out of mental wards, and hospices, Boone had met very few fellow sufferers who didn't cleave to some talisman, some object or keepsake to stand guard at the gates of their heads and hearts. He'd learned quickly not to despise such charms. *Whatever gets you through the night* was an axiom he understood from hard experience. Most of these safeguards against chaos were personal to those who wielded them. Trinkets, keys, books, and photographs: mementos of good times treasured as defense against bad. But some belonged to the collective mind. They were words he would hear more than once: nonsense rhymes whose rhythms kept the pain at bay, names of gods.

Among them, Midian.

He'd heard the name of that place spoken maybe half a dozen times by people he'd met on the way through, usually those whose strength was all burned up. When they called on Midian it was as a place of refuge, a place to be carried away to. And more: a place where whatever sins they'd committed—real or imagined—would be forgiven them. Boone didn't know the origins of this mythology nor had he ever been interested enough to inquire. He had not been in need of forgiveness, or so he thought. Now he knew better. He had plenty to seek cleansing of, obscenities his mind had kept from him until Decker had brought them to light, which no agency he knew could lift from him. He had joined another class of creature.

Midian called.

Locked up in his misery, he'd not been aware that someone else now shared the white room with him until he heard the rasping voice.

"Midian . . ."

He thought at first it was another voice from the past, like Lori's. But when it came again it was not at his shoulder, as hers had been, but from across the room. He opened his eyes, the left lid gummy with blood from a cut on his temple, and looked toward the speaker. Another of the night's walking wounded, apparently, brought in for mending and left to fend for himself until some patchwork could be done. He was sitting in the corner of the room farthest from the door, on which his wild eyes were fixed as though at any moment his savior would step into view. It was virtually impossible to guess anything of his age or true appearance: dirt and caked blood concealed both. I must look as bad or worse, Boone thought. He didn't much mind; people were always staring at him. In their present state he and the man in the corner were the kind folks crossed the street to avoid.

But whereas he, in his jeans and his scuffed boots and black T-shirt, was just another nobody, there were some signs about the other man that marked him out. The long coat he wore had a monkish severity to it; his gray hair pulled back tight on his scalp hung to the middle of his back in a plaited ponytail. There was jewelry at his neck, almost hidden by his high collar, and on his thumbs two artificial nails that looked to be silver, curled into hooks.

Finally, there was that name, rising from the man again.

". . . Will you take me," he asked softly, "take me to Midian?"

His eyes had not left the door for an instant. It seemed he was oblivious to Boone, until without warning, he turned his wounded head and spat across the room. The blood-marbled phlegm hit the floor at Boone's feet.

"Get the fuck out of here," he said. "You're keeping them from me. They won't come while you're here."

Boone was too weary to argue and too bruised to get up. He let the man rant.

"Get out!" he said again. "They won't show themselves to the likes of you. Don't you see that?"

Boone put his head back and tried to keep the man's pain from invading him.

"Shit!" the other said. "I've missed them. *I've missed them!*"

He stood up and crossed to the window. Outside there was solid darkness.

"They passed by," he murmured, suddenly plaintive. The next moment he was a yard from Boone, grinning through the dirt.

"Got anything for the pain?" he wanted to know.

"The nurse gave me something," Boone replied.

The man spat again; not at Boone this time, but at the floor.

"*Drink*, man," he said, "have you got a drink?"

"No."

The grin evaporated instantly, and the face began to crumple up as tears overtook him. He turned away from Boone, sobbing, his litany begun again.

"Why won't they take me? Why won't they come for me?"

"Maybe they'll come later," Boone said, "when I've gone."

The man looked back at him.

"What do you know?" he said.

Very little was the answer, but Boone kept that fact to himself. There were enough fragments of Midian's mythology in his head to have him eager for more. Wasn't it a place where those who had run out of refuges could find a home? And wasn't that *his* condition now? He had no source of comfort left. Not Decker, not Lori, not even Death. Even though Midian was just another talisman, he wanted to hear its story recited.

"Tell me," he said.

"I asked you what you know," the other man replied, catching the flesh beneath his unshaven chin with the hook of his left hand.

"I know it takes away the pain," Boone replied.

"And?"

"I know it turns nobody away."

"Not true," came the response.

"No?"

"If it turned nobody away you think I wouldn't be there already? You think it wouldn't be the biggest city on earth? Of course it turns people away...."

The man's tear-brightened eyes were fixed on Boone. *Does he realize I know nothing?* Boone wondered. It seemed not. The man talked on, content to debate the secret. Or more particularly, his fear of it.

"I don't go because I may not be worthy," he said. "And they don't forgive that easily. They don't forgive at all. You know what they do . . . to those who aren't worthy?"

Boone was less interested in Midian's rites of passage than in the man's certainty that it existed at all. He didn't speak of Midian as a lunatic's Shangri-la, but as a place to be found, and entered, and made peace with.

"Do you know how to get there?" he asked.

The man looked away. As he broke eye contact a surge of panic rose in Boone: the bastard was going to keep the rest of the story to himself.

"I need to know," Boone said.

The other man looked up again.

"I can see that," he said, and there was a twist in his voice that suggested the spectacle of Boone's despair entertained him. "It's northwest of Athabasca," the man replied.

"Yes?"

"That's what I heard."

"That's empty country," Boone said. "You could wander forever, 'less you've got a map."

"Midian's on no map," the man said. "You look east of Peace River, near Shere Neck, north of Dwyer."

There was no taint of doubt in this recitation of directions. He believed in Midian's existence as much, perhaps more, than the four walls he was bound by.

"What's your name?" Boone asked.

The question seemed to flummox him. It had been a long time since anyone had cared to ask him his name.

"Narcisse," he said finally. "You?"

"Aaron Boone. Nobody ever calls me Aaron. Only Boone."

"Aaron," said the other, "where d'you hear about Midian?"

"Same place you did," Boone said. "Same place anyone hears. From others. People in pain."

"Monsters," said Narcisse.

Boone hadn't thought of them as such, but perhaps to dispassionate eyes they were, the ranters and the weepers, unable to keep their nightmares under lock and key.

"They're the only ones welcome in Midian," Narcisse explained; "if you're not a beast, you're a victim. That's true, isn't it? You can only be one or the other. That's why I don't dare go unescorted. I wait for friends to come for me."

"People who went already?"

"That's right," Narcisse said. "Some of them alive. Some of them who died, and went after."

Boone wasn't certain he was hearing this story correctly.

"Went *after?*" he said.

"Don't you have anything for the pain, man?" Narcisse said, his tone veering again, this time to the wheedling.

"I've got some pills," Boone said, remembering Decker's supply. "Do you want those?"

"Anything you got."

Boone was content to be relieved of them. They'd kept his head in chains, driving him to the point where he didn't care if he lived or died. Now he did. He had a place to go, where he might find someone at last who understood the horrors he was enduring. He would not need the pills to get to Midian. He'd need strength, and the will to be forgiven. The latter he had. The former his wounded body would have to find.

"Where are they?" said Narcisse, appetite igniting his features.

Boone's leather jacket had been peeled from his back when he'd first been admitted, for a cursory examination of the damage he'd done himself. It hung on the back of a chair, a twice discarded skin. He plunged his hand into the inside pocket but found to his shock that the familiar bottle was not there.

"Someone's been through my jacket."

He rummaged through the rest of the pockets. All of them were empty. Lori's notes, his wallet, the pills: all gone. It took him seconds only to realize why they'd want evidence of who he was and the consequence of that. He'd attempted suicide; no doubt they thought him prepared to do the same again. In his wallet was Decker's address. The doctor was probably already on his way to collect his erring patient and deliver him to the police. Once in the hands of the law he'd never see Midian.

"You said there were *pills!*" Narcisse yelled.

"They've been taken!"

Narcisse snatched the jacket from Boone's hands, and began to tear at it.

"*Where?*" he yelled. "*Where?*"

His face was once more crumpling up as he realized he was not going to get a fix of peace. He dropped the jacket and backed away from Boone, his tears beginning again, but sliding down his face to meet a broad smile.

"I know what you're doing," he said, pointing at Boone. Laughter and sobs were coming in equal measure. "Midian sent you. To see if I'm worthy. You came to see if I was one of you or not!"

He offered Boone no chance to contradict, his elation spiraling into hysteria.

"I'm sitting here praying for someone to come, *begging,* and you're here all the time, watching me shit myself. Watching me *shit!*"

He laughed hard. Then, deadly serious, he said, "I never doubted. Never once. I always knew somebody'd come. But I was expecting a face I recognized. Marvin maybe. I should have known they'd send someone new. Stands to reason. And you *saw,* right? You *heard.* I'm not ashamed. They never made me ashamed. You ask anyone. They tried. Over and over. They got in my fucking head and tried to take me apart, tried to take the Wild Ones out of me. But I held on. I knew you'd come sooner or later, and I wanted to be ready. That's why I wear these."

He thrust his thumbs up in front of his face. "So I could show you."

He turned his head right and left.

"Want to see?" he said.

He needed no reply. His hands were already up to either side of his face, the hooks touching the skin at the base of each ear. Boone watched, words of denial or appeal redundant. This was a moment Narcisse had rehearsed countless times; he was not about to be denied it. There was no sound as the hooks, razor sharp, slit his skin, but blood began to flow instantly, down his neck and arms. The expression on his face didn't change, it merely intensified: a mask in which comic muse and tragic were united. Then, fingers spread to either side of his face, he steadily drew the razor hooks down the line of his jaw. He had a surgeon's precision. The wounds opened with perfect symmetry, until the twin hooks met at his chin.

Only then did he drop one hand to his side, blood dripping from hook and wrist, the other moving across his face to seek the flap of skin his work had opened.

"You want to see," he said again.

Boone murmured:

"Don't."

It went unheard. With a sharp, upward jerk, Narcisse detached the mask of skin from the muscle beneath, and began to tear, uncovering his true face.

From behind him, Boone heard somebody scream. The door had been opened and one of the nursing staff stood on the threshold. He saw from the corner of his eye: her face whiter than her uniform, her mouth open wide, and beyond her the corridor, and freedom. But he couldn't bring himself to look away from Narcisse, not while the blood filling the air between them kept the revelation from view. He wanted to see the man's secret face: the Wild One beneath the skin that made him fit for Midian's ease. The red rain was dispersing. The air began to clear. He saw the face now, a little, but couldn't make sense of its complexity. Was that a beast's anatomy that knotted up and snarled in front of him, or human tissue agonized by self-mutilation? A moment more, and he'd know—

Then, someone had hold of him, seizing his arms and dragging him toward the door. He glimpsed Narcisse raising the weapons of his hands to keep his saviors at bay, then the uniforms were upon him, and he was eclipsed. In the rush of the moment Boone took his chance. He pushed the nurse from him, snatched up his leather jacket, and ran for the unguarded door. His bruised body was not prepared for violent action. He stumbled, nausea and darting pains in his bruised limbs vying for the honor of bringing him to his knees, but the sight of Narcisse surrounded and tethered was enough to give him strength. He was away down the hall before anyone had a chance to come after him.

As he headed for the door to the night, he heard Narcisse's voice raised in protest, a howl of rage that was pitifully human.

4

ΠECROPOLIS

I

Though the distance from Calgary to Athabasca was little more than three hundred miles, the journey took a traveler to the borders of another world. North of here the highways were few, the inhabitants fewer still. The rich prairie lands of the province steadily gave way to forest, marshland, and wilderness. It also marked the limits of Boone's experience. A short stint as a truck driver, in his early twenties, had taken him as far as Bonnyville to the southeast, Barrhead to the southwest, and Athabasca itself. But the territory beyond was unknown to him except as names on a map. Or more correctly, as an absence of names. There were great stretches of land here that were dotted only with small farming settlements, one of which bore the name Narcisse had used: Shere Neck.

The map that carried this information he found, along with enough change to buy himself a bottle of brandy, in five minutes of theft on the outskirts of Calgary. He rifled three vehicles left in an underground parking facility and was away, mapped and moneyed, before the source of the car alarms had been traced by security.

The rain washed his face; his bloodied T-shirt he dumped, happy to have his beloved jacket next to his skin. Then he found himself a ride to Edmonton, and another that took him through Athabasca to High Prairie. It was easy.

2

Easy? To go in search of a place he'd only heard rumor of among lunatics? Perhaps not easy. But it was necessary, even inevitable. From the moment the truck he'd chosen to die beneath had cast him aside, this journey had been beckoning. Perhaps from long before that, only he'd never seen the invitation. The sense he had of its *rightness* might almost have made a fatalist of him. If Midian existed and was willing to embrace him, then he was traveling to a place where he would finally find some self-comprehension and peace. If not—if it existed only as a talisman for the frightened and the lost—then that too was *right*, and he would meet whatever extinction awaited him, searching for a nowhere. Better that than the pills, better that than Decker's fruitless pursuit of rhymes and reasons.

The doctor's quest to root out the monster in Boone had been bound to fail. That much was clear as the skies overhead. Boone the man and Boone the monster could not be divided. They were one; they traveled the same road in the same mind and body. And whatever lay at the end of that road, death or glory, would be the fate of both.

3

East of Peace River, Narcisse had said, near the town of Shere Neck, north of Dwyer.

He had to sleep rough in High Prairie; the following morning he found a ride to Peace River. The driver was in her late fifties, proud of the region she'd known since childhood and happy to give him a quick geography lesson. He made no mention of Midian, but Dwyer and Shere Neck she knew—the latter a town of five thousand souls away to the east of Highway 67. He'd have saved himself a good two hundred miles if he'd not traveled as far as High Prairie, he was told, but taken himself north earlier. No matter, she said; she knew a place in Peace River where the farmers stopped off to eat before heading back to their homesteads. He'd find a ride there, to take him where he wanted to go.

Got people there? she asked. He said he had.

It was close to dusk by the time the last of his rides dropped him a mile or so shy of Dwyer. He watched the truck take a gravel road off into the deepening blue, then began to walk the short distance to the town. A night of sleeping rough and traveling in farm vehicles on roads that had seen better days had taken its toll on his already battered system. It took him an hour to come within sight of the outskirts of Dwyer, by which time night had fallen completely. Fate was once again on his side. Without the darkness he might not have seen the lights flashing ahead, not in welcome but in warning.

The police were here before him; three or four cars, he judged. It was possible they were in pursuit of someone else entirely but he doubted it. More likely Narcisse, lost to himself, had told the law what he'd told Boone. In which case this was a reception committee. They were probably already searching for him, house to house. And if here, in Shere Neck too. He was expected.

Thankful for the cover of the night, he made his way off the road and into the middle of a rapeseed field, where he could lie and think through his next move. There was certainly no wisdom in trying to go into Dwyer. Better he set off for Midian now, putting his hunger and weariness aside and trusting to the stars and his instinct to give him directions.

He got up and headed off in what he judged to be a northerly direction. He knew very well he might miss his destination by miles with such rough bearings to travel by, or just as easily fail to see it in the darkness. No matter; he had no other choice, which was a kind of comfort to him.

In his five-minute spree as thief he'd not found a watch to steal, so the only sense he had of time passing was the slow progression of the constellations overhead. The air became cold, then bitter, but he kept up his painful pace, avoiding the roads wherever possible, though they would have been easier to walk than the plowed and seeded ground. This caution proved well founded at one point when two police vehicles, bookending a black limousine, slid all but silently down a road he had a minute ago crossed. He had no evidence whatsoever for the feeling that seized him as the cars passed by, but he sensed more than strongly that the limo's passenger was Decker, the good doctor, still in pursuit of *understanding*.

4

Then, Midian.

Out of nowhere, Midian. One moment the night ahead was featureless darkness, the next there was a cluster of buildings on the horizon, their painted walls glimmering gray blue in the starlight. Boone stood for several minutes and studied the scene. There was no light burning in any window or on any porch. By now it was surely well after midnight, and the men and women of the town, with work to rise to the following morning, would be in bed. But not one single light? That struck him as strange. Small Midian might be—forgotten by mapmakers and signpost writers alike—but did it not lay claim to one insomniac, or a child who needed the comfort of a lamp burning through the night hours? More probably they were in wait for him—Decker and the law—concealed in the shadows until he was foolish enough to step into the trap. The simplest solution would be to turn tail and leave them to their vigil, but he had little enough energy left. If he retreated now, how long would he have to wait before attempting a return, every hour making recognition and arrest more likely?

He decided to skirt the edge of the town and get some sense of the lay of the land. If he could find no evidence of a police presence, then he'd enter and take the consequences. He hadn't come all this way to turn back.

Midian revealed nothing of itself as he moved around its southeastern flank, except perhaps its emptiness. Not only could he see no sign of police vehicles in the streets or secreted between the houses, he could see no automobile of any kind: no truck, no farm vehicle. He began to wonder if the town was one of those religious communities he'd read of, whose dogmas denied them electricity or the combustion engine.

But as he climbed toward the spine of a small hill on the summit of which Midian stood, a second and plainer explanation occurred. There was nobody *in* Midian. The thought stopped him in his tracks. He stared across at the houses, searching for some evidence of decay, but he could see none. The roofs were intact as far as he could make out; there were no buildings that appeared on the verge of collapse. Yet, with the night so quiet he could hear the whoosh of falling stars overhead, he could hear *nothing* from the town. If somebody in Midian had moaned in his sleep, the night would have brought the sound his way, but there was only silence.

Midian was a ghost town.

Never in his life had he felt such desolation. He stood like a dog returned home to find its masters gone, not knowing what his life now meant or would ever mean again.

It took him several minutes to uproot himself and continue his circuit of the town. Twenty yards on from where he'd stood, however, the height of the hill gave him sight of a scene more mysterious even than the vacant Midian.

On the far side of the town lay a cemetery. His vantage point gave him an uninterrupted view of it, despite the high walls that bounded the place. Presumably it had been built to serve the entire region, for it was massively larger than a town Midian's size could ever have required. Many of the mausoleums were of impressive scale, that much was clear even from a distance. The layout of avenues, trees, and tombs lent the cemetery the appearance of a small city.

Boone began down the slope of the hill toward it, his route taking him well clear of the town itself. After the adrenaline rush of finding and approaching Midian, he felt his reserves of strength failing fast; the pain and exhaustion that expectation had numbed now returned with a vengeance. It could not be long, he knew, before his muscles gave out completely and he collapsed. Perhaps behind the cemetery's walls he'd be able to find a niche to conceal himself from his pursuers and rest his bones.

There were two means of access. A small gate in the side wall and large double gates that faced toward the town. He chose the former. It was latched but not locked. He gently pushed it open and stepped inside. The impression he'd had from the hill of the cemetery as city was here confirmed, the mausoleums rising house-high around him. Their scale and, now that he could study them close up, their elaborate decor puzzled him. What great families had occupied the town or its surrounds, moneyed enough to bury their dead in such splendor? The small communities of the prairie clung to the land as their sustenance but it seldom made them rich; and on the few occasions when it did, with oil or gold, never in such numbers. Yet here were magnificent tombs, avenue upon avenue of them, built in all manner of styles from the classical to the baroque, and marked—though he was not certain his fatigued senses were telling him the truth—with motifs from warring theologies.

It was beyond him. He needed sleep. The tombs had been standing a century or more; the puzzle would still be there at dawn.

He found himself a bed out of sight between two graves and lay his head down. The spring growth of grass smelled sweet. He'd slept on far worse pillows, and would again.

5

A DİFFERENT APE

The sound of an animal woke him, its growls finding their way into floating dreams and calling him down to earth. He opened his eyes and sat up. He couldn't see the dog but he heard it still. Was it behind him? The proximity of the tombs threw echoes back and forth. Very slowly, he turned to look over his shoulder. The darkness was deep, but did not quite conceal a large beast, its species impossible to read. There was no misinterpreting the threat from its throat, however. It didn't like his scrutiny, to judge by the tenor of its growls.

"Hey, boy . . ." he said softly, "it's OK."

Ligaments creaking, he started to stand up, knowing that if he stayed on the ground, the animal had easy access to his throat. His limbs had stiffened lying on the cold ground; he moved like a geriatric. Perhaps it was this that kept the animal from attacking, for it simply watched him, the crescents of the whites of its eyes—the only detail he could make out—widening as its gaze followed him into a standing position. Once on his feet he turned to face the creature, which began to move toward him. There was something in its advance that made him think it was wounded. He could hear it dragging one of its limbs behind it, its head low, its stride ragged.

He had words of comfort on his lips when an arm hooked about his neck, taking breath and words away.

"Move and I gut you."

With the threat, a second arm slid around his body, the fingers digging into his belly with such force he had no doubt the man would make the threat good with his bare hand.

Boone took a shallow breath. Even that minor motion brought a tightening of the death grip at neck and abdomen. He felt blood run down his belly and into his jeans.

"Who the fuck are you?" the voice demanded.

"My name's Boone. I came here . . . I came to find Midian."

Did the hold on his belly relax a little when he named his purpose?

"Why?" a second voice now demanded. It took Boone no more than a heartbeat to realize that the voice had come from the shadows ahead of him, where the wounded beast stood. Indeed *from* the beast.

"My friend asked you a question," said the voice at his ear. "Answer him."

Boone, disoriented by the attack, fixed his gaze again on whatever occupied the shadows and found himself doubting his eyes. The head of his questioner was not *solid*; it seemed almost to be *inhaling* its redundant features, their substance darkening and flowing through socket and nostrils and mouth back into itself.

All thought of his jeopardy disappeared; what seized him now was elation. *Narcisse had not lied.* Here was the transforming truth of that.

"I came to be among you," he said, answering the miracle's question. "I came because I belong here."

A question emerged from the soft laughter behind him.

"What does he look like, Peloquin?"

The thing had drunk its beast-face down. There were human features beneath, set on a body more reptile than mammal. That limb he dragged behind him was a tail, his wounded lope the gait of a low-slung lizard. That too was under review as the tremor of change moved down its jutting spine.

"He looks like a Natural," Peloquin replied, "not that that means much."

Why could his attacker not see for himself? Boone wondered.

He glanced down at the hand on his belly. It had six fingers, tipped not with nails but with claws, now buried half an inch in his muscle.

"Don't kill me," he said, "I've come a long way to be here."

"Hear that, Jackie?" said Peloquin, thrusting from the ground with his four legs to stand upright in front of Boone. His eyes, now level with Boone's, were bright blue. His breath was as hot as the blast from an open furnace.

"What kind of beast are you, then?" Boone wanted to know. The transformation was all but finished. The man beneath the monster was nothing remarkable. Forty, lean, and sallow-skinned.

"We should take him below," said Jackie. "Lylesburg will want to see him."

"Probably," said Peloquin. "But I think we'd be wasting his time. This is a Natural, Jackie. I can smell 'em."

"I've spilled blood . . ." Boone murmured. "Killed eleven people."

The blue eyes perused him. There was humor in them.

"I don't think so," Peloquin said.

"It's not up to us," Jackie put in. "You can't judge him."

"I've got eyes in my head, haven't I?" said Peloquin. "I know a clean man when I see one." He wagged his finger at Boone. "You're not Nightbreed," he said. "You're meat. That's what you are. Meat for the beast." The humor drained from his expression as he spoke and *hunger* replaced it.

"We can't do this," the other creature protested.

"Who'll know?" said Peloquin. "Who'll *ever* know?"

"We're breaking the law."

Peloquin seemed indifferent to that. He bared his teeth, dark smoke oozing from the gaps and rising up over his face. Boone knew what was coming next. The man was breathing *out* what he'd moments ago inhaled; his lizard self. The proportions of his head were already altering subtly, as though his skull were dismantling and reorganizing beneath the hood of his flesh.

"You can't kill me!" he said, "I belong with you."

Was there a denial out of the smoke in front of him? If so it was lost in translation. There was to be no further debate. The beast intended to eat him. He felt a sharp pain in his belly, and glanced down to see the clawed hand detach itself from his flesh. The hold at his neck slipped, and the creature behind him said:

"*Go.*"

He needed no persuasion. Before Peloquin could complete his reconstruction, Boone slid from Jackie's embrace and ran. Any sense of direction he might have had was forfeited in the desperation of the moment, a desperation fueled by a roar of fury from the hungry beast, and the sound—almost instant, it seemed—of pursuit.

The Necropolis was a maze. He ran blindly, ducking right and left wherever an opening offered itself, but he didn't need to look over his shoulder to know that the devourer was closing on him. He heard its accusation in his head as he ran:

You're not Nightbreed. You're meat. Meat for the beast.

The words were an agony more profound than the ache in his legs or his lungs. Even here, among the monsters of Midian, he *did not belong*. And if not here, where? He was running, as prey had always run when the hungry were on its heels, but it was a race he couldn't win.

He stopped. He turned.

Peloquin was five or six yards behind him, his body still human, naked, and vulnerable, but the head entirely bestial, the mouth wide and ringed with teeth like thorns. He too stopped running, perhaps expecting Boone to draw a weapon. When none was forthcoming, he raised his arms toward his victim. Behind him, Jackie stumbled into view and Boone had his first glimpse of the man. Or was it *men*? There were two faces on his lumpen head, the features of both utterly distorted: eyes dislodged so they looked everywhere but ahead, mouths collided into a single gash, noses slits without bones. It was the face of a freak-show fetus.

Jackie tried one last appeal but Peloquin's outstretched arms were already transforming from fingertip to elbow, their delicacy giving way to formidable power.

Before the muscle was fixed he came at Boone, leaping to bring his victim down. Boone fell before him. It was too late now to regret his passivity. He felt the claws tear at his jacket to bare the good flesh of his chest. Peloquin raised his head and *grinned*, an expression this mouth was not made for; then he bit. The teeth were not long but many. They hurt less than Boone had expected, until Peloquin pulled back, tearing away a mouthful of muscle, taking skin and nipple with it.

The pain shocked Boone from resignation; he began to thrash beneath Peloquin's weight. But the beast spat the morsel from its maw and came back for better, exhaling the smell of blood in its prey's face. There was reason for the exhalation; on its next breath it would suck Boone's heart and lungs from his chest. He cried out for help, and it came. Before the fatal breath could be drawn, Jackie seized hold of Peloquin and dragged him from his sustenance. Boone felt the weight of the creature lifted, and through the blur of agony saw his champion wrestling with Peloquin, their thrashing limbs intertwined. He didn't wait to cheer the victor. Pressing his palm to the wound on his chest, he got to his feet.

There was no safety for him here; Peloquin was surely not the only occupant with a taste for human meat. He could feel others watching him as he staggered through the Necropolis, waiting for him to falter and fall so they could take him with impunity.

Yet his system, traumatized as it was, didn't fail. There was a vigor in his muscles he'd not felt since he'd done violence to himself, a thought that repulsed him now as it had never before. Even the wound, throbbing beneath his hand, had its *life*, and was celebrating it. The pain had gone, replaced not by numbness but by a sensitivity that was almost erotic, tempting Boone to reach into his chest and stroke his heart. Entertained by such nonsenses he let instinct guide his feet and it brought him to the double gates. The latch defeated his blood-slicked hands so he climbed, scaling the gates with an ease that brought laughter to his throat. Then he was off up toward Midian, running not for fear of pursuit but for the pleasure his limbs took in movement and his senses in speed.

6

FEET OF CLAY

The town was indeed empty, as he'd known it must be. Though the houses had seemed in good shape at half a mile's distance, closer scrutiny showed them to be much the worse for being left unoccupied for the cycle of seasons. Though the feeling of well-being still suffused him, he feared that loss of blood would undo him in time. He needed something to bind his wound, however primitive. In search of a length of curtaining or a piece of forsaken bed linen, he opened the door of one of the houses and plunged into the darkness within.

He hadn't been aware, until he was inside, how strangely attenuated his senses had become. His eyes pierced the gloom readily, discovering the pitiful debris the sometime tenants had left behind, all dusted by the dry earth years of prairie had borne in through the broken window and the ill-fitting door. There was cloth to be found, a length of damp, stained linen that he tore between teeth and right hand into strips while keeping his left upon the wound.

He was in that process when he heard the creak of boards on the stoop. He let the bandaging drop from his teeth. The door stood open. On the threshold a silhouetted man, whose name Boone knew though the face was all darkness. It was Decker's cologne he smelled, Decker's heartbeat he heard, Decker's sweat he tasted on the air between them.

"So," said the doctor, "here you are."

There were forces mustering in the starlit street. With ears preternaturally sharp, Boone caught the sound of nervous whispers, of wind passed by churning bowels, and of weapons cocked ready to bring the lunatic down should he try to slip them.

"How did you find me?" he said.

"Narcisse, was it," Decker said, "your friend at the hospital?"

"Is he dead?"

"I'm afraid so. He died fighting."

Decker took a step into the house.

"You're hurt," he said. "What did you do to yourself?"

Something prevented Boone from replying. Was it that the mysteries of Midian were so bizarre he'd not be believed? Or that their nature was not Decker's business? Not the latter surely. Decker's commitment to comprehending the monstrous could not be in doubt. Who better than to share the revelation with? Yet he hesitated.

"Tell me," Decker said again, "how did you get the wound?"

"Later," said Boone.

"There'll be no later. I think you know that."

"I'll survive," Boone said. "This isn't as bad as it looks. At least it doesn't feel bad."

"I don't mean the wound. I mean the police. They're waiting for you."

"I know."

"And you're not going to come quietly, are you?"

Boone was no longer sure. Decker's voice reminded him so much of being safe, he almost believed it would be possible again, if the doctor wanted to make it so.

But there was no talk of safety from Decker now. Only of death.

"You're a multiple murderer, Boone. Desperate. Dangerous. It was tough persuading them to let me near you."

"I'm glad you did."

"I'm glad too," Decker replied. "I wanted a chance to say good-bye."

"Why does it have to be this way?"

"You know why."

He didn't, not really. What he did know, more and more certainly, was that Peloquin had told the truth.

You're not Nightbreed, he'd said.

Nor was he; he was innocent.

"I killed nobody," he murmured.

"*I* know that," Decker replied.

"That's why I couldn't remember any of the rooms. I was never *there*."

"But you remember now," Decker said.

"Only because—" Boone stopped, and stared at the man in the charcoal suit, "because you showed me."

"*Taught* you," Decker corrected him.

Boone kept staring, waiting for an explanation that wasn't the one in his head. It couldn't be Decker. Decker was Reason, Decker was Calm.

"There are two children dead in Westlock tonight," the doctor was saying. "They're blaming you."

"I've never been to Westlock," Boone protested.

"But I have," Decker replied. "I made sure they saw the pictures, the men out there. Child murderers are the worst. It'd be better you died here than be turned over to them."

"You?" Boone said. "You did it?"

"Yes."

"All of them?"

"And more."

"Why?"

Decker pondered on this a moment.

"Because I like it," he said flatly.

He still looked so sane in his well-cut suit. Even his face, which Boone could see clearly now, bore no visible clue to the lunacy beneath. Who would have doubted, seeing the bloodied man and the clean, which was the lunatic and which his healer? But appearances deceived. It was only the monster, the child of Midian, who actually altered its flesh to parade its true self. The rest hid behind their calm and plotted the deaths of children.

Decker drew a gun from inside his jacket.

"They armed me," he said, "in case you lost control."

His hand trembled, but at such a distance he could scarcely miss. In moments it would be over. The bullet would fly and he'd be dead, with so many mysteries unsolved. The wound, Midian, Decker.

There was no other moment but now. Flinging the cloth he still held at Decker, he threw himself aside behind it. Decker fired, the shot filling the room with sound and light. By the time the cloth hit the ground, Boone was at the door. As he came within a yard of it, the gun's light flashed again. And an instant after, the sound. And with the sound a blow to Boone's back that threw him forward, out through the door and onto the stoop.

Decker's shout came with him.

"He's armed!"

Boone heard the shadows prepare to bring him down. He raised his arms in sign of surrender, opened his mouth to protest his innocence.

The men gathered behind their cars saw only his bloodied hands; guilt enough. They fired.

Boone heard the bullets coming his way—two from the left, three from the right, and one from straight ahead, aimed at his heart. He had time to wonder at how slow they were, and how musical. Then they struck him: upper thigh, groin, spleen, shoulder, cheek, and heart. He stood upright for several seconds, then somebody fired again and nervous trigger fingers unleashed a second volley. Two of these shots went wide. The rest hit home: abdomen, knee, two to the chest, one to the temple. This time he fell.

As he hit the ground he felt the wound Peloquin had given him convulse like a second heart, its presence curiously comforting in his dwindling moments.

Somewhere nearby he heard Decker's voice and his footsteps approaching as he emerged from the house to peruse the body.

"Got the bastard," somebody said.

"You sure he's dead?"

"He's dead," Decker said.

No, I'm not, Boone thought.

Then thought no more.

PART TWO

DEATH'S
A BITCH

The miraculous too is born,
has its season, and dies . . .

—CARMEL SANDS, *ORTHODOXIES*

7

ROUGH ROADS

I

Knowing Boone was gone from her was bad enough, but what came after was so much worse. First, of course, there'd been that telephone call. She'd met Philip Decker only once and didn't recognize his voice until he identified himself.

"I've got some bad news, I'm afraid."

"You've found Boone."

"Yes."

"He's hurt?"

There was a pause. She knew before the silence was broken what came next.

"I'm afraid he's dead, Lori."

There it was, the news she'd half known was coming, because she'd been too happy and it couldn't last. Boone had changed her life beyond all recognition. His death would do the same.

She thanked the doctor for the kindness of telling her himself, rather than leaving the duty to the police. Then she put the phone down, and waited to believe it.

There were those among her peers who said she'd never have been courted by a man like Boone if he'd been sane, meaning not that his illness made him choose blindly but that a face like his, which inspired such fawning in those susceptible to faces, would have been in the company of like beauty had the mind behind it not been unbalanced. These remarks bit deep, because in her heart of hearts she thought them true. Boone had little by way of possessions, but his face was his glory, demanding a devotion to its study that embarrassed and discomfited him. It gave him no pleasure to be stared at. Indeed Lori had more than once feared he'd scar himself in the hope of spoiling whatever drew attention to him, an urge rehearsed in his total lack of interest in his appearance. She'd known him to go days without showering, weeks without shaving, half a year without a haircut. It did little to dissuade the devotees. He haunted them because *he* in his turn was haunted; simple as that.

She didn't waste time trying to persuade her friends of the fact. Indeed she kept conversation about him to the minimum, particularly when talk turned to sex. She'd slept with Boone three times only, each occasion a disaster. She knew what the gossips would make of that. But his tender, eager way with her suggested his overtures were more than dutiful. He simply couldn't carry them through, which fact made him rage and fall into such depression she'd come to hold herself back, cooling their exchanges so as not to invite further failure.

She dreamt of him often though, scenarios that were unequivocally sexual. No symbolism here. Just she and Boone in bare rooms, fucking. Sometimes there were people beating on the doors to get in and see, but they never did. He belonged to her completely, in all his beauty and his wretchedness.

But only in dreams. Now more than ever, only in dreams.

Their story together was over. There'd be no more dark days when his conversation was a circle of defeat, no moments of sudden sunshine because she'd chanced upon some phrase that gave him hope. She'd not been unprepared for an abrupt end. But nothing like this. No Boone unmasked as a killer and shot down in a town she'd never heard of. This was the wrong ending.

But bad as it was, there was worse to follow.

After the telephone call there'd been the inevitable questioning by the police: had she ever suspected him of criminal activities? Had he ever been violent in his dealings with her? She told them a dozen times he'd never touched her except in love, and then only with coaxing. They seemed to find an unspoken confirmation in her account of his tentativeness, exchanging knowing looks as she made a blushing account of their lovemaking. When they'd finished with their questions they asked her if she would identify the body. She agreed to the duty. Though she'd been warned it would be unpleasant, she wanted a good-bye.

But Boone's body had disappeared.

At first nobody would tell her why the identification process was being delayed; she was fobbed off with excuses that didn't quite ring true. Finally, however, they had no option but to tell her the truth. The corpse, which had been left in the police mortuary overnight, had simply vanished. Nobody knew how it had been stolen—the mortuary had been locked up and there was no sign of forced entry—or indeed why. A search was under way, but to judge by the harassed faces that delivered this news, there didn't seem to be much hope held out of finding the body snatchers. The inquest on Aaron Boone would have to proceed without a corpse.

2

That he might never be laid to rest tormented her. The thought of his body as some pervert's plaything, or worse, some terrible icon, haunted her night and day. Her power to imagine what uses his poor flesh might be put to shocked her. Her mind's downward spiral of morbidity made her fearful—for the first time in her life—of her own mental processes.

Boone had been a mystery in life, his affection a miracle that gave her a sense of herself she never had. Now, in death, that mystery deepened. It seemed she'd not known him at all, even in those moments of traumatic lucidity between them, when he'd been ready to break his skull open and she'd coaxed the distress from him; even then he'd been hiding a secret life of murder from her.

It scarcely seemed possible. When she pictured him now, making idiot faces at her or weeping in her lap, the thought that she'd never known him properly was like a physical hurt. Somehow she had to heal that hurt or be prepared to bear the wound of his betrayal forever. She had to know *why* his other life had taken him off to the back of beyond. Maybe the best solution was to go looking where he'd been found: in Midian. Perhaps there she'd find the mystery answered.

The police had instructed her not to leave Calgary until after the inquest, but she was a creature of impulse. She'd woken at three in the morning with the idea of going to Midian. She was packing by five, and an hour after dawn heading north on Highway 2.

3

Things went well at first. It was good to be away from the office—where she'd be missed, but what the hell?—and the apartment, with all its reminders of her time with Boone. She wasn't quite driving blind, but damn near it; no map marked any town called Midian. She'd heard mention of other towns, however, in exchanges between the police. Shere Neck was one she remembered—and that *was* marked on the maps. She made that her target.

She knew little or nothing about the landscape she was crossing. Her family had come from Toronto—the civilized East as her mother had called it to the day she died, resenting her husband for the move that had taken them into the hinterland. The prejudice had rubbed off. The sight of wheat fields stretching as far as the eye could see had never done much for Lori's imagination, and nothing she saw as she drove changed her mind. The grain was being left to grow, its planters and reapers about other business. The sheer monotony of it wearied her more than she'd anticipated. She broke her journey at McLennan, an hour's drive short of Peace River, and slept a full night undisturbed on a motel bed, to be up and off again good and early the next morning. She'd make Shere Neck by noon, she estimated.

Things didn't quite work out that way, however. Somewhere east of Peace River she lost her bearings and had to drive forty miles in what she suspected was the wrong direction till she found a gas station and someone to help her on her way.

There were twin boys playing with plastic armies in the dirt of the station office step. Their father, whose blond hair they shared, ground a cigarette out among the battalions and crossed to the car.

"What can I get you?"

"Gas, please. And some information?"

"It'll cost you," he said, not smiling.

"I'm looking for a town called Shere Neck. Do you know it?"

The war games had escalated behind him. He turned on the children.

"Will you shut up?" he said.

The boys fell silent until he turned back to Lori. Too many years of working outdoors in the summer sun had aged him prematurely.

"What do you want Shere Neck for?" he said.

"I'm trying . . . to track somebody."

"That so?" he replied, plainly intrigued. He offered her a grin designed for better teeth. "Anyone I know?" he said. "We don't get too many strangers through here."

There was no harm in asking, she supposed. She reached back into the car and fetched a photograph from her bag.

"You didn't ever see this man, I suppose?"

Armageddon was looming at the step. Before looking at Boone's photograph he turned on the children.

"I told you to *shut the fuck up!*" he said, then turned back to study the picture. His response was immediate. "You know who this guy is?"

Lori hesitated. The raw face before her was scowling. It was too late to claim ignorance, however, "Yes," she said, trying not to sound offensive, "I know who it is."

"And you know what he did?" The man's lip curled as he spoke. "There were pictures of him. I saw them." Again, he turned on the children. "Will you *shut up?*"

"It wasn't me," one of the pair protested.

"I don't give a fuck who it was!" came the reply.

He moved toward them, arm raised. They were out from his shadow in seconds, forsaking the armies in fear of him. His rage at the children and his disgust at the picture were welded into one revulsion now.

"A fucking animal," he said, turning to Lori, "that's what he was. A fucking animal."

He thrust the tainted photograph back at her.

"Damn good thing they took him out. What you wanna do, go bless the spot?"

She claimed the photograph from his oily fingers without replying, but he read her expression well enough. Unbowed he continued his tirade.

"Man like that should be put down like a *dog*, lady. Like a fucking dog."

She retreated before his vehemence, her hands trembling so much she could barely open the car door.

"Don't you want no gas?" he suddenly said.

"Go to hell," she replied.

He looked bewildered.

"What's your problem?" he spat back.

She turned on the ignition, muttering a prayer that the car would not play dead. She was in luck. Driving away at speed, she glanced in her mirror to see the man shouting after her through the dust she'd kicked up.

She didn't know where his anger had come from, but she knew where it would go: to the children. No use to fret about it. The world was full of brutal fathers and tyrannical mothers, and come to that, cruel and uncaring children. It was the way of things. She couldn't police the species.

Relief at her escape kept any other response at bay for ten minutes, but then it ran out, and a trembling overtook her, so violent she had to stop at the first sign of civilization and find somewhere to calm herself down. There was a small diner among the dozen or so stores, where she ordered coffee and a sugar fix of pie, then retired to the rest room to splash some cold water on her flushed cheeks. Solitude was the only cue her tears needed. Staring at her blotchy, agitated features in the cracked mirror, she began to sob so deeply, nothing—not even the entrance of another customer—could shame her into stopping.

The newcomer didn't do as Lori would have done in such circumstances and withdraw. Instead, catching Lori's eye in the mirror, she said, "What is it? Men or money?"

Lori wiped the tears away with her fingers.

"I'm sorry," she said.

"When I cry," the girl said, putting a comb through her hennaed hair, "it's only over men or money."

"Oh." The girl's unabashed curiosity helped hold fresh tears at bay. "A man," Lori said.

"Leave you, did he?"

"Not exactly."

"Jesus," said the girl, "did he come back? That's even worse."

The remark earned a tiny smile from Lori.

"It's usually the ones you don't want, right?" the girl went on. "You tell 'em to piss off, they just keep coming back, like dogs—"

Mention of dogs reminded Lori of the scene at the garage, and she felt tears mustering again.

"Oh, shut up, Sheryl," the newcomer chided herself, "you're making it worse."

"No," said Lori. "No really. I need to talk."
Sheryl smiled.

Sheryl Margaret Clark was her name, and she could have coaxed gossip
from angels. By their second hour of conversation and their fifth coffee,
Lori had told her the whole story, from her first meeting with Boone to
the moment she and Sheryl had exchanged looks in the mirror. Sheryl
herself had a story to tell—more comedy than tragedy—about her lover's
passion for cars and hers for his brother, which had ended in hard words
and parting. She was on the road to clear her head.

"I've not done this since I was a kid," she said, "just going where the
fancy takes me. I've forgotten how good it feels. Maybe we could go on
together. To Shere Neck. I've always wanted to see the place."

"Is that right?"

Sheryl laughed.

"No. But it's as good a destination as any. All directions being equal
to the fancy-free."

8

WHERE HE FELL

So they traveled on together. They had taken directions from the owner of the diner, who claimed he had a better than vague idea of Midian's whereabouts. The instructions were good. Their route took them through Shere Neck, which was bigger than Lori had expected, and on down an unmarked road that in theory led to Midian.

"Why d'you wanna go there?" the diner owner had wanted to know. "Nobody goes there anymore. It's empty."

"I'm writing an article on the gold rush," Sheryl had replied, an enthusiastic liar. "*She's* sight-seeing."

"Some sight," came the response.

The remark had been made ironically, but it was truer than its speaker had known. It was late afternoon, the light golden on the gravel road, when the town came into view, and until they were in the streets themselves they were certain this could not be the right place, because what ghost town ever looked so welcoming? Once out of the sun, however, that impression changed. There was something forlornly romantic about the deserted houses, but finally the sight was dispiriting and not a little eerie. Seeing the place, Lori's first thought was:

Why would Boone come here?

Her second:

He didn't come of his own volition. He was chased. It was an accident that he was here at all.

They parked the car in the middle of the main street, which, give or take an alleyway, was the only street.

"No need to lock it," Sheryl said. "Ain't anybody coming to steal it."

Now that they were here, Lori was gladder than ever of Sheryl's company. Her verve and good humor were an affront to this somber place; they kept whatever haunted it at bay.

Ghosts could be laid with laughter; misery was made of sterner stuff. It was so easy to imagine Boone here, alone and confused, knowing his pursuers were closing on him. It was easier still to find the place where they'd shot him down. The holes the stray bullets had made were ringed with chalk marks; smears and splashes of blood had soaked into the planks of the porch. She stood off from the spot for several minutes, unable to approach it, yet equally unable to retreat. Sheryl had tactfully taken herself off exploring: there was nobody to break the hypnotic hold the sight of his deathbed had upon her.

She would miss him forever. Yet there were no tears. Perhaps she'd sobbed them out back in the diner rest room. What she felt instead, fueling her loss, was the mystery of how a man she'd known and loved—or loved and thought she'd known—could have died here for crimes she'd never have suspected him of. Perhaps it was the anger she felt toward him that prevented tears, knowing that despite his professions of love he'd hidden so much from her and was now beyond the reach of her demands for explanation. Could he not at least have left a sign? She found herself staring at the bloodstains, wondering if eyes more acute than hers might have found some meaning in them. If prophecies could be read from the dregs in a coffee cup, surely the last mark Boone had made on the world carried some significance. But she was no interpreter. The signs were just more of many unsolved mysteries, chief among them the feeling she voiced aloud as she stared at the stairs:

"I still love you, Boone."

Now *there* was a puzzle, that despite her anger and her bewilderment she'd have traded the life that was left in her just to have him walk out through that door now and embrace her.

But there was no reply to her declaration. No wraith breath against her cheek, no sigh against her inner ear. If Boone was still here in some phantom form he was mute and breathless, not released by death, but its prisoner.

Somebody spoke her name. She looked up.

"—don't you think?" Sheryl was saying.

"I'm sorry?"

"Time we went," Sheryl repeated. "Don't you think it's time we went?"

"Oh."

"You don't mind me saying, you look like shit."

"Thanks."

Lori put her hand out, in need of steadying. Sheryl grasped it.

"You've seen all you need to, honey," she said.

"Yes . . ."

"Let it go."

"You know it still doesn't seem quite *real*," Lori said. "Even standing here. Even seeing the place. I can't quite believe it. How can he be so . . . *irretrievable?* There should be some way we could *reach*, don't you think, some way to reach and touch them?"

"Who?"

"The dead. Otherwise it's all nonsense, isn't it? It's all sadistic nonsense." She broke her hold with Sheryl, put her hand to her brow, and rubbed it with her fingertips.

"I'm sorry," she said, "I'm not making much sense, am I?"

"Honestly? No."

Lori proffered an apologetic look.

"Listen," Sheryl said, "the old town's not what it used to be. I think we should get out of here and leave it to fall apart. Whadda you say?"

"I'd vote for that."

"I keep thinking . . ." Sheryl stopped.

"What?"

"I just don't like the company very much," she said. "I don't mean you," she added hurriedly.

"Who, then?"

"All these dead folk," she said.

"What dead folk?"

"Over the hill. There's a bloody cemetery."

"Really?"

"It's not ideal viewing in your state of mind," Sheryl said hurriedly. But she could tell by the expression on Lori's face she shouldn't have volunteered the information.

"You don't want to see," she said, "really you don't."

"Just a minute or two," Lori said.

"If we stay much longer we'll be driving back in the dark."

"I'll never come here again."

"Oh sure. You should see the sights. Great sights. Dead people's houses."

Lori made a small smile.

"I'll be quick," she said, starting down the street in the direction of the cemetery. Sheryl hesitated. She'd left her sweater in the car and was getting chilly. But all the time she'd been here she hadn't been able to dislodge the suspicion that they were being watched. With dusk close she didn't want to be alone in the street.

"Wait for me," she said, and caught up with Lori, who was already in sight of the graveyard wall.

"Why's it so big?" Lori wondered aloud.

"Lord knows. Maybe they all died out at once."

"So many? It's just a little town."

"True."

"And look at the size of the tombs."

"I should be impressed?"

"Did you go in?"

"No. And I don't much want to."

"Just a little way."

"Where have I heard that before?"

There was no reply from Lori. She was at the cemetery gates now, reaching through the ironwork to operate the latch. She succeeded. Pushing one of the gates open far enough to slip through, she entered. Reluctantly, Sheryl followed.

"Why so many?" Lori said again. It wasn't simply curiosity that had her voice the question, it was that this strange spectacle made her wonder again if Boone had simply been cornered here by accident or whether Midian had been his *destination*. Was somebody buried here he'd come hoping to find alive or at whose grave he'd wanted to confess his crimes? Though it was all conjecture, the avenues of tombs seemed to offer some faint hope of comprehension the blood he'd shed would not have supplied had she studied it till the sky fell.

"It's late," Sheryl reminded her.

"Yes."

"And I'm cold."

"Are you?"

"I'd like to *go*, Lori."

"Oh . . . I'm sorry. Yes. Of course. It's getting too dark to see much anyhow."

"You noticed."

They started back up the hill toward the town, Sheryl setting the pace.

What little light remained was almost gone by the time they reached the outskirts of the town. Letting Sheryl march on to the car, Lori stopped to take one final look at the cemetery. From this vantage point it resembled a fortress. Perhaps the high walls kept animals out, though it seemed an unnecessary precaution. The dead were surely secure beneath their memorial stones. More likely the walls were the mourners' way to keep the dead from having power over them. Within those gates the ground was sacred to the departed, tended in their name. Outside, the world belonged to the living, who had nothing left to learn from those they'd lost.

She was not so arrogant. There was much she wanted to say to the dead tonight, and much to hear. That was the pity of it.

She returned to the car oddly exhilarated. It was only once the doors were locked and the engine running that Sheryl said, "There's been somebody watching us."

"You sure?"

"I swear. I saw him just as I got to the car."

She was rubbing her breasts vigorously. "Jesus, my nipples get numb when I'm cold."

"What did he look like?" Lori said.

Sheryl shrugged. "Too dark to see," she said. "Doesn't matter now. Like you said, we won't be coming back here again."

True, Lori thought. They could drive away down a straight road and never look back. Maybe the deceased citizens of Midian envied them that.

9

TOUCHED

I

I t wasn't difficult to choose their accommodation in Shere Neck; there were only two places available, and one was already full to brimming with buyers and sellers for a farm-machinery sale that had just taken place, some of the spillage occupying the rooms at the other establishment: the Sweetgrass Inn. Had it not been for Sheryl's way with a smile they might have been turned away from there too, but after some debate a twin-bedded room was found that they could share. It was plain but comfortable.

"You know what my mother used to tell me?" said Sheryl, as she unpacked her toiletries in the bathroom.

"What?"

"She used to say, 'There's a man out there for you, Sheryl; he's walking around with your name on.' Mind you this is from a woman who'd been looking for her particular man for thirty years and never found him. But she was always stuck on this romantic notion. You know, the man of your dreams is just around the next corner. And she stuck me on it too, damn her."

"Still?"

"Oh yeah. I'm still looking. You'd think I'd know better, after what I've been through. You want to shower first?"

"No. You go ahead."

A party had started up in the next room, the walls too thin to muffle much of the noise. While Sheryl took her shower, Lori lay on the bed and turned the events of the day over in her head. The exercise didn't last long. The next thing she knew, she was being stirred from sleep by Sheryl, who'd showered and was ready for a night on the town.

"You coming?" she wanted to know.

"I'm too tired," Lori said. "You go have a good time."

"If there's a good time to be had," said Sheryl ruefully.

"You'll find it," Lori said. "Give 'em something to talk about."

Sheryl promised she would, and left Lori to rest, but the edge had been taken off her fatigue. She could do no more than doze, and even that was interrupted at intervals by loud bursts of drunken hilarity from the adjacent room.

She got up to go in search of a soda machine and ice, returning with her calorie-free nightcap to a less than peaceful bed. She'd take a leisurely bath, she decided, until drink or fatigue quieted the neighbors. Immersed to her neck in hot water, she felt her muscles unknotting, and by the time she emerged she felt a good deal mellower. The bathroom had no fan, so both the mirrors had steamed up. She was grateful for their discretion. The catalog of her frailties was quite long enough without another round of self-scrutiny to swell it. Her neck was too thick, her face too thin, her eyes too large, her nose too small. In essence she was one excess upon another, and any attempt on her part to undo the damage merely exacerbated it. Her hair, which she grew long to cover the sins of her neck, was so luxuriant and so dark her face looked sickly in its frame. Her mouth, which was her mother's mouth to the last flute, was naturally, even indecently, red, but taming its color with a pale lipstick merely made her eyes look vaster and more vulnerable than ever.

It wasn't that the sum of her features was unattractive. She'd had more than her share of men at her feet. No, the trouble was she didn't look the way she felt. It was a *sweet* face, and she wasn't sweet, didn't want to *be* sweet, or *thought of* as sweet. Perhaps the powerful feelings that had touched her in the last few hours—seeing the blood, seeing the tombs—would make their mark in time. She hoped so. The memory of them moved in her still, and she was richer for them, however painful they'd been.

Still naked, she wandered back into the bedroom. As she'd hoped, the celebrants next door had quieted down. The music was no longer rock 'n' roll, but something smoochy. She sat on the edge of the bed and ran her palms back and forth over her breasts, enjoying their smoothness. Her breath had taken on the slow rhythm of the music through the wall, music for dancing groin to groin, mouth to mouth. She lay back on the bed, her right hand sliding down her body. She could smell several months' accrual of cigarette smoke in the coverlet she lay on. It made the room seem almost a public place, with its nightly comings and goings. The thought of her nakedness in such a room, and the smell of her skin's cleanliness on this stale bed, was acutely arousing.

She eased her first and middle fingers into her cunt, raising her hips a little to meet the exploration. This was a joy she offered herself all too seldom; her Catholic upbringing had put guilt between her instinct and her fingertips. But tonight she was a different woman. She found the gasping places quickly, putting her feet on the edge of the bed and spreading her legs wide to give both hands a chance to play.

It wasn't Boone she pictured as the first waves of gooseflesh came. Dead men were bad lovers. Better she forgot him. His face had been pretty, but she'd never kiss it again. His cock had been pretty too, but she'd never stroke it, or have it in her again. All she had was herself, and pleasure for pleasure's sake. That was what she pictured now: the very act she was performing. A clean body naked on a stale bed. A woman in a strange room enjoying her own strange self.

The rhythm of the music no longer moved her. She had her own rhythm, rising and falling, rising and falling, each time climbing higher. There was no peak. Just height after height, till she was running with sweat and gorged on sensation. She lay still for several minutes. Then, knowing sleep was quickly overtaking her and that she could scarcely pass the night in her present position, she threw off all the covers but a single sheet, put her head on the pillow, and fell into the space behind her closed eyes.

2

The sweat on her body cooled beneath the thin sheet. In sleep she was at Midian's Necropolis, the wind coming to meet her down its avenues from all directions at once—north, south, east, and west—chilling her as it whipped her hair above her head and ran up inside her blouse.

The wind was not invisible. It had a texture, as though it carried a weight of dust, the motes steadily gumming up her eyes and sealing her nose, finding its way into her underwear and up into her body by those routes too.

It was only as the dust blinded her completely that she realized what it was—the remains of the dead, the ancient dead, blown on contrary winds from pyramids and mausoleums, from vaults and dolmen, charnel houses and crematoria. Coffin dust and human ash and bone pounded to bits, all blown to Midian and catching her at the crossroads.

She felt the dead inside her. Behind her lids, in her throat, carried up toward her womb. And despite the chill and the fury of the four storms, she had no fear of them, nor desire to expel them. They sought her warmth and her womanliness. She would not reject them.

"Where's Boone?" she asked in her dream, assuming the dead would know. He was one of their number, after all.

She knew he was not far from her, but the wind was getting stronger, buffeting her from all directions, howling around her head.

"Boone?" she said again. "I want Boone. Bring him to me."

The wind heard her. Its howling grew louder.

But somebody else was nearby, distracting her from hearing its reply.

"He's dead, Lori," the voice said.

She tried to ignore the idiot voice, and concentrate on interpreting the wind. But she'd lost her place in the conversation, and had to begin again.

"It's Boone I want," she said. "Bring me—"

"*No!*"

Again, that damn voice.

She tried a third time, but the violence of the wind had become another violence; she was being shaken.

"Lori! Wake up!"

She clung to sleep, to the dream of wind. It might yet tell her what she needed to know if she could resist the assault of consciousness a moment longer.

"Boone!" she called again, but the winds were receding from her and taking the dead with them. She felt the itch of their exit from her veins and senses. What knowledge they had to impart was going with them. She was powerless to hold them.

"*Lori.*"

Gone now, all of them gone. Carried away on the storm.

She had no choice but to open her eyes, knowing they would find Sheryl, mere flesh and blood, sitting at the end of the bed and smiling at her.

"Nightmare?" she said.

"No. Not really."

"You were calling his name."

"I know."

"You should have come out with me," Sheryl said, "get him out of your system."

"Maybe."

Sheryl was beaming; she clearly had news to tell.

"You met somebody?" Lori guessed.

Sheryl's smile became a grin.

"Who'd have thought it?" she said. "Mother may have been right after all."

"That good?"

"That good."

"Tell all."

"There's not much to tell. I just went out to find a bar, and I met this great guy. Who'd have thought it?" she said again. "In the middle of the damn prairies? Love comes looking for me."

She could barely contain her enthusiasm as she gave Lori a complete account of the night's romance. The man's name was Curtis, a banker, born in Vancouver, divorced and recently moved to Edmonton. They were perfect complementaries, she said: star signs, tastes in food and drink, family background. And better still, though they'd talked for hours he'd not once tried to persuade her out of her underwear. He was a gentleman: articulate, intelligent, and yearning for the sophisticated life of the West Coast, to which he'd intimated he'd return if he could find the right companion. Maybe she was it.

"I'm going to see him again tomorrow night," Sheryl said. "Maybe even stay over a few weeks if things go well."

"They will," Lori replied. "You deserve some good times."

"Are you going back to Calgary tomorrow?" Sheryl asked.

Yes was the reply her mind was readying. But the dream was there before her, answering quite differently.

"I think I'll go back to Midian first," it said. "I want to see the place one more time."

Sheryl pulled a face.

"Please don't ask me to go," she said. "I'm not up for another visit."

"No problem," Lori replied. "I'm happy to go alone."

10
SUΠ AΠD SHADE

The sky was cloudless over Midian, the air effervescent. All the fretfulness she'd felt during her first visit here had disappeared. Though this was still the town where Boone had died, she could not hate it for that. Rather the reverse: she and it were allies, both marked by the man's passing.

It was not the town itself she'd come to visit, however; it was the graveyard, and it did not disappoint her. The sun gleamed on the mausoleums, the sharp shadows flattering their elaborate decor. Even the grass that sprouted between the tombs was a more brilliant green today. There was no wind from any quarter, no breath of the dream storms, bringing the dead. Within the high walls there was an extraordinary stillness, as if the outside world no longer existed. Here was a place sacred to the dead, who were *not* the living ceased, but almost another species, requiring rites and prayers that belonged uniquely to them. She was surrounded on every side by such signs: epitaphs in English, French, Polish, and Russian, images of veiled women and shattered urns, saints whose martyrdom she could only guess at, stone dogs sleeping upon their masters' tombs—all the symbolism that accompanied this other people. And the more she explored, the more she found herself asking the question she'd posed the day before: why was the cemetery so big? And why, as became apparent the more tombs she studied, were there so many nationalities laid here? She thought of her dream, of the wind that had come from all quarters of the earth. It was as if there'd been something prophetic in it. The thought didn't worry her. If that was the way the world worked—by omens and prophecies—then it was at least a *system*, and she had lived too long without one. Love had failed her; perhaps this would not.

It took her an hour, wandering down the hushed avenues, to reach the back wall of the cemetery, against which she found a row of animals' graves—cats interred beside birds, dogs beside cats, at peace with each other as common clay. It was an odd sight. Though she knew of other animal cemeteries, she'd never heard of pets being laid in the same consecrated ground as their owners. But then should she be surprised at anything here? The place was a law unto itself, built far from any who would care or condemn.

Turning from the back wall, she could see no sign of the front gate, nor could she remember which of the avenues led back there. It didn't matter. She felt secure in the emptiness of the place, and there was a good deal she wanted to see: sepulchers whose architecture, towering over its fellows, invited admiration. Choosing a route that would take in half a dozen of the most promising, she began an idling return journey. The sun was warmer by the minute now, as it climbed toward noon. Though her pace was slow she broke out into a sweat and her throat became steadily drier. It would be no short drive to find somewhere to quench her thirst. But parched throat or no, she didn't hurry. She knew she'd never come here again. She intended to leave with her memories well stocked.

Along the way were several tombs that had been virtually overtaken by saplings planted in front of them. Evergreens mostly, reminders of the life eternal, the trees flourished in the seclusion of the walls, fed well on rich soil. In some cases their spreading roots had cracked the very memorials they'd been planted to offer shade and protection. These scenes of verdancy and ruin she found particularly poignant. She was lingering at one when the perfect silence was broken.

Hidden in the foliage somebody, or some*thing*, was panting. She automatically stepped out of the tree's shadow and into the hot sun. Shock made her heart beat furiously, its thump deafening her to the sound that had excited it. She had to wait for a few moments and listen hard to be sure she'd not imagined the sound. There was no error. Something was in hiding beneath the branches of the tree, which were so weighed by their burden of leaves they almost touched the ground. The sound, now that she listened more carefully, was not human; nor was it healthy. Its roughness and raggedness suggested a dying animal.

She stood in the heat of the sun for a minute or more, just staring into the mass of foliage and shadow, trying to catch some sight of the creature. Occasionally there was a movement: a body vainly trying to right itself, a desperate pawing at the ground as the creature tried to rise. Its helplessness touched her. If she failed to do what she could for it the animal would certainly perish, knowing—this was the thought that moved her to action—that someone had heard its agony and passed it by.

She stepped back into the shadow. For a moment the panting stopped completely. Perhaps the creature was fearful of her and, reading her approach as aggression, preparing some final act of defense. Readying herself to retreat before claws and teeth, she parted the outer twigs and peered through the mesh of branches. Her first impression was not one of sight or sound but of *smell*: a bittersweet scent that was not unpleasant, its source the pale-flanked creature she now made out in the murk, gazing at her wide-eyed. It was a young animal, she guessed, but of no species she could name. A wild cat of some kind, perhaps, but the skin resembled deer hide rather than fur. It watched her warily, its neck barely able to support the weight of its delicately marked head. Even as she returned its gaze it seemed to give up on life. Its eyes closed and its head sank to the ground.

The resilience of the branches defied any further approach. Rather than attempting to bend them aside, she began to break them in order to get to the failing creature. They were living wood, and fought back. Halfway through the thicket a particularly truculent branch snapped back in her face with such stinging force it brought a shout of pain from her. She put her hand to her cheek. The skin to the right of her mouth was broken. Dabbing the blood away she attacked the branch with fresh vigor, at last coming within reach of the animal. It was almost beyond responding to her touch, its eyes momentarily fluttering open as she stroked its flank, then closing again. There was no sign that she could see of a wound, but the body beneath her hand was feverish and full of tremors.

As she struggled to pick the animal up it began to urinate, wetting her hands and blouse, but she drew it to her nevertheless, a dead weight in her arms. Beyond the spasms that ran through its nervous system there was no power left in its muscles. Its limbs hung limply, its head the same. Only the smell she'd first encountered had any strength, intensifying as the creature's final moments approached.

Something like a sob reached her ears. She froze.

Again, the sound. Off to her left, some way, and barely suppressed. She stepped back, out of the shadow of the tree, bringing the dying animal with her. As the sunlight fell on the creature it responded with a violence that utterly belied its apparent frailty, its limbs jerking madly. She stepped back into the shade, instinct telling her the brightness was responsible. Only then did she look again in the direction from which the sob had come.

The door of one of the mausoleums farther down the avenue—a massive structure of cracked marble—stood ajar, and in the column of darkness beyond she could vaguely make out a human figure. Vaguely, because it was dressed in black and seemed to be veiled.

She could make no sense of this scenario. The dying animal tormented by light, the sobbing woman—surely a woman—in the doorway, dressed for mourning.

"Who are you?" she called out.

The mourner seemed to shrink back into the shadows as she was addressed, then regretted the move and approached the open door again, but so very tentatively the connection between animal and woman became clear.

She's afraid of the sun *too*, Lori thought. They belonged together, animal and mourner, the woman sobbing for the creature Lori had in her arms.

She looked at the pavement that lay between where she stood and the mausoleum. Could she get to the door of the tomb without having to step back into the sun, and so hasten the creature's demise? Perhaps, with care. Planning her route before she moved, she started to cross toward the mausoleum, using the shadows like stepping-stones. She didn't look up at the door—her attention was wholly focused on keeping the animal from the light—but she could feel the mourner's presence, willing her on. Once the woman gave voice, not with a word but with a soft sound, a cradle-side sound, addressed not to Lori but to the dying animal.

With the mausoleum door three or four yards from her, Lori dared to look up. The woman in the door could be patient no longer. She reached out from her refuge, her arms bared as the garment she wore rode back, her flesh exposed to the sunlight. The skin was white—as ice, as paper—but only for an instant. As the fingers stretched to relieve Lori of her burden, they darkened and swelled as though instantly bruised. The mourner made a cry of pain and almost fell back into the tomb as she withdrew her arms, but not before the skin broke and trails of dust—yellowish, like pollen—burst from her fingers and fell through the sunlight onto the patio.

Seconds later, Lori was at the door, then through it into the safety of the darkness beyond. The room was no more than an antechamber. Two doors led from it: one into a chapel of some sort, the other below ground. The woman in mourning was standing at this second door, which was open, as far from the wounding light as she could get. In her haste, her veil had fallen. The face beneath was fine-boned, and thin almost to the point of being wasted, lending additional force to her eyes, which caught, even in the darkest corner of the room, some trace of light from the open door, so that they seemed almost to glow.

Lori felt no trace of fear. It was the other woman who trembled as she nursed her sunstruck hands, her gaze moving from Lori's bewildered face to the animal.

"I'm afraid it's dead," Lori said, not knowing what disease afflicted this woman, but recognizing her grief from all too recent memory.

"No . . ." the woman said with quiet conviction, "she can't die."

Her words were statement not entreaty, but the stillness in Lori's arms contradicted such certainty. If the creature wasn't yet dead it was surely beyond recall.

"Will you bring her to me?" the woman asked.

Lori hesitated. Though the weight of the body was making her arms ache, and she wanted the duty done, she didn't want to cross the chamber.

"Please," the woman said, reaching out with wounded hands.

Relenting, Lori left the comfort of the door and the sunlit patio beyond. She'd taken only two or three steps, however, when she heard the sound of whispering. There could only be one source: the stairs. There were people in the crypt. She stopped walking, childhood superstitions rising up in her. Fear of tombs, fear of stairs *descending*, fear of the Underworld.

"It's nobody," the woman said, her face pained. "Please, bring me Babette."

As if to further reassure Lori, she took a step away from the stairs, murmuring to the animal she'd called Babette. Either the words, or the woman's proximity, or perhaps the cool darkness of the chamber, won a response from the creature: a tremor ran down its spine like an electrical charge, so strong Lori almost lost hold of it. The woman's murmurs grew louder, as if she were chiding the dying thing, her anxiety to claim it suddenly urgent. But there was an impasse. Lori was no more willing to approach the entrance to the crypt than the woman was to come another step toward the outer door, and in the seconds of stasis the animal found new life. One of its claws seized Lori's breast as it began to writhe in her embrace.

The chiding became a shout—

"*Babette!*"

—but if the creature heard, it didn't care to listen. Its motion became more violent: a mingling of fit and sensuality. One moment it shuddered as though tortured, the next it moved like a snake sloughing off its skin.

"*Don't look, don't look!*" she heard the woman say, but Lori wasn't about to take her eyes off this horrendous dance. Nor could she give the creature over to the woman's charge; while the claw gripped her so tightly any attempt to separate them would draw blood.

But that *Don't look!* had purpose. Now it was Lori's turn to raise her voice in panic, as she realized that what was taking place in her arms defied all reason.

"*Jesus God!*"

The animal was changing before her eyes. In the luxury of slough and spasm it was losing its bestiality, not by reordering its anatomy but by liquefying its whole self—through to the bone—until what had been solid was a tumble of matter. Here was the origin of the bittersweet scent she'd met beneath the tree: the stuff of the beast's dissolution. In the moment it lost its coherence, the matter was ready to be out of her grasp, but somehow the essence of the thing—its will, perhaps, perhaps its *soul*—drew it back for the business of remaking. The last part of the beast to melt was the claw, its disintegration sending a throb of pleasure through Lori's body. It did not distract her from the fact that she was released. Horrified, she couldn't get what she held from her embrace fast enough, tipping it into the mourner's outstretched arms like so much excrement.

"*Jesus,*" she said, backing away, "*Jesus, Jesus.*"

There was no horror on the woman's face, however, only joy. Tears of

welcome rolled down her pale cheeks, and fell into the melting pot she
held. Lori looked away toward the sunlight. After the gloom of the interior it was blinding. She was momentarily disoriented, and closed her
eyes to allow herself a reprieve from both tomb and light.

It was sobbing that made her open her eyes. Not the woman this
time, but a child, a girl of four or five, lying naked where the muck of
transformation had been.

"Babette," the woman said.

Impossible, reason replied. This thin white child could not be the
animal she'd rescued from beneath the tree. It was sleight of hand, or
some idiot delusion she'd foisted upon herself. Impossible, all impossible.

"She likes to play outside," the woman was saying, looking up from
the child at Lori. "And I tell her: never, never in the sun. Never play in
the sun. But she's a child. She doesn't understand."

Impossible, reason repeated. But somewhere in her gut Lori had
already given up trying to deny. The animal had been real. The transformation had been real. Now here was a living child, weeping in her
mother's arms. She too was real. Every moment she wasted saying No to
what she *knew*, was a moment lost to comprehension. That her world-
view couldn't contain such a mystery without shattering was its liability,
and a problem for another day. For now she simply wanted to be away,
into the sunlight where she knew these shape shifters feared to follow.
Not daring to take her eyes off them until she was in the sun, she reached
out to the wall to guide her tentative backward steps. But Babette's
mother wanted to hold her awhile longer.

"I owe you something . . ." she said.

"No," Lori replied, "I don't . . . want anything . . . from you."

She felt the urge to express her revulsion, but the scene of reunion
before her—the child reaching up to touch her mother's chin, her sobs
passing—were so tender. Disgust became bewilderment, fear, confusion.

"Let me help you," the woman said. "I know why you came here."

"I doubt it," Lori said.

"Don't waste your time here," the woman replied. "There's nothing
for you here. Midian's a home for the Nightbreed. Only the Nightbreed."

Her voice had dropped in volume; it was barely above a whisper.

"The Nightbreed?" Lori said, more loudly.

The woman looked pained.

"Shh . . ." she said. "I shouldn't be telling you this. But I owe you this much at least."

Lori had stopped her retreat to the door. Her instinct was telling her to wait.

"Do you know a man called Boone?" she said.

The woman opened her mouth to reply, her face a mass of contrary feelings. She wanted to answer, that much was clear, but fear prevented her from speaking. It didn't matter. Her hesitation was answer enough. She *did* know Boone, or had.

"Rachel."

A voice rose from the door that led down into the earth. A man's voice.

"Come away," it demanded, "you've nothing to tell."

The woman looked toward the stairs.

"Mr. Lylesburg," she said, her tone formal, "she saved Babette."

"We know," came the reply from the darkness, "we saw. Still, you must come away."

We, Lori thought. How many others were there below ground, how many more of the *Nightbreed*?

Taking confidence from the proximity of the open door, she challenged the voice that was attempting to silence her informant.

"I saved the child," she said. "I think I deserve something for that."

There was a silence from the darkness, then a point of heated ash brightened in its midst and Lori realized that Mr. Lylesburg was standing almost at the top of the stairs, where the light from outside should have illuminated him, albeit poorly, but that somehow the shadows were clotted about him, leaving him invisible but for his cigarette.

"The child has no life to save," he said to Lori, "but what she has is yours, if you want it." He paused. "Do you want it? If you do, take her. She belongs to you."

The notion of this exchange horrified her.

"What do you take me for?" she said.

"I don't know," Lylesburg replied. "You were the one who demanded recompense."

"I just want some questions answered," Lori protested. "I don't want the child. I'm not a savage."

"No," the voice said softly, "no, you're not. So go. You've no business here."

He drew on the cigarette and by its tiny light Lori glimpsed the speaker's features. She sensed that he willingly revealed himself in this moment, dropping the veil of shadow for a handful of instants to meet her gaze face-to-face. He, like Rachel, was wasted, his gauntness more acute because his bones were large and made for solid cladding. Now, with his eyes sunk into their sockets, and the muscles of his face all too plain beneath papery skin, it was the sweep of his brow that dominated, furrowed and sickly.

"This was never intended," he said. "You weren't meant to see."

"I know that," Lori replied.

"Then you also know that to speak of this will bring dire consequences."

"Don't threaten me."

"Not for you," Lylesburg said. "for *us*."

She felt a twinge of shame at her misunderstanding. She wasn't the vulnerable one, she who could walk in the sunlight.

"I won't say anything," she told him.

"I thank you," he said.

He drew on his cigarette again, and the dark smoke took his face from view.

"What's below," he said from behind the veil, "remains below."

Rachel sighed softly at this, gazing down at the child as she rocked it gently.

"Come away," Lylesburg told her, and the shadows that concealed him moved off down the stairs.

"I have to go," Rachel said, and turned to follow. "Forget you were ever here. There's nothing you can do. You heard Mr. Lylesburg. What's below—"

"—remains below. Yes, I heard."

"Midian's for the Breed. There's no one here who needs you—"

"Just tell me," Lori requested, "is Boone here?"

Rachel was already at the top of the stairs, and now began to descend.

"He is, isn't he?" Lori said, forsaking the safety of the open door and crossing the chamber toward Rachel. "You people stole the body!"

It made some terrible, macabre sense. Those tomb dwellers, this Nightbreed, keeping Boone from being laid to rest.

"You *did! You stole him!*"

Rachel paused and looked back up at Lori, her face barely visible in the blackness of the stairs.

"We stole nothing," she said, her reply without rancor.

"*So where is he?*" Lori demanded.

Rachel turned away, and the shadows took her completely from view.

"*Tell me! Please God!*" Lori yelled down after her. Suddenly she was crying, in a turmoil of rage and fear and frustration. "*Tell me, please!*"

Desperation carried her down the stairs after Rachel, her shouts becoming appeals.

"Wait . . . talk to me . . ."

She took three steps, then a fourth. On the fifth she stopped, or rather her body stopped, the muscles of her legs becoming rigid without her instruction, refusing to carry her another step into the darkness of the crypt. Her skin was suddenly crawling with gooseflesh, her pulse thumping in her ears. No force of will could overrule the animal imperative forbidding her to descend: all she could do was stand rooted to the spot and stare into the depths. Even her tears had suddenly dried and the saliva gone from her mouth, so she could no more speak than walk. Not that she wanted to call down into the darkness now, for fear the forces there would answer her summons. Though she could see nothing of them her gut knew they were more terrible by far than Rachel and her beast-child. Shape shifting was almost a natural act beside the skills these others had to hand. She felt their perversity as a quality of the air. She breathed it in and out. It scoured her lungs and hurried her heart.

If they had Boone's corpse as a plaything it was beyond reclamation. She would have to take comfort from the hope that his spirit was somewhere brighter.

Defeated, she took a step backward. The shadows seemed unwilling to relinquish her, however. She felt them weave themselves into her blouse and hook themselves on her eyelashes, a thousand tiny holds upon her, slowing her retreat.

"I won't tell anyone," she murmured. "Please let me go."

But the shadows held on, their power a promise of retribution if she defied them.

"I promise," she said. "What more can I do?"

And suddenly, they capitulated. She hadn't realized how strong their claim was until it was withdrawn. She stumbled backward, falling up the stairs into the light of the antechamber. Turning her back on the crypt, she fled for the door and out into the sun.

It was too bright. She covered her eyes, holding herself upright by gripping the stone portico so that she could accustom herself to its violence. It took several minutes, standing against the mausoleum, shaking and rigid by turn. Only when she felt able to see through half-closed eyes did she attempt to walk, her route back to the main gate a farrago of cul-de-sacs and missed turnings.

By the time she reached it, however, she'd more or less accustomed herself to the brutality of light and sky. Her body was still not back at her mind's disposal, however. Her legs refused to carry her more than a few paces up the hill to Midian without threatening to drop her to the ground. Her system, overdosed on adrenaline, was cavorting. But at least she was alive. For a short while there on the stairs it had been touch and go. The shadows that had held her by lash and thread could have taken her, she had no doubt of that. Claimed her for the Underworld and snuffed her out. Why had they released her? Perhaps because she'd saved the child, perhaps because she'd sworn silence and they'd trusted her. Neither, however, seemed the motives of monsters, and she had to believe that what lived beneath Midian's cemetery deserved that name. Who other than monsters made their nests among the dead? They might call themselves the Nightbreed, but neither words nor gestures of good faith could disguise their true nature.

She had escaped demons—things of rot and wickedness—and she would have offered up a prayer of thanks for her deliverance if the sky had not been so wide and bright, and so plainly devoid of deities to hear.

PART THREE

DARK AGES

. . . out on the town, with two skins. The leather and the flesh. Three if you count the fore. All out to be touched tonight, yessir. All ready to be rubbed and nuzzled and loved tonight, yessir.

—CHARLES KYD, HANGING BY A THREAD

11

THE STALKING
GROUND

I

Driving back to Shere Neck, the radio turned up to a deafening level both to confirm her existence and keep it from straying, she became more certain by the mile that promises notwithstanding she'd not be able to conceal the experience from Sheryl. How could it not be obvious in her face, in her voice? Such fears proved groundless. Either she was better at concealment than she'd thought, or Sheryl was more insensitive. Either way, Sheryl asked only the most perfunctory questions about Lori's return visit to Midian before moving on to talk of Curtis.

"I want you to meet him," she said, "just to be sure I'm not dreaming."

"I'm going to go home, Sheryl," Lori said.

"Not tonight, surely. It's too late."

She was right; the day was too advanced for Lori to contemplate a homeward trip. Nor could she fabricate a reason for denying Sheryl's request without offending.

"You won't feel like a lemon, I promise," Sheryl said. "He said he wanted to meet you. I've told him all about you. Well . . . not all. But enough, you know, about how we met." She made a forlorn face. "Say you'll come," she said.

"I'll come."

"Fabulous! I'll call him right now."

While Sheryl went about making her call, Lori took a shower. There was news of the night's arrangements within two minutes.

"He'll meet us at this restaurant he knows, around eight," Sheryl hollered. "He'll even find a friend for you—"

"No, Sheryl—"

"I think he was just kidding," came the reply. Sheryl appeared at the bathroom door. "He's got a funny sense of humor," she said. "You know, when you're not sure if someone's making a joke or not? He's like that."

Great, Lori thought, a failed comedian. But there was something undeniably comforting about coming back to Sheryl and this girlish passion. Her endless talk of Curtis—none of which gave Lori more than a street artist's portrait of the man: all surface and no insight—was the perfect distraction from thoughts of Midian and its revelations. The early evening was so filled with good humor, and the ritual of preparing for a night on the town, that on occasion Lori found herself wondering if all that had happened in the Necropolis had not been a hallucination. But she had evidence that confirmed the memory; the cut beside her mouth from that wayward branch. It was little enough sign, but the sharp hurt of it kept her from doubting her sanity. She *had* been to Midian. She *had* held the shape shifter in her arms, and stood on the crypt stairs gazing into a miasma so profound it could have rotted the faith of a saint.

Though the unholy world beneath the cemetery was as far from Sheryl and her whirlwind romance as night from day, it was no less real for that. In time she would have to address that reality, find a place for it, though it defied all logic. For now, she would keep it in mind, with the cut as its guardian, and enjoy the pleasures of the evening ahead.

2

"It's a joke," said Sheryl, as they stood outside the Hudson Bay Sunset. "Didn't I tell you he had this weird sense of humor?"

The restaurant he'd named had been completely gutted by fire, several weeks ago, to judge by the state of the timbers.

"Are you sure you got the right address?" Lori asked.

Sheryl laughed.

"I tell you it's one of his jokes," she said.

"So we've laughed," said Lori. "When do we get to eat?"

"He's probably watching us," Sheryl said, her good humor slightly forced.

Lori looked around for some sign of the voyeur. Though there was nothing to fear on the streets of a town like this, even on a Saturday night, the neighborhood was far from welcoming. Every other shop along the block was closed up and the sidewalks completely deserted in both directions. It was no place they wanted to linger.

"I don't see him," Lori said.

"Neither do I."

"So what do we do now?" Lori asked, doing her best to keep any trace of irritation from her voice. If this was Curtis the Beau's idea of a good time, Sheryl's taste had to be in doubt; but then who was she to judge, who'd loved and lost a psycho?

"He's got to be here somewhere," Sheryl said hopefully. "Curtis?" she called out, pushing open the heat-blistered door.

"Why don't we wait for him out here, Sheryl?"

"He's probably inside."

"The place could be dangerous."

Her appeal was ignored.

"*Sheryl.*"

"I hear you. I'm OK." She was already immersed in the darkness of the interior. The smell of burned wood and fabric stung Lori's nostrils.

"Curtis?" she heard Sheryl call.

A car went past, its engine badly tuned. The passenger, a youth, prematurely balding, leaned out of the window.

"Need any help?"

"No thanks," Lori yelled back, not certain if the question was small-town courtesy or a come-on. Probably the latter, she decided, as the car picked up speed and disappeared; people were the same all over. Her mood, which had improved by leaps and bounds since she'd been back in Sheryl's company, was rapidly souring. She didn't like being on this empty street, with what little was left of the day sliding toward extinction. The night, which had always been a place of promise, belonged too much to the Breed, who had taken its name for themselves. And why not? All darkness was one darkness in the end. Of heart or heavens, one darkness. Even now, in Midian, they'd be dragging back the doors of the mausoleums, knowing the starlight would not wither them. She shuddered at the thought.

Off down one of the streets she heard the car engine rev up and roar, then a squeal of brakes. Were the Good Samaritans coming round for a second look?

"Sheryl," she called out, "where are you?"

The joke—if joke it had been and not Sheryl's error—had long since lost what questionable humor it had. She wanted to get back into the car and *drive*, back to the hotel if necessary.

"Sheryl? Are you there?"

There was laughter from the interior of the building, Sheryl's gurgling laughter. Suspecting now her compliance in this fiasco, Lori stepped through the door in search of the tricksters.

The laughter came again, then broke off as Sheryl said, *"Curtis,"* in a tone of mock indignation that decayed into further inane laughter. So the great lover *was* here. Lori half contemplated returning to the street, getting back into the car, and leaving them to their damn fool games. But the thought of the evening alone in the hotel room, listening to more partying, spurred her on through an assault course of burned furniture.

Had it not been for the brightness of floor tiles throwing the streetlight up toward the cage of ceiling beams, she might not have risked advancing far. But ahead she could dimly see the archway through which Sheryl's laughter had floated. She made her way toward it. All sound had ceased. They were watching her every tentative step. She felt their scrutiny.

"Come on, guys," she said, "joke's over. I'm hungry."

There was no reply. Behind her, on the street, she heard the Samaritans yelling. Retreat was not advisable. She advanced, stepping through the archway.

Her first thought was: he only told half a lie, this *was* a restaurant. The exploration had taken her into a kitchen, where probably the fire had started. It too was tiled in white, surfaces smoke-stained but still bright enough to lend the whole interior, which was large, an odd luminescence. She stood in the doorway and scanned the room. The largest of the stoves was placed in the center, racks of shining utensils still hanging above it, truncating her view. The jokers had to be in hiding on the other side of the range; it was the only refuge the room offered.

Despite her anxieties, she felt an echo here of remembered games of hide-and-seek. The first game, because the simplest. How she'd loved to be terrorized by her father, chased and caught. If only he were here in hiding now, she found herself thinking, waiting to embrace her. But cancer had long since caught him by the throat.

"Sheryl?" she said, "I give up. Where are you?"

Even as she spoke, her advance brought her within sight of one of the players, and the game ended.

Sheryl was not in hiding, unless death was hiding. She was crouched against the stove, the darkness around her too wet for shadow, her head thrown back, her face slashed open.

"Jesus God."

Behind Lori, a sound. Somebody coming to find her. Too late to hide. She'd be caught. And not by loving arms, not by her father, playing the monster. This was the monster itself.

She turned to see its face before it took her, but running at her was a sewing-box doll: zipper for mouth, buttons for eyes, all sewn on white linen and tied around the monster's face so tightly his saliva darkened a patch around his mouth. She was denied the face but not the teeth. He held them above his head, gleaming knives, their blades fine as grass stalks, sweeping down to stab out her eyes. She threw herself out of their reach but he was after her in an instant, the mouth behind the zipper calling her name.

"Better get it over with, Lori."

The blades were coming at her again, but she was quicker. The Mask didn't seem too hurried; he closed on her with a steady step, his confidence obscene.

"Sheryl had the right idea," he said. "She just stood there and let it happen."

"Fuck you."

"Later, maybe."

He ran one of the blades along the row of hanging pots, striking squeals and sparks.

"Later, when you're a little colder."

He laughed, the zipper gaping.

"There's something to look forward to."

She let him talk, while trying to get some sense of what escape routes lay open to her. The fire door was blocked by burned timbers: her only exit was the arch through which she'd entered, and the Mask stood between her and it, sharpening his teeth on each other.

He started toward her again. No jibes from him now; the time for talk was over. As he closed on her she thought of Midian. Surely she'd not survived its terrors to be hacked to death by some lone psycho?

Fuck him!

As the knives slid toward her she snatched a pot from the rack above the range and brought it up to meet his face. It connected squarely. Her strength shocked her. The Mask reeled, dropping one of his blades. There was no sound from behind the linen, however. He merely transferred the remaining blade from right hand to left, shook his head as if to stop it singing, and came at her again, at a rush. She barely had time to raise the pan in defense. The blade slid down it and met her hand. For a moment there was no pain, nor even blood. Then both came in profusion, the pan falling from her hand at her feet. Now he made a sound, a cooing sound, the tilt of his head suggesting that it was the blood he was staring at as it ran from the wound he'd fathered.

She looked toward the door, calculating the time it would take to get there against his speed of pursuit. But before she could act, the Mask began his last advance. The knife was not raised. Nor was his voice, when he spoke.

"Lori," he said, "we must talk, you and me."

"Keep the fuck away."

To her amazement he obeyed the instruction. She seized what little time this offered to claim his other blade from the floor. She was less competent with her unwounded hand, but he was a large target. She could do him damage, preferably through the heart.

"That's what I killed Sheryl with," he said. "I'd put it down if I were you."

The steel was sticky in her palm.

"Yes, that slit little Sheryl, ear to ear," he went on. "And now you've got your prints all over it. You should have worn gloves, like me."

The thought of what the blade had done appalled her, but she wasn't about to drop it and stand unarmed.

"Of course, you could always blame Boone," the Mask was saying. "Tell the police he did it."

"How do you know about Boone?" she said. Hadn't Sheryl sworn she'd told her paramour nothing?

"You know where he is?" the Mask stated.

"He's dead," she replied.

The sewing-box face denied it with a shake.

"No, I'm afraid not. He got up and walked. God knows how. But he got up and walked. Can you imagine that? The man was pumped full of bullets. You saw the blood he shed—"

He was watching us all the time, she thought. *He followed us to Midian that first day.* But why? That was what she couldn't make sense of; *why?*

"—all that blood, all those bullets, and still he wouldn't lie down dead."

"Somebody stole the body," she said.

"No," came the reply, "that's not the way it was."

"Who the hell *are* you?"

"Good question. No reason why you shouldn't have an answer."

His hand went up to his face and he pulled off the mask. Beneath was Decker, sweaty and smiling.

"I wish I'd brought my camera," he said, "the look on your face."

The shock made her gape like a fish. Decker was Curtis, Sheryl's Mister Right."

"Why?" she demanded.

"Why what?"

"Why did you kill Sheryl?"

"For the same reason I killed all the others," he said lightly, as though the question hadn't much vexed him. Then, deadly serious: "For the fun of it, of course. For the pleasure. We used to talk a lot about *why*, Boone and me. Digging deep, you know, trying to understand. But when it really comes down to it, I do it because I like it."

"Boone was innocent."

"*Is* innocent, wherever he's hiding. Which is a problem, because he knows the real facts, and one of these days he might find someone to convince of the truth."

"So you want to stop him?"

"Wouldn't you? All the trouble I went to so he could die a guilty man. I even put a bullet in him myself and he still gets up and walks away."

"They told me he was dead. They were certain."

"The mortuary was unlocked from the *inside*. Did they tell you that? His fingerprints were on the handle, his footprints on the floor; did they tell you *that?* No, of course not. But I'm telling you. I know. *Boone is alive.* And your death is going to bring him out of hiding, I'll bet on it. He'll have to show himself."

Slowly, as he spoke, he was raising the knife.

"If it's only to mourn."

Suddenly he was at her. She put the blade that had killed Sheryl between her and his approach. It slowed him, but he didn't stop coming.

"Could you really do it?" he said to her. "I don't think so. And I speak from experience. People are *squeamish* even when their lives are at stake. And that knife, of course, it's already been blunted on poor Sheryl. You'll have to really dig to make some impression on me."

He spoke almost playfully, still advancing.

"I'd like to see you try, though," he said. "I really would. Like to see you try."

Out of the corner of her eye she was aware that she'd come abreast of piled plates mere inches from her elbow. Might they offer her time enough to get to the door? she wondered. In knife-to-knife combat with this maniac she'd lose, no doubt of it. But she might yet outwit him.

"Come on. Try me. Kill me if you can. For Boone. For poor, mad Boone—"

As the words became laughter, she threw her wounded hand out toward the plates, hooked them round, and flung them onto the floor in front of Decker. A second pile followed, and a third, china shards flying up in all directions. He took a step back, his hands going up to his face to protect himself, and she took the chance while she had it, bolting for the archway. She got through it and into the restaurant itself before she heard his pursuit. By that time she had sufficient lead to reach the outer door and fling herself through it, onto the street. Once on the sidewalk she immediately turned and faced the door through which he would come. But he had no intention of following her into the light.

"Clever bitch," he said from the darkness. "I'll get you. When I've got Boone I'll come back for you. You just count the breaths till then."

Eyes still fixed on the door, she backed off down the sidewalk toward the car. Only now did she realize that she still carried the murder weapon, her grip so strong she felt almost glued to it. She had no choice but to take it with her, and give it, and her evidence, to the police. Back to the car, she opened the door and got in, only looking away from the burned-out building when the locks were on. Then she threw the knife onto the floor in front of the passenger seat, started the engine, and drove.

3

The choice before her came down to this: the police or Midian. A night of interrogation or a return to the Necropolis. If she chose the former she would not be able to warn Boone of Decker's pursuit. But then suppose Decker had been lying and Boone had not survived the bullets? She'd not only be fleeing from the scene of a murder but putting herself within reach of the Nightbreeders, and uselessly.

Yesterday she would have chosen to go to the law. She would have trusted that its procedures would make all these mysteries come clear, that they would believe her story and bring Decker to justice. But yesterday she'd thought beasts were beasts, and children, children; she'd thought that only the dead lived in the earth, and that they were peaceful there. She'd thought doctors healed, and that when the madman's mask was raised she would say, "But of course, that's a madman's face."

All wrong, all so wrong. Yesterday's assumptions were gone to the wind. Anything might be true.

Boone might be alive.

She drove to Midian.

12
ABOVE AПD BELOW

I

Visions came to meet her down the highway, brought on by the aftereffects of shock and the loss of blood from her bound but wounded hand. They began like snow blown toward the windshield, flakes of brightness that defied the glass and flew past her, whining as they went. As her dreamy state worsened, she seemed to see faces flying at her, and commas of life like fetuses, which whispered as they tumbled past. The spectacle did not distress her; quite the reverse. It seemed to confirm a scenario her hallucinating mind had created: that she, like Boone, was living a charmed life. Nothing could harm her, not tonight. Though her cut hand was now so numb it could no longer grip the wheel, leaving her to navigate an unlit road one-handed, and at speed, fate had not let her survive Decker's attack only to kill her on the highway.

There was a reunion in the air. That was why the visions came, racing into the headlights, and skipping over the car to burst above her in showers of white lights. They were welcoming her.

To Midian.

2

Once she looked in the mirror and thought she glimpsed a car behind her, its lights turned off. But when she looked again it had gone. Perhaps it had never been there. Ahead lay the town, its houses blinded by her headlights. She drove down the main street all the way to the graveyard gates.

The mingled intoxications of blood loss and exhaustion had dulled all fear of this place. If she could survive the malice of the living she could surely survive the dead, or their companions. And Boone was here; that hope had hardened into certainty as she drove. Boone was here, and finally she'd be able to take him into her arms.

She stumbled out of the car, and almost fell flat on her face.

Get up, she told herself.

The lights were still coming at her, though she was no longer moving, but now all trace of detail in them had vanished. There was only the brightness, its ferocity threatening to wash the whole world away. Knowing total collapse was imminent she crossed to the gates, calling Boone's name. She had an answer immediately, though not the one she sought.

"He's here?" somebody said. "Boone is *here?*"

Clinging to the gate she turned her leaden head, and through the surf of light saw Decker, standing a few yards from her. Behind him, his lightless car. Even in her dizzied state she understood how she'd been manipulated. Decker had allowed her to escape, knowing she'd seek out his enemy.

Stupid! she told herself.

"Well, yes. But then, what were you to do? No doubt you thought you might save him."

She had neither the strength nor the wit to resist the man. Relinquishing the support of the gates, she staggered into the cemetery.

"*Boone!*" she yelled. "*Boone!*"

Decker didn't come after her quickly; he had no need. She was a wounded animal going in search of another wounded animal. Glancing behind her she saw him checking his gun by the light of his headlights. Then he pushed the gate wider and came in pursuit.

She could barely see the avenues in front of her for the bursts of light in her head. She was like a blind woman, sobbing as she stumbled, no longer even certain if Decker was behind her or in front. Any moment he would dispatch her. One bullet, and her charmed life would end.

3

In the ground below, the Breed heard her arrival, their senses attuned to panic and despair. They knew the hunter's tread too; they'd heard it behind them all too often. Now they waited, pitying the woman in her last moments but too covetous of their refuge to put it at risk. There were few enough hiding places left where the monstrous might find peace. They'd not endanger their hermitage for a human life.

Still it pained them, hearing her pleas and her calls. And for one of their number the sound was almost beyond endurance.

"Let me go to her."

"You can't. You know you can't."

"I can kill him. Who's to know he was ever here?"

"He won't be alone. There'll be others waiting outside the walls. Remember how they came for you."

"I can't let her die."

"Boone! Please God—"

It was worse than anything he'd suffered, hearing her calling him and knowing Midian's law wouldn't let him answer.

"Listen to her, for God's sake!" he said. "Listen."

"You made promises when we took you in," Lylesburg reminded him.

"I know. I understand."

"I wonder if you do. They weren't demanded lightly, Boone. Break them and you belong nowhere. Not with us. Not with them."

"You're asking me to listen to her die."

"So block your ears. It'll soon be over."

4

She could no longer find the breath to call his name. No matter. He wasn't here. Or if he was, he was dead in the earth, and corrupted. Beyond help, in the giving or the taking.

She was alone, and the man with the gun was closing on her.

Decker took the mask from his pocket, the button mask he felt so safe behind. Oh, the number of times in those tiresome days with Boone, teaching him the dates and the places of the murders he was inheriting, when Decker's pride had almost brimmed over and he'd itched to reclaim the crimes. But he needed the scapegoat more than the quick thrill of confession, to keep suspicion at bay. Boone's admitting to the crimes wouldn't have been an end to it all, of course. In time the Mask would start speaking to its owner again, demanding to be bloodied, and the killings would have to begin afresh. But not until Decker had found himself another name, and another city to set up his store in. Boone had spoiled those well-laid plans, but he'd get no chance to tell what he knew. Ol' Button Face would see to that.

Decker pulled the mask on. It smelled of his excitement. As soon as he breathed in he got a hard. Not the little sex-hard, but the death-hard, the murder-hard. It sniffed the air for him, even through the thickness of his trousers and underwear. It smelled the victim that ran ahead of him. The Mask didn't care that his prey was female; he got the murder-hard for anyone. In his time he'd had a heat for old men, pissing their pants as they went down in front of him; for girls, sometimes; sometimes women; even children. Ol' Button Face looked with the same cross-threaded eyes on the whole of humanity.

This one, this woman in the dark up ahead, meant no more to the Mask than any of the others. Once they started to panic and bleed, they were all the same. He followed her with steady step; that was one of Button Head's trademarks, the executioner's tread. And she fled before him, her pleas deteriorating into snot and gasps. Though she hadn't got breath to call for her hero, no doubt she prayed he'd still come for her. Poor bitch. Didn't she know they never showed? He'd heard them all called upon in his time, begged for, bargained with, the Holy Fathers and Mothers, the champions, the interceders; none of them ever showed.

But her agony would be over soon. A shot through the back of the head to bring her down, and then he'd take the big knife, the heavy knife, to her face, the way he did with all of them. Crisscross, crisscross, like the threads in his eye, till there was nothing left to look at but meat.

Ah! She was falling. Too tired to run any farther.

He opened Ol' Button Head's steel mouth, and spoke to the fallen girl—

"Be still," he said. "It's quicker that way."

She tried to get up one final time, but her legs had given out completely, and the wash of whiteness was practically all-consuming. Giddily, she

turned her head in the direction of Decker's voice, and in a trough
between the white waves she saw that he'd put his mask back on. Its face
was a death's head.

He raised the gun—

In the ground beneath her, she felt tremors. Was it the sound of a
shot, perhaps? She couldn't see the gun any longer, or even Decker. One
final wave had washed him from sight. But her body felt the earth rock,
and through the whine in her head she heard somebody calling the name
of the man she'd hoped to find here.

Boone!

She didn't hear an answer—perhaps there wasn't one—but the call
came again, as if summoning him back into the earth.

Before she could muster the last of her power to counter the call, her
good arm gave out beneath her and she was facedown on the ground.

Button Head walked toward his quarry, disappointed that the woman
would not be conscious to hear his final benediction. He liked to offer a
few words of insight at the penultimate moment, words he never planned
but that came like poetry from the zipper mouth. On occasion they'd
laughed at his sermon, and that had made him cruel. But if they cried,
and they often did, then he took it in good part and made certain the last
moment, the *very* last, was swift and painless.

He kicked the woman over onto her back to see if he could raise her
from her sleep. And yes, her eyes flickered open slightly.

"Good," he said, pointing the gun at her face.

As he felt wisdom coming to his lips he heard the growl. It drew his
gaze off the woman for a moment. A soundless wind had risen from
somewhere and was shaking the trees. There was complaint in the
ground beneath his feet.

The Mask was untouched. Wandering in tomb yards didn't raise a
hair on his neck. He was the New Death, tomorrow's face today: what
harm could dust do him?

He laughed at the melodrama of it. Threw back his head and
laughed.

At his feet the woman started moaning. Time to shut her up. He took
aim at her open mouth.

As he recognized the word she was shaping, the dark ahead of him
divided, and that word stepped out of hiding.

"Boone," she'd said.

It was.

He emerged from the shadow of the shaking trees, dressed just as the Mask remembered, in dirty T-shirt and jeans. But there was a brightness in his eyes the Mask did not remember, and he walked—despite the bullets he'd taken—like a man who'd never known an ache in his life.

Mystery enough. But there was more. Even as he stepped into view he began to *change*, breathing out a veil of smoke that took his flesh for fantasy.

This was the scapegoat, yet not. So much *not*.

The Mask looked down at the woman to confirm that they shared this vision, but she had fallen into unconsciousness. He had to trust what the cross-sewn eyes told him, and they told him terrors.

The sinews of Boone's arms and neck were rippling with light and darkness; his fingers were growing larger; his face, behind the smoke he exhaled, seemed to be running with dazzling filaments that described a hidden form within his head that muscle and bone were conforming to.

And out of the confusion, a voice. It was not the voice the Mask remembered. No scapegoat's voice, hushed with guilt. It was a yell of fury.

"You're a dead man, Decker!" the monster cried.

The Mask hated that name, that *Decker*. The man was just some old flame he'd fucked once in a while. In a heat like this, with the murderhard so strong, Ol' Button Head could barely remember whether Dr. Decker was alive or dead.

Still the monster called him by that name.

"You hear me, *Decker?*" he said.

Bastard thing, the Mask thought. Misbegotten, half-aborted bastard thing. He pointed the gun at its heart. It had finished breathing transformations, and stood before its enemy complete, if a thing born on a butcher's slab could ever be called complete. Mothered by a she-wolf, fathered by a clown, it was ridiculous to a fault. There'd be no benediction for this one, the Mask decided. Only phlegm on its hybrid face when it was dead on the ground.

Without further thought, he fired. The bullet opened a hole in the center of Boone's T-shirt and in the changed flesh beneath, but the creature only grinned.

"You tried that already, Decker," Boone said. "Don't you ever learn?"

"*I'm not Decker*," the Mask replied, and fired again. Another hole opened up beside the first but no blood came from either.

Boone had begun to advance on the gun. No last, faltering step but a steady approach which the Mask recognized as his own executioner's tread. He could smell the filth of the beast even through the linen across his face. It was bittersweet, and sickened him.

"Be still," the monster said, "it's quicker that way."

The stolen step was insult enough, but to hear the purity of his own words from that unnatural throat drove the Mask to distraction. He shrieked against the cloth and aimed the gun at Boone's mouth. But before he could blow out the offending tongue, Boone's swollen hands reached and took hold of the gun. Even as it was snatched from him the Mask pulled the trigger, firing against Boone's hand. The bullets blew off his smallest finger. The expression on his face darkened with displeasure. He dragged the gun out of the Mask's hands and flung it away. Then he reached for his mutilator and drew him close.

Faced with imminent extinction, the Mask and its wearer divided. Ol' Button Head did not believe he could ever die. Decker did. His teeth grated against the cage across his mouth as he began to beg.

"Boone . . . you don't know what you're doing."

He felt the mask tighten over his head in fury at his cowardice, but he talked on, trying to find that even tone he had used to calm this man once upon a time.

"You're diseased, Boone."

Don't beg, he heard the Mask saying, *don't you* dare *beg*.

"And you can heal me, can you?" the monster said.

"Oh yes," Decker replied. "Oh certainly. Just give me a little time."

Boone's wounded hand stroked the mask.

"Why do you hide behind this thing?" he asked.

"It *makes* me hide. I don't want to, but it makes me."

The Mask's fury knew no bounds. It shrieked in Decker's head, hearing him betray his master. If he survived tonight it would demand the vilest compensation for these lies. He'd pay it gladly tomorrow. But he had to outwit the beast to live that long.

"You must feel the same as me," he said, "behind that skin you have to wear."

"The same?" said Boone.

"Trapped. Made to spill blood. You don't want to spill blood any more than I do."

"You don't understand," Boone said, "I'm not *behind* this face. I *am* this face."

Decker shook his head.

"I don't think so. I think that somewhere you're still Boone."

"Boone is dead. Boone was shot down in front of you. Remember? You put bullets in him yourself."

"But you survived."

"Not alive."

Decker's bulk had been trembling. Now it stopped. Every muscle in his body became rigid as the explanation for these mysteries came clear.

"You drove me into the hands of monsters, Decker. And I became one. Not your kind of monster. Not the soulless kind." He drew Decker very close, his face inches from the mask. "I'm dead, Decker. Your bullets mean nothing to me. I've got Midian in my veins. That means I'll heal myself over and over. But you—"

The hand stroking the mask now gripped the fabric.

"—you, Decker . . . when you die, you die. And I want to see your face when it happens."

Boone pulled at the mask. It was tied on securely and wouldn't come. He had to get his claws into the warp and woof to tear it open and uncover the sweaty facts beneath. How many hours had he spent watching this face, hanging on its every flicker of approbation? So much wasted time. This was the healer's true condition: lost and weak and weeping.

"I was afraid," Decker said. "You understand that, don't you? They were going to find me, punish me. I needed someone to blame."

"You chose the wrong man."

"*Man?*" said a soft voice from the darkness. "You call yourself a man?"

Boone stood corrected.

"Monster," he said.

Laughter followed. Then: "Well, are you going to kill him or not?"

Boone looked away from Decker to the speaker squatting on the tomb. His face was a mass of scar tissue.

"Does he remember me?" the man asked Boone.

"I don't know. Do you?" Boone demanded of Decker. "His name's Narcisse."

Decker just stared.

"Another of Midian's tribe," Boone said.

"I was never quite certain I belonged," Narcisse mused. "Not till I was picking the bullets from my face. Kept thinking I was dreaming it all."

"Afraid," said Boone.

"I was. You know what they do to natural men."

Boone nodded.

"So kill him," Narcisse said. "Eat out his eyes or I'll do it for you."

"Not till I get a confession from him."

"Confession," said Decker, his eyes widening at the thought of reprieve. "If that's what you want, say the word."

He began rummaging in his jacket as if looking for a pen.

"What the fuck's the use of a confession?" Narcisse said. "You think anybody's ever gonna forgive you now? Look at yourself!"

He jumped down off the tomb.

"Look," he whispered, "if Lylesburg knows I came up here he'll have me out. Just give me his eyes, for old time's sake. Then the rest's yours."

"Don't let him touch me," Decker begged Boone. "Anything you want . . . full confession . . . anything. But keep him off me!"

Too late: Narcisse was already reaching for him, with or without Boone's permission. Boone attempted to keep him at bay with his free hand, but the man was too eager for revenge to be blocked. He forced himself between Boone and his prey.

"Look your last," he grinned, raising his hooked thumbs.

But Decker's rummaging hadn't been all panic. As the hooks came at his eyes he drew the big knife out of hiding in his jacket and thrust it into his attacker's belly. He'd made long and sober study of his craft. The cut he gave Narcisse was a disemboweling maneuver learned from the Japanese: deep into the intestines and up toward the navel, drawing the blade two-handed against the weight of meat. Narcisse cried out—more in memory of pain than in pain itself.

In one smooth motion Decker pulled the big knife out, knowing from research in the field that the well-packed contents were bound to follow. He wasn't wrong. Narcisse's gut uncoiled, falling like a flesh apron to its owner's knees. The wounding—which would have dropped a living man to the ground on the spot—merely made a clown of Narcisse. Howling in disgust at the sight of his innards, he clutched at Boone.

"Help me," he hollered, "I'm coming undone."

Decker took the moment. While Boone was held fast he fled toward the gates. There wasn't much ground to cover. By the time Boone had struggled free of Narcisse, the enemy was within sight of unconsecrated earth. Boone gave chase, but before he was even halfway to the gates he heard Decker's car door slam, and the engine rev. The doctor was away. Damn it, *away!*

"What the fuck do I do with this?" Boone heard Narcisse sob. He turned from the gates. The man had his guts looped between his hands like so much knitting.

"Go below," Boone said flatly. It was useless to curse Narcisse for his interference. "Somebody'll help you," he said. "I can't. They'll know I was up here."

"You think they don't know already?" Boone replied. "They know everything."

He was no longer concerned about Narcisse. It was the body sprawled on the walkway that had claimed his attentions. In his hunger to terrorize Decker he'd forgotten Lori entirely.

"They'll throw us both out," Narcisse was saying.

"Maybe," said Boone.

"What will we do?"

"Just go below," Boone said wearily. "Tell Mr. Lylesburg I led you astray."

"You did?" said Narcisse. Then, warming to the idea, "Yes, I think you did."

Carrying his guts, he limped away.

Boone knelt beside Lori. Her scent made him dizzy; the softness of her skin beneath his palms was almost overpowering. She was still alive, her pulse strong despite the traumas she must have endured at Decker's hand. As he gazed on her gentle face, the thought that she might wake and see him in the shape he'd inherited from Peloquin's bite distressed him beyond measure. In Decker's presence he'd been proud to call himself a *monster*: to parade his Nightbreed self. But now, looking at the woman he had loved and had been loved by in return for his frailty and his humanity, he was ashamed.

He inhaled, his will making flesh smoke, which his lungs drew back into his body. It was a process as strange in its ease as its nature. How quickly he'd become accustomed to what he'd once have called miraculous.

But he was no wonder, not compared with this woman. The fact that she'd enough faith to come looking for him with death on her heels was more than any natural man could hope for, and, for one such as himself, a true miracle.

Her humanity made him proud of what he'd been, and could still pretend to be.

So it was in human form he picked her up and tenderly carried her underground.

13

THE PROPHETIC CHILD

Lori listened to the fury of the voices.

"*You cheated us!*"

The first was Lylesburg.

"*I had no choice!*"

The second, Boone.

"*So Midian's put at risk for your finer feelings?*"

"*Decker won't tell anyone,*" Boone responded. "*What's he going to say? That he tried to kill a girl and a dead man stopped him? Talk sense.*"

"*So suddenly you're the expert. A few days here and you're rewriting the law. Well, do it somewhere else, Boone. Take the woman and leave.*"

Lori wanted to open her eyes and go to Boone, calm him before his anger made him say or do something stupid. But her body was numb. Even the muscles of her face wouldn't respond to instruction. All she could do was lie still and listen as the argument raged.

"*I belong here,*" Boone said. "*I'm Nightbreed now.*"

"*Not any longer.*"

"*I can't live out there.*"

"*We did. For generations we took our chances in the natural world, and it nearly extinguished us. Now you come along and damn near destroy our one hope of surviving. If Midian's unearthed, you and the woman will be responsible. Think of that on your travels.*"

There was a long silence. Then Boone said:

"*Let me make amends.*"

"*Too late. The law makes no exceptions. The other one goes too.*"

"*Narcisse? No. You'll break his heart. He spent half his life waiting to come here.*"

"*The decision's made.*"

"*Who by? You? Or Baphomet?*"

At the sound of that name Lori felt a chill. The word meant nothing to her, but clearly it did to others nearby. She heard whispers echoing around her, repeated phrases like words of worship.

"*I demand to speak with it,*" Boone said.

"*Out of the question.*"

"*What are you afraid of? Losing your grip on your tribe? I want to see Baphomet. If you want to try and stop me, do it now.*"

As Boone threw the challenge down, Lori's eyes opened. There was a vaulted roof above her, where last there'd been sky. It was painted with stars, however, more fireworks than celestial bodies, catherine wheels throwing off sparks as they rolled across the stone heavens.

She inclined her head a little. She was in a crypt. There were sealed coffins on every side of her, upended against the walls. To her left a profusion of squat candles, their wax grimy, their flame as weak as she. To her right, Babette, sitting cross-legged on the floor, watching her intently. The child was dressed completely in black, her eyes catching the candlelight and steadying its flicker. She was not pretty. Her face was too solemn for prettiness. Even in the smile she offered Lori, seeing her wake, couldn't mellow the sadness in her features. Lori did her best to return the welcoming look, but wasn't certain her muscles were yet obeying her.

"It was a bad hurt he did us," Babette said.

Lori assumed she meant Boone. But the child's next words put her right.

"Rachel made it clean. Now it doesn't sting."

She raised her right hand. It was bandaged with dark linen around thumb and forefinger.

"Nor you either."

Mustering her will, Lori raised her own right hand from her side. It was bandaged identically.

"Where . . . is Rachel?" Lori asked, her voice barely audible to herself. Babette heard the question clearly, however.

"Somewhere near," she said.

"Could you get her for me?"

Babette's perpetual frown deepened.

"Are you here forever?" she asked.

"No," came the reply, not from Lori but from Rachel, who had appeared at the door, "no she's not. She's going to be away very soon."

"Why?" said Babette.

"I heard Lylesburg," Lori murmured.

"*Mister* Lylesburg," Rachel said, crossing to where Lori lay. "Boone broke his word going overground to fetch you. He's put us all in danger."

Lori understood only a fraction of Midian's story, but enough to know that the maxim she'd first heard from Lylesburg's lips—*"What's below remains below"* was not some idle catchphrase. It was a law the inhabitants of Midian had sworn to live by or else forfeit their place here.

"Can you help me?" she asked. She felt vulnerable lying on the floor.

It wasn't Rachel who came to her aid, however, but Babette, by laying her small, bandaged hand on Lori's stomach. Her system responded instantly to the child's touch, all trace of numbness leaving her body at once. She remembered the same sensation, or its like, from her last encounter with the girl: that feeling of transferred power that had moved through her when the beast had dissolved in her arms.

"She's formed quite a bond with you," Rachel said.

"So it seems." Lori sat up. "Is she hurt?"

"Why don't you ask *me?*" Babette said. "I'm here too."

"I'm sorry," Lori said, chastened. "Did you get cut too?"

"No. But I felt your hurt."

"She's empathic," Rachel said. "She feels what others feel, particularly if she has some emotional connection with them."

"I knew you were coming here," Babette said, "I saw through your eyes. And you can see through mine."

"Is that true?" Lori asked Rachel.

"Believe her," came the reply.

Lori wasn't quite certain she was ready to get to her feet yet, but she decided to put her body to the test. It was easier than she'd expected. She stood up readily, her limbs strong, her head clear.

"Will you take me to Boone?" she requested.

"If that's what you want."

"He was here all along, wasn't he?" she said.

"Yes."

"Who brought him?"

"Brought him?"

"To Midian."

"Nobody."

"He was almost dead," Lori said. "Somebody must have got him out of the mortuary."

"You still don't understand, do you?" said Rachel grimly.

"About Midian? No, not really."

"Not just Midian. About Boone, and why he is here."

"He thinks he's Nightbreed," Lori said.

"He *was,* until he broke his word."

"So we'll go," Lori replied. "That's what Lylesburg wants, isn't it? And I've got no wish to stay."

"Where will you go?" Rachel asked.

"I don't know. Maybe back to Calgary. It shouldn't be so hard to prove Decker's the guilty man. Then we can start over."

Rachel shook her head.

"That won't be possible," she said.

"Why not? Have you got some prior claim on him?"

"He came here because he's one of us."

"*Us.* Meaning what?" Lori replied sharply. She was tired of evasion and innuendo. "Who are you? Sick people living in the dark. Boone isn't sick. He's a sane man. A sane, healthy man."

"I suggest you ask him how healthy he feels," was Rachel's retort.

"Oh, I will, when the time comes."

Babette was not untouched by this exchange of contempt.

"You mustn't go," she said to Lori.

"I have to."

"Not into the light." She took fierce hold of Lori's sleeve. "I can't come with you there."

"She has to go," Rachel said, reaching over to prize her child loose. "She doesn't belong with us."

Babette held fast.

"You *can,*" she said, looking up at Lori. "It's easy."

"She doesn't want to," Rachel said.

Babette looked up at Lori.

"Is that true?" she asked.

"Tell her," Rachel said, taking plain satisfaction in Lori's discomfort, "tell her she's one of the sick people."

"But we live forever," Babette said. She glanced at her mother. "Don't we?"

"Some of us."

"*All* of us. If we want to. Live forever and ever. And one day, when the sun goes out—"

"*Enough!*" said Rachel.

But Babette had more to say.

"—when the sun goes out and there's only night, we'll live on the earth. It'll be ours."

Now it was Rachel's turn to be ill at ease.

"She doesn't know what she's saying," the woman muttered.

"I think she knows very well," Lori replied.

The proximity of Babette, and the thought that she had some bond with the child, suddenly chilled her. What little peace her rational mind had made with Midian was rapidly crumbling. She wanted more than anything to be away from here, from children who talked of the end of the world, from candles and coffins and the life of the tomb.

"Where's Boone?" she said to Rachel.

"Gone to the Tabernacle. To Baphomet."

"What is Baphomet?"

Rachel made a ritualisitic gesture at mention of Baphomet, touching her forefinger to tongue and heart. It was so familiar to her, and so often performed, Lori doubted she even knew she'd done it.

"Baphomet is the Baptizer," she said. "Who Made Midian. Who called us here."

Finger touched tongue and heart again.

"Will you take me to the Tabernacle?" Lori asked.

Rachel's reply was a plain and simple "No."

"Direct me at least."

"I'll take you," Babette volunteered.

"No, you won't," Rachel said, this time snatching the child's hand from Lori's sleeve with such speed Babette had no chance to resist.

"I've paid my debt to you," Rachel said, "healing the wound. We've no more business together."

She took hold of Babette and lifted the child up into her arms. Babette squirmed in her mother's embrace so as to look back at Lori.

"I want you to see beautiful things for me."

"Be quiet," Rachel chided.

"What *you* see *I'll* see."

Lori nodded.

"Yes?" Babette said.

"Yes."

Before her child could utter another mournful word, Rachel had carried her out of the room, leaving Lori to the company of the coffins.

She threw her head back and exhaled slowly. Calm, she thought, be calm. It'll be over soon.

The painted stars cavorted overhead, seeming to turn as she watched. Was their riot just the artist's fancy, she wondered, or was this the way the sky looked to the Breed, when they stepped out of their mausoleums at night to take the air?

Better not to know. It was bad enough that these creatures had children and art; that they might also have *vision* was too dangerous a thought to entertain.

When first she'd encountered them, halfway down the stairs into this Underworld, she'd feared for her life. She still did, in some hushed corner of herself. Not that it would be taken away, but that it would be *changed;* that somehow they'd taint her with their rites and visions, so she'd not be able to scrub them from her mind.

The sooner she was out of here, with Boone beside her, the sooner she'd be back in Calgary. The streetlights were bright there. They tamed the stars.

Reassured by the thought, she went in search of the Baptizer.

14

TABERNACLE

This was the true Midian. Not the empty town on the hill, not even the Necropolis above her, but this network of tunnels and chambers, which presumably spread beneath the entire cemetery. Some of the tombs were occupied only by the undisturbed dead, their caskets laid on shelves to molder: were these the first occupants of the cemetery, laid to rest here before the Nightbreed had taken possession? Or were they Breed who had died from their half-life, caught in the sun, perhaps, or withered by longing? Whichever, they were in the minority. Most of the chambers were tenanted by more vital souls, their quarters lit by lamps or candles, or on occasion by the occupant itself: a being that burned with its own light.

Only once did Lori glimpse such an entity, supine on a mattress in the corner of its boudoir. It was naked, corpulent and sexless, its sagging body a motley of dark, oily skin and larval eruptions that seeped phosphorescence, soaking its simple bed. It seemed every other doorway let on to some fragment as mysterious. Was it simply disgust that made her stomach flip, seeing the stigmatic in full flood, with sharp-toothed adherents sucking noisily at her wounds? Or excitement, confronting the legend of the vampire in the flesh? And what was she to make of the man whose body broke into birds when he saw her watching? Or the dog-headed painter who turned from his fresco and beckoned her to join his apprentice mixing paint? Or the machine beasts running up the walls on caliper legs? After a dozen corridors she no longer knew horror from fascination. Perhaps she'd never known.

She might have spent days lost and seeing the sights, but luck or instinct brought her close enough to Boone that further progress was blocked. It was Lylesburg's shadow that appeared before her, seeming to step from the solid wall.

"You may go no farther."

"I intend to find Boone," she told him.

"You're not to blame in this," Lylesburg said. "That's completely understood. But you must in turn understand: what Boone did has put us all in danger—"

"Then let me speak to him. We'll get out of here together."

"That might have been possible a little while ago," Lylesburg said, the voice emerging from his shadow-coat as measured and authoritative as ever.

"And now?"

"He's beyond my recall. And yours too. He's made appeal to another force entirely."

Even as he spoke, there was noise from farther down the catacomb, a din the like of which Lori had never heard. For an instant she felt certain an earthquake was its source; the sound seemed to be *in* and *of* the earth around them. But as the second wave began she heard something animal in it: a moan of pain, perhaps, or of ecstasy. Surely this was Baphomet—*Who Made Midian*, Rachel had said. What other voice could shake the very fabric of the place?

Lylesburg confirmed the belief.

"*That* is what Boone has gone to parley with," he said, "or so he thinks."

"Let me go to him."

"It's already devoured him," Lylesburg said, "taken him into the flame."

"I want to see for myself," Lori demanded.

Unwilling to delay a moment longer she pushed past Lylesburg, expecting resistance. But her hands sank into the darkness he wore and touched the wall behind him. He had no substance. He couldn't keep her from going anywhere.

"It will kill you too," she heard him warn as she ran in pursuit of the sound. Though it was all around her, she sensed its source. Every step she took it got louder and more complex, layers of raw sound, each of which touched a different part of her: head, heart, groin.

A quick backward glance confirmed what she'd already guessed: that Lylesburg had made no attempt to follow. She turned a corner, and another, the undercurrents in the voice still multiplying, until she was walking against them as if in a high wind, head down, shoulders hunched.

There were no chambers now along the passageway and consequently no lights. There was a glow up ahead, however—fitful and cold, but bright enough to illuminate both the ground she stumbled over, which was bare earth, and the silvery frost on the walls.

"Boone?" she shouted. "Are you there? Boone?"

After what Lylesburg had said she didn't hope too hard for an answer, but she got one. His voice came to meet her from the core of light and sound ahead. But all she heard through the din was:

"*Don't*—"

Don't *what?* she wondered. Don't come any farther? Don't leave me here?

She slowed her pace, and called again, but the noise the Baptizer was making virtually drowned out the sound of her own voice, never mind a reply. Having come so far, she had to go forward, not knowing if his call had been warning or encouragement.

Ahead, the passageway became a slope—a steep slope. She halted at the top and squinted into the brightness. The din Baphomet was making eroded the walls of the slope and carried the dust up into her face. Tears began to fill her eyes to wash the grit away, but it kept coming. Deafened by voice, blinded by dust, she teetered on the lip of the slope, unable to go forward or back.

Suddenly, the Baptizer fell silent, the layers of sound all dying at once.

The hush that followed was more alarming than the din that had preceded it. Had it shut its mouth because it knew it had a trespasser in its midst? She held her breath, afraid to utter a sound.

At the bottom of the slope was a sacred place, she had not the slightest doubt of that. Standing in the great cathedrals of Europe with her mother, years before, gazing at the windows and the altars, she'd felt nothing approaching the surge of recognition she felt now. Nor in all her life—dreaming or awake—had such contradictory impulses run in her. She wanted to flee the place with a passion—wanted to forsake it and forget it, and yet it *summoned*. It was not Boone's presence there that called her but the pull of the holy, or the unholy, or the two in one, and it wouldn't be resisted.

Her tears had cleared the dust from her eyes now. She had no excuse but cowardice to remain where she stood. She began down the slope. It was a descent of thirty yards, but she'd covered no more than a third of it when a familiar figure staggered into view at the bottom.

The last time she'd seen Boone had been overground, as he emerged to confront Decker. In the seconds before she'd passed out she'd seen him as never before: like a man who'd forgotten pain and defeat entirely. Not so now. He could barely hold himself upright.

She whispered his name, the word gathering weight as it tumbled toward him.

He heard, and raised his head toward her. Even in his worst times, when she'd rocked him and held him to keep the terrors at bay, she'd not seen such grief on his face as she saw now. Tears coming and coming, his features so crumpled with sorrow they were like a baby's.

She began the descent again, every sound her feet made, every tiny breath she took multiplied by the acoustics of the slope.

Seeing her approach he left off holding himself up to wave her away, but in doing so lost his only means of support and fell heavily. She picked up her pace, careless now of the noise she was making. Whatever power occupied the pit at the bottom, it knew she was there. Most likely it knew her history. In a way she hoped it did. She wasn't afraid of its judgment. She had loving reason for her trespass; she came weaponless and alone. If Baphomet was indeed the architect of Midian, then it understood vulnerability, and would not act against her. She was within five yards of Boone by now. He was attempting to roll himself onto his back.

"Wait!" she said, distressed by his desperation.

He didn't look her way, however. It was Baphomet his eyes went to, once he got onto his back. Her gaze went with her, into a room with walls of frozen earth, and a floor the same, the latter split from corner to corner, and a fissure opened in it from which a flame column rose four or five times the size of a man. There was bitter cold off it rather than heat, and no reassuring flicker in its heart. Instead its innards churned upon themselves, turning over and over some freight of stuff which she failed to recognize at first, but her appalled stare rapidly interpreted.

There was a *body* in the fire, hacked limb from limb, human enough that she recognized it as flesh, but no more than that. Baphomet's doing presumably, some torment visited on a transgressor.

Boone said the Baptizer's name even now, and she readied herself for sight of its face. She had it too, but from *inside* the flame, as the creature there—not dead, but alive, not Midian's subject, but its creator—rolled its head over in the turmoil of flame and looked her way.

This was *Baphomet*. This diced and divided thing. Seeing its face, she screamed. No story or movie screen, no desolation, no bliss, had prepared her for the maker of Midian. Sacred it must be, as anything so extreme must be sacred. A thing beyond things. Beyond love or hatred or their sum, beyond the beautiful or the monstrous or *their* sum. Beyond, finally, her mind's power to comprehend or catalog. In the instant she looked away from it she had already blanked every fraction of the sight from conscious memory and locked it where no torment or entreaty would ever make her look again.

She hadn't known her own strength till the frenzy to be out of its presence had her hauling Boone to his feet and dragging him up the slope. He could do little to help her. The time he'd spent in the Baptizer's presence had driven all but the rags of power from his muscles. It seemed to Lori that it took an age staggering up to the head of the slope, the flame's icy light throwing their shadows before them like prophecies.

The passageway above was deserted. She had half expected Lylesburg to be in wait somewhere with more solid cohorts, but the silence of the chamber below had spread throughout the tunnel. Once she'd hauled Boone a few yards from the summit of the slope, she halted, her lungs burning with the effort of bearing him up. He was emerging from the daze of grief or terror she'd found him in.

"Do you know a way out of here?" she asked him.

"I think so," he said.

"You're going to have to give me some help. I can't support you much longer."

He nodded, then looked back at the entrance to Baphomet's pit.

"What did you see?" he asked.

"Nothing."

"Good."

He covered his face with his hands. One of his fingers was missing, she saw, the wound fresh. He seemed indifferent to it, however, so she asked no questions but concentrated on encouraging him to move. He was reluctant, almost sullen in the aftermath of high emotion, but she chivied him along, until they reached a steep stairway that took them up through one of the mausoleums and into the night.

The air smelled of *distance* after the confinement of the earth, but rather than linger to enjoy it, she insisted they get out of the cemetery, threading their way through the maze of tombs to the gate. There Boone halted.

"The car's just outside," she said.

He was shuddering, though the night was quite warm.

"I can't . . ." he said.

"Can't what?"

"I belong here."

"No, you don't," she said, "you belong with me. We belong with each other."

She stood close to him, but his head was turned toward the shadow. She took hold of his face in her hands and pulled his gaze round upon her.

"We belong to each other, Boone. That's why you're alive. Don't you see? After all this. After all we've been through. We've survived."

"It's not that easy."

"I know that. We've both had terrible times. I understand things can't be the same. I wouldn't want them to be."

"You don't know . . ." he began.

"Then you'll tell me," she said, "when the time's right. You have to forget Midian, Boone. It's already forgotten you."

The shudders were not cold, but the precursors of tears, which broke now.

"I can't go," he said, "I can't go."

"We've got no choice," she reminded him. "All we've got is each other."

The pain of his hurt was almost bending him double.

"Stand up, Boone," she said. "Put your arms around me. The Breed don't want you; they don't need you. I do. Boone. Please."

Slowly he drew himself upright, and embraced her.

"Tight," she told him. "Hold me tight, Boone."

His grip tightened. When she dropped her hands from his face to reciprocate, his gaze did not now return to the Necropolis. He looked at her.

"We're going to go back to the inn and pick up my things, yes? We have to do that. There are letters, photographs—lots of stuff we don't want anyone finding."

"Then?" he said.

"Then we find somewhere to go where no one will look for us, and work out a way to prove you innocent."

"I don't like the light," he said.

"Then we'll stay out of it," she replied. "Till you've got this damn place in perspective."

She couldn't find anything in his face resembling an echo of her optimism. His eyes shone, but that was only the dregs of his tears. The rest of him was so *cold*, so much still a part of Midian's darkness. She didn't wonder at that. After all this night (and the days that had preceded it) had brought, she was surprised to find such capacity for hope in herself. But it was there, strong as a heartbeat.

"I love you, Boone," she said, not expecting an answer.

Maybe in time he'd speak up. If not words of love, at least of explanation. And if he didn't, or *couldn't*, it was not so bad. She had better than explanations. She had the fact of him, the flesh of him. His body was solid in her arms. Whatever claim Midian had upon his memories, Lylesburg had been perfectly explicit: he would never be allowed to return there. Instead he would be beside her again at night, his simple presence more precious than any display of passion.

And as time went by she'd persuade him from the torments of Midian, as she had from the self-inflicted torments of his lunacy. She hadn't failed in that, as Decker's deceits had convinced her she had. Boone had not concealed a secret life from her; he was innocent. As was she. Innocents both, which fact had brought them alive through this precarious night and into the safety of the day.

PART FOUR

SAINTS AND SINNERS

You want my advice!
Kiss the Devil, eat the worm.

—JAN DE MOOY,
ANOTHER MATTER; OR, MAN REMADE

15

THE TOLL

I

The sun rose like a stripper, keeping its glory well covered by cloud till it seemed there'd be no show at all, then casting off its rags one by one. As the light grew, so did Boone's discomfort. Rummaging in the glove compartment Lori rooted out a pair of sunglasses, which Boone put on to keep the worst of the light from his sensitized eyes. Even then he had to keep his head down, his face averted from the brightening East.

They spoke scarcely at all. Lori was too concerned to keep her weary mind on the task of driving, and Boone made no attempt to break the silence. He had thoughts of his own, but none that he could have articulated to the woman at his side. In the past Lori had meant a great deal to him, he knew, but making contact with those feelings now was beyond him. He felt utterly removed from his life with her, indeed from life at all. Through the years of his sickness he'd clung always to the threads of consequence he saw in living: how one action resulted in another, this feeling in that. He'd got through, albeit with stumbling steps, by seeing how the path behind him became the one ahead. Now he could see neither forward nor backward, except dimly.

Clearest in his head, Baphomet, the Divided One. Of all Midian's occupants it was the most powerful and the most vulnerable, taken apart by ancient enemies but preserved, suffering and suffering, in the flame Lylesburg had called the Trial Fire. Boone had gone into Baphomet's pit, hoping to argue his case, but it was the Baptizer that had spoken oracles from a severed head. He could not now remember its pronouncements but he knew the news had been grim.

Among his memories of the whole and the human, sharpest was that of Decker. He could piece together several fragments of their shared history and knew it should enrage him, but he could not find it in himself to hate the man who'd led him to Midian's deeps, any more than he could love the woman who'd brought him out of them. They were part of some other biography, not quite *his*.

What Lori understood of his condition he didn't know, but he suspected she remained for the most part ignorant. Whatever she guessed, she seemed content to accept him as he was, and in a simple, animal way he needed her presence too much to risk telling her the truth, assuming that he could have found the words. He was as much and as little as he was. Man. Monster. Dead. Alive. In Midian he'd seen all these states in a single creature: they were, most likely, all true of him. The only people who might have helped him understand how such contraries could coexist were behind him, in the Necropolis. They'd only begun the long, long process of educating him in Midian's history when he'd defied them. Now he was exiled from their presence forever, and he'd never know.

There was a paradox. Lylesburg had warned him clearly enough as they'd stood together in the tunnels and listened to Lori's cries for help, told him unequivocally that if he broke cover he broke his covenant with the Breed.

"*Remember what you are now,*" he'd said. "*You can't save her and keep our refuge. So you have to let her die.*"

Yet he couldn't. Though Lori belonged in another life, a life he'd lost forever, he couldn't leave her to the fiend. What that meant, if anything, was beyond his capacity to grasp right now. These few circling thoughts aside, he was sealed in the moment he was living, and the next moment, and the moment after that; moving second by second through his life as the car moved over the road, ignorant of the place it had been and blind to where it was headed.

2

They were almost within sight of the Sweetgrass Inn when it occurred to Lori that if Sheryl's body had been found at the Hudson Bay Sunset there was a chance their destination would already be crawling with police.

She stopped the car.

"What's wrong?" Boone asked.

She told him.

"Perhaps it'd be safer if I went there alone," she said; "if it's safe I'll get my things and come back for you."

"No," he said, "that's not so good."

She couldn't see his eyes behind the sunglasses, but his voice carried fear in it.

"I'll be quick," she said.

"No."

"Why not?"

"It's better we stay together," he replied. He put his hands over his face, as he had at Midian's gates. "Don't leave me alone," he said, his voice hushed. "I don't know where I am, Lori. I don't even know *who* I am. Stay with me."

She leaned over to him and kissed the back of his hand. He let both fall from his face. She kissed his cheek, then his mouth. They drove on together to the inn.

In fact her fears proved groundless. If Sheryl's body had indeed been located overnight—which was perhaps unlikely given its location—no connection had been made with the inn. Indeed, not only were there no police to bar their way, there was little sign of life at all, only a dog yapping in one of the upper rooms and a baby crying somewhere. Even the lobby was deserted, the desk clerk too occupied with the "Morning Show" to keep his post. The sound of laughter and music followed them through the hall and up the stairs to the second floor. Despite the ease of it, by the time they'd reached the room Lori's hands were trembling so much she could scarcely align the key with the lock. She turned to Boone for assistance, only to discover that he was no longer close behind her but lingering at the top of the stairs, looking back and forth along the corridor. Again she cursed the sunglasses, which prevented her reading his feelings with any certainty. At least until he backed against the wall, his fingers seeking some purchase though there was none to be had.

"What's the problem, Boone?"

"There's nobody here," he returned.

"Well, that's good for us, isn't it?"

"But I can smell . . ."

"What can you smell?"

He shook his head.

"*Tell me.*"

"I smell *blood.*"

"Where? Where from?"

He made no answer, nor did he look her way, but stared off down the corridor.

"I'll be quick," she told him. "Just stay where you are, and I'll be back with you."

Going down on her haunches she clumsily fitted key to lock, then stood up and opened the door. There was no scent of blood from the room, only the stale perfume of the previous night. It reminded her instantly of Sheryl. Less than twenty-four hours ago she'd been laughing in this very room, and talking of her killer as the man of her dreams.

Thinking of which, Lori looked back toward Boone. He was still pressed against the wall, as if it were the only way to be certain the world wasn't toppling. Leaving him to it, she stepped into the room and got about her packing. First into the bathroom to collect her toiletries, and then back into the bedroom to gather her strewn clothes. It was only as she put her bag on the bed to pack it that she saw the crack in the wall. It was as if something had hit it from the other side, very hard. The plaster had come away in clods and littered the floor between the twin beds. She stared at the crack a moment. Had the party got so riotous they'd started throwing the furniture around?

Curious, she crossed to the wall. It was little more than a plaster-board partition, and the impact from the far side had actually opened a hole in it. She pulled a piece of loose plaster away and put her eye to the aperture.

The curtains were still drawn in the room beyond, but the sun was strong enough to penetrate, lending the air an ocher gloom. Last night's party must have been even more debauched than the one the night before, she thought. Wine stains on the walls, and the celebrants still asleep on the floor.

But the smell: it wasn't wine.

She stepped back from the wall, her stomach turning.

Fruit spilled no such juice—

Another step.

—flesh did. And if it was blood she smelled, then it was blood she saw, and if it was blood she saw, then the sleepers were not sleeping, because who lies down in an abattoir? Only the dead.

She went quickly to the door. Down the corridor Boone was no longer standing but crouched against the wall, hugging his knees. His face, as he turned to her, was full of distressing tics.

"Get up," she told him.

"I smell blood," he said softly.

"You're right. So get up. Quickly. Help me."

But he was rigid, rooted to the floor. She knew this posture of old: hunched in a corner, shivering like a beaten dog. In the past she'd had comforting words to offer, but there was no time for such solace now. Perhaps someone had survived the bloodbath in the next room. If so, she had to help, with Boone or without. She turned the handle of the slaughterhouse door and opened it.

As the smell of death came out to meet her Boone started to moan.

". . . *blood* . . ." she heard him say.

Everywhere, blood. She stood and stared for a full minute before forcing herself over the threshold to search for some sign of life. But even the most cursory glance at each of the corpses confirmed that the same nightmare had claimed all six. She knew his name too. He'd left his mark, wiping their features out with his knives the way he had Sheryl's. Three of the six he'd caught in flagrante delicto. Two men and a woman, partially undressed and slumped over each other on the bed, their entanglements fatal. Hand over her mouth to keep the smell out and the sobs in, she retreated from the room, the taste of her stomach in her throat. As she stepped out into the corridor her peripheral vision caught sight of Boone. He wasn't sitting any longer, but moving purposefully down the passageway toward her.

"We have . . . to get . . . out," she said.

He made no sign that he'd even heard her voice, but moved past her toward the open door.

"Decker . . ." she said, "it was Decker."

He still offered no reply.

"Talk to me, Boone."

He murmured something—

"He could still be here," she said. "We have to hurry."

—but he was already stepping inside to view the carnage at closer quarters. She had no desire to look again. Instead she returned to the adjacent room to finish her hurried packing. As she went about it she heard Boone moving around the room next door, his breathing almost pained. Afraid of leaving him on his own for any time, she gave up on trying to collect all but the most telling items—the photographs and an address book chief among them—and that done, went out into the corridor.

The din of police sirens was there to meet her, their panic fueling hers. Though the cars were still some way off she couldn't doubt their destination. Louder with every whoop, they were coming to the Sweetgrass, hot for the guilty.

She called for Boone.

"I'm finished!" she said. "Let's get going!"

There was no reply from the room.

"Boone?"

She went to the door, trying to keep her eyes off the bodies. Boone was on the far side of the room, silhouetted against the curtains. His breath was no longer audible.

"Do you hear me?" she said.

He didn't move a muscle. She could read no expression on his face—it was too dark—but she could see that he'd taken the sunglasses off.

"We haven't got much time," she said. "Will you come on?"

As she spoke, he exhaled. It was no normal breath; she knew that even before the smoke started from his throat. As it came he raised his hands to his mouth as if to stop it, but at his chin they halted and began to convulse.

"*Get out,*" he said, on the same breath that brought the smoke.

She couldn't move, or even take her eyes off him. The murk was not so thick she couldn't see the change coming, his face reordering itself behind the veil, light burning in his arms and climbing his neck in waves to melt the bones of his head.

"*I don't want you to see,*" he begged her, his voice deteriorating.

Too late. She'd seen the man with fire in his flesh at Midian, and the dog-headed painter, and more besides: Boone had all their diseases in his system, undoing his humanity before her eyes. He was the stuff of nightmares. No wonder he howled, head thrown back as his face was forfeited.

The sound was almost canceled by the sirens, however. They could be no more than a minute from the door. If she went now she might still outpace them.

In front of her, Boone was done, or undone, entirely. He lowered his head, remnants of smoke evaporating around him. Then he began to move, his new sinews bearing him lightly.

Even now she hoped he understood his jeopardy and was coming to the door to be saved. But it was to the dead he moved, where the ménage à trois still lay, and before she had the wit to look away, one of his clawed hands was reaching down and claiming a body from the heap, drawing it up toward his mouth.

"No, Boone!" she shrieked. "*No!*"

Her voice found him, or a part that was still Boone, lost in the chaos of this monster. He let the meat drop a little and looked up at her. His eyes were still blue, and they were full of tears.

She started toward him.

"Don't," she begged.

For an instant he seemed to weigh up love and appetite. Then he forgot her, and lifted the human meat to his lips. She didn't watch his jaws close on it, but the sound reached her, and it was all she could do to stay conscious, hearing him tear and chew.

From below, brakes screeching, doors slamming. In moments they'd have the building surrounded, blocking any hope of escape; moments later they'd be coming up the stairs. She had no choice but to leave the beast to its hunger. Boone was lost to her.

She elected not to return the way they'd come, but to take the back stairs. The decision was well made; even as she turned the corner of the upper corridor she heard the police at the other end, rapping on doors. Almost immediately afterward she heard the sound of forced entry from above, and exclamations of disgust. This couldn't be on finding Boone; he wasn't behind a locked door. Clearly they'd discovered something *else* on the upper corridor. She didn't need to hear the morning news to know what. Her instinct told her how thorough Decker had been the night before. There *was* a dog alive somewhere in the building, and he'd over-looked a baby in his heat, but the rest he'd taken. He'd come straight back from his failure at Midian and killed every living soul in the place.

Above and below, the investigating officers were discovering that very fact, and the shock of it made them incompetent. Lori had no difficulty slipping out of the building and away into the scrub at the back. Only as she reached the cover of the trees did one of the cops appear round the corner of the building, but even he had business other than the search. Once out of sight of his colleagues he threw up his breakfast in the dirt, then scrupulously wiped his mouth with his handkerchief and went back to the job at hand.

Secure that they wouldn't start a search of the exterior until they'd finished inside, she waited. What would they do to Boone when they found him? Shoot him down, most likely. There was nothing she could think of to prevent it. But the minutes passed, and though there were shouts from within, there was no sound of gunfire. They must have found him by now. Maybe she'd get a better grasp of what had happened from the front of the building.

The inn was shielded on three sides by shrubbery and trees. It wasn't difficult to make her way through the undergrowth to the flank, her movement countered by an influx of rifle-bearing cops from the front, to take up stations at the rear exit. Two more patrol cars were arriving at the scene. The first contained further armed troopers, the second a selection of interested parties. Two ambulance vans followed.

They'll need more, she thought grimly. *A lot more.*

Though the congregation of so many cars and armed men had attracted an audience of passersby, the scene at the front was subdued, even casual. There were as many men standing and staring at the building as moving to enter and explore it. They grasped the point now. The place was a two-story coffin. More people had been murdered here in one night than had died by violence in Shere Neck over its entire existence. Anyone here this bright morning was part of history. The knowledge hushed them.

Her attention went from the witnesses to a knot of people standing around the lead car. A break in the circle of debaters allowed her a glimpse of the man at its center. Sober-suited, polished spectacles glinting in the sun, Decker held court. What was he arguing for, a chance to coax his patient out into the open air? If that was his pitch he was being overruled by the only member of the circle in uniform, Shere Neck's police chief, presumably, who dismissed his appeal with a wave of the hand, then stepped out of the argument entirely. From a distance it was impossible to read Decker's response, but he seemed perfectly in control of himself, leaning to speak into the ear of one of the others, who nodded sagely at the whispered remark.

Last night Lori had seen Decker the madman unmasked. Now she wanted to unmask him again, strip away this facade of civilized concern. But how? If she stepped out of hiding and challenged him—tried to begin to explain all that she'd seen in the last twenty-four hours—they'd be measuring her up for a straitjacket before she'd taken a second breath.

He was the one in the well-cut suit, with the doctorate and the friends in high places; *he* was the *man*, the voice of reason and analysis, while she—mere woman!—what credentials did she have? Lover of a lunatic and a sometime beast? Decker's midnight face was quite secure.

There was a sudden eruption of shouts from inside the building. On an order from their chief, the troopers outside leveled their weapons at the front door; the rest retired a few yards. Two cops, pistols aimed at someone inside, backed out of the door. A beat later, Boone, his hands cuffed in front of him, was pushed into the light. It nearly blinded him. He tried to turn from its brilliance back into the shadows, but there were two armed men following who pressed him forward.

There was no sign remaining of the creature Lori had seen him become, but there was ample reminder of his hunger. Blood glued his T-shirt to his chest and spattered his face and arms.

There was some applause from the audience, uniformed and otherwise, at the sight of the killer chained. Decker joined it, nodding and smiling, as Boone was led away, head averted from the sun, and put into the back of one of the cars.

Lori watched the scene with so many feelings grappling for her attention. Relief that Boone had not been shot on sight, mingled with horror at what she now knew he was; rage at Decker's performance, and disgust at those who were taken in by it.

So many masks. Was she the only one who had no secret life, no other self in marrow or mind? If not, then perhaps she had no place in this game of *appearances*; perhaps Boone and Decker were the true lovers here, swapping blows and faces but *necessary* to each other.

And she'd hugged this man, demanded he embrace her, put her lips to his face. She could never do that again, knowing what lay in wait behind his lips, behind his eyes. She could never *kiss the beast*.

So why did the thought make her heart hammer?

16

ΠOW OR ΠEVER

I

"What are you telling me? That there's more of these people involved? Some kind of cult?"

Decker drew breath to deliver his warning about Midian again. The troopers called their chief everything but his name behind his back. Five minutes in his presence and Decker knew why, and he was plotting the man's dismemberment. But not today. The day he needed Irwin Eigerman, and Eigerman, did he but know it, needed him. While daylight lasted Midian was vulnerable, but they had to be swift. It was already one o'clock. Nightfall might still be a good distance away, but so was Midian. To get a task force out there to uproot the place was the work of several hours and every minute lost to argument was a minute lost to action.

"Beneath the cemetery," Decker said, beginning again at the place he'd begun half an hour before.

Eigerman scarcely made a pretense of listening. His euphoria had increased in direct proportion to the number of bodies brought out of the Sweetgrass Inn, a count that presently stood at sixteen. He had hopes for more. The only human survivor was a year-old baby found in a tumble of blood-soaked sheets. He'd taken her out of the building himself, for the benefit of the cameras. Tomorrow the country would know his name.

None of this would have been possible without Decker's tip-off, of course, which was why he was humoring the man, though at this stage in

CABAL 119

proceedings, with interviewers and flashbulbs calling, he was damned if he was going to go after a few freaks who liked corpses for company, which was what Decker was suggesting he do.

He took out his comb and began to rake over his thinning crop, in the hope of fooling the cameras. He was no beauty, he knew. Should it ever slip his mind he had Annie to remind him. You look like a sow, she was fond of remarking, usually before bedtime on a Saturday night. But then people saw what they wanted to see. After today, he'd look like a hero.

"Are you listening?" Decker said.

"I hear you. There's folks grave robbing. I hear you."

"Not grave robbing. Not *folks.*"

"Freaks," Eigerman said. "I seen 'em."

"Not the likes of these."

"You're not saying any of them were at the Sweetgrass, are you?"

"No."

"We've got the man responsible right here?"

"Yes."

"Under lock and key."

"Yes. But there are others in Midian."

"Murderers?"

"Probably."

"You're not sure?"

"Just get some of your people out there."

"What's the hurry?"

"If I told you once I told you a dozen times."

"So tell me again."

"They have to be rounded up by daylight."

"What are they? Some kind of bloodsuckers?" He chuckled to himself. "That what they are?"

"In a manner of speaking," Decker replied.

"Well, in a manner of speaking I gotta tell you, it's gonna have to wait. I got people want to interview me, Doctor. Can't leave them begging. It's not polite."

"Fuck polite. You've got deputies, haven't you? Or is this a one-cop town?"

Eigerman clearly bridled at this.

"I've got deputies."

"Then may I suggest you dispatch some of them to Midian?"

"To do what?"

"Dig around."

"That's probably consecrated ground, mister," Eigerman replied, "that's holy."

"What's under it isn't," Decker replied, with a gravity that had Eigerman silenced. "You trusted me once, Irwin," he said, "and you caught a killer. Trust me again. You have to turn Midian upside down."

2

There had been terrors, yes, but the old imperatives remained the same: the body had to eat, had to sleep. After leaving the Sweetgrass Inn, Lori satisfied the first of these, wandering the streets until she found a suitably anonymous and busy store, then buying a collection of instant-gratification foods: doughnuts, custard-filled and Dutch apple, chocolate milk, cheese. Then she sat in the sun and ate, her numbed mind unable to think much beyond the simple business of biting, chewing, and swallowing. The food made her so sleepy she couldn't have prevented her lids falling if she'd tried. When she woke, her side of the street, which had been bathed in sunshine, was in shadow. The stone step was chilly, and her body ached. But the food and the rest, however primitive, had done her some good. Her thought processes were a little more in order.

She had little cause for optimism, that was certain, but the situation had been bleaker when she'd first come through this town, on her way to find the spot where Boone had fallen. Then she'd believed the man she loved was dead; it had been a widow's pilgrimage. Now at least he was alive, though God alone knew what horror, contracted in the tombs of Midian, possessed him. Given that fact, it was perhaps good that he was safe in the hands of the law, the slow process of which would give her time to think through their problems. Most urgent of those, a way to unmask Decker. No one could kill so many without leaving some trace of evidence. Perhaps back at the restaurant where he'd murdered Sheryl. She doubted he'd lead the police there as he'd led them to the inn. It would seem too like complicity with the accused, knowing all the murder sites. He'd wait for the other corpse to be found by accident, knowing the crime would be ascribed to Boone. Which meant—*perhaps*—the site was untouched, and she might still find some clue that would incriminate him, or at very least open a crack in that controlled face of his.

Returning to where Sheryl had died, and where she'd endured Decker's provocations, would be no picnic, but it was the only alternative to defeat she had.

She went quickly. By daylight she had a hope of getting up the courage to step through that burned-out door. By night it would be another matter.

3

Decker watched as Eigerman briefed his deputies, four men who shared with their chief the looks of bullies made good.

"Now I trust our source," he said magnanimously, throwing a look back at Decker, "and if he tells me something bad's going down in Midian, then I think that's worth listening to. I want you to dig around a little. See what you can see."

"What exactly are we looking for?" one of the number wanted to know. His name was Pettine. A forty-year-old with the wide, empty face of a comedian's foil, and a voice too loud and a belly too big.

"Anything weird," Eigerman told him.

"Like people been messing with the dead?" the youngest of the four said.

"Could be, Tommy," Eigerman said.

"It's more than that," Decker put in. "I believe Boone's got friends in the cemetery."

"A fuckwit like that has friends?" Pettine said. "Sure as shit wanna know what *they* look like."

"Well, you bring 'em back, boys."

"And if they won't come?"

"What are you asking, Tommy?"

"Do we use force?"

"Do unto others, boy, before they do unto you."

"They're good men," Eigerman told Decker, when the quartet had been dispatched. "If there's anything to find there, they'll find it."

"Good enough."

"I'm going to see the prisoner. You want to come?"

"I've seen as much of Boone as I ever want to see."

"No problem," Eigerman said, and left Decker to his calculations.

He'd almost elected to go with the troopers to Midian, but there was too much work to do here preparing the ground for the revelations ahead. There would *be* revelations. Though so far Boone had declined to respond to even the simplest inquiries, he'd break his silence eventually, and when he did Decker would have questions asked of him. There was no chance any of Boone's accusations could stick—the man had been found with human meat in his mouth, bloodied from head to foot—but there were elements of recent events that confounded even Decker, and until every variable had been pinned down and understood, he would fret.

What, for instance, had happened to Boone? How had the scapegoat filled with bullets and filed as dead become the ravening monster he'd almost lost his life to the night before? Boone had even claimed he was *dead,* for Christ's sake—and in the chill of the moment Decker had almost shared the psychosis. Now he saw more clearly. Eigerman was right. They *were* freaks, albeit stranger than the usual stuff. Things in defiance of nature, to be poked from under their stones and soaked in gasoline. He'd happily strike the match himself.

"Decker?"

He turned from his thoughts to find Eigerman closing the door on the babble of journalists outside. All trace of his former confidence had fled. He was sweating profusely.

"OK, what the fuck's going on?"

"Do we have a problem, Irwin?"

"Shit alive, do we have a problem."

"Boone?"

"Of course Boone."

"What?"

"The doctors have just looked him over. That's procedure."

"And?"

"How many times did you shoot him? Three, four?"

"Yeah, maybe."

"Well, the bullets are still in him."

"I'm not that surprised," Decker said. "I told you we're not dealing with ordinary people here. What are the doctors saying? He should be dead?"

"He *is* dead."

"When?"

"I don't mean lying-down dead, shithead," Eigerman said. "I mean sitting-in-my-fucking-cell dead. I mean his heart isn't beating."

"That's impossible."

"I've got two fuckers telling me the man is walking dead, and inviting me to listen for myself. You wanna tell me about that, *Doctor?*"

17

DELIRIUM

Lori stood across the street from the burned-out restaurant and watched it for five minutes to see if there was any sign of activity. There was none. Only now, in the full light of day, did she realize just how run-down this neighborhood was. Decker had chosen well. The chance of anyone having seen him enter or leave the place the night before was most likely zero. Even in the middle of the afternoon no pedestrian passed along the street in either direction, and the few vehicles that used the thoroughfare were speeding on their way to somewhere more promising.

Something about the scene—perhaps the heat of the sun in contrast to Sheryl's unmarked grave—brought her solitary adventure in Midian back to her, or more particularly, her encounter with Babette. It wasn't just her mind's eye that conjured the girl. It seemed her whole body was reliving their first meeting. She could feel the weight of the beast she'd picked up from beneath the tree against her breast. Its labored breathing was in her ears, its bittersweetness pricked her nostrils.

The sensations came with such force they almost constituted a *summoning*: past jeopardy signaling present. She seemed to *see* the child looking up at her from her arms, though she'd never carried Babette in human form. The child's mouth was opening and closing, forming an appeal Lori could not read from lips alone.

Then, like a cinema screen blanked out in midmovie, the images disappeared, and she was left with one set of sensations; the street, the sun, the burned-out building ahead.

There was no purpose in putting off the evil moment any longer. She crossed the street, mounted the sidewalk, and, without allowing herself to slow her step by a beat, went through the carbonized door frame into the murk beyond. So quickly dark! So quickly cold! One step out of the sunlight, and she was in another world. Her pace slowed a little now as she negotiated the maze of debris that lay between the front door and the kitchen. Fixed clearly in her mind was her sole intention: to turn up some shred of evidence that would convict Decker. She had to keep all other thoughts at bay: revulsion, grief, fear. She had to be cool and calm. Play Decker's game.

Girding herself, she stepped through the archway.

Not into the kitchen, however: into *Midian*.

She knew the moment it happened where she was—the chill and the dark of the tombs was unmistakable. The kitchen had simply vanished: every tile.

Across the chamber from her stood Rachel, looking up at the roof, distress on her face. For a moment she glanced at Lori, registering no surprise at her presence. Then she returned to watching and listening.

"What's wrong?" Lori said.

"Hush," Rachel said sharply, then seemed to regret her harshness and opened her arms. "Come to me, child," she said.

Child. So that was it. She wasn't in Midian, she was in Babette, seeing with the child's eyes. The memories she'd felt so strongly on the street had been a prelude to a union of minds.

"Is this real?" she said.

"Real?" Rachel whispered. "Of course it's real . . ."

Her words faltered, and she looked at her daughter with inquiry on her face.

"Babette?" she said.

"No . . ." Lori replied.

"Babette, what have you done?"

She moved toward the child, who backed away from her. Her view through these stolen eyes brought a taste of the past back. Rachel seemed impossibly tall, her approach ungainly.

"What have you done?" she asked a second time.

"I've brought her," the girl said, "to see."

Rachel's face became furious. She snatched at her daughter's arm.

But the child was too quick for her. Before she could be caught she'd scooted away, out of Rachel's reach. Lori's mind's eye went with her, dizzied by the ride.

"Come back here," Rachel whispered.

Babette ignored the instructions and took to the tunnels, ducking round corner after corner with the ease of one who knew the labyrinth back to front. The route took runner and passenger off the main thoroughfares and into darker, narrower passages, until Babette was certain she was not being pursued. They had come to an opening in the wall, too small to allow adult passage. Babette clambered through, into a space no larger than a refrigerator and as cold; this was the child's hideaway. Here she sat to draw breath, her sensitive eyes able to pierce the total darkness. Her few treasures were gathered around her. A doll made of grasses and crowned with spring flowers, two bird skulls, a small collection of stones. For all her otherness, Babette was in this like any child: sensitive, ritualistic. Here was her world. That she'd let Lori see it was no small compliment.

But she hadn't brought Lori here simply to see her hoard. There were voices overhead, close enough to be heard clearly.

"*Who-ee!* Will you look at this shit? You could hide a fuckin' army here."

"Don't say it, Cas."

"Shittin' your pants, Tommy?"

"Nope."

"Sure smells like it."

"Fuck you."

"Shut up, the both of you. We've got work to do."

"Where do we start?"

"We look for any signs of disturbance."

"There's people here. I feel 'em. Decker was right."

"So let's get the fuckers out where we can see 'em."

"You mean . . . *go down?* I ain't going down."

"No need."

"So how the fuck do we bring 'em up, asshole?"

The reply wasn't a word but a shot, ringing off stone.

"Be like shootin' fish in a barrel," somebody said. "If they won't come up they can stay down there permanent."

"Saves digging a grave!"

Who are these people? Lori thought. No sooner had she asked the question than Babette was up and clambering into a narrow duct that led off her playroom. It was barely large enough to accommodate her small body; a twinge of claustrophobia touched Lori. But there was compensation. Daylight up ahead, and the fragrance of the open air, which, warming Babette's skin, warmed Lori too.

The passage was apparently some kind of drainage system. The child squirmed through an accumulation of debris, pausing only to turn over the corpse of a shrew that had died in the duct. The voices from overground were distressingly close.

"I say we just start here and open up every damn tomb till we find something to take home."

"Nothing here I wanna take home."

"Shit, Pettine, I want *prisoners!* As many of the fuckers as we can get."

"Shouldn't we call in first?" a fourth speaker now asked. This dissenting voice had not so far been heard in the exchanges. "Maybe the chief's got fresh instructions for us."

"Fuck the chief," Pettine said.

"Only if he says *please,*" came the response from Cas.

Amid the laughter that followed there were several other remarks exchanged, obscenities mostly. It was Pettine who silenced the hilarity.

"OK, let's get the fuck on with it."

"Sooner the better," said Cas. "Ready, Tommy?"

"I'm always ready."

The source of the light Babette was crawling toward now became apparent: a latticed grille in the side of the tunnel.

Keep out of the sun, Lori found herself thinking.

It's all right, Babette's thoughts replied. Clearly this wasn't the first time she'd used the spyhole. The grille offered a view of the avenues but was so placed in the mausoleum wall that direct sunlight did not fall through it. Babette put her face close to the grille to get a clearer grasp of the scene outside.

Lori could see three of the four speakers. All were in uniform, all—despite their brave talk—looked like men who could think of a dozen better places to be than this. Even in broad daylight, armed to the teeth and safe in the sun, they were ill at ease. It wasn't difficult to guess why. Had they come to take prisoners from a tenement block, there'd be none of the half glances and nervous tics on display here. But this was Death's territory, and they felt like trespassers.

In any other circumstances she would have taken some delight in their discomfiture. But not here, not now. She knew what men afraid, and afraid of their fear, were capable of.

They'll find us, she heard Babette think.

Let's hope not, her thoughts replied.

But they will, the child said. *The Prophetic says so.*

Who?

Babette's answer was an image of a creature Lori had glimpsed when she'd gone in pursuit of Boone in the tunnels: the beast with larval wounds, lying on a mattress in an empty cell. Now she glimpsed it in different circumstances, lifted up above the heads of a congregation by two Breed, down whose sweating arms the creature's burning blood coursed. It was speaking, though she couldn't hear its words. Prophecies, she presumed, and among them, this scene.

They'll find us, and try to kill us all, the child thought.

And will they?

The child was silent.

Will they, Babette?

The Prophetic can't see, because it's one of those who'll die. Maybe I'll die too.

The thought had no voice, so came as pure feeling, a wave of sadness that Lori had no way to resist or heal.

One of the men, Lori now noticed, had sidled toward his colleague, and was surreptitiously pointing at a tomb to their right. Its door stood slightly ajar. There was movement within. Lori could see what was coming; so could the child. She felt a shudder run down Babette's spine, felt her fingers curl around the lattice, gripping it in anticipation of the horror ahead. Suddenly the two men were at the tomb door, and kicking it wide. There was a cry from within; somebody fell. The lead cop was inside in seconds, followed by his partner, the din alerting the third and fourth to the tomb door.

"Out of the way!" the cop inside yelled. The trooper stepped back, and with a grin of satisfaction on his face, the arresting officer dragged his prisoner out of hiding, his colleague kicking from behind.

Lori caught only a glimpse of their victim, but quick-eyed Babette named him with a thought.

Ohnaka.

"On your knees, asshole," the cop bringing up the rear demanded, and kicked the legs from under the prisoner. The man went down, bowing his head to keep the sun from breaching the defense of his wide-brimmed hat.

"Good work, Gibbs," Pettine grinned.

"So where's the rest of them?" the youngest of the four, a skinny kid with a coxcomb, demanded.

"Underground, Tommy," the fourth man announced, "that's what Eigerman said."

Gibbs closed in on Ohnaka.

"We'll get fuckface to show us," he said. He looked up at Tommy's companion: a short, wide man. "You're good with the questions, Cas."

"Ain't nobody ever said no to me," the man replied. "True or false?"

"True," said Gibbs.

"You want this man on your case?" Pettine asked Ohnaka. The prisoner said nothing.

"Don't think he heard," Gibbs said. "You ask him, Cas."

"Sure enough."

"Ask him *hard*."

Cas approached Ohnaka, reaching down and snatching the brimmed hat from his head. Instantly, Ohnaka began to scream.

"Shut the fuck up!" Cas yelled at him, kicking him in the belly.

Ohnaka went on screaming, his arms crossed over his bald head to keep the sun off it as he clambered to his feet. Desperate for the succor of the dark, he started back toward the open door, but young Tommy was already there to block his way.

"Good man, Tommy!" Pettine hollered. "Go get him, Cas!"

Forced back into the sun, Ohnaka had begun to shudder as though a fit had seized him.

"What the fuck?" said Gibbs.

The prisoner's arms no longer had the strength to protect his head. They fell to his sides, smoking, leaving Tommy to look straight into his face. The boy cop didn't speak. He just took two stumbling steps backward, dropping his rifle as he did so.

"What are you doin', dickhead?" Pettine yelled. Then he reached and took hold of Ohnaka's arm to prevent him claiming the dropped weapon. In the confusion of the moment it was difficult for Lori to see what happened next, but it seemed Ohnaka's flesh gave way. There was a cry of disgust from Cas, and one of fury from Pettine as he pulled his hand away, dropping a fistful of fabric and dust.

"What the fuck?" Tommy shouted. "What the fuck? What the fuck?"

"Shut up!" Gibbs told him, but the boy had lost control. Over and over, the same question:

"What the fuck?"

Unmoved by Tommy's panic, Cas went in to beat Ohnaka back down to his knees. The blow he delivered did more than he intended. It broke Ohnaka's arm at the elbow, and the limb fell off at Tommy's feet. His shouts gave way to puking. Even Cas backed off, shaking his head in disbelief.

Ohnaka was past the point of no return. His legs buckled beneath him, his body growing frailer and frailer beneath the assault of the sun. But it was his face turned now toward Pettine—that brought the loudest shouts, as the flesh dropped away and smoke rose from his eye sockets as though his brain were on fire.

He no longer howled. There was no strength in his body left for that. He simply sank to the ground, head thrown back as if to invite the sun's speed, and have the agony over. Before he hit the paving some final stitch in his being snapped with a sound like a shot. His decaying remains flew apart in a burst of blood-dust and bones.

Lori willed Babette to look away, as much for her own sake as that of the child. But she refused to avert her eyes. Even when the horror was over—Ohnaka's body spread in pieces across the avenue—she still pressed her face to the grille, as if to know this death by sunlight in all its particulars. Nor could Lori look away while the child stared on. She shared every quiver in Babette's limbs, tasted the tears she was holding back, so as not to let them cloud her vision. Ohnaka was dead, but his executioners were not finished with their business yet. While there was more to see, the child kept watching.

Tommy was trying to wipe spattered puke from the front of his uniform. Pettine was kicking over a fragment of Ohnaka's corpse; Cas was taking a cigarette from Gibbs's breast pocket.

"Gimme a light, will you?" he said. Gibbs dug his trembling hand into his trouser pocket for matches, his eyes fixed on the smoking remains.

"Never saw nothin' like that before," Pettine said, almost casually.

"You shit yourself this time, Tommy?" Gibbs said.

"Fuck you," came the reply. Tommy's fair skin was flushed red. "Cas said we should have called the chief," he said. "He was right."

"What the fuck does Eigerman know?" Pettine commented, and spat into the red dust at his feet.

"You see the face on that fucker?" Tommy said. "You see the way it looked at me? I was near dead, I tell you. He would have had me."

"What's going on here?" Cas said.

Gibbs had the answer almost right.

"Sunlight," he replied. "I heard there's diseases like that. It was the sun got him."

"No way, man," said Cas, "I never seen or heard of nothin' like that."

"Well, we seen and heard it *now*," said Pettine with more than a little satisfaction. "It weren't no hallucination."

"So what do we do?" Gibbs wanted to know. He was having difficulty getting the match in his shaking fingers to the cigarette between his lips.

"We look for more," said Pettine, "and we *keep* looking."

"I ain't," said Tommy. "I'm calling the fuckin' chief. We don't know how many of these freaks there are. There could be hundreds. You said so yourself. Hide a fuckin' army, you said."

"What are you so scared of?" Gibbs replied. "You saw what the sun did to it."

"Yeah. And what happens when the sun goes down, fuckwit?" was Tommy's retort.

The match flame burned Gibbs's fingers. He dropped it with a curse.

"I seen the movies," Tommy said. "Things come out at night."

Judging by the look on Gibbs's face, he'd seen the same movies.

"Maybe you *should* call up some help," he said, "just in case."

Lori's thoughts spoke hurriedly to the child.

You must warn Rachel. Tell her what we've seen.

They know already, came the child's reply.

Tell them anyway. Forget me! Tell them, Babette, before it's too late.

I don't want to leave you.

I can't help you, Babette. I don't belong with you. I'm—

She tried to prevent the thought coming, but it was too late.

—I'm normal. The sun won't kill me the way it'll kill you. I'm alive. I'm human. I don't belong with you.

She had no opportunity to qualify this hurried response. Contact was broken instantly—the view from Babette's eyes disappearing—and Lori found herself standing on the threshold of the kitchen.

The sound of flies was loud in her head. Their buzzing was no echo of Midian, but the real thing. They were circling the room ahead of her. She knew all too well what scent had brought them here, egg-laden and hungry; and she knew with equal certainty that after all she'd seen in Midian she couldn't bear to take another step toward the corpse on the floor. There was too much death in her world, inside her head and out. If she didn't escape it she'd go mad. She had to get back into the open air where she could breathe freely. Maybe find some unremarkable shop girl to talk to: about the weather, about the price of sanitary napkins; anything as long as it was banal, predictable.

But the flies wanted to buzz in her ears. She tried to swat them away. Still they came *at* her and *at* her, their wings buttered with death, their feet red with it.

"Let me alone," she sobbed. But her excitement drew them in larger and still larger numbers; they rose at the sound of her voice from their dining table behind the ovens. Her mind struggled to take hold of the reality she'd been thrown back into, her body to turn and leave the kitchen.

Both mind and body failed. The cloud of flies came at her, their numbers now so large they were a darkness unto themselves. Dimly she realized that such a multiplicity was impossible and that her mind in its confusion was creating this terror. But the thought was too far from her to keep the madness at bay; her reason reached for it, and reached, but the cloud was upon her now. She felt their feet on her arms and face, leaving trails of whatever they'd been dabbling in: Sheryl's blood, Sheryl's bile, Sheryl's sweat and tears. There were so many of them they could not all find flesh to occupy, so they began to force their way between her lips and crawl up her nostrils and across her eyes.

Once, in a dream of Midian, hadn't the dead come as dust, from all four corners of the world? And hadn't she stood in the middle of the storm—caressed, eroded—and been happy to know that the dead were on the wind? Now came the companion dream: horror to the splendor of the first. A world of flies to match that world of dust, a world of incomprehension and blindness, of the dead without burial, and without a wind to carry them away. Only flies to feast on them, to lie in them and make more flies.

And matching dust against flies, she knew which she favored, knew, as consciousness went out of her completely, that if Midian died—and she let it—if Pettine and Gibbs and their friends dug up the Nightbreeds' refuge, then *she*, dust herself one day, and touched by Midian's condition—would have nowhere to be carried, and would belong, body and soul, to the flies.

Then she hit the tiles.

18

THE WRATH OF
THE RIGHTEOUS

I

For Eigerman bright ideas and excretion were inextricably linked; he did all his best thinking with his trousers around his ankles. More than once, in his cups, he'd explained to any who'd listen that world peace and a cure for cancer could be achieved overnight if the wise and the good would just sit down and take a crap together.

Sober, the thought of sharing that most private of functions would have appalled him. The can was a place for solitary endeavor, where those weighed down by high office could snatch a little time to sit and meditate upon their burdens.

He studied the graffiti on the door in front of him. There was nothing new among the obscenities, which was reassuring. Just the same old itches needing to be scratched. It gave him courage in the face of his problems.

Which were essentially twofold. First, he had a dead man in custody. That, like the graffiti, was an old story. But zombies belonged in the late movie, as sodomy did on a lavatory wall. They had no place in the real world. Which brought him to the second problem: the panicked call from Tommy Caan, reporting that something bad was going down in Midian. To those two, on reflection, he now added a third: Decker. He wore a fine suit and he talked fine talk, but there was something unwholesome about him. Eigerman hadn't admitted the suspicion to himself until now, sitting on the crapper, but it was plain as his dick, once he thought about it. The bastard knew more than he was telling: not just about Dead Man

Boone, but about Midian and whatever was going on there. If he was setting Shere Neck's finest up for a fall, then there'd come a reckoning time,
sure as shit, and he'd regret it.

Meanwhile the chief had to make some decisions. He'd begun the day
a hero, leading the arrest of the Calgary Killer, but instinct told him events
could very quickly get out of hand. There were so many imponderables in
all of this, so many questions to which he had no answers. There was an easy
way out, of course. He could call up his superiors in Edmonton and pass the
whole fuck-up along to them to deal with. But if he gave away the problem
he also gave the glory. The alternative was to act now—before nightfall,
Tommy had kept saying, and how far was that? Three, four hours—to root
out the abominations of Midian. If he succeeded he'd double his helping of
accolades. In one day he'd not only have brought a human evil to justice but
scoured the cesspit in which it had found succor: an appealing notion.

But again the unanswered questions raised their heads, and they
weren't pretty. If the doctors who'd examined Boone and reports coming
out of Midian were to be trusted, then things he'd heard only in stories
were true today. Did he really want to pit his wits against dead men who
walked and beasts that sunlight killed?

He sat and crapped and weighed up the alternatives. It took him half
an hour, but he finally came to a decision. As usual, once the sweat was
over, it looked very simple. Perhaps today the world was not quite the way
it had been yesterday. Tomorrow, God willing, it would be its old self: dead
men dead, and sodomy on the walls where it belonged. If he didn't seize
his chance to become a man of destiny there wouldn't be another, at least
not till he was too old to do more than tend his hemorrhoids. This was a
God-given opportunity to show his mettle. He couldn't afford to ignore it.

With new conviction in his gut he wiped his ass, hauled up his pants,
flushed the crapper, and went out to meet the challenge head-on.

2

"I want volunteers, Cormack, who'll come out to Midian with me and get
digging."

"How soon do you need them?"

"*Now*. We don't have much time. Start with the bars. Take Holliday
with you."

"What are we telling them it's for?"

Eigerman mused on this a moment: what to *tell*.

"Say we're looking for grave robbers. That'll get a sizable turnout. Anyone with a gun and a shovel's eligible. I want 'em mustered in an hour. Less if you can do it."

Decker smiled as Cormack went on his way.

"You happy now?" Eigerman said.

"I'm pleased to see you've taken my advice."

"Your advice, shit."

Decker just smiled.

"Get the fuck out of here," Eigerman said. "I've got work to do. Come back when you've found yourself a gun."

"I just might do that."

Eigerman watched him leave, then picked up the phone. There was a number he'd been thinking about dialing since he'd made up his mind to go into Midian, a number he hadn't had reason to call in a long time. He dialed it now. In seconds, Father Ashbery was on the line.

"You sound breathless, Father."

Ashbery knew who his caller was without need of prompting.

"Eigerman."

"Got it in one. What have you been up to?"

"I've been out running."

"Good idea. Sweat out the dirty thoughts."

"What do you want?"

"What do you think I want? A priest."

"I've done nothing."

"That's not what I hear."

"I'm not paying, Eigerman. God forgave me my sins."

"Not in question."

"So leave me alone."

"Don't hang up!"

Ashbery was quick to detect the sudden anxiety in Eigerman's voice.

"Well, well," he said.

"What?"

"You've got a problem."

"Maybe both of us do."

"Meaning?"

"I want you here real quick, with whatever you've got in the way of crucifixes and holy water."

"What for?"

"Trust me."

Ashbery laughed.

"I'm not at your beck and call any longer, Eigerman. I've got a flock to tend."

"So do it for them."

"What are you talking about?"

"You preach the Day of Judgment, right? Well they're warming up for it over in Midian."

"Who are?"

"I don't know who and I don't know why. All I know is, we need a little holiness on our side, and you're the only priest I've got."

"You're on your own, Eigerman."

"I don't think you're listening. I'm talking serious shit here."

"I'm not playing any of your damn fool games."

"I mean it, Ashbery. If you don't come of your own accord, I'll make you."

"I burned the negative, Eigerman. I'm a free man."

"I kept copies."

There was silence from the Father. Then, "You swore."

"I lied."

"You're a bastard, Eigerman."

"And you wear lacy underwear. So how soon can you be here?"

Silence.

"Ashbery, I asked a question."

"Give me an hour."

"You've got forty-five minutes."

"Fuck you."

"That's what I like: a God-fearing lady."

3

Must be the hot weather, Eigerman thought when he saw how many men Cormack and Holliday had rounded up in the space of sixty minutes. Hot weather always got folks itchy: for fornication maybe, or killing. And Shere Neck being what it was, and fornication not being so easy to get just whenever you wanted it. The hunger to do some shooting was well up today. There were twenty men gathered outside in the sun, and three or four women coming along for the ride, plus Ashbery and his holy water.

There'd been two more calls from Midian in that hour. One from Tommy, who was ordered back into the cemetery to help Pettine contain the enemy until reinforcements arrived, the second from Pettine himself, informing Eigerman that there'd been an escape bid made by one of Midian's occupants. He'd slipped away through the main gate while accomplices created a diversion. The nature of this diversion not only explained Pettine's choking as he delivered his report, but also why they'd failed to give chase. Somebody had ignited the tires of the cars. The conflagration was quickly consuming the vehicles, including the radio upon which the report was being made. Pettine was in the process of explaining that there would be no further bulletins when the airwaves went dead.

Eigerman kept this information to himself, for fear it cooled anyone's appetite for the adventure ahead. Killing was all fine, but he wasn't so sure there'd be quite so many ready to roll now if it was common knowledge that some of the bastards were ready to fight back.

As the convoy moved off he looked at his watch. They had maybe two and a half hours of good light left before dusk began to settle in. Three-quarters of an hour to Midian, which left an hour and three-quarters to get these fuckers dealt with before the enemy had night on its side. That was long enough if they were organized about it. Best to treat it like a regular shakedown, Eigerman supposed. Drive the bastards out into the light and see what happened. If they came apart at the seams, the way piss pants Tommy had kept saying, then that was all the proof a judge would need that these creatures were unholy as hell. If not—if Decker was lying, Pettine on dope again, and all this a fool's errand—he'd find someone to shoot so it wasn't all a wasted journey. Might just turn around and put a bullet through the zombie in Cell Five, the man with no pulse and blood on his face.

Either way, he wouldn't let the day end without tears.

PART FIVE

THE GOOD NIGHT

No sword shall touch you.
Unless it be mine.

—ANONYMOUS, LOVER'S OATH

19

A FRIENDLESS FACE

I

Why did she have to wake? Why did there have to be a coming to? Couldn't she just sink and sink, further into the nowhere she'd taken refuge in? But it didn't want her. She rose from it, unwillingly, and into the old pain of living and dying.

The flies had gone. That at least was something. She got to her feet, her body cumbersome, an embarrassment. As she made an attempt to dust the dirt from her clothes she heard the voice calling her name. For a ghastly moment she thought the voice was Sheryl's, that the flies had succeeded in their ambition and driven her to lunacy. But when it came a second time she put another name to it: Babette. The child was calling her. Turning her back on the kitchen she picked up her bag and started through the debris toward the street. The light had changed since she'd made the first crossing; hours had passed while she'd debated with sleep. Her watch, broken in the fall, refused to tell how many.

It was still balmy on the street, but the heat of noon had long passed. The afternoon was winding down. It could not be long until dusk.

She began to walk, not once looking back at the restaurant. Whatever crisis of reality had overcome her there, Babette's voice had called her from it, and she felt oddly buoyant, as though something about the way the world worked had come clear.

She knew what it was without having to think too hard. Some vital part of her, heart or head or both, had made its peace with Midian and all it contained. Nothing in the chambers had been as agonizing as what she'd confronted in the burned-out building: the loneliness of Sheryl's body, the stench of creeping decay, the inevitability of it all. Against that the monsters of Midian—transforming, rearranging, ambassadors of tomorrow's flesh and reminders of yesterday's—seemed full of possibilities. Weren't there, among those creatures, faculties she envied? The power to fly, to be transformed, to know the condition of beasts, to defy death?

All that she'd coveted or envied in others of her species now seemed valueless. Dreams of the perfected anatomy—the soap opera face, the centerfold body—had distracted her with promises of true happiness. Empty promises. Flesh could not keep its glamour, or eyes their sheen. They would go to nothing soon.

But the monsters were forever. Part of her forbidden self. Her dark, transforming midnight self. She longed to be numbered among them.

There was still much she had to come to terms with, not least their appetite for human flesh, which she'd witnessed firsthand at the Sweetgrass Inn. But she could learn to understand. In a real sense she had no choice. She'd been touched by a knowledge that had changed her inner landscape out of all recognition. There was no way back to the bland pastures of adolescence and early womanhood. She had to go forward. And tonight that meant along this empty street, to see what the coming night had in store.

The idling engine of a car on the opposite side of the road drew her attention. She glanced across at it. Its windows were all wound up— despite the warmth of the air—which struck her as odd. She could not see the driver; both windows and windshield were too thick with grime. But an uncomfortable suspicion was growing in her. Clearly the occupant was waiting for someone. And given that there was nobody else on the street, that someone was most likely her.

If so, the driver could only be one man, for only one knew that she had a reason to be here: Decker.

She started to run.

The engine revved. She glanced behind her. The car was moving off from its parking place, slowly. He had no reason to hurry. There was no sign of life along the street. No doubt there *was* help to be had, if only she knew which direction to run. But the car had already halved the distance between them. Though she knew she couldn't outrun it, she ran anyway, the engine louder and louder behind her. She heard the tire walls squeal against the sidewalk. Then the car appeared at her side, keeping pace with her yard for yard.

The door opened. She ran on. The car kept its companion pace, the door scraping the concrete.

Then, from within, the invitation.

"Get in."

Bastard, to be *so* calm.

"Get in, will you, before we're arrested."

It wasn't Decker. The realization was not a slow burn but a sudden comprehension: it *wasn't* Decker speaking from the car. She stopped running, her whole body heaving with the effort of catching her breath.

The car also stopped.

"Get in," the driver said again.

"Who . . . ?" she tried to say, but her lungs were too jealous of her breath to provide the words.

The answer came anyway.

"Friend of Boone's."

Still she hung back from the open door.

"Babette told me how to find you," the man went on.

"Babette?"

"Will you *get in?* We've got work to do."

She approached the door. As she did so, the man said, "Don't scream."

She didn't have the breath to make a sound, but she certainly had the *inclination*, when her eyes fell on the face in the gloom of the car. This was one of Midian's creatures, no doubt, but not a brother to the fabulous things she'd seen in the tunnels. The man's appearance was horrendous, his face raw and red, like uncooked liver. Had it been any other way she might have distrusted it, knowing what she knew about pretenders. But this creature could pretend nothing: his wound was a vicious honesty.

"My name's Narcisse," he said. "Will you shut the door, please? It keeps the light out. And the flies."

2

His story, or at least its essentials, took two and a half blocks to tell. How he'd first met with Boone in the hospital, how he'd later gone to Midian and once more encountered Boone, how together they'd broken

Midian's laws, trespassing overground. He had a souvenir of that adventure, he told her; a wound in his belly the like of which a lady should never have to set eyes upon.

"So they exiled you, like Boone?" she said.

"They tried to," he told her. "But I hung on there, hoping I could maybe get myself a pardon. Then when the troopers came, I thought: well, we brought this on the place. I should try and find Boone. Try and stop what we started."

"The sun doesn't kill you?"

"Maybe I've not been dead long enough, but no—I can bear it."

"You know Boone's in prison?"

"Yeah, I know. That's why I got the child to help me find you. I'm thinking together we can get him out."

"How in God's name do we do that?"

"I don't know," Narcisse confessed. "But we'd damn well better try. And be quick about it. They'll have people out at Midian by now, digging it up."

"Even if we can free Boone, I don't see what he can do."

"He went into the Baptizer's chamber," Narcisse replied, his finger going to lip and heart. "He spoke with Baphomet. From what I hear nobody other than Lylesburg ever did that before and survived. I'm figuring the Baptizer had some tricks to pass on. Something that'll help us stop the destruction."

Lori pictured Boone's terrified face as he stumbled from the chamber.

"I don't think Baphomet told him anything," Lori said. "He barely escaped alive."

Narcisse laughed.

"He *escaped,* didn't he? You think the Baptizer would have allowed that if there hadn't been a reason for it?"

"All right . . . so how do we get access to him? They'll have him guarded within an inch of his life."

Narcisse smiled.

"What's so funny?"

"You forget what he *is* now," Narcisse said. "He's got powers."

"I don't *forget,*" Lori replied, "I simply don't *know.*"

"He didn't tell you?"

"No."

"He went to Midian because he thought he'd shed blood—"

"I guessed that much."

"He hadn't, of course. He was guiltless. Which made him meat."

"You mean he was attacked?"

"Almost killed. But he escaped, at least as far as the town."

"Where Decker was waiting for him," Lori said, finishing the story, or beginning it. "He was damn lucky that none of the shots killed him."

Narcisse's smile, which had more or less lingered on his face since Lori's remark about Boone being guarded within an inch of his life, disappeared.

"What do you mean," he said, "none of the shots killed him? What do you think took him back to Midian? Why do you think they opened the tombs to him the second time?"

She stared at him blankly.

"I don't follow," she said, hoping she didn't. "What are you telling me?"

"He was bitten by Peloquin," Narcisse said, "bitten and infected. The balm got into his blood . . ." He stopped speaking. "You want me to go on?"

"Yes."

"The balm got into his blood. Gave him the powers. Gave him the hunger. And allowed him to get up off the slab and go walking. . . ."

His words had grown soft by the end of his statement, in response to the shock on Lori's face.

"He's dead?" she murmured.

Narcisse nodded.

"I thought you understood that," he said. "I thought you were making a joke before . . . about his being . . ." The remark trailed into silence.

"This is too much," Lori said. Her fist had closed on the door handle, but she lacked the strength to pull on it. "Too much."

"Dead isn't bad," Narcisse said. "It isn't even that different. It's just . . . unexpected."

"Are you speaking from experience?"

"Yes."

Her hand dropped from the door. Every last ounce of strength had gone from her.

"Don't give up on me now," Narcisse said.

Dead, all dead. In her arms, in her mind.

"Lori. Speak to me. Say something, if it's only goodbye."

"How . . . can . . . you *joke* about it?" she asked him.

"If it's not funny, what is it? Sad. Don't want to be sad. Smile, will you? We're going to save lover-boy, you and me."

She didn't reply.

"Do I take silence as consent?"

Still she made no answer.

"Then I do."

20

DRIVEΠ

I

Eigerman had been to Midian only once before, when providing backup for the Calgary force in their pursuit of Boone. It had been then that he'd met Decker—who'd been the hero of that day, risking his life to try and coax his patient out of hiding. He'd failed, of course. The whole thing had ended in Boone's summary execution as he stepped out into plain sight. If ever a man should have lain down and died, it was that man. Eigerman had never seen so many bullets in one lump of flesh. But Boone hadn't lain down. At least hadn't stayed down. He'd gone walkabout, with no heartbeat and flesh the color of raw fish.

Sickening stuff. It made Eigerman's hide crawl to think of it. Not that he was about to admit that fact to anyone. Not even to his passengers in the backseat, the priest and the doctor, both of whom had secrets of their own. Ashbery's he knew. The man liked to dress in women's dainties, which fact Eigerman had chanced upon and used as leverage when he'd needed sanctification of a sin or two of his own. But Decker's secrets remained a mystery. His face betrayed nothing, even to an eye as practiced in the recognition of guilt as Eigerman's.

Reangling the mirror, the chief looked at Ashbery, who shot him a sullen glance.

"Ever exorcise anyone?" he asked the priest.

"No."

"Ever watch it done?"

Again, "No."

"You do *believe*, though," Eigerman said.

"In *what?*"

"In heaven and hell, for Christ's sake."

"Define your terms."

"Huh?"

"What do you *mean* by heaven and hell?"

"Jesus, I don't want a fucking debate. You're a priest, Ashbery. You're supposed to believe in the Devil. Isn't that right, Decker?"

The doctor grunted. Eigerman pushed a little harder.

"Everyone's seen stuff they can't explain, haven't they? Especially doctors, right? You've had patients speaking in tongues—"

"I can't say that I have," Decker replied.

"Is that right? It's all perfectly scientific, is it?"

"I'd say so."

"You'd say so. And what would you say about Boone?" Eigerman pressed. "Is being a fucking zombie scientific too?"

"I don't know," Decker murmured.

"Well, will you look at this? I've got a priest who doesn't believe in the Devil, and a doctor who doesn't know science from his asshole. That makes me feel real comfortable."

Decker didn't respond. Ashbery did.

"You really think there's something up ahead, don't you?" he said. "You're sweating a flood."

"Don't push, sweetheart," Eigerman said, "just dig out your little book of exorcisms. I want those freaks sent back wherever the fuck they came from. You're supposed to know how."

"There are other explanations these days, Eigerman," Ashbery replied. "This isn't Salem. We're not going to a burning."

Eigerman turned his attention back to Decker, floating his next question lightly.

"What do you think, Doc? Think maybe we should try putting the zombie on the couch? Ask him if he ever wanted to fuck his sister?" Eigerman threw a look at Ashbery. "Or dress in her underwear?"

"I think we *are* going to Salem," Decker replied. There was an undercurrent in his voice Eigerman hadn't heard before. "And I also think you don't give a fuck what I believe or don't believe. You're going to burn them out anyway."

"Right on," Eigerman said with a throaty laugh.

"*And* I think Ashbery's right. You're *terrified.*"

That silenced the laugh.

"Asshole," Eigerman said quietly.

They drove the rest of the way in silence, Eigerman setting a new pace for the convoy, Decker watching the light getting frailer with every moment, and Ashbery, after a few minutes of introspection, leafing through his book of prayers, turning the onionskin pages at speed, looking for the Rites of Expulsion.

2

Pettine was waiting for them fifty yards from the Necropolis gate, his face dirtied by smoke from the cars, which were still burning.

"What's the situation?" Eigerman wanted to know.

Pettine glanced back toward the cemetery.

"There's been no sign of movement in there since the escape. But we've *heard* stuff."

"Like what?"

"Like we're sitting on a termite hill," Pettine said. "There's things moving around underground. No doubt about that. You can feel it as much as hear it."

Decker joined the debate, cutting Pettine off in midflow to address Eigerman.

"We've got an hour and twenty minutes before the sun sets."

"I can count," Eigerman replied.

"So are we going to get digging?"

"When *I* say so, Decker."

"Decker's right, chief," Pettine said. "It's sun these bastards are afraid of. I tell you, I don't think we want to be here at nightfall. There's a lot of them down there."

"We'll be here as long as it takes to clear this shit up," said Eigerman. "How many gates are there?"

"Two. The big one, and another on the northeast side."

"All right. So it shouldn't be difficult to contain them. Get one of the trucks in front of the main gate, and we'll post men at intervals around the wall just to make sure nobody gets out. Once they're sealed in we make our approach."

"See you brought some insurance," Pettine commented, looking at Ashbery.

"Damn right."

Eigerman turned to the priest.

"You can bless water, right? Make it holy?"

"Yes."

"So do it. Any water we can find. Bless it. Spread it among the men. It may do some good if bullets don't. And you, Decker, stay out of the fucking way. This is police business now."

Orders given, Eigerman walked down toward the cemetery gates. Crossing the dusty ground he rapidly understood what Pettine had meant by *a termite hill*. There was something going on below ground. He even thought he heard voices, bringing visions of premature burial to mind. He'd seen that once, or its consequences. Done the spadework disinterring a woman who'd been heard screaming underground. She'd had reason: she'd given birth and died in her coffin. The child, a freak, had survived. Ended up in an asylum, probably. Or here perhaps, in the earth with the rest of the motherfuckers.

If so, he could count the minutes left of his sick life on his six-fingered hand. Soon as they showed their heads, Eigerman would kick them right back where they came from, bullets in their brain. So let them come. He wasn't afraid. Let them come. Let them try to dig their way out.

His heel was waiting.

3

Decker watched the organization of the troops until it began to make him uneasy. Then he withdrew up the hill a little. He loathed being an observer of other men's labor. It made him feel impotent. It made him long to show them *his* power. And that was always a dangerous urge. The only eyes that could stare safely at his murder-hard were eyes about to glaze, and even then he had to erase them after they'd looked, for fear they'd tell what they'd seen.

He turned his back on the cemetery and entertained himself with plans for the future. With Boone's trial over, he'd be free to begin the Mask's work afresh. He looked forward to that with a passion. He'd go farther afield from now on. Find slaughtering places in Manitoba and Saskatchewan, or maybe over in Vancouver. He became hot with pleasure just thinking about it. From the briefcase he was carrying he could almost hear Button Face sigh through his silver teeth.

"*Hush,*" he found himself telling the Mask.

"What's that?"

Decker turned. Pettine was standing a yard from him.

"Did you say something?" the cop wanted to know.

He'll go to the wall, the Mask said.

"Yes," Decker replied.

"I didn't hear."

"Just talking to myself."

Pettine shrugged.

"Word from the chief. He says we're about to move in. Do you want to give a hand?"

I'm ready, the Mask said.

"No," said Decker.

"Don't blame you. Are you just a head doctor?"

"Yes. Why?"

"Think we might need some medics before too long. They're not going to give up without a fight."

"I can't help. Don't even like the sight of blood."

There was laughter from the briefcase, so loud Decker was certain Pettine would hear. But no.

"You'd better keep your distance, then," he said, and turned away to head back to the field of action.

Decker drew the bag up toward his chest and held it tight in his arms. From inside he could hear the zipper opening and closing, opening and closing.

"Shut the fuck up," he whispered.

Don't lock me away, the Mask whined. *Not tonight of all nights. If you don't like the sight of blood let me look for you.*

"I can't."

You owe me, it said. *You denied me in Midian, remember?*

"I had no choice."

You have now. You can give me some air. You know you'd like it.

"I'd be seen."

Soon, then.

Decker didn't reply.

Soon! the Mask yelled.

"Hush."

Just say it.

"... please ..."

Say it.

"Yes. *Soon.*"

21
THAT DESIRE

I

Two men had been left on duty at the station to guard the prisoner in Cell Five. Eigerman had given them explicit instructions. They were not on any account to unlock the cell door, whatever noises they heard from within. Nor was any outside agency—judge, doctor, or the Good Lord Himself—to be given access to the prisoner. And to enforce these edicts, should enforcement be necessary, troopers Cormack and Koestenbaum had been given the keys to the arsenal, and carte blanche to use extreme measures should the security of the station be in jeopardy. They weren't surprised. Shere Neck would most likely never see another prisoner so certain to find his way into the annals of atrocity as Boone. If he were to be sprung from custody, Eigerman's good name would be cursed from coast to coast.

But there was more to the story than that, and both of them knew it. Though the chief had not been explicit about the condition of the prisoner, rumors had been rife. The man was in some way *freakish*, possessed of powers that made him dangerous, even behind a locked and bolted door.

Cormack was grateful, then, to have been left to guard the front of the station, while Koestenbaum watched the cell itself. The whole place was a fortress. Every window and door sealed. Now it was simply a question of sitting it out, rifle at the ready, until the cavalry returned from Midian.

It wouldn't be long. The kind of human garbage they'd be likely to find at Midian—addicts, perverts, radicals—would be rounded up in a few hours, and the convoy on its way back to relieve the sentinels. Then tomorrow there'd be a force up from Calgary to take possession of the prisoner, and things would settle back into their regular pattern. Cormack wasn't in the policing business to sit and sweat the way he was now—he was in it for the easy feeling that came on a summer night when he could drive down to the corner of South and Emmett, and coerce one of the professionals to put her face in his lap for half an hour. That was what he liked the law for. Not this fortress-under-siege shit.

"Help me," somebody said.

He heard the words quite clearly. The speaker—a woman—was just outside the front door.

"Help me, *please.*"

The appeal was so pitiful he couldn't ignore it. Rifle cocked, he went to the door. There was no glass in it, not even a spyhole, so he couldn't see the speaker on the step. But he heard her again. First a sob, then a soft rapping, which was failing even as it came.

"You'll have to go someplace else," he said. "I can't help you right now."

"I'm hurt," she seemed to say, but he wasn't sure. He put his ear to the door.

"Did ya hear me?" he asked. "I can't help you. Go on down to the drugstore."

There was not even a sob by way of reply. Only the faintest of breaths.

Cormack liked women, liked to play the boss man and breadwinner. Even the hero, as long as it didn't cost him too much sweat. It went against the grain not to open the door to a woman begging for help. She'd sounded young and desperate. It was not his heart that hardened, thinking of her vulnerability. Checking first that Koestenbaum wasn't in sight to witness his defiance of Eigerman's orders, he whispered, "Hold on," and unbolted the door top and bottom.

He'd only opened it an inch and a hand darted through, its thumb slashing his face. The wound missed his eye by a centimeter, but the spurting blood turned half the world red. Semiblind, he was thrown backward as the force on the other side of the door threw it open. He didn't let the rifle go, however. He fired, first at the woman (the shot went wide), then at her companion, who ran at him, half-crouching to avoid the bullets. The second shot, though as wild as the first, brought blood. Not his target's, however. It was his own boot, and the good flesh and bone inside, that was spattered across the floor.

"Jesus Fucking Christ!"

In his horror he let the rifle drop from his fingers. Knowing he'd not be able to bend and snatch it up again without losing his balance, he turned and started to hop toward the desk, where his gun lay.

But Silver Thumbs was already there, swallowing the bullets like vitamin pills.

Denied his defenses, and knowing he could not stay vertical for more than a few seconds, he began to howl.

2

Outside Cell Five, Koestenbaum held his post. He had his orders. Whatever happened beyond the door into the station itself he was to stand guard by the cell, defending it from any and every assault. That he was determined to do, however much Cormack yelled.

Grinding out his cigarette he drew the shutter in the cell door aside and put his eyes to the peephole. The killer had moved in the last few minutes, edging into the corner by degrees, as if hunted by a patch of weak sunlight that fell through the tiny window high above him. Now he could go no farther. He was wedged in the corner, wrapped up in himself. Movement aside, he looked much as he had all along: like wreckage. No danger to anyone.

Appearances deceived, of course; Koestenbaum had been in uniform too long to be naive about that. But he knew a defeated man when he saw one. Boone didn't even look up when Cormack let out another yelp. He just watched the crawling sunlight from the corner of his eye and shook.

Koestenbaum slammed the peephole shut and turned back to watch the door through which Cormack's attackers—whoever they were—had to come. They'd find him ready and waiting, guns blazing.

He didn't have long to contemplate his last stand, as a blast blew out the lock and half the door with it, shards and smoke filling the air. He fired into the confusion, seeing somebody coming at him. The man was tossing away the rifle he'd used to blow the door, and was raising his hands, which *glinted* as they swept toward Koestenbaum's eyes. The trooper hesitated long enough to catch sight of his assailant's face—like something that should have been under bandages or six feet of earth—then he fired. The bullet struck its target, but slowed the man not a jot, and before he could fire a second time he was up against the wall, with the raw face inches from his. Now he saw all too clearly what glinted in the man's hands. A hook hovered an inch from the gleam of his left eye. There was another at his groin.

"Which do you want to live without?" the man said.

"No need," said a woman's voice, before Koestenbaum had a chance to choose between sight and sex.

"Let me," Narcisse said.

"Don't let him," Koestenbaum murmured. "Please . . . don't let him."

The woman came into view now. The parts of her that showed seemed natural enough, but he wouldn't have wanted to lay bets on what she looked like under her blouse. More tits than a bitch, most likely. He was in the hands of freaks.

"Where's Boone?" she said.

There was no purpose in risking his balls, eye or otherwise. They'd find the prisoner with or without his help.

"Here," he said, glancing back toward Cell Five.

"And the keys?"

"On my belt."

The woman reached down and took the keys from him.

"Which one?" she said.

"Blue tag," he replied.

"Thank you."

She moved past him to the door.

"Wait—" Koestenbaum said.

"What?" she said.

"—make him let me alone."

"Narcisse," she said.

The hook was withdrawn from his eye, but the one at his groin remained, pricking him.

"We have to be quick," Narcisse said.

"I know," the woman replied.

Koestenbaum heard the door swing open. He glanced round to see her stepping into the cell. As he looked back the fist came at his face, and he dropped to the floor with his jaw broken in three places.

3

Cormack had suffered the same summary blow, but he'd been already toppling when it came, and instead of knocking him solidly into unconsciousness it had merely left him in a daze, from which he quickly shook himself. He crawled to the door and hauled himself, hand over hand, to his feet. Then he stumbled out into the street. The rush of homeward traffic was over, but there were still vehicles passing in both directions, and the sight of a toeless trooper hobbling into the middle of the street, arms raised, was enough to bring the flow of traffic to a squealing halt.

But even as the drivers and their passengers stepped out of the trucks and cars to come to his assistance, Cormack felt the delayed shock of his self-wounding closing his system down. The words his helpers were mouthing to him reached his befuddled mind as nonsense.

He thought (hoped) somebody had said, *"I'll get a gun,"* but he couldn't be sure.

He hoped (prayed) his lolling tongue had told them where to find the felons, but he was even less sure of that.

As the ring of faces faded around him, however, he realized his seeping foot would have left a trail that would lead them back to the transgressors. Comforted, he passed out.

4

"Boone," she said.

His sallow body, bared to the waist—scarred and missing a nipple— shuddered as she spoke his name. But he didn't look up at her.

"Get him going, will you?"

Narcisse was at the door, staring at the prisoner.

"Not with you yelling, I won't," she told him. "Leave us alone a little while, huh?"

"No time for fucky fucky."

"Just get out."

"OK." He raised his arms in mock surrender. "I'm going."

He closed the door. It was just her and Boone now. The living and the dead.

"Get up," she told him.

He did nothing but shudder.

"Will you get up? We don't have that much time."

"So leave me," he said.

She ignored the sentiment but not the fact that he'd broken his silence.

"Talk to me," she said.

"You shouldn't have come back," he said, defeat in his every word. "You put yourself at risk for nothing."

She hadn't expected this. Anger maybe, that she'd left him to be captured at the Sweetgrass Inn. Suspicion even, that she'd come here with someone from Midian. But not this mumbling, broken creature slumped in a corner like a boxer who'd fought a dozen too many fights. Where was the man she'd seen at the inn, changing the order of his very flesh in front of her? Where was the casual strength she'd seen, and the appetite? He scarcely seemed capable of lifting his own head, never mind meat to his lips.

That was the issue, she suddenly understood. That forbidden flesh.

"I can still taste it," he said.

There was such shame in his voice; the human he'd been was repulsed by the thing he'd become.

"You weren't answerable," she told him. "You weren't in control of yourself."

"I am now," he replied. His nails dug into the muscle of his forearms, she saw, as though he were holding himself down. "I'm not going to let go. I'm going to wait here till they come to string me up."

"That won't do any good, Boone," she reminded him.

"*Jesus* . . ." The word decayed into tears. "You know everything?"

"Yes, Narcisse told me. You're dead. So why wish a hanging on yourself? They can't kill you."

"They'll find a way," he said. "Take off my head. Blow out my brains."

"Don't talk like that!"

"They have to finish me, Lori. Put me out of my misery."

"I don't want you out of your misery," she said.

"But I do!" he replied, looking up at her for the first time. Seeing his face, she remembered how many had doted on him, and understood why. Pain could have no more persuasive apologists than his bones, his eyes.

"I want *out*," he said. "Out of this body. Out of this life."

"You can't. Midian needs you. It's being destroyed, Boone."

"Let it go! Let it all go. Midian's just a hole in the ground, full of things that should lie down and be dead. They know that, all of 'em. They just haven't got the balls to do what's right."

"Nothing's right," she found herself saying (how far she'd come to this bleak relativity), "except what you feel and know."

His small fury abated. The sadness that replaced it was more profound than ever.

"I *feel* dead," he said, "I *know* nothing."

"That's not true," she replied, taking the first steps toward him she'd taken since entering the cell. He flinched as if he expected her to strike him.

"You *know* me," she said. "You *feel* me."

She took hold of his arm and pulled it up toward her. He didn't have time to make a fist. She lay his palm on her stomach.

"You think you disgust me, Boone? You think you horrify me? You don't."

She drew his hand up toward her breasts.

"I still want you, Boone. Midian wants you too, but I want you more. I want you cold, if that's the way you are. I want you dead, if that's the way you are. And *I'll* come to you if you won't come to me. I'll let them shoot me down."

"*No*," he said.

Her grip on his hand was light now. He could have slipped it, but he chose to leave his touch upon her, with only the thin fabric of her blouse intervening. She wished she could dissolve it at will, have his hand stroking the skin between her breasts.

"They're going to come for us sooner or later," she said.

Nor was she bluffing. There were voices from outside. A lynch mob gathering. Maybe the monsters *were* forever. But so were their persecutors.

"They'll destroy us both, Boone. You for what you are. Me for loving you. And I'll never hold you again. I don't want that, Boone. I don't want us dust in the same wind. I want us *flesh*."

Her tongue had outstripped her intention. She hadn't meant to say it so plainly. But it was said now, and true. She wasn't ashamed of it.

"I won't let you deny me, Boone," she told him. The words were their own engine. They drove her hand to Boone's cold scalp. She snatched a fist of his thick hair.

He didn't resist her. Instead the hand on her chest closed on the blouse, and he went down onto his knees in front of her, pressing his face to her crotch, licking at it as if to tongue her clean of clothes and enter her with spit and spirit all in one.

She was wet beneath the fabric. He smelled her heat for him. Knew what she'd said was no lie. He kissed her cunt, or the cloth that hid her cunt, over and over and over.

"Forgive yourself, Boone," she said.

He nodded.

She took tighter hold on his hair, and pulled him away from the bliss of her scent.

"*Say it,*" she told him. "*Say you forgive yourself.*"

He looked up from his pleasure, and she could see before he spoke the weight of shame had gone from his face. Behind his sudden smile she met the monster's eyes, *dark,* and darkening still as he delved for it.

The look made her ache.

"Please . . ." she murmured, "love me."

He pulled at her blouse. It tore. His hand was through the gap in one smooth motion, and beneath her bra to her breast. This was madness, of course. The mob would be upon them if they didn't get out quickly. But then madness had drawn her into this circle of dust and flies in the first place; why be surprised that her journey had brought her round to this *new* insanity? Better this than life without him. Better this than practically anything.

He was getting to his feet, teasing her tit from hiding, putting his cold mouth to her hot nipple, flicking it, licking it, tongue and teeth in perfect play. Death had made a lover of him. Given him knowledge of flesh and how to rouse it, made him easy with the body's mysteries. He was everywhere about her, working his hips against hers in slow grinding circles—trailing his tongue from her breasts to the sweat bowl between her clavicles, and up along the ridge of her throat to her chin, thence to her mouth.

Only once in her life had there been such wrenching hunger in her. In New York, years before, she'd met and fucked with a man whose name she'd never known, but whose hands and lips seemed to know her better than herself.

"Have a drink with me?" she'd said, when they'd unglued themselves.

He'd told her *no* almost pityingly, as though someone so ignorant of the rules was bound for grief. So she'd watched him dress and leave, angry with herself for asking, and with him for such practiced detachment. But she'd dreamt of him a dozen times in the weeks after, revisiting their squalid moments together, hungry for them again.

She had them here. Boone was the lover of that dark corner, perfected. Cool and feverish, urgent and studied. She knew his name this time, but he was still strange to her. And in the fervor of his possession, and in her heat for him, she felt that other lover, and all the lovers who'd come and gone before him, burned up. It was only their ash in her now, where their tongues and cocks had been, and she had power over them completely.

Boone was unzipping himself. She took his length in her hand. Now it was his turn to sigh as she ran her fingers along the underside of his erection, up from his balls to where the ring of his circumcision scar bore a nugget of tender flesh. She stroked him there, tiny movements to match the measure of his tongue back and forth between her lips. Then, on the same sudden impulse, the teasing time was over. He was lifting her skirt, tearing at her underwear, his fingers going where only hers had been for too long. She pushed him back against the wall, pulled his jeans down to midthigh. Then, one arm hooked around his shoulders, the other hand enjoying the silk of his cock before it was out of sight, she took him inside. He resisted her speed, a delicious war of want which had her at screaming pitch in seconds. She was never so open, nor had ever needed to be. He filled her to overflowing.

Then it really began. After the promises, the proof. Bracing his upper back against the wall he angled himself so as to throw his fuck up into her, her weight its own insistence. She licked his face. He grinned. She spat in it. He laughed and spat back.

"*Yes,*" she said. "*Yes. Go on. Yes.*"

All she could manage was affirmatives. Yes to his spittle, yes to his cock, yes to this life in death, and joy in life in death forever and ever.

His answer was honey-hipped, wordless labor, teeth clenched, brow plowed. The expression on his face made her cunt spasm. To see him shut his eyes against her pleasure, to know that the sight of her bliss took him too close to be countenanced. They had such power each over each. She demanded his motion with motion of her own, one hand gripping the brick beside his head so she could raise herself along his length and then impale herself again. There was no finer hurt. She wished it could never stop.

But there was a voice at the door. She could hear it through her whining head.

"*Quickly.*"

It was Narcisse.

"*Quickly.*" Boone heard him too, and the din behind his voice as the lynchers gathered. He matched her new rhythm, up to meet her descent.

"Open your eyes," she said.

He obeyed, grinning at the command. It was too much for him, meeting her eyes. Too much for her, meeting his. The pact struck, they parted till her cunt only sucked at the head of his cock—so slicked it might slip from her—then closed on each other for one final stroke.

The joy of it made her cry out, but he choked her yell with his tongue, sealing their eruption inside their mouths. Not so below. Undammed after months, his come overflowed and ran down her legs, its course colder than his scalp or kisses.

It was Narcisse who brought them back from their world of two into that of many. The door was now open. He was watching them without embarrassment.

"Finished?" he wanted to know.

Boone wiped his lips back and forth on Lori's, spreading their saliva from cheek to cheek.

"For now," he said, looking only at her.

"So can we get going?" Narcisse said.

"Whenever. Wherever."

"Midian," came the instant reply.

"Midian, then."

The lovers drew apart. Lori pulled up her underwear. Boone tried to get his cock, still hard, behind his zip.

"There's quite a mob out there," Narcisse said. "How the hell are we going to get past them?"

"They're all the same," Boone said, "all afraid."

Lori, her back turned to Boone, felt a change in the air around her. A shadow was climbing the walls to left and right, spreading over her back, kissing her nape, her spine, her buttocks, and what lay between. It was Boone's darkness. He was in it to its length and breadth.

Even Narcisse was agog.

"Holy shit," he muttered, then flung the door wide to let the night go running.

5

The mob was itching for fun. Those with guns and rifles had brought them from their cars, those with the luck to have been traveling with rope in their trunks were practicing knots, and those without rope or guns had picked up stones. For justification they needed to look no farther than the spattered remains of Cormack's foot, spread on the station floor. The leaders of the group—who'd established themselves immediately by natural selection (they had louder voices and more powerful weapons)—were treading this red ground when a noise from the vicinity of the cells drew their attention.

Somebody at the back of the crowd started shouting, "*Shoot the bastards down!*"

It was not Boone's shadow the leaders' hungry eyes first alighted upon. It was Narcisse. His ruined face brought a gasp of disgust from several of the throng, and shouts for his dispatch from many more.

"*Shoot the fucker!*"

"*Through the heart!*"

The leaders didn't hesitate. Three of them fired. One of them hit the man, the bullet catching Narcisse in the shoulder and passing straight through him. There was a cheer from the mob. Encouraged by this first wounding they surged into the station in still greater numbers, those at the back eager to see the bloodletting, those at the front mostly blind to the fact that their target had not shed a single drop. He hadn't fallen either; that they *did* see. And now one or two acted to put that to rights, firing a volley at Narcisse. Most of the shots went wide, but not all.

As the third bullet struck home, however, a roar of fury shook the room, exploding the lamp on the desk and bringing dust from the ceiling.

Hearing it, one or two of those just crossing the threshold changed their minds. Suddenly careless of what their neighbors might think, they began to dig their way out into the open air. It was still light on the street;

there was warmth to cancel the chill of fear that ran down every human spine hearing that cry. But for those at the head of the mob there was no retreat. The door was jammed. All they could do was stand their ground and aim their weapons, as the roarer emerged from the darkness at the back of the station.

One of the men had been a witness at the Sweetgrass Inn that morning, and knew the man who now came into sight as the killer he'd seen arrested. Knew his name too.

"That's him!" he started to yell. "That's Boone!"

The man who'd fired the first shot to strike Narcisse aimed his rifle. *"Bring him down!"* somebody shouted.

The man fired.

Boone had been shot before, and shot, and shot. This little bullet entering his chest and nicking his silent heart was nothing. He laughed it off and kept coming, feeling the change in him as he breathed it out. His substance was fluid. It broke into droplets and became something new; part the beast he'd inherited from Peloquin, part a shade warrior, like Lylesburg; part Boone the lunatic, content with his visions at last. And oh! The pleasure of it, feeling this possibility liberated and forgiven, the pleasure of bearing down on this human herd and seeing it break before him.

He smelled their heat and hungered for it. He saw their terror and took strength from it. They stole such authority for themselves, these people. Made themselves arbiters of good and bad, natural and unnatural, justifying their cruelty with spurious laws. Now they saw a simpler law at work as their bowels remembered the oldest fear: of being *prey*.

They fled before him, panic spreading throughout their unruly ranks. The rifles and the stones were forgotten in the chaos, as howls for blood became howls for escape. Trampling each other in their haste, they clawed and fought their way into the street.

One of the riflemen stood his ground, or else was rooted to it in shock. Whichever, the weapon was dashed from his grip by Boone's swelling hand, and the man flung himself into the throng of people to escape further confrontation.

Daylight still ruled the street outside, and Boone was loath to step into it, but Narcisse was indifferent to such niceties. With the route cleared he made his way out into the light, weaving through the fleeing crowd unnoticed, until he reached the car.

There was some regrouping of forces going on, Boone could see. A knot of people on the far sidewalk, comforted by the sunlight and their distance from the beast, talking heatedly together as though they might rally. Dropped weapons were being claimed from the ground. It could only be a matter of time before the shock of Boone's transformation died away and they renewed their assault.

But Narcisse was swift. He was in the car and revving it by the time Lori reached the step. Boone held her back, the touch of his shadow (which he trailed like smoke) more than enough to cancel any lingering fear she might have had of his reworked flesh. Indeed, she found herself imagining what it would be like to fuck with him in this configuration, to spread herself for the shadow and the beast at its heart.

The car was at the door now, squealing to a halt in a cloud of its own fumes.

"*Go!*" Boone said, pitching her through the door, his shadow covering the sidewalk to confound the enemy's sights. With reason. A shot blew out the back window even as she threw herself into the car; a barrage of stones followed.

Boone was at her side already, and slamming the door.

"They're going to come after us!" Narcisse said.

"Let them," was Boone's response.

"To Midian?"

"It's no secret now."

"True."

Narcisse put his foot down and the car was away.

"We'll lead them to hell," said Boone as a quartet of vehicles began to give chase, "if that's where they want to go."

His voice was guttural from the throat of the creature he'd become, but the laugh that followed was Boone's laugh, as though it had always belonged to this beast, a humor more ecstatic than his humanity had room for, that had finally found its purpose and its face.

22

TRIUMPH OF
THE MASK

I

If he never saw another day like today, Eigerman thought, he'd have little to complain about to the Lord when he was eventually called. First the sight of Boone in chains. Then bringing the baby out to meet the cameras, knowing his face would be on the cover of every newspaper across the country tomorrow morning. And now this: the glorious sight of Midian in flames.

It had been Pettine's notion, and a damn good one, to pour lighted gasoline down the gullets of the tombs, to drive whatever was underground up into the light. It had worked better than either of them had anticipated. Once the smoke began to thicken and the fires to spread, the enemy had no choice but to exit their cesspit into the open air, where God's good sun took many of them apart at a stroke.

Not all, however. Some of them had time to prepare for their emergence, protecting themselves against the light by whatever desperate means they could. Their invention was in vain. The pyre was sealed: gates guarded, walls manned. Unable to escape skyward with wings and heads covered against the sun, they were driven back into the conflagration.

In other circumstances Eigerman might not have allowed himself to enjoy the spectacle as openly as he did. But these creatures weren't human—that much was apparent even from a safe distance. They were miscreated fuckheads, no two the same, and he was sure the saints themselves would have laughed to see them bested. Putting down the devil was the Lord's own sport.

But it couldn't last forever. Night would soon be falling. When it did their strongest defense against the enemy would drop out of sight and the tide might turn. They'd have to leave the bonfire to burn overnight, and return at dawn to dig the survivors out of their niches and finish them off. With crosses and holy water securing the walls and gates, there'd be little chance of any escaping before daybreak. He wasn't sure what power was working to subdue the monsters: fire, water, daylight, faith: all, or some combination of these. It didn't matter. All that concerned him was that he had the power to crack their heads. A shout from down the hill broke Eigerman's train of thought.

"You've got to stop this!"

It was Ashbery. It looked as though he'd been standing too close to the flames. His face was half-cooked, basted in sweat.

"Stop what?" Eigerman yelled back.

"This massacre."

"I see no massacre."

Ashbery was within a couple of yards of Eigerman, but he still had to shout over the noise from below: the din of the freaks and the fires punctuated now and again by louder dins as the heat broke a slab, or brought a mausoleum down.

"They don't stand a chance!" Ashbery hollered.

"They're not supposed to," Eigerman pointed out.

"But you don't know who's down there! Eigerman! . . . *You don't know who you're killing!"*

The chief grinned.

"I know damn well," he said, a look in his eyes that Ashbery had only ever seen in mad dogs. "I'm killing the dead, and how can that be wrong? Eh? *Answer me, Ashbery.* How can it be wrong to make the dead lie down and *stay dead?"*

"There's children down there, Eigerman," Ashbery replied, jabbing a finger in the direction of Midian.

"Oh yes. With eyes like headlights! And teeth! You seen the teeth on those fuckers? That's the Devil's children, Ashbery."

"You're out of your mind."

"You haven't got the balls to believe that, have you? You haven't got balls at all!"

He took a step toward the priest and caught hold of the black cassock.

"Maybe you're more like *them* than us," he said. "Is that what it is, Ashbery? Feel the call of the wild, do you?"

Ashbery wrested his robes from Eigerman's grip. They tore.

"All right . . ." he said, "I tried reasoning with you. If you've got such God-fearing executioners, then maybe a man of God can stop them."

"You leave my men alone!" Eigerman said.

But Ashbery was already halfway down the hill, his voice carried above the tumult.

"*Stop!*" he yelled. "*Lay down your weapons!*"

Center stage in front of the main gates he was visible to a good number of Eigerman's army, and though few, if any, had stepped into a church since their wedding or their baptism, they listened now. They wanted some explanation of the sights the last hour had provided, sights they'd happily have fled from but that some urge they barely recognized as their own kept them at the wall, childhood prayers on their lips.

Eigerman knew their loyalty was only his by default. They didn't obey him because they loved the law. They obeyed because they were more afraid of retreating in front of their companions than of doing the job. They obeyed because they couldn't defy the ant-under-the-magnifying-glass fascination of watching helpless things go bang. They obeyed because obeying was simpler than not.

Ashbery might change their minds. He had the robes, he had the rhetoric. If he wasn't stopped he might still spoil the day.

Eigerman took his gun from his holster and followed the priest down the hill. Ashbery saw him coming, saw the gun in his hand.

He raised his voice still louder.

"This isn't what God wants!" he yelled. "And it's not what you want either. You don't want innocent blood on your hands."

Priest to the bitter end, Eigerman thought, laying on the guilt.

"Shut your mouth, faggot," he hollered.

Ashbery had no intention of doing so.

"They're not animals in there," he said, "they're people! And you're killing them just because this lunatic tells you to."

His words carried weight, even among the atheists. He was voicing a doubt more than one had entertained but none had dared express. Half a dozen of the nonuniformed began to retire toward their cars, all enthusiasm for the extermination drained. One of Eigerman's men also withdrew from his station at the gate, his slow retreat becoming a run as the chief fired a shot in his direction.

"*Stand your ground!*" he bellowed. But the man was away, lost in the smoke.

Eigerman turned his fury back on Ashbery.

"Got some bad news," he said, advancing toward the priest.

Ashbery looked to right and left for someone willing to defend him, but nobody moved.

"You going to watch him kill me?" he appealed. "For God's sake, won't somebody help me?"

Eigerman leveled his gun. Ashbery had no intention of attempting to outrun the bullet. He dropped to his knees.

"Our Father . . ." he began.

"You're on your own, cocksucker," Eigerman purred. "Nobody's listening."

"Not true," somebody said.

"Huh?"

The prayer faltered.

"*I'm* listening."

Eigerman turned his back on the priest. A figure loomed in the smoke ten yards from him. He pointed the gun in the newcomer's direction.

"Who are you?"

"Sun's almost set," the other said.

"One more step and I'll shoot you."

"So shoot," said the man, and took a step toward the gun. The tatters of smoke that clung to him blew away, and the prisoner in Cell Five walked into Eigerman's sights, his skin bright, his eyes brighter. He was stark naked. There was a bullet hole in the middle of his chest, and more wounds besides, decorating his body.

"Dead," Eigerman said.

"You bet."

"Jesus Lord."

He backed off a step, and another.

"Ten minutes, maybe, before sundown," Boone said. "Then the world's ours."

Eigerman shook his head.

"You're not getting me," he said. "I won't let you get me!"

His backward steps multiplied, and suddenly he was away at speed, not looking behind him. Had he done so, he would have seen that Boone was not interested in pursuit. He was moving instead toward the besieged gates of Midian. Ashbery was still on the ground there.

"*Get up,*" Boone told him.

"If you're going to kill me, do it, will you?" Ashbery said. "Get it over with."

"Why should I kill you?" Boone said.

"I'm a priest."

"So?"

"You're a monster."

"And you're not?"

Ashbery looked up at Boone.

"Me?"

"There's lace under the robe," Boone said.

Ashbery pulled together the tear in his cassock.

"Why hide it?"

"Let me alone."

"Forgive yourself," Boone said, "I did."

He walked on past Ashbery to the gates.

"Wait!" the priest said.

"I'd get going if I were you. They don't like the robes in Midian. Bad memories."

"I want to see," Ashbery said.

"Why?"

"Please. Take me with you."

"It's your risk."

"I'll take it."

2

From a distance it was hard to be sure what was going on down at the cemetery gates, but of two facts the doctor was sure: Boone had returned and somehow bested Eigerman. At the first sight of his arrival Decker had taken shelter in one of the police vehicles. There he sat now, briefcase in hand, trying to plot his next action.

It was difficult, with two voices each counseling different things.

His public self demanded retreat before events became any more dangerous.

Leave now, it said. *Just drive away. Let them all die together.*

There was wisdom in this. With night almost fallen, and Boone there to rally them, Midian's hosts might still triumph. If they did, and they found Decker, his heart would be ripped from his chest.

But there was another voice demanding his attention.

Stay, said the voice of the Mask, rising from the case on his lap.

You've denied me here once already, it said.

So he had, knowing when he did it there'd come a time for repaying the debt.

"Not now," he whispered.

Now, it said.

He knew rational argument carried no weight against its hunger, nor did pleading.

Use your eyes, it said. *I've got work to do.*

What did it see that he didn't? He stared out through the window.

Don't you see her?

Now he did. In his fascination with Boone, naked at the gates, he'd missed the other newcomer to the field: Boone's woman.

Do you see the bitch? the Mask said.

"I see her."

Perfect timing, eh? In this chaos who's going to see me finish her off? Nobody. And with her gone there'll be no one left who knows our secret.

"There's still Boone."

He'll never testify, the Mask laughed. *He's a dead man, for Christ's sake. What's a zombie's word worth, tell me that?*

"Nothing," Decker said.

Exactly. He's no danger to us. But the woman is. Let me silence her.

"Suppose you're seen?"

Suppose I am, the Mask said. *They'll think I was one of Midian's clan all along.*

"Not you," Decker said.

The thought of his precious Other being confused with the degenerates of Midian nauseated him.

"You're pure," he said.

Let me prove it, the Mask coaxed.

"Just the woman?"

Just the woman. Then we'll leave.

He knew the advice made sense. They'd never have a better opportunity for killing the bitch.

He started to unlock the case. Inside, the Mask grew agitated.

Quickly, or we'll lose her.

His fingers slid on the dial as he ran the numbers of the lock.

Quickly, damn you.

The final digit clicked into place. The lock sprang open.

Ol' Button Face was never more beautiful.

3

Though Boone had advised Lori to stay with Narcisse, the sight of
Midian in flames was enough to draw her companion away from the
safety of the hill and down toward the cemetery gates. Lori went with
him a little way, but her presence seemed to intrude upon his grief, so
she hung back a few paces, and in the smoke and deepening twilight was
soon divided from him.

The scene before her was one of utter confusion. Any attempt to
complete the assault on the Necropolis had ceased since Boone had sent
Eigerman running. Both his men and their civilian support had retreated
from around the walls. Some had already driven away, most likely fearing
what would happen when the sun sank over the horizon. Most remained,
however, prepared to beat a retreat if necessary, but mesmerized by the
spectacle of destruction. Her gaze went from one to another, looking for
some sign of what they were feeling, but every face was blank. They
looked like death masks, she thought, wiped of response. Except that she
knew the dead now. She walked with them, talked with them, saw them
feel and weep. Who then were the *real* dead? The silent-hearted, who
still knew pain, or their glassy-eyed tormentors?

A break in the smoke uncovered the sun, teetering on the rim of the
world. The red light dazzled her. She closed her eyes against it.

In the darkness, she heard a breath a little way behind her. She
opened her eyes and began to turn, knowing harm was coming. Too late
to slip it. The Mask was a yard from her, and closing.

She had only seconds before the knife found her, but it was long
enough to see the Mask as she'd never seen it before. Here was the
blankness on the faces she'd studied perfectly perfected, the human

fiend made myth. No use to call it *Decker*. It wasn't Decker. No use to call it anything. It was as far beyond names as she was beyond power to tame it.

It slashed her arm. Once, and again.

There were no taunts from it this time. It had come only to dispatch her.

The wounds stung. Instinctively she put her hand to them, her motion giving him opportunity to kick the legs from under her. She had no time to cushion her fall. The impact emptied her lungs. Sobbing for breath, she turned her face to the ground to keep it from the knife. The earth seemed to shudder beneath her. Illusion, surely. Yet it came again.

She glanced up at the Mask. He too had felt the tremors and was looking toward the cemetery. His distraction would be her only reprieve; she had to take it. Rolling out of his shadow, she got to her feet. There was no sign of Narcisse or Rachel, nor much hope of help from the death masks who'd forsaken their vigil and were hurrying away from the smoke as the tremors intensified. Fixing her eyes on the gate through which Boone had stepped, she stumbled down the hill, the dusty soil dancing at her feet.

The source of the agitation was Midian, its cue the disappearance of the sun, and with it the light that had trapped the Breed underground. It was their noise that made the ground shake, as they destroyed their refuge. What was below could remain below no longer.

The Nightbreed were rising.

The knowledge didn't persuade her from her course. Whatever was loose inside the gate she'd long ago made her peace with it, and might expect mercy. From the horror at her back, matching her stride for stride, she could expect none.

There were only the fires from the tombs up ahead to light her way now, a way strewn with the debris of the siege: gasoline cans, shovels, discarded weapons. She was almost at the gates before she caught sight of Babette, standing close to the wall, her face terror-stricken.

"*Run!*" she yelled, afraid the Mask would wound the child.

Babette did as she was told, her body seeming to melt into beast as she turned and fled through the gates. Lori came a few paces after her, but by the time she was over the threshold the child had already gone, lost down the smoke-filled avenues. The tremors here were strong enough to unseat the paving stones and topple the mausoleums, as though some force underground—Baphomet, perhaps, Who Made Midian—was shaking its foundations to bring the place to ruin. She hadn't anticipated such violence; her chances of surviving the cataclysm were slim.

But better to be buried in the rubble than succumb to the Mask. And be flattered, at the end, that Fate had at least offered her a choice of extinctions.

23

THE HARROWING

I

In the cell back at Shere Neck memories of Midian's labyrinth had tormented Boone. Closing his eyes against the sun he'd found himself lost here, only to open them again and find the maze echoed in the whorls of his fingertips and the veins on his arms. Veins in which no heat ran, reminders, like Midian, of his shame.

Lori had broken that spell of despair, coming to him not begging but *demanding* he forgive himself.

Now, back in the avenues from which his monstrous condition had sprung, he felt her love for him like the life his body no longer possessed.

He needed its comfort in the pandemonium. The Nightbreed were not simply bringing Midian down, they were erasing all clue to their nature or keepsake of their passing. He saw them at work on every side, laboring to finish what Eigerman's scourge had begun. Gathering up the pieces of their dead and throwing them into the flames, burning their beds, their clothes, anything they couldn't take with them.

These were not the only preparations for escape. He glimpsed the Breed in forms he'd never before had the honor to see: unfurling wings, unfolding limbs. One becoming many (a man, a flock), many becoming one (three lovers, a cloud). All around, the rites of departure.

Ashbery was still at Boone's side, agog.

"Where are they going?"

"I'm too late," Boone said. "They're leaving Midian."

The lid of a tomb ahead flew off and a ghost form rose like a rocket into the night sky.

"Beautiful," Ashbery said. "What are they? Why have I never known them?"

Boone shook his head. He had no way to describe the Breed that were not the old ways. They didn't belong to hell, nor yet to heaven. They were what the species he'd once belonged to could not bear to be. The *un*-people, the *anti*-tribe, humanity's sack unpicked and sewn together again with the moon inside.

And now, before he'd had a chance to know them—and by knowing them, know *himself*—he was losing them. They were finding transport in their cells, and rising to the night.

"Too late," he said again, the pain of this parting bringing tears to his eyes.

The escapes were gathering momentum. On every side doors were being thrown wide and slabs overturned as the spirits ascended in innumerable forms. Not all flew. Some went as goat or tiger, racing through the flames to the gate. Most went alone, but some—whose fecundity neither death nor Midian had slowed—went with families of six or more, their littlest in their arms. He was witnessing, he knew, the passing of an age, the end of which had begun the moment he'd first stepped on Midian's soil. He was the maker of this devastation, though he'd set no fire and toppled no tomb. He had brought men to Midian. In doing so, he'd destroyed it. Even Lori could not persuade him to forgive himself that. The thought might have tempted him to the flames had he not heard the child calling his name.

She was only human enough to use words; the rest was beast.

"*Lori*," she said.

"What about her?"

"The Mask has her."

The Mask? She could only mean Decker.

"*Where?*"

2

Close, and closer still.

Knowing she couldn't outpace him she tried instead to out*dare* him, going where she hoped he would not. But he was too hot for her life to be shaken off. He followed her into territory where the ground erupted beneath their feet and smoking stone rained around them.

It was not his voice that called her, however.

"Lori! This way!"

She chanced a desperate look, and there—*God love him!*—was Narcisse, beckoning. She veered off the pathway, or what was left of it, toward him, ducking between two mausoleums as their stained glass blew, and a stream of shadow, pricked with eyes, left its hiding place for the stars. It was like a piece of night sky itself, she marveled. It belonged in the heavens.

The sight slowed her pace by an all but fatal step. The Mask closed the gap between them and snatched at her blouse. She threw herself forward to avoid the stab she knew must follow, the fabric tearing as she fell. This time he had her. Even as she reached for the wall to haul herself to her feet she felt his gloved hand at her nape.

"*Fuckhead?*" somebody shouted.

She looked up to see Narcisse at the other end of the passage between the mausoleums. He'd clearly caught Decker's attention. The hold on her neck was relaxing. It wasn't enough for her to squirm free, but if Narcisse could only keep up his distraction he might do the trick.

"*Got something for you,*" he said, and took his hands from his pocket to display the silver hooks on his thumbs.

He struck the hooks together. They sparked.

Decker let Lori's neck slip from his fingers. She slid out of his reach and began to stumble toward Narcisse. He was moving down the passage toward her, or rather toward *Decker,* on whom his eyes were fixed.

"Don't—" she gasped. "He's dangerous."

Narcisse heard her—he *grinned* at the warning—but he made no reply. He just moved on past her to intercept the killer.

Lori glanced back. As the pair came within a yard of each other the Mask dragged a second knife, its blade as broad as a machete, from his jacket. Before Narcisse had a chance to defend himself, the butcher delivered a swift downward stroke that separated Narcisse's left hand from his wrist in a single cut. Shaking his head, Narcisse took a backward step, but the Mask matched his retreat, raising the machete a second time and bringing it down on his victim's skull. The blow divided Narcisse's head from scalp to neck. It was a wound even a dead man could not survive. Narcisse's body began to shake, and then—like

Ohnaka trapped in sunlight—he came apart with a crack, a chorus of howls and sighs emerging, then taking flight.

Lori let out a sob, but stifled anything more. There was no time to mourn. If she waited to shed a single tear the Mask would claim her, and Narcisse's sacrifice would have been for nothing. She started to back away, the walls shaking to either side of her, knowing she should simply run but unable to detach herself from the sight of the Mask's depravity. Rooting amid the carnage he skewered half of Narcisse's head on the finer of his blades, then rested the knife on his shoulder, trophy and all, before renewing his pursuit.

Now she ran out of the shadow of the mausoleums and back onto the main avenue. Even if memory could have offered a guide to her whereabouts, all the monuments had gone to the same rubble; she could not tell north from south. It was all one in the end. Whichever way she turned the same ruin and the same pursuer. If he would come after her forever and forever—*and he would*—what was the use of living in fear of him? Let him have his sharp way. Her heart beat too hard to be pressed any further.

But even as she resigned herself to his knife, the stretch of paving between her and her slaughterer cracked open, a plume of smoke shielding her from the Mask. An instant later the whole avenue opened up. She fell. Not to the ground. There was no ground. But into the earth—

3

"—falling!" the child said.

The shock of it almost toppled her from Boone's shoulders. His hands went up to support her. She took fiercer hold of his hair.

"Steady?" he said.

"Yes."

She wouldn't countenance Ashbery accompanying them. He'd been left to fend for himself in the maelstrom while they went looking for Lori.

"Ahead," she said, directing her mount. "Not very far."

The fires were dying down, having devoured all they could get their tongues to. Confronted with cold brick all they could do was lick it black, then gutter out. But the tremors from below had not ceased. Their motions still ground stone on stone. And beneath the reverberations there was another sound, which Boone didn't so much hear as *feel*: in his gut and balls and teeth.

The child turned his head with her reins.

"That way," she said.

The diminishing fires made progress easier; their brightness hadn't suited Boone's eyes. Now he went more quickly, though the avenues had been plowed by the quake and he trod turned earth.

"How far?" he asked.

"Hush," she told him.

"What?"

"Stand still."

"You hear it too?" he said.

"Yes."

"What is it?"

She didn't answer at first, but listened again.

Then she said, *"Baphomet."*

In his hours of imprisonment he'd thought more than once of the Baptizer's chamber, of the cold time he'd spent witness to the divided God. Hadn't it spoken prophecies to him, whispered in his head and demanded he listen? It had seen this ruin. It had told him Midian's last hour was imminent. Yet there'd been no accusations, though it must have known that it spoke to the man responsible. Instead it had seemed almost *intimate*, which had terrified him more than any assault. He could not be the confidant of divinities. He'd come to appeal to Baphomet as one of the newly dead requesting a place in the earth. But he'd been greeted like an actor in some future drama. Called by another name, even. He'd wanted none of it. Not the auguries, not the name. He'd fought them, turning his back on the Baptizer, stumbling away, shaking the whispers from his head.

In that he'd not succeeded. At the thought of Baphomet's presence, its words, and that name, were back like Furies.

You're Cabal, it had said.

He'd denied it then, he denied it now. Much as he pitied Baphomet's tragedy, knowing it couldn't escape this destruction in its wounded condition, he had more urgent claims upon his sympathies.

He couldn't save the Baptizer. But he could save Lori.

"She's there!" the child said.

"Which way?"

"Straight ahead. Look!"

There was only chaos visible. The avenue in front of them had been split open; light and smoke poured up through the ruptured ground. There was no sign of anything living.

"I don't see her," he said.

"She's underground," the child replied. "In the pit."

"Direct me, then."

"I can't go any farther."

"Why not?"

"Put me down. I've taken you as far as I can." A barely suppressed panic had crept into her voice. *"Put me down,"* she insisted.

Boone dropped to his haunches, and the child slid off his shoulders.

"What's wrong?" he said.

"I mustn't go with you. It's not allowed."

After the havoc they'd come through, her distress was bewildering.

"What are you afraid of?" he said.

"I can't look," she replied, "not at the Baptizer."

"It's here?"

She nodded, retreating from him as new violence opened the fissure ahead even wider.

"Go to Lori," she told him. "Bring her out. You're all she has."

Then she was gone, two legs becoming four as she fled, leaving Boone to the pit.

4

Lori's consciousness flickered out as she fell. When she came round, seconds later, she was lying halfway up, or down, a steep slope. The roof above her was still intact, but badly fractured, the cracks opening even as she watched, presaging total collapse. If she didn't move quickly she'd be buried alive. She looked toward the head of the slope. The cross tunnel was open to the sky. She began to crawl toward it, earth cascading down on her head, the walls creaking as they were pressed to surrender.

"Not yet . . ." she murmured, *"please, not yet . . ."*

It was only as she came within six feet of the summit that her dazed senses recognized the slope. She'd carried Boone up this very incline once, away from the power that resided in the chamber at the bottom.

Was it still there, watching her scrabblings? Or was this whole cataclysm evidence of its departure, the architect's farewell? She couldn't feel its surveillance, but then she could feel very little. Her body and mind functioned because instinct told them to. There was life at the top of the slope. Inch by wracking inch she was crawling to meet it.

Another minute and she reached the tunnel, or its roofless remains. She lay on her back for a time, staring up at the sky. With her breath regained she got to her feet and examined her wounded arm. The cuts were gummed up with dirt, but at least the blood had ceased to flow.

As she coaxed her legs to move, something fell in front of her, wet in the dirt. Narcisse looked up at her with half a face. She sobbed his name, turning her eyes to meet the Mask. He straddled the tunnel like a gravedigger, then dropped down to join her.

The spike was aimed at her heart. Had she been stronger it would have struck home, but the earth at the head of the slope gave way beneath her backward step and she had no power to keep herself from falling, head over heels, back down the incline—

Her cry gave Boone direction. He clambered over upended slabs of paving into the exposed tunnels, then through the maze of toppled walls and dying fires toward her. It was not her figure he saw in the passage ahead, however, turning to meet him with knives at the ready.

It was the doctor, at last.

From the precarious safety of the slope Lori saw the Mask turn from her, diverted from its purpose. She had managed to arrest her fall by catching hold of a crack in the wall with her good hand, which did its duty long enough for her to glimpse Boone in the passageway above. She'd seen what the machete had done to Narcisse. Even the dead had their mortality. But before she could utter any word of warning to Boone a wave of cold power mounted the slope behind her. Baphomet had not vacated its flame. It was there still, its grasp unpicking her fingers from the wall.

Unable to resist it, she slid backward down the slope into the erupting chamber.

The ecstasies of the Breed hadn't tainted Decker. He came at Boone like an abattoir worker to finish a slaughter he'd been called from: without flourish, without passion.

He struck quickly, with no signal of his intention. The thin blade ran straight through Boone's neck.

To disarm the enemy Boone simply stepped away from him. The knife slid through Decker's fingers, still caught in Boone's flesh. The doctor made no attempt to claim it back. Instead he took a two-handed grip on the skull splitter. Now there was some sound from him: a low moan that broke into gasps as he threw himself forward to dispatch his victim.

Boone ducked the slicing blow, and the blade embedded itself in the tunnel wall. Earth spattered them both as Decker pulled it free. Then he swung again, this time missing his target's face by a finger length.

Caught off balance, Boone almost fell, and his downcast eyes chanced on Decker's trophy. He couldn't mistake that maimed face. Narcisse, cut up and dead in the dirt.

"*You bastard!*" he roared.

Decker paused for a moment and watched Boone. Then he spoke. Not with his own voice, but with someone else's, a grinning whine of a voice.

"You can die," it said.

As he spoke he swung the blade back and forth, not attempting to touch Boone, merely to demonstrate his authority. The blade whined like the voice, the music of a fly in a coffin, to and fro between the walls.

Boone retreated before the display with mortal terror in his gut. Decker was right. The dead *could* die.

He drew breath, through mouth and punctured throat. He'd made a near fatal error, staying human in the presence of the Mask. And why? From some absurd idea that this final confrontation should be man to man, that they'd trade words as they fought, and he'd undo the doctor's ego before he undid his life.

It wouldn't be that way. This wasn't a patient's revenge on his corrupted healer: this was a beast and a butcher, tooth to knife.

He exhaled, and the truth in his cells came forth like honey. His nerves ran with bliss; his body throbbed as it swelled. In life he'd never felt so alive as he did at these moments, stripping off his humanity and dressing for the night.

"*No more . . .*" he said, and let the beast come from him everywhere.

Decker raised his machete to undo the enemy before the change had been completed. But Boone didn't wait. Still transforming, he tore at the butcher's face, taking off the mask—buttons, zipper, and all—to uncover the infirmities beneath.

Decker howled at being revealed, putting his hand up to his face to half cover it against the beast's stare.

Boone snatched the mask up from the ground and began to tear it apart, his claws shredding the linen. Decker's howls mounted. Dropping his hand from his face he began to swipe at Boone with insane abandon. The blade caught Boone's chest, slicing it open, but as it returned for a second cut, Boone dropped the rags and blocked the blow, carrying Decker's arm against the wall with such force he broke the bones. The machete fell to the ground, and Boone reached out for Decker's face.

The steep howl stopped as the claws came at him. The mouth closed. The features slackened. For an instant Boone was looking at a face he'd studied for hours, hanging on its every word. At that thought his hand went from face to neck and he seized Decker's windpipe, which had funded so many lies. He closed his fist, his claws piercing the meat of Decker's throat. Then he pulled. The machinery came out in a wash of blood. Decker's eyes widened, fixed on his silencer. Boone pulled again, and again. The eyes glazed. The body jerked, and jerked, then started to sag.

Boone didn't let it drop. He held it as in a dance, and undid the flesh and bone as he'd undone the mask, clots of Decker's body striking the walls. There was only the dimmest memory of Decker's crimes against him in his head now. He tore with a Breed's zeal, taking monstrous satisfaction in a monstrous act. When he'd done his worst he dropped the wreckage to the earth, and finished the dance with his partner underfoot.

There'd be no rising from the grave for this body. No hope of earthly resurrection. Even in the full flood of his attack, Boone had withheld the bite that would have passed life after death into Decker's system. His flesh belonged only to the flies and their children, his reputation to the vagaries of those who chose to tell his story. Boone didn't care. If he never shrugged off the crimes Decker had hung around his neck it scarcely mattered now. He was no longer innocent. With this slaughter he became the killer Decker had persuaded him he was. In murdering the prophet he made the prophecy true.

He let the body lie, and went to seek Lori. There was only one place

she could have gone: down the slope into Baphomet's chamber. There
was pattern in this, he saw. The Baptizer had *brought* her here, unknit-
ting the ground beneath her feet so as to bring Boone after.

The flame its divided body occupied threw a cold glamour up into
his face. He started down the slope toward it, dressed in the blood of his
enemy.

24

CABAL

1

Lost in the wasteland, Ashbery was found by a light flickering up from between the fractured paving stones. Its beams were bitterly cold, and sticky in a way light had no right to be, adhering to his sleeve and hand before fading away. Intrigued, he tracked its source from one eruption to another, each point brighter than the one before.

A scholar in his youth, he would have known the name Baphomet had somebody whispered it to him, and understood why the light, springing from the deity's flame, exercised such a claim upon him. He would have known the deity as god and goddess in one body. Would have known too how its worshipers had suffered for their idol, burned as heretics or for crimes against nature. He might have feared a power that demanded such homage, and wisely.

But there was nobody to tell him. There was only the light, drawing him on.

2

The Baptizer was not alone in its chamber, Boone found. He counted eleven members of the Breed around the walls, kneeling blindfolded with their backs to the flame. Among them, Lylesburg and Rachel.

On the ground to the right of the door lay Lori. There was blood on her arm and on her face, and her eyes were closed. But even as he went to her aid the thing in the flame set its eyes on him, turning him round with an icy touch. It had business with him, which it was not about to postpone.

Approach, it said, *of your own free will*.

He was afraid. The flame from the ground was twice the size it had been when last he'd entered, battering the roof of the chamber. Fragments of earth, turned to either ice or ash, fell in a glittering rain and littered the floor. A dozen yards from the flame the assault of its energies was brutal. Yet Baphomet *invited* him closer.

You're safe, it said. *You come in the blood of your enemy. It'll keep you warm.*

He took a step toward the fire. Though he'd suffered bullet and blade in his life since death, and felt none of them, he felt the chill from Baphomet's flame plainly enough. It pricked his nakedness, made frost patterns on his eyes. But Baphomet's words were no empty promise. The blood he wore grew hot as the air around him grew colder. He took comfort from it and braved the last few steps.

The weapon, Baphomet said, *discard it*.

He'd forgotten the knife in his neck. He drew it out of his flesh and threw it aside.

Closer still, the Baptizer said.

The flame's fury concealed all but glimpses of its freight, but enough to confirm what his first encounter with Baphomet had taught him: that if this deity had made creatures in its own image, then he'd never set eyes on them. Even in dreams, nothing that approached the Baptizer. It was one of one.

Suddenly some part of it reached for him out of the flame. Whether limb, or organ, or both he had no chance to see. It snatched at his neck and hair and pulled him toward the fire. Decker's blood didn't shield him now; the ice scorched his face. Yet there was no fighting free. It immersed his head in the flame, holding him fast. He knew what this was the instant the fire closed around his head: *Baptism*.

And to confirm that belief, Baphomet's voice in his head.

You are Cabal, it said.

The pain was mellowing. Boone opened his mouth to draw breath, and the fire coursed down his throat and into his belly and lungs, then through his whole system. It carried his new name with it, baptizing him inside out.

He was no longer Boone. He was Cabal. An alliance of many.

From this cleansing on he would be capable of heat and blood and making children: that was in Baphomet's gift, and the deity gave it. But he would be frail too, or frailer. Not just because he bled, but because he was charged with purpose.

I must be hidden tonight, Baphomet said. *We all have enemies, but mine have lived longer and learned more cruelty than most. I will be taken from here and hidden from them.*

Now the presence of the Breed made sense. They'd remained behind to take a fraction of the Baptizer with them and conceal it from whatever forces came in pursuit.

This is your doing, Cabal, Baphomet said. *I don't accuse you. It was bound to happen. No refuge is forever. But I charge you—*

"Yes?" he said. "tell me."

Rebuild what you've destroyed.

"A new Midian?"

No.

"What, then?"

You must discover for us, in the human world.

"Help me," he said.

I can't. From here on, it's you must help me. You've undone the world. Now you must remake it.

There were shudders in the flame. The Rites of Baptism were almost over.

"How do I begin?" Cabal said.

Heal me, Baphomet replied. *Find me, and heal me. Save me from my enemies.*

The voice that had first addressed him had changed its nature utterly. All trace of demand had gone from it. There was only this prayer to be healed, and kept from harm, delivered softly at his ear. Even the leash on his head had been slipped, leaving him free to look left and right. A call he hadn't heard had summoned Baphomet's attendants from the wall. Despite their blindfolds they walked with steady steps to the edge of the flame, which had lost much of its ferocity. They'd raised their arms, over which shrouds were draped, and the flame wall broke as pieces of Baphomet's body were dropped into the travelers' waiting arms, to be wrapped up instantly and put from sight.

This parting of piece from piece was agonizing. Cabal felt the pain as his own, filling him up until it was almost beyond enduring. To escape it he began to retreat from the flame.

But as he did so the one piece yet to be claimed tumbled into view in front of his face. Baphomet's head. It turned to him, vast and white, its symmetry fabulous. His entire body rose to it: gaze, spittle, and prick. His heart began to beat, healing its damaged wing with its first throb. His congealed blood liquefied like a saint's relics, and began to run. His testicles tightened; sperm ran up his cock. He ejaculated into the flame, pearls of semen carried up past his eyes to touch the Baptizer's face.

Then the rendezvous was over. He stumbled out of the fire as Lylesburg—the last of the adherents in the chamber—received the head from the flames and wrapped it up.

Its tenants departed, the flame's ferocity redoubled. Cabal stumbled back as it unleashed itself with terrifying vigor—

On the ground above, Ashbery felt the force build, and tried to retreat from it, but his mind was full of what he'd spied upon, and its weight slowed him. The fire caught him, sweeping him up as it hurtled heavenward. He shrieked at its touch and at the aftertaste of Baphomet that flooded his system. His many masks were burned away. The robes first, then the lace he'd not been able to pass a day of his adult life without wearing. Next the sexual anatomy he'd never much enjoyed. And finally, his flesh, scrubbing him clean. He fell back to earth more naked than he'd been in his mother's womb, and blind. The impact smashed his legs and arms beyond repair.

Below, Cabal shook himself from the daze of revelation. The fire had blown a hole in the roof of the chamber, and was spreading from it in all directions. It would consume flesh as easily as earth or stone. They had to be out of here before it found them. Lori was awake. From the suspicion in her eyes as he approached, it was plain she'd seen the Baptism, and feared him.

"It's me," he told her. "It's still me."

He offered her a hand. She took it, and he pulled her to her feet.

"I'll carry you," he said.

She shook her head. Her eyes had gone from him to something on the floor behind him. He followed her gaze. Decker's blade lay close to the fissure, where the man he'd been before the Baptism had cast it aside.

"You want it?" he said.

"Yes."

Shielding his head from the debris he retraced his steps and picked it up.

"Is he dead?" she asked, as he came back to her.

"He's dead."

There was no sign of the corpse to verify his claim. The tunnel, collapsing on itself, had already buried him, as it was burying all of Midian. A tomb for the tombs.

With so much already leveled it wasn't difficult to find their way out to the main gates. They saw no sign of Midian's inhabitants on their way. Either the fire had consumed their remains or rubble and earth covered them.

Just outside the gate, left where they could not fail to find it, was a reminder for Lori of one whom she prayed had escaped unharmed. Babette's doll—woven from grasses and crowned with spring flowers—lay in a small ring of stones. As Lori's fingers made contact with the toy it seemed she saw one final time through the child's eyes—a landscape moving by as somebody speeded her away to safety. The glimpse was all too brief. She had no time to pass a prayer for good fortune along to the child before the vision was startled from her by a noise at her back. She turned to see that the pillars that had supported Midian's gates were beginning to topple. Boone snatched her arm as the two stone slabs struck each other, teetered head to head like matched wrestlers, then fell sideways to hit the ground where moments before Lori and Boone had stood.

3

Though he had no watch to read the hour, Boone had a clear sense—Baphomet's gift, perhaps—of how long they had until daybreak. In his mind's eye he could see the planet, a clock face decorated with seas, the magical divide of night from day creeping around it.

He had no fear of the sun's appearance on the horizon. His Baptism had given him a strength denied his brothers and sisters. The sun wouldn't kill him. This he knew without question. Undoubtedly it would be a discomfort to him. Moonrise would always be a more welcome sight than daybreak. But his work wouldn't be confined to the night hours. He wouldn't need to hide his head from the sun the way his fellow Breed were obliged to. Even now they'd be looking for a place of refuge before morning broke.

He imagined them in the sky over America, or running beside its highways, groups dividing when some among them grew tired or found a likely haven, the rest moving on, more desperate by the moment. Silently he wished them safe journeys and secure harbor.

More: he promised he would find them again with time. Gather them up and unite them as Midian had done. Unwittingly, he'd harmed them. Now he had to heal that harm, however long it took.

"I have to start tonight," he told Lori. "Or their trails will be cold. Then I'll never find them."

"You're not going without me, Boone."

"I'm not Boone any longer," he told her.

"Why?"

They sat on the hill overlooking the Necropolis, and he recited to her all he'd learned at the Baptism. Hard lessons, which he had too few words to communicate. She was weary, and shivering, but she wouldn't let him stop.

"Go on . . ." she'd kept saying, when he'd faltered. "Tell me everything."

She knew most of it. She'd been Baphomet's instrument as much as he, or more. Part of the prophecy. Without her he'd never have returned to Midian to save it, and to fail. The consequence of that return and that failure was the task before him.

Yet she revolted.

"You can't leave me," she said. "Not after all that's happened."

She put her hand on his leg.

"Remember the cell . . ." she murmured.

He looked at her.

"You told me to forgive myself. And it was good advice. But it doesn't mean I can turn my back on what happened here. Baphomet, Lylesburg, all of them . . . I destroyed the only home they ever had."

"*You* didn't destroy it."

"If I'd never come here, it'd still be standing," he replied. "I have to undo that damage."

"So take me with you," she said. "We'll go together."

"It can't be that way. You're alive, Lori. I'm not. You're still human. I'm not."

"You can change that."

"What are you saying?"

"You can make me the same as you. It's not difficult. One bite and Peloquin changed you forever. So change *me*."

"I can't."

"You *won't*, you mean."

She turned the point of Decker's blade in the dirt.

"You don't want to be with me. Simple as that, isn't it?" She made a small, tight-lipped smile. "Haven't you got the guts to say it?"

"When I've finished my work . . ." he answered. "Maybe then."

"Oh, in a hundred years or so?" she murmured, tears beginning. "You'll come back for me then, will you? Dig me up. Kiss me all over. Tell me you would have come sooner, but the days just kept *slipping by*."

"*Lori.*"

"Shut up," she said. "Don't give me any more excuses. They're just insults." She studied the blade, not him. "You've got your reasons. I think they stink, but you keep hold of them. You're going to need something to cling to."

He didn't move.

"What are you waiting for? I'm not going to tell you it's all right. Just go. I never want to set eyes on you again."

He stood up. Her anger hurt, but it was easier than tears. He backed away three or four paces, then—understanding that she wouldn't grant him a smile or even a look—he turned from her.

Only then did she glance up. His eyes were averted. It was now or never. She put the point of Decker's blade to her belly. She knew she couldn't drive it home with only one hand, so she went onto her knees, wedged the handle into the dirt, and let her body weight carry her down onto the blade. It hurt horribly. She yelled in pain.

He turned to find her writhing, her good blood pouring out into the soil. He ran back to her, turning her over. The death spasms were already in her.

"*I lied,*" she murmured. "Boone . . . I lied. You're all I ever want to see."

"Don't die," he said. "Oh, God in heaven, don't die."

"So stop me."

"I don't know how."

"Kill me. Bite me . . . give me the balm."

Pain twisted up her face. She gasped.

"Or let me die, if you can't take me with you. That's better than living without you."

He cradled her, tears dropping onto her face. Her pupils were turning up beneath her lids. Her tongue was twitching at her lips. In seconds she'd be gone, he knew. Once dead, she'd be beyond his power of recall.

"Is . . . it . . . *no?*" she said. She wasn't seeing him any longer.

He opened his mouth to provide his answer, raising her neck to his bite. Her skin smelled sour. He bit deep into the muscle, her blood meaty on his tongue, the balm rising in his throat to enter her bloodstream. But the shudders in her body had already ceased. She slumped in his embrace.

He raised his head from her torn neck, swallowing what he'd taken. He'd waited too long. Damn him. She was his mentor and his confessor, and he'd let her slip from him. Death had been upon her before he'd had time to turn sting into promise.

Appalled at this last and most lamentable failure, he lay her down on the ground in front of him.

As he drew his arms out from beneath her, she opened her eyes.

"I'll never leave you," she said.

25

ABIDE WITH ME

I

It was Pettine who found Ashbery, but it was Eigerman who recognized the remnants for the man they'd been. The priest still had life in him, a fact—given the severity of his injuries—that verged on the miraculous. Both his legs were amputated in the days following, and one of his arms up to midbicep. He didn't emerge from his coma after the operations, nor did he die, though every surgeon opined that his chances were virtually zero. But the same fire that had maimed him had lent him an unnatural fortitude. Against all the odds, he endured.

He was not alone through the nights and days of unconsciousness. Eigerman was at his side twenty hours out of every twenty-four, waiting like a dog at a table for some scrap from above, certain that the priest could lead him to the evil that had undone both their lives.

He got more than he bargained for. When Ashbery finally rose from the deep, after two months of teetering on extinction, he rose voluble. Insane, but voluble. He named Baphomet. He named Cabal. He told, in the hieroglyphs of the hopelessly lunatic, of how the Breed had taken the pieces of their divinity's body and hidden them. More than that. He said he could find them again. Touched by the Baptizer's fire and its survivor, he wanted the touch again.

"I can smell God," he'd say, over and over.

"Can you take us to Him?" Eigerman asked.

The answer was always yes.

"I'll be your eyes, then," Eigerman volunteered. "We'll go together."

Nobody else wanted the evidence Ashbery offered; there were too many nonsenses to be accounted for as it was, without adding to the burden on reality. The authorities gladly let Eigerman have custody of the priest. They deserved each other, was the common opinion. Not one sane cell between them.

Ashbery was utterly dependent on Eigerman: incapable, at least at the beginning, of feeding, shitting, or washing without help. Repugnant as it was to tend the imbecile, Eigerman knew Ashbery was a God-given gift. Through him he might yet revenge himself for the humiliations of Midian's last hours. Coded in Ashbery's rantings were clues to the enemy's whereabouts. With time he'd decipher them.

And when he did—oh, *when he did*—there would come such a day of reckoning the Last Trump would pale beside.

2

The visitors came by night, stealthily, and took refuge wherever they could find it.

Some revisited haunts their forebears had favored, towns under wide skies where believers still sang on Sunday and the picket fences were painted every spring. Others took to the cities: to Toronto, Washington, Chicago, hoping to avoid detection better where the streets were fullest, and yesterday's corruption today's commerce. In such a place their presence might not be noticed for a year, or two or three. But not forever. Whether they'd taken refuge in city canyon or bayou or dust bowl, none pretended this was a permanent residence. They would be discovered in time, and rooted out. There was a new frenzy abroad, particularly among their old enemies the Christians, who were a daily spectacle, talking of their martyr and calling for purges in His name. The moment they discovered the Breed in their midst the persecutions would begin again.

So discretion was the by-word. They would take meat only when the hunger became crippling, and only then victims who were unlikely to be missed. They would refrain from infecting others, so as not to advertise their presence. If one was found, no other would risk exposure by going to his aid. Hard laws to live by, but not as hard as the consequences of breaking them.

The rest was patience, and they were well used to that. Their liberator would come eventually, if they could only survive the wait. Few had any clue as to the shape he'd come in. But all knew his name.

Cabal, he was called, *Who Unmade Midian.*

Their prayers were full of him. *On the next wind, let him come. If not now, then tomorrow.*

They might not have prayed so passionately had they known what a sea change his coming would bring. They might not have prayed at all had they known they prayed to themselves. But these were revelations for a later day. For now, they had simpler concerns. Keeping the children from the roofs at night, the bereaved from crying out too loud, the young in summer from falling in love with the human.

It was a life.

THE LIFE
OF DEATH

The newspaper was the first edition of the day, and Elaine devoured it from cover to cover as she sat in the hospital waiting room. An animal thought to be a panther—which had terrorized the neighborhood of Epping Forest for two months—had been shot and found to be a wild dog. Archaeologists in the Sudan had discovered bone fragments which they opined might lead to a complete reappraisal of Man's origins. A young woman who had once danced with minor royalty had been found murdered near Clapham; a solo round-the-world yachtsman was missing; recently excited hopes of a cure for the common cold had been dashed. She read the global bulletins and the trivia with equal fervor—anything to keep her mind off the examination ahead—but today's news seemed very like yesterday's; only the names had been changed.

Dr. Sennett informed her that she was healing well, both inside and out, and was quite fit to return to her full responsibilities whenever she felt psychologically resilient enough. She should make another appointment for the first week of the new year, he told her, and come back for a final examination then. She left him washing his hands of her.

The thought of getting straight onto the bus and heading back to her rooms was repugnant after so much time sitting and waiting. She would walk a stop or two along the route, she decided. The exercise would be good for her, and the December day, though far from warm, was bright.

Her plans proved overambitious, however. After only a few minutes of walking, her lower abdomen began to ache, and she started to feel nauseated, so she turned off the main road to seek out a place where she could rest and drink some tea. She should eat too, she knew, though she had never had much appetite, and had less still since the operation. Her wanderings were rewarded. She found a small restaurant which, though it was twelve fifty-five, was not enjoying a roaring lunchtime trade. A small woman with unashamedly artificial red hair served her tea and a mushroom omelet. She did her best to eat, but didn't get very far. The waitress was plainly concerned.

"Something wrong with the food?" she said, somewhat testily.

"Oh no," Elaine reassured her. "It's just me."

The waitress looked offended nevertheless.

"I'd like some more tea though, if I may?" Elaine said.

She pushed the plate away from her, hoping the waitress would claim it soon. The sight of the meal congealing on the patternless plate was doing nothing for her mood. She hated this unwelcome sensitivity in herself: it was absurd that a plate of uneaten eggs should bring these doldrums on, but she couldn't help herself. She found everywhere little echoes of her own loss. In the death, by a benign November and then the sudden frosts, of the bulbs in her windowsill box, in the thought of the wild dog she'd read of that morning, shot in Epping Forest.

The waitress returned with fresh tea, but failed to take the plate. Elaine called her back, requesting that she do so. Grudgingly, she obliged.

There were no other customers left in the place now, other than Elaine, and the waitress busied herself with removing the lunchtime menus from the tables and replacing them with those for the evening. Elaine sat staring out of the window. Veils of blue-gray smoke had crept down the street in recent minutes, solidifying the sunlight.

"They're burning again," the waitress said. "Damn smell gets everywhere."

"What are they burning?"

"Used to be the community center. They're knocking it down and building a new one. It's a waste of taxpayers' money."

The smoke was indeed creeping into the restaurant. Elaine did not find it offensive; it was sweetly redolent of autumn, her favorite season. Intrigued, she finished her tea, paid for her meal, and then elected to wander along and find the source of the smoke. She didn't have far to walk. At the end of the street was a small square; the demolition site dominated it. There was one surprise, however. The building that the waitress had described as a community center was in fact a church, or had been. The lead and slates had already been stripped off the roof, leaving the joists bare to the sky; the windows had been denuded of glass; the turf had gone from the lawn at the side of the building, and two trees had been felled there. It was their pyre which provided the tantalizing scent.

She doubted if the building had ever been beautiful, but there was enough of its structure remaining for her to suppose it might have had charm. Its weathered stone was now completely at variance with the brick and concrete that surrounded it, but its besieged situation (the workmen laboring to undo it, the bulldozer on hand, hungry for rubble) gave it a certain glamour.

One or two of the workmen noticed her standing watching them, but none made any move to stop her as she walked across the square to the front porch of the church and peered inside. The interior, stripped of its decorative stonework, of pulpit, pews, font and the rest, was simply a stone room, completely lacking in atmosphere or authority. Somebody, however, had found a source of interest here. At the far end of the church a man stood with his back to Elaine, staring intently at the ground. Hearing footsteps behind him, he looked round guiltily.

"Oh," he said, "I won't be a moment."

"It's all right—" Elaine said. "I think we're probably both trespassing."

The man nodded. He was dressed soberly—even drearily—but for his green bow tie. His features, despite the garb and the gray hairs of a man in middle age, were curiously unlined, as though neither smile nor frown much ruffled their perfect indifference.

"Sad, isn't it?" he said. "Seeing a place like this."

"Did you know the church as it used to be?"

"I came in on occasion," he said, "but it was never very popular."

"What's it called?"

"All Saints. It was built in the late seventeenth century, I believe. Are you fond of churches?"

"Not particularly. It was just that I saw the smoke and . . ."

"Everybody likes a demolition scene," he said.

"Yes," she replied, "I suppose that's true."

"It's like watching a funeral. Better them than us, eh?"

She murmured something in agreement, her mind flitting elsewhere. Back to the hospital. To her pain and her present healing. To her life saved only by losing the capacity for further life. *Better them than us.*

"My name's Kavanagh," he said, covering the short distance between them, his hand extended.

"How do you do?" she said. "I'm Elaine Rider."

"Elaine," he said. "Charming."

"Are you just taking a final look at the place before it comes down?"

"That's right. I've been looking at the inscriptions on the floor stones. Some of them are most eloquent." He brushed a fragment of timber off one of the tablets with his foot. "It seems such a loss. I'm sure they'll just smash the stones to smithereens when they start to pull the floor up—"

She looked down at the patchwork of tablets beneath her feet. Not all were marked, and of those that were, many simply carried names and dates. There were some inscriptions, however. One, to the left of where Kavanagh was standing, carried an all but eroded relief of crossed shinbones, like drumsticks, and the abrupt motto: *Redeem the time.*

"I think there must have been a crypt under here at some time," Kavanagh said.

"Oh. I see. And these are the people who were buried there."

"Well, I can't think of any other reason for the inscriptions, can you? I was thinking of asking the workmen . . ." He paused in midsentence. ". . . You'll probably think this positively morbid of me . . ."

"What?"

"Well, just to preserve one or two of the finer stones from being destroyed."

"I don't think that's morbid," she said. "They're very beautiful."

He was evidently encouraged by her response. "Maybe I should speak with them now," he said. "Would you excuse me for a moment?"

He left her standing in the nave like a forsaken bride, while he went out to quiz one of the workmen. She wandered down to where the altar had been, reading the names as she went. Who knew or cared about these people's resting places now? Dead two hundred years and more, and gone away not into loving posterity but into oblivion. And suddenly the unarticulated hopes for an afterlife she had nursed through her thirty-four years slipped away; she was no longer weighed down by some vague ambition for heaven. One day, perhaps *this* day, she would die, just as these people had died, and it wouldn't matter a jot. There was nothing to come, nothing to aspire to, nothing to dream of. She stood in a patch of smoke-thickened sun, thinking of this, and was almost happy.

Kavanagh returned from his exchanges with the foreman.

"There is indeed a crypt," he said, "but it hasn't been emptied yet."

"Oh."

They were still underfoot, she thought. Dust and bones.

"Apparently they're having some difficulty getting into it. All the entrances have been sealed up. That's why they're digging around the foundations. To find another way in."

"Are crypts normally sealed up?"

"Not as thoroughly as this one."

"Maybe there was no more room," she said.

Kavanagh took the comment quite seriously. "Maybe," he said.

"Will they give you one of the stones?"

He shook his head. "It's not up to them to say. These are just Council lackeys. Apparently they have a firm of professional excavators to come in and shift the bodies to new burial sites. It all has to be done with due decorum."

"Much they care," Elaine said, looking down at the stones again.

"I must agree," Kavanagh replied. "It all seems in excess of the facts. But then perhaps we're not God-fearing enough."

"Probably."

"Anyhow, they told me to come back in a day or two's time, and ask the removal men."

She laughed at the thought of the dead moving house, packing up their goods and chattels. Kavanagh was pleased to have made a joke, even if it had been unintentional. Riding on the crest of this success, he said, "I wonder, may I take you for a drink?"

"I wouldn't be very good company, I'm afraid," she said. "I'm really very tired."

"We could perhaps meet later," he said.

She looked away from his eager face. He was pleasant enough, in his uneventful way. She liked his green bow tie—surely a joke at the expense of his own drabness. She liked his seriousness too. But she couldn't face the idea of drinking with him, at least not tonight. She made her apologies, and explained that she'd been ill recently and hadn't recovered her stamina.

"Another night, perhaps?" he inquired gently. The lack of aggression in his courtship was persuasive, and she said:

"That would be nice. Thank you."

Before they parted they exchanged telephone numbers. He seemed charmingly excited by the thought of their meeting again; it made her feel, despite all that had been taken from her, that she still had her sex.

She returned to the flat to find both a parcel from Mitch and a hungry cat on the doorstep. She fed the demanding animal, then made herself some coffee and opened the parcel. In it, cocooned in several layers of tissue paper, she found a silk scarf, chosen with Mitch's uncanny eye for her taste. The note along with it simply said: *It's your color. I love you. Mitch.* She wanted to pick up the telephone on the spot and talk to him, but somehow the thought of hearing his voice seemed dangerous. Too close to the hurt, perhaps. He would ask her how she felt, and she would reply that she was well, and he would insist: yes, but *really?*, and she would say: I'm empty; they took out half my innards, damn you, and I'll never have your children or anybody else's, so that's the end of that, isn't it? Even thinking about their talking she felt tears threaten, and in a fit of inexplicable rage she wrapped the scarf up in the desiccated paper and buried it at the back of her deepest drawer. Damn him for trying to make things better now, when at the time she'd most needed him all he'd talked of was fatherhood, and how her tumors would deny it him.

It was a clear evening—the sky's cold skin stretched to breaking point. She did not want to draw the curtains in the front room, even though passersby would stare in, because the deepening blue was too fine to miss. So she sat at the window and watched the dark come. Only when the last change had been wrought did she close off the chill.

She had no appetite, but she made herself some food nevertheless, and sat down to watch television as she ate. The food unfinished, she laid down her tray and dozed, the programs filtering through to her intermittently. Some witless comedian whose merest cough sent his audience into paroxysms, a natural history program on life in the Serengeti, the news. She had read all that she needed to know that morning: the headlines hadn't changed.

One item, however, did pique her curiosity: an interview with the solo yachtsman, Michael Maybury, who had been picked up that day after two weeks adrift in the Pacific. The interview was being beamed from Australia, and the contact was bad; the image of Maybury's bearded and sun-scorched face was constantly threatened with being snowed out. The picture little mattered: the account he gave of his failed voyage was riveting in sound alone, and in particular an event that seemed to distress him afresh even as he told it. He had been becalmed, and as his vessel lacked a motor had been obliged to wait for wind. It had not come. A week had gone by with his hardly moving a kilometer from the same spot of listless ocean; no bird or passing ship broke the monotony. With every hour that passed, his claustrophobia grew, and on the eighth day it reached panic proportions, so he let himself over the side of the yacht and swam away from the vessel, a lifeline tied about his middle, in order to escape the same few yards of deck. But once away from the yacht, and treading the still, warm water, he had no desire to go back. Why not untie the knot, he'd thought to himself, and float away.

"What made you change your mind?" the interviewer asked.

Here Maybury frowned. He had clearly reached the crux of his story, but didn't want to finish it. The interviewer repeated the question.

At last, hesitantly, the sailor responded. "I looked back at the yacht," he said, "and I saw somebody on the deck."

The interviewer, not certain that he'd heard correctly, said, "Somebody on the deck?"

"That's right," Maybury replied. "Somebody was there. I saw a figure quite clearly, moving around."

"Did you . . . did you recognize this stowaway?" the question came.

Maybury's face closed down, sensing that his story was being treated with mild sarcasm.

"Who was it?" the interviewer pressed.

"I don't know," Maybury said. "Death, I suppose."

The questioner was momentarily at a loss for words.

"But of course you returned to the boat, eventually."

"Of course."

"And there was no sign of anybody?"

Maybury glanced up at the interviewer, and a look of contempt crossed his face.

"I'd survived, hadn't I?" he said.

The interviewer mumbled something about not understanding his point.

"I didn't drown," Maybury said. "I could have died then, if I'd wanted to. Slipped off the rope and drowned."

"But you didn't. And the next day—"

"The next day the wind picked up."

"It's an extraordinary story," the interviewer said, content that the stickiest part of the exchange was now safely bypassed. "You must be looking forward to seeing your family again for Christmas . . ."

Elaine didn't hear the final exchange of pleasantries. Her imagination was tied by a fine rope to the room she was sitting in; her fingers toyed with the knot. If Death could find a boat in the wastes of the Pacific, how much easier it must be to find her. To sit with her, perhaps, as she slept. To watch her as she went about her mourning. She stood up and turned the television off. The flat was suddenly silent. She questioned the hush impatiently, but it held no sign of guests, welcome or unwelcome.

As she listened, she could taste salt water. Ocean, no doubt.

She had been offered several refuges in which to convalesce when she came out of the hospital. Her father had invited her up to Aberdeen; her sister Rachel had made several appeals for her to spend a few weeks in Buckinghamshire; there had even been a pitiful telephone call from Mitch, in which he had talked of their holidaying together. She had rejected them all, telling them that she wanted to reestablish the rhythm of her previous life as soon as possible: to return to her job, to her working colleagues and friends. In fact, her reasons had gone deeper than that. She had *feared* their sympathies, feared that she would be held too close in their affections and quickly come to rely upon them. Her streak of independence, which had first brought her to this unfriendly city, was in studied defiance of her smothering appetite for security. If she gave in to those loving appeals she knew she would take root in domestic soil and not look up and out again for another year. In which time, what adventures might have passed her by?

Instead she had returned to work as soon as she felt able, hoping that although she had not taken on all her former responsibilities the familiar routines would help her to reestablish a normal life. But the sleight of hand was not entirely successful. Every few days something would happen—she would overhear some remark, or catch a look that she was not intended to see—that made her realize she was being treated with a rehearsed caution, that her colleagues viewed her as being fundamentally changed by her illness. It had made her angry. She'd wanted to spit her suspicions in their faces, tell them that she and her uterus were not synonymous, and that the removal of one did not imply the eclipse of the other.

But today, returning to the office, she was not so certain they weren't correct. She felt as though she hadn't slept in weeks, though in fact she was sleeping long and deeply every night. Her eyesight was blurred, and there was a curious remoteness about her experiences that day that she associated with extreme fatigue, as if she were drifting further and further from the work on her desk, from her sensations, from her very thoughts. Twice that morning she caught herself speaking and then wondered who it was who was conceiving of these words. It certainly wasn't *her*; she was too busy listening.

And then, an hour after lunch, things had suddenly taken a turn for the worse. She had been called into her supervisor's office and asked to sit down.

"Are you all right, Elaine?" Mr. Chimes had asked.

"Yes," she'd told him. "I'm fine."

"There's been some concern—"

"About what?"

Chimes looked slightly embarrassed. "Your behavior," he finally said. "Please don't think I'm prying, Elaine. It's just that if you need some further time to recuperate—"

"There's nothing wrong with me."

"But your weeping—"

"What?"

"The way you've been crying today. It concerns us."

"Cry?" she'd said. "I don't cry."

The supervisor seemed baffled. "But you've been crying all day. You're crying now."

Elaine put a tentative hand to her cheek. And yes, yes, she *was* crying. Her cheek was wet. She'd stood up, shocked at her own conduct.

"I didn't . . . I didn't know," she said. Though the words sounded preposterous, they were true. She *hadn't* known. Only now, with the fact pointed out, did she taste tears in her throat and sinuses, and with that taste came a memory of when this eccentricity had begun: in front of the television the night before.

"Why don't you take the rest of the day off?"

"Yes."

"Take the rest of the week, if you'd like," Chimes said. "You're a valued member of staff, Elaine; I don't have to tell you that. We don't want you coming to any harm."

This last remark struck home with stinging force. Did they think she was verging on suicide? Was that why she was treated with kid gloves? They were only tears she was shedding, for God's sake, and she was so indifferent to them she had not even known they were falling.

"I'll go home," she said. "Thank you for your . . . concern."

The supervisor looked at her with some dismay. "It must have been a very traumatic experience," he said. "We all understand, we really do. If you feel you want to talk about it at any time—"

She declined, but thanked him again and left the office.

Face-to-face with herself in the mirror of the women's toilet she realized just how bad she looked. Her skin was flushed, her eyes swollen. She did what she could to conceal the signs of this painless grief, then picked up her coat and started home. As she reached the Underground station she knew that returning to the empty flat would not be a wise idea. She would brood, she would sleep (so much sleep of late, and so perfectly dreamless), but she would not improve her mental condition by either route. It was the bell of Holy Innocents, tolling in the clear afternoon, that reminded her of the smoke and the square and Mr. Kavanagh. There, she decided, was a fit place for her to walk. She could enjoy the sunlight, and think. Maybe she would meet her admirer again.

She found her way back to All Saints easily enough, but there was disappointment awaiting her. The demolition site had been cordoned off, the boundary marked by a row of posts, a red fluorescent ribbon looped between them. The site was guarded by no less than four policemen, who were ushering pedestrians toward a detour around the square. The workers and their hammers had been exiled from the shadows of All Saints and now a very different selection of people—suited and academic—occupied the zone beyond the ribbon, some in furrowed conversation, others standing on the muddy ground and staring up quizzically at the derelict church. The south transept and much of the area around it had been curtained off from public view by an arrangement of tarpaulins and black plastic sheeting. Occasionally somebody would emerge from behind this veil and consult with others on the site. All who did so, she noted, were wearing gloves; one or two were also masked. It was as though they were performing some ad hoc surgery in the shelter of the screen. A tumor, perhaps, in the bowels of All Saints.

She approached one of the officers. "What's going on?"

"The foundations are unstable," he told her. "Apparently the place could fall down at any moment."

"Why are they wearing masks?"

"It's just a precaution against the dust."

She didn't argue, though this explanation struck her as unlikely.

"If you want to get through to Temple Street you'll have to go round the back," the officer said.

What she really wanted to do was to stand and watch the proceedings, but the proximity of the uniformed quartet intimidated her, and she decided to give up and go home. As she began to make her way back to the main road she caught sight of a familiar figure crossing the end of an adjacent street. It was unmistakably Kavanagh. She called after him, though he had already disappeared, and was pleased to see him step back into view and return a nod to her.

"Well, well," he said as he came down to meet her, "I didn't expect to see you again so soon."

"I came to watch the rest of the demolition," she said.

His face was ruddy with the cold, and his eyes were shining.

"I'm so pleased," he said. "Do you want to have some afternoon tea? There's a place just around the corner."

"I'd like that."

As they walked she asked him if he knew what was going on at All Saints.

"It's the crypt," he said, confirming her suspicions.

"They opened it?"

"They certainly found a way in. I was here this morning—"

"About your stones?"

"That's right. They were already putting up the tarpaulins then."

"Some of them were wearing masks."

"It won't smell very fresh down there. Not after so long."

Thinking of the curtain of tarpaulin drawn between her and the mystery within, she said, "I wonder what it's like."

"A wonderland," Kavanagh replied.

It was an odd response, and she didn't query it, at least not on the spot. But later, when they'd sat and talked together for an hour, and she felt easier with him, she returned to the comment.

"What you said about the crypt . . ."

"Yes?"

"About it being a wonderland."

"Did I say that?" he replied, somewhat sheepishly. "What must you think of me?"

"I was just puzzled. Wondered what you meant."

"I like places where the dead are," he said. "I always have. Cemeteries can be very beautiful, don't you think? Mausoleums and tombs, all the fine craftsmanship that goes into those places. Even the dead may sometimes reward closer scrutiny." He looked at her to see if he had strayed beyond her taste threshold, but seeing that she only looked at him with quiet fascination, continued. "They can be very beautiful on occasion. It's a sort of glamour they have. It's a shame it's wasted on morticians and funeral directors." He made a small mischievous grin. "I'm sure there's much to be seen in that crypt. Strange sights. Wonderful sights."

"I only ever saw one dead person. My grandmother. I was very young at the time . . ."

"I trust it was a pivotal experience."

"I don't think so. In fact I scarcely remember it at all. I only remember how everybody cried."

"Ah."

He nodded sagely.

"So selfish," he said. "Don't you think? Spoiling a farewell with snot and sobs." Again he looked at her to gauge the response; again he was satisfied that she would not take offense. "We cry for ourselves, don't we? Not for the dead. The dead are past caring."

She made a small, soft, "Yes," and then, more loudly, "My God, yes. That's right. Always for ourselves . . ."

"You see how much the dead can teach, just by lying there, twiddling their thumb bones?"

She laughed; he joined her in laughter. She had misjudged him on that initial meeting, thinking his face unused to smiles; it was not. But his features, when the laughter died, swiftly regained that eerie quiescence she had first noticed.

When, after a further half hour of his laconic remarks, he told her he had appointments to keep and had to be on his way, she thanked him for his company, and said:

"Nobody's made me laugh so much in weeks. I'm grateful."

"You *should* laugh," he told her. "It suits you." Then added, "You have beautiful teeth."

She thought of this odd remark when he'd gone, as she did of a dozen others he had made through the afternoon. He was undoubtedly one of the most offbeat individuals she'd ever encountered, but he had come into her life—with his eagerness to talk of crypts and the dead and the beauty of her teeth—at just the right moment. He was the perfect distraction from her buried sorrows, making her present aberrations seem minor stuff beside his own. When she started home she was in high spirits. If she had not known herself better she might have thought herself half in love with him.

On the journey back, and later that evening, she thought particularly of the joke he had made about the dead twiddling their thumb bones, and that thought led inevitably to the mysteries that lay out of sight in the crypt. Her curiosity, once aroused, was not easily silenced; it grew on her steadily that she badly wanted to slip through that cordon of ribbon and see the burial chamber with her own eyes. It was a desire she would never previously have admitted to herself. (How many times had she walked from the site of an accident, telling herself to control the shameful inquisitiveness she felt?) But Kavanagh had legitimized her appetite with his flagrant enthusiasm for things funereal. Now, with the taboo shed, she wanted to go back to All Saints and look Death in its face; then next time she saw Kavanagh she would have some stories to tell of her own. The idea, no sooner budded, came to full flower, and in the middle of the evening she dressed for the street again and headed back toward the square.

She didn't reach All Saints until well after eleven-thirty, but there were still signs of activity at the site. Lights, mounted on stands and on the wall of the church itself, poured illumination on the scene. A trio of technicians, Kavanagh's so-called removal men, stood outside the tarpaulin shelter, their faces drawn with fatigue, their breath clouding the frosty air. She stayed out of sight and watched the scene. She was growing steadily colder, and her scars had begun to ache, but it was apparent that the night's work on the crypt was more or less over. After some brief exchange with the police, the technicians departed. They had extinguished all but one of the floodlights, leaving the site—church, tarpaulin, and rimy mud—in grim chiaroscuro.

The two officers who had been on guard were not overconscientious in their duties. What idiot, they apparently reasoned, would come grave robbing at this hour, and in such temperatures? After a few minutes of keeping a foot-stamping vigil, they withdrew to the relative comfort of the workmen's hut. When they did not reemerge, Elaine crept out of hiding and moved as cautiously as possible to the ribbon that divided one zone from the other. A radio had been turned on in the hut; its noise (music for lovers from dusk to dawn, the distant voice purred) covered her crackling advance across the frozen earth.

Once beyond the cordon, and into the forbidden territory beyond, she was not so hesitant. She swiftly crossed the hard ground, its wheel-plowed furrows like concrete, into the lee of the church. The floodlight was dazzling; by it her breath appeared as solid as yesterday's smoke had seemed. Behind her, the music for lovers murmured on. No one emerged from the hut to summon her from her trespassing. No alarm bells rang. She reached the edge of the tarpaulin curtain without incident, and peered at the scene concealed behind it.

The demolition men, under very specific instructions to judge by the care they had taken in their labors, had dug fully eight feet down the side of All Saints, exposing the foundations. In so doing they had uncovered an entrance to the burial chamber that previous hands had been at pains to conceal. Not only had earth been piled up against the flank of the church to hide the entrance, but also the crypt door had been removed, and stone masons had sealed the entire aperture up. This had clearly been done at some speed; their handiwork was far from ordered. They had simply filled the entrance up with any stone or brick that had come to hand, and plastered coarse mortar over their endeavors. Into this mortar—though the design had been spoiled by the excavations—some artisan had scrawled a six-foot cross.

All their efforts in securing the crypt, and marking the mortar to keep the godless out, had gone for nothing, however. The seal had been broken—the mortar hacked at, the stones torn away. There was now a small hole in the middle of the doorway, large enough for one person to gain access to the interior. Elaine had no hesitation in climbing down the slope to the breached wall, and then squirming through.

She had predicted the darkness she met on the other side, and had brought with her a cigarette lighter Mitch had given her three years ago. She flicked it on. The flame was small; she turned up the wick, and by the swelling light investigated the space ahead of her. It was not the crypt itself she had stepped into but a narrow vestibule of some kind: a yard or so in front of her was another wall, and another door. This one had not been replaced with bricks, though into its solid timbers a second cross had been gouged. She approached the door. The lock had been removed—by the investigators presumably—and the door then held shut again with a rope binding. This had been done quickly, by tired fingers. She did not find the rope difficult to untie, though it required both hands, and so had to be effected in the dark.

As she worked the knot free, she heard voices. The policemen—damn them—had left the seclusion of their hut and come out into the bitter night to do their rounds. She let the rope be, and pressed herself against the inside wall of the vestibule. The officers' voices were becoming louder: talking of their children, and the escalating cost of Christmas joy. Now they were within yards of the crypt entrance, standing, or so she guessed, in the shelter of the tarpaulin. They made no attempt to descend the slope, however, but finished their cursory inspection on the lip of the earthworks, then turned back. Their voices faded.

Satisfied that they were out of sight and hearing of her, she reignited the flame and returned to the door. It was large and brutally heavy; her first attempt at hauling it open met with little success. She tried again, and this time it moved, grating across the grit on the vestibule floor. Once it was open the vital inches required for her to squeeze through, she eased her straining. The lighter guttered as though a breath had blown from within; the flame briefly burned not yellow but electric blue. She didn't pause to admire it, but slid into the promised wonderland.

Now the flame fed—became livid—and for an instant its sudden brightness took her sight away. She pressed the corners of her eyes to clear them, and looked again.

So this was Death. There was none of the art or the glamour Kavanagh had talked of, no calm laying out of shrouded beauties on cool marble sheets, no elaborate reliquaries, nor aphorisms on the nature of human frailty: not even names and dates. In most cases, the corpses lacked even coffins.

The crypt was a charnel house. Bodies had been thrown in heaps on every side; entire families pressed into niches that were designed to hold a single casket, dozens more left where hasty and careless hands had tossed them. The scene—though absolutely still—was rife with panic. It was there in the faces that stared from the piles of dead: mouths wide in silent protest, sockets in which eyes had withered gaping in shock at such treatment. It was there too in the way the system of burial had degenerated from the ordered arrangement of caskets at the far end of the crypt to the haphazard piling of crudely made coffins, their wood unplaned, their lids unmarked but for a scrawled cross, and thence—finally—to this hurried heaping of unhoused carcasses, all concern for dignity, perhaps even for the rites of passage, forgotten in the rising hysteria.

There had been a disaster, of that she could have no doubt, a sudden influx of bodies—men, women, children (there was a baby at her feet who could not have lived a day)—who had died in such escalating numbers that there was not even time to close their eyelids before they were shunted away into this pit. Perhaps the coffin makers had also died, and were thrown here among their clients; the shroud sewers too, and the priests. All gone in one apocalyptic month (or week), their surviving relatives too shocked or too frightened to consider the niceties, but only eager to have the dead thrust out of sight where they would never have to look on their flesh again.

There was much of that flesh still in evidence. The sealing of the crypt, closing it off from the decaying air, had kept the occupants intact. Now, with the violation of this secret chamber, the heat of decay had been rekindled, and the tissues were deteriorating afresh. Everywhere she saw rot at work, making sores and suppurations, blisters and pustules. She raised the flame to see better, though the stench of spoilage was beginning to crowd upon her and make her dizzy. Everywhere her eyes traveled she seemed to alight upon some pitiful sight. Two children lay together as if sleeping in each other's arms; a woman whose last act, it appeared, had been to paint her sickened face so as to die more fit for the marriage bed than the grave.

She could not help but stare, though her fascination cheated them of privacy. There was so much to see and remember. She could never be the same, could she, having viewed these scenes? One corpse—lying half-hidden beneath another—drew her particular attention: a woman whose long chestnut-colored hair flowed from her scalp so copiously. Elaine envied it. She moved closer to get a better look, and then, putting the last of her squeamishness to flight, took hold of the body thrown across the woman and hauled it away. The flesh of the corpse was greasy to the touch and left her fingers stained, but she was not distressed. The uncovered corpse lay with her legs wide, but the constant weight of her companion had bent them into an impossible configuration. The wound that had killed her had bloodied her thighs, and glued her skirt to her abdomen and groin. Had she miscarried, Elaine wondered, or had some disease devoured her there?

She stared and stared, bending close to study the faraway look on the woman's rotted face. Such a place to lie, she thought, with your blood still shaming you. She would tell Kavanagh, when next she saw him, how wrong he had been with his sentimental tales of calm beneath the sod.

She had seen enough, more than enough. She wiped her hands upon her coat and made her way back to the door, closing it behind her and knotting up the rope again as she had found it. Then she climbed the slope into the clean air. The policemen were nowhere in sight, and she slipped away unseen, like a shadow's shadow.

There was nothing for her to feel, once she had mastered her initial disgust, and that twinge of pity she'd felt seeing the children and the woman with the chestnut hair; and even those responses—even the pity and the repugnance—were quite manageable. She had felt both more acutely seeing a dog run down by a car than she had standing in the crypt of All Saints, despite the horrid displays on every side. When she lay her head down to sleep that night, and realized that she was neither trembling nor nauseated, she felt strong. What was there to fear in all the world if the spectacle of mortality she had just witnessed could be borne so readily? She slept deeply, and woke refreshed.

She went back to work that morning, apologizing to Chimes for her behavior of the previous day, and reassuring him that she was now feeling happier than she'd felt in months. In order to prove her rehabilitation she was as gregarious as she could be, striking up conversations with neglected acquaintances, and giving her smile a ready airing. This met with some initial resistance; she could sense her colleagues doubting that this bout of sunshine actually meant a summer. But when the mood was sustained throughout the day and through the day following, they began to respond more readily. By Thursday it was as though the tears of earlier in the week had never been shed. People told her how well she was look-

ing. It was true; her mirror confirmed the rumors. Her eyes shone, her
skin shone. She was a picture of vitality.

On Thursday afternoon she was sitting at her desk, working through
a backlog of inquiries, when one of the secretaries appeared from the
corridor and began to babble. Somebody went to the woman's aid;
through the sobs it was apparent she was talking about Bernice, a woman
Elaine knew well enough to exchange smiles with on the stairs, but no
better. There had been an accident, it seemed; the woman was talking
about blood on the floor. Elaine got up and joined those who were making their way out to see what the fuss was about. The supervisor was
already standing outside the women's lavatories, vainly instructing the
curious to keep clear. Somebody else—another witness, it seemed—was
offering her account of events:

"She was just standing there, and suddenly she started to shake. I
thought she was having a fit. Blood started to come from her nose. Then
from her mouth. Pouring out."

"There's nothing to see," Chimes insisted. "Please keep back." But
he was substantially ignored. Blankets were being brought to wrap
around the woman, and as soon as the toilet door was opened again the
sightseers pressed forward. Elaine caught sight of a form moving about
on the toilet floor as if convulsed by cramps; she had no wish to see any
more. Leaving the others to throng the corridor, talking loudly of Bernice
as if she were already dead, Elaine returned to her desk. She had so
much to do, so many wasted, grieving days to catch up on. An apt phrase
flitted into her head. *Redeem the time.* She wrote the three words in her
notebook as a reminder. Where did they come from? She couldn't recall.
It didn't matter. Sometimes there was wisdom in forgetting.

Kavanagh rang her that evening and invited her out to dinner the following night. She had to decline, however, eager as she was to discuss
her recent exploits, because a small party was being thrown by several of
her friends, to celebrate her return to health. Would he care to join
them? she asked. He thanked her for the invitation, but replied that
large numbers of people had always intimidated him. She told him not
to be foolish, that her circle would be pleased to meet him, and she to
show him off, but he replied he would only put in an appearance if his
ego felt the equal of it, and that if he didn't show up he hoped she
wouldn't be offended. She soothed such fears. Before the conversation

came to an end she slyly mentioned that next time they met she had a tale to tell.

The following day brought unhappy news. Bernice had died in the early hours of Friday morning, without ever regaining consciousness. The cause of death was as yet unverified, but the office gossips concurred that she had never been a strong woman—always the first among the secretaries to catch a cold and the last to shake it off. There was also some talk, though traded less loudly, about her personal behavior. She had been generous with her favors it appeared, and injudicious in her choice of partners. With venereal diseases reaching epidemic proportions, was that not the likeliest explanation for the death?

The news, though it kept the rumormongers in business, was not good for general morale. Two girls went sick that morning, and at lunchtime it seemed that Elaine was the only member of staff with an appetite. She compensated for the lack in her colleagues, however. She had a fierce hunger in her; her body almost seemed to ache for sustenance. It was a good feeling after so many months of lassitude. When she looked around at the worn faces at the table she felt utterly apart from them: from their tittle-tattle and their trivial opinions, from the way their talk circled on the suddenness of Bernice's death as though they had not given the subject a moment's thought in years, and were amazed that their neglect had not rendered it extinct.

Elaine knew better. She had come close to death so often in the recent past: during the months leading up to her hysterectomy, when the tumors had suddenly doubled in size as though sensing that they were plotted against; on the operating table, when twice the surgeons thought they'd lost her; and most recently, in the crypt, face-to-face with those gawping carcasses. Death was everywhere. That they should be so startled by its entrance into their charmless circle struck her as almost comical. She ate lustily, and let them talk in whispers.

They gathered for her party at Reuben's house—Elaine, Hermione, Sam and Nellwyn, Josh and Sonja. It was a good night, a chance to pick up on how mutual friends were faring, how statuses and ambitions were on the change. Everyone got drunk very quickly; tongues already loosened by familiarity became progressively looser. Nellwyn led a tearful toast to Elaine; Josh and Sonja had a short but acrimonious exchange on the subject of evangelism; Reuben did his impersonations of fellow barristers. It was like old times, except that memory had yet to improve it. Kavanagh did not put in an appearance, and Elaine was glad of it. Despite her protestations when speaking to him she knew he would have felt out of place in such close-knit company.

About half-past midnight, when the room had settled into a number of quiet exchanges, Hermione mentioned the yachtsman. Though she was almost across the room, Elaine heard the sailor's name mentioned quite distinctly. She broke off her conversation with Nellwyn and picked her way through the sprawling limbs to join Hermione and Sam.

"I heard you talking about Maybury," she said.

"Yes," said Hermione, "Sam and I were just saying how strange it all was—"

"I saw him on the news," Elaine said.

"Sad story, isn't it?" Sam commented. "The way it happened."

"Why sad?"

"Him saying that: about Death being on the boat with him—"

"—And then dying," Hermione said.

"Dying?" said Elaine. "When was this?"

"It was in all the papers."

"I haven't been concentrating that much," Elaine replied. "What happened?"

"He was killed," Sam said. "They were taking him to the airport to fly him home, and there was an accident. He was killed just like that." He snapped his middle finger and thumb. "Out like a light."

"So sad," said Hermione.

She glanced at Elaine, and a frown crept across her face. The look baffled Elaine until—with that same shock of recognition she'd felt in Chimes's office, discovering her tears—she realized that she was smiling.

So the sailor was dead.

When the party broke up in the early hours of Saturday morning— when the embraces and the kisses were over and she was home again— she thought over the Maybury interview she'd heard, summoning a face scorched by the sun and eyes peeled by the waters he'd almost been lost to, thinking of his mixture of detachment and faint embarrassment as he'd told the tale of his stowaway. And, of course, those final words of his, when pressed to identify the stranger:

"Death, I suppose," he'd said.

He'd been right.

She woke up late on Saturday morning, without the anticipated hangover. There was a letter from Mitch. She didn't open it, but left it on the mantelpiece for an idle moment later in the day. The first snow of winter was in the wind, though it was too wet to make any serious impression on the streets. The chill was biting enough, however, to judge by the scowls on the faces of passersby. She felt oddly immune from it, however. Though she had no heating on in the flat she walked around in her bathrobe, and barefoot, as though she had a fire stoked in her belly.

After coffee she went through to wash. There was a spider clot of hair in the plughole; she fished it out and dropped it down the lavatory, then returned to the sink. Since the removal of the dressings she had studiously avoided any close scrutiny of her body, but today her qualms and her vanity seemed to have disappeared. She stripped off her robe and looked herself over critically.

She was pleased with what she saw. Her breasts were full and dark, her skin had a pleasing sheen to it, her pubic hair had regrown more lushly than ever. The scars themselves still looked and felt tender, but her eyes read their lividness as a sign of her cunt's ambition, as though any day now her sex would grow from anus to navel (and beyond perhaps), opening her up, making her terrible.

It was paradoxical, surely, that it was only now, when the surgeons had emptied her out, that she should feel so ripe, so resplendent. She stood for fully half an hour in front of the mirror admiring herself, her thoughts drifting off. Eventually she returned to the chore of washing. That done, she went back into the front room, still naked. She had no desire to conceal herself; quite the other way about. It was all she could do to prevent herself from stepping out into the snow and giving the whole street something to remember her by.

She crossed to the window, thinking a dozen foolish thoughts. The snow had thickened. Through the flurries she caught a movement in the alley between the houses opposite. Somebody was there, watching her, though she couldn't see who. She didn't mind. She stood peeping at the peeper, wondering if he would have the courage to show himself, but he did not.

She watched for several minutes before she realized that her brazenness had frightened him away. Disappointed, she wandered back to the bedroom and got dressed. It was time she found herself something to eat; she had that familiar fierce hunger upon her. The fridge was practically empty. She would have to go out and stock up for the weekend.

Supermarkets were circuses, especially on a Saturday, but her mood was far too buoyant to be depressed by having to make her way through the crowds. Today she even found some pleasure in these scenes of conspicuous consumption: in the shopping carts and the baskets heaped high with foodstuffs, and the children greedy-eyed as they approached the confectionery, and tearful if denied it, and the wives weighing up the merits of a leg of mutton while their husbands watched the girls on the staff with eyes no less calculating.

She purchased twice as much food for the weekend as she would normally have done in a full week, her appetite driven to distraction by the smells from the delicatessen and fresh-meat counters. By the time she reached the house she was almost shaking with the anticipation of sustenance. As she put the bags down on the front step and fumbled for her keys, she heard a car door slam behind her.

"Elaine?"

It was Hermione. The red wine she'd consumed the previous night had left her looking blotchy and stale.

"Are you feeling all right?" Elaine asked.

"The point is, are you?" Hermione wanted to know.

"Yes, I'm fine. Why shouldn't I be?"

Hermione returned a harried look. "Sonja's gone down with some kind of food poisoning, and so's Reuben. I just came round to see that you were all right."

"As I say, fine."

"I don't understand it."

"What about Nellwyn and Dick?"

"I couldn't get an answer at their place. But Reuben's in a bad way. They've taken him into the hospital for tests."

"Do you want to come in and have a cup of coffee?"

"No thanks, I've got to get back to see Sonja. I just didn't like to think of your being on your own if you'd gone down with it too."

Elaine smiled. "You're an angel," she said, and kissed Hermione on the cheek. The gesture seemed to startle the other woman. For some reason she stepped back, the kiss exchanged, staring at Elaine with a vague puzzlement in her eyes.

"I must . . . I must go," she said, fixing her face as though it would betray her.

"I'll call you later in the day," Elaine said, "and find out how they're doing."

"Fine."

Hermione turned away and crossed the pavement to her car. Though she made a cursory attempt to conceal the gesture, Elaine caught sight of putting her fingers to the spot on her cheek where she had been kissed and scratching at it, as if to eradicate the contact.

It was not the season for flies, but those that had survived the recent cold buzzed around in the kitchen as Elaine selected some bread, smoked ham, and garlic sausage from her purchases, and sat down to eat. She was ravenous. In five minutes or less she had devoured the meats and made substantial inroads into the loaf, and her hunger was scarcely tamed. Settling to a dessert of figs and cheese, she thought of the paltry omelet she'd been unable to finish that day after the visit to the hospital. One thought led to another; from omelet to smoke to the square to Kavanagh to her most recent visit to the church, and thinking of the place she was suddenly seized by an enthusiasm to see it one final time before it was entirely leveled. She was probably too late already. The bodies would have been parceled up and removed, the crypt decontaminated and scoured; the walls would be rubble. But she knew she would not be satisfied until she had seen it for herself.

Even after a meal which would have sickened her with its excess a few days before, she felt light-headed as she set out for All Saints, almost as though she were drunk. Not the maudlin drunkenness she had been prone to when with Mitch, but a euphoria which made her feel well-nigh invulnerable, as if she had at last located some bright and incorruptible part of herself, and no harm would ever befall her again.

She had prepared herself for finding All Saints in ruins, but she did not. The building still stood, its walls untouched, its beams still dividing the sky. Perhaps it too could not be toppled, she mused; perhaps she and it were twin immortals. The suspicion was reinforced by the gaggle of fresh worshipers the church had attracted. The police guard had trebled since the day she'd been here, and the tarpaulin that had shielded the crypt entrance from sight was now a vast tent, supported by scaffolding, which entirely encompassed the flank of the building. The altar servers, standing in close proximity to the tent, wore masks and gloves; the high priests—the chosen few who were actually allowed into the Holy of Holies—were entirely garbed in protective suits.

She watched from the cordon: the signs and genuflections between the devotees, the sluicing down of the suited men as they emerged from behind the veil, the fine spray of fumigants which filled the air like bitter incense.

Another onlooker was quizzing one of the officers.

"Why the suits?"

"In case it's contagious," the reply came.

"After all these years?"

"They don't know what they've got in there."

"Diseases don't last, do they?"

"It's a plague pit," the officer said. "They're just being cautious."

Elaine listened to the exchange, and her tongue itched to speak. She could save them their investigations with a few words. After all, she was living proof that whatever pestilence had destroyed the families in the crypt, it was no longer virulent. She had breathed that air, she had touched that moldy flesh, and she felt healthier now than she had in years. But they would not thank her for her revelations, would they? They were too engrossed in their rituals, perhaps even excited by the discovery of such horrors, their turmoil fueled and fired by the possibility that this death was still living. She would not be so unsporting as to sour their enthusiasm with a confession of her own rare good health.

Instead she turned her back on the priests and their rites, on the drizzle of incense in the air, and began to walk away from the square. As she looked up from her thoughts she glimpsed a familiar figure watching her from the corner of the adjacent street. He turned away as she glanced up, but it was undoubtedly Kavanagh. She called to him and went to the corner, but he was walking smartly away from her, head bowed. Again she called after him, and now he turned—a patently false look of surprise pasted onto his face—and retrod his escape route to greet her.

"Have you heard what they've found?" she asked him.

"Oh yes," he replied. Despite the familiarity they'd last enjoyed she was reminded now of her first impression of him: that he was not a man much conversant with feeling.

"Now you'll never get your stones," she said.

"I suppose not," he replied, not overtly concerned at the loss.

She wanted to tell him that she'd seen the plague pit with her own eyes, hoping the news would bring a gleam to his face, but the corner of this sunlit street was an inappropriate spot for such talk. Besides, it was almost as if he knew. He looked at her so oddly, the warmth of their previous meeting entirely gone.

"Why did you come back?" he asked her.

"Just to see," she replied.

"I'm flattered."

"Flattered?"

"That my enthusiasm for mausoleums is infectious."

Still he watched her, and she, returning his look, was conscious of how cold his eyes were, and how perfectly shiny. They might have been glass, she thought, and his skin suede, glued like a hood over the subtle architecture of his skull.

"I should go," she said.

"Business or pleasure?"

"Neither," she told him. "One or two of my friends are ill."

"Ah."

She had the impression that he wanted to be away, that it was only fear of foolishness that kept him from running from her.

"Perhaps I'll see you again," she said. "Sometime."

"I'm sure," he replied, gratefully taking his cue and retreating along the street. "And to your friends—my best regards."

Even if she had wanted to pass Kavanagh's good wishes along to Reuben and Sonja, she could not have done so. Hermione did not answer the telephone, nor did any of the others. The closest she came was to leave a message with Reuben's answering service.

The light-headedness she'd felt earlier in the day developed into a strange dreaminess as the afternoon inched toward evening. She ate again, but the feast did nothing to keep the fugue state from deepening. She felt quite well; that sense of inviolability that had come upon her was still intact. But time and again as the day wore on she found herself standing on the threshold of a room not knowing why she had come there, or watching the light dwindle in the street outside without being quite certain if she was the viewer or the thing viewed. She was happy with her company though, as the flies were happy. They kept buzzing attendance even though the dark fell.

About seven in the evening she heard a car draw up outside, and the bell rang. She went to the door of her flat, but couldn't muster the inquisitiveness to open it, step out into the hallway, and admit callers. It would be Hermione again, most probably, and she didn't have any appetite for gloomy talk. Didn't want anybody's company, in fact, but that of the flies.

The callers insisted on the bell; the more they insisted the more determined she became not to reply. She slid down the wall beside the flat door and listened to the muted debate that now began on the step. It wasn't Hermione, it was nobody she recognized. Now they systematically rang the bells of the flats above, until Mr. Prudhoe came down from the top flat, talking to himself as he went, and opened the door to them. Of the conversation that followed she caught sufficient only to grasp the urgency of their mission, but her disheveled mind hadn't the persistence to attend to the details. They persuaded Prudhoe to allow them into the hallway. They approached the door of her flat and rapped upon it, calling her name. She didn't reply. They rapped again, exchanging words of frustration. She wondered if they could hear her smiling in the darkness. At last—after a further exchange with Prudhoe—they left her to herself.

She didn't know how long she sat on her haunches beside the door, but when she stood up again her lower limbs were entirely numb, and she was hungry. She ate voraciously, more or less finishing off all the purchases of that morning. The flies seemed to have procreated in the intervening hours; they crawled on the table and picked at her slops. She let them eat. They too had their lives to live.

Finally she decided to take some air. No sooner had she stepped out of her flat, however, than the vigilant Prudhoe was at the top of the stairs and calling down to her.

"Miss Rider. Wait a moment. I have a message for you."

She contemplated closing the door on him, but she knew he would not rest until he had delivered his communiqué. He hurried down the stairs—a Cassandra in shabby slippers.

"There were policemen here," he announced before he had even reached the bottom step. "They were looking for you."

"Oh," she said. "Did they say what they wanted?"

"To talk to you. *Urgently*. Two of your friends—"

"What about them?"

"They died," he said. "This afternoon. They had some kind of disease."

He had a sheet of notepaper in his hand. This he now passed over to her, relinquishing his hold an instant before she took it.

"They left that number for you to call," he said. "You're to contact them as soon as possible." His message delivered, he was already retiring up the stairs again.

Elaine looked down at the sheet of paper with its scrawled figures. By the time she'd read the seven digits, Prudhoe had disappeared.

She went back into the flat. For some reason she wasn't thinking of Reuben or Sonja—who, it seemed, she would not see again—but of the sailor, Maybury, who'd seen Death and escaped it only to have it follow him like a loyal dog, waiting its moment to leap and lick his face. She sat beside the phone and stared at the numbers on the sheet, and then at the fingers that held the sheet and at the hands that held the fingers. Was the touch that hung so innocently at the end of her arms now lethal? Was that what the detectives had come to tell her, that her friends were dead by *her* good offices? If so, how many others had she brushed against and breathed upon in the days since her pestilential education at the crypt? In the street, in the bus, in the supermarket: at work, at play. She thought of Bernice, lying on the toilet floor, and of Hermione, rubbing the spot where she had been kissed as if knowing some scourge had been passed along to her. And suddenly she *knew*, knew in her marrow, that her pursuers were right in their suspicions, and that all these dreamy days she had been nurturing a fatal child. Hence her hunger, hence the glow of fulfillment she felt.

She put down the note and sat in the semidarkness, trying to work out precisely the plague's location. Was it in her fingertips, in her belly, in her eyes? None, and yet all of these. Her first assumption had been wrong. It wasn't a child at all: she didn't carry it in some particular cell. It was *everywhere*. She and it were synonymous. That being so, there could be no slicing out of the offending part, as they had sliced out her tumors and all that had been devoured by them. Not that she would escape their attentions for that fact. They had come looking for her, hadn't they, to take her back into the custody of sterile rooms, to deprive her of her opinions and dignity, to make her fit only for their loveless investigations? The thought revolted her; she would rather die as the chestnut-haired woman in the crypt had died, sprawled in agonies, than submit to them again. She tore up the sheet of paper and let the litter drop.

It was too late for solutions anyway. The removal men had opened the door and found Death waiting on the other side, eager for daylight. She was its agent, and it—in its wisdom—had granted her immunity, had given her strength and a dreamy rapture, had taken her fear away. She, in return, had spread its word, and there was no undoing those labors: not now. All the dozens, maybe hundreds of people whom she'd contaminated in the last few days would have gone back to their families and friends, to their workplaces and their places of recreation, and spread the word yet further. They would have passed its fatal promise to their children as they tucked them into bed, and to their mates in the act of love. Priests had no doubt given it with Communion, shopkeepers with change of a five-pound note.

While she was thinking of this—of the disease spreading like fire in tinder—the doorbell rang again. They had come back for her. And, as before, they were ringing the other bells in the house. She could hear Prudhoe coming downstairs. This time he would know she was in. He would tell them so. They would hammer at the door, and when she refused to answer—

As Prudhoe opened the front door she unlocked the back. As she slipped into the yard she heard voices at the flat door, and then their rapping and their demands. She unbolted the yard gate and fled into the darkness of the alleyway. She was already out of hearing range by the time they had beaten down the door.

She wanted most of all to go back to All Saints, but she knew that such a tactic would only invite arrest. They would expect her to follow that route, counting upon her adherence to the first cause. But she wanted to see Death's face again, now more than ever. To speak with it. To debate its strategies. *Their* strategies. To ask why it had chosen her.

She emerged from the alleyway and watched the goings-on at the front of the house from the corner of the street. This time there were more than two men; she counted four at least, moving in and out of the house. What were they doing? Peeking through her underwear and her love letters, most probably, examining the sheets on her bed for stray hairs, and the mirror for traces of her reflection. But even if they turned the flat upside down, if they examined every print and pronoun, they wouldn't find the clues they sought. Let them search. The lover had escaped. Only her tearstains remained, and flies at the light bulb to sing her praises.

THE LIFE OF DEATH 227

The night was starry, but as she walked down to the center of the city, the brightness of the Christmas illuminations festooning trees and buildings canceled out their light. Most of the stores were well closed by this hour, but a good number of window-shoppers still idled along the pavements. She soon tired of the displays, however, of the baubles and the dummies, and made her way off the main road and into the side streets. It was darker here, which suited her abstracted state of mind. The sound of music and laughter escaped through open bar doors; an argument erupted in an upstairs gaming room: blows were exchanged; in one door-way two lovers defied discretion; in another, a man pissed with the gusto of a horse.

It was only now, in the relative hush of these backwaters, that she realized she was not alone. Footsteps followed her, keeping a cautious distance, but never straying far. Had the trackers followed her? Were they hemming her in even now, preparing to snatch her into their closed order? If so, flight would only delay the inevitable. Better to confront them now, and dare them to come within range of her pollution. She slid into hiding and listened as the footsteps approached, then stepped into view.

It was not the law, but Kavanagh. Her initial shock was almost imme-diately superseded by a sudden comprehension of *why* he had pursued her. She studied him. His skin was pulled so tight over his skull she could see the bone gleam in the dismal light. How, her whirling thoughts demanded, had she not recognized him sooner, not realized at that first meeting, when he'd talked of the dead and their glamour, that he spoke as their Maker?

"I followed you," he said.

"All the way from the house?"

He nodded.

"What did they tell you?" he asked her. "The policemen. What did they say?"

"Nothing I hadn't already guessed," she replied.

"You knew?"

"In a manner of speaking. I must have done, in my heart of hearts. Remember our first conversation?"

He murmured that he did.

"All you said about Death. Such egotism."

He grinned suddenly, showing more bone.

"Yes," he said. "What must you think of me?"

"It made a kind of sense to me, even then. I didn't know why at the time. Didn't know what the future would bring—"

"What does it bring?" he inquired of her softly.

She shrugged. "Death's been waiting for me all this time, am I right?"

"Oh yes," he said, pleased by her understanding of the situation between them. He took a step toward her, and reached to touch her face.

"You are remarkable," he said.

"Not really."

"But to be so unmoved by it all. So cold."

"What's to be afraid of?" she said. He stroked her cheek. She almost expected his hood of skin to come unbuttoned then, and the marbles that played in his sockets to tumble out and smash. But he kept his disguise intact, for appearance' sake.

"I want you," he told her.

"Yes," she said. Of course he did. It had been in his every word from the beginning, but she hadn't had the wit to comprehend it. Every love story was—at the last—a story of death; this was what the poets insisted. Why should it be any less true the other way about?

They could not go back to his house; the officers would be there too, he told her, for they must know of the romance between them. Nor, of course, could they return to her flat. So they found a small hotel in the vicinity and took a room there. Even in the dingy lift he took the liberty of stroking her hair, and then, finding her compliant, put his hand upon her breast.

The room was sparsely furnished, but was lent some measure of charm by a splash of colored lights from a Christmas tree in the street below. Her lover didn't take his eyes off her for a single moment, as if even now he expected her to turn tail and run at the merest flaw in his behavior. He needn't have concerned himself; his treatment of her left little cause for complaint. His kisses were insistent but not overpowering; his undressing of her—except for the fumbling (a nice human touch, she thought)—was a model of finesse and sweet solemnity.

She was surprised that he had not known about her scar, only because she had come to believe this intimacy had begun on the operating table, when twice she had gone into his arms, and twice been denied them by the surgeon's bullying. But perhaps, being no sentimentalist, he had forgotten that first meeting. Whatever the reason, he looked to be upset when he slipped off her dress, and there was a trembling interval when she thought he would reject her. But the moment passed, and now he reached down to her abdomen and ran his fingers along the scar.

"It's beautiful," he said.

She was happy.

"I almost died under the anesthetic," she told him.

"That would have been a waste," he said, reaching up her body and working at her breast. It seemed to arouse him, for his voice was more guttural when next he spoke. "What did they tell you?" he asked her, moving his hands up to the soft channel behind her clavicle, and stroking her there. She had not been touched in months, except by disinfected hands; his delicacy woke shivers in her. She was so engrossed in pleasure that she failed to reply to his question. He asked again as he moved between her legs.

"What did they tell you?"

Through a haze of anticipation she said, "They left a number for me to ring. So that I could be helped . . ."

"But you didn't want help?"

"No," she breathed. "Why should I?"

She half saw his smile, though her eyes wanted to flicker closed entirely. His appearance failed to stir any passion in her; indeed there was much about his disguise (that absurd bow tie, for one) which she thought ridiculous. With her eyes closed, however, she could forget such petty details; she could strip the hood off and imagine him pure. When she thought of him that way her mind pirouetted.

He took his hands from her; she opened her eyes. He was fumbling with his belt. As he did so somebody shouted in the street outside. His head jerked in the direction of the window; his body tensed. She was surprised at his sudden concern.

"It's all right," she said.

He leaned forward and put his hand to her throat.

"Be quiet," he instructed.

She looked up into his face. He had begun to sweat. The exchanges in the street went on for a few minutes longer; it was simply two late-night gamblers parting. He realized his error now.

"I thought I heard—"

"What?"

"—I thought I heard them calling my name."

"Who would do that?" she inquired fondly. "Nobody knows we're here."

He looked away from the window. All purposefulness had abruptly drained from him; after the instant of fear his features had slackened. He looked almost stupid.

"They came close," he said, "but they never found me."

"Close?"

"Coming to you." He laid his head on her breasts. "So *very* close," he murmured. She could hear her pulse in her head. "But I'm swift," he said, "and invisible."

His hand strayed back down to her scar, and farther.

"And always neat," he added.

She sighed as he stroked her.

"They admire me for that, I'm sure. Don't you think they must admire me? For being so neat?"

She remembered the chaos of the crypt, its indignities, its disorders.

"Not always . . ." she said.

He stopped stroking her.

"*Oh yes,*" he said. "Oh yes. I never spill blood. That's a rule of mine. *Never* spill blood."

She smiled at his boasts. She would tell him now—though surely he already knew—about her visit to All Saints, and the handiwork of his that she'd seen there.

"Sometimes you can't help blood being spilled," she said; "I don't hold it against you."

At these words, he began to tremble.

"What did they tell you about me? What *lies?*"

"Nothing," she said, mystified by his response. "What could they know?"

"I'm a professional," he said to her, his hand moving back up to her face. She felt intentionality in him again. A seriousness in his weight as he pressed closer upon her.

"I won't have them lie about me," he said. "I won't have it."

He lifted his head from her chest and looked at her.

"All I do is stop the drummer," he said.

"The drummer?"

"I have to stop him cleanly. In his tracks."

The wash of colors from the lights below painted his face one moment red, the next green, the next yellow, unadulterated hues, as in a child's paint box.

"I won't have them tell lies about me," he said again. "To say I spill blood."

"They told me nothing," she assured him. He had given up his pillow entirely, and now moved to straddle her. His hands were done with tender touches.

"Shall I show you how clean I am?" he said. "How easily I stop the drummer?"

Before she could reply, his hands closed around her neck. She had no time even to gasp, let alone shout. His thumbs were expert; they found her windpipe and pressed. She heard the drummer quicken its rhythm in her ears. "It's quick, and clean," he was telling her, the colors still coming in predictable sequence. Red, green, yellow, red, green, yellow.

There was an error here, she knew, a terrible misunderstanding which she couldn't quite fathom. She struggled to make some sense of it.

"I don't understand," she tried to tell him, but her bruised larynx could produce no more than a gargling sound.

"Too late for excuses," he said, shaking his head. "You came to me, remember? You want the drummer stopped. Why else did you come?" His grip tightened yet further. She had the sensation of her face swelling, of the blood throbbing to jump from her eyes.

"Don't you see that they came to warn you about me?" he said, frowning as he labored. "They came to seduce you away from me by telling you I spilled blood."

"No." She squeezed the syllable out of her last breath, but he only pressed harder to cancel her denial.

The drummer was deafeningly loud now; though Kavanagh's mouth still opened and closed, she could no longer hear what he was telling her. It mattered little. She realized now that he was not Death, not the clean-boned guardian she'd waited for. In her eagerness, she had given herself into the hands of a common killer, a street-corner Cain. She wanted to spit contempt at him, but her consciousness was slipping, the room, the lights, the face all throbbing to the drummer's beat. And then it all stopped.

She looked down on the bed. Her body lay sprawled across it. One desperate hand had clutched at the sheet, and clutched still, though there was no life left in it. Her tongue protruded, there was spittle on her blue lips. But (as he had promised) there was no blood.

She hovered, her presence failing even to bring a breeze to the cobwebs in this corner of the ceiling, and watched while Kavanagh observed the rituals of his crime. He was bending over the body, whispering in its ear as he rearranged it on the tangled sheets. Then he unbuttoned himself and unveiled that bone whose inflammation was the sincerest form of flattery. What followed was comical in its gracelessness; as her body was comical, with its scars and its places where age puckered and plucked at it. She watched his ungainly attempts at congress quite remotely. His buttocks were pale, and imprinted with the marks his underwear had left; their motion put her in mind of a mechanical toy.

He kissed her as he worked, and swallowed the pestilence with her spittle; his hands came off her body gritty with her contagious cells. He knew none of this, of course. He was perfectly innocent of what corruption he embraced, and took into himself with every uninspired thrust.

At last, he finished. There was no gasp, no cry. He simply stopped his clockwork motion and climbed off her, wiping himself with the edge of the sheet, and buttoning himself up again.

Guides were calling her. She had journeys to make, reunions to look forward to. But she did not want to go, at least not yet. She steered the vehicle of her spirit to a fresh vantage point, where she could better see Kavanagh's face. Her sight, or whatever sense this condition granted her, saw clearly how his features were painted over a groundwork of muscle, and how, beneath that intricate scheme, the bones sheened. Ah, the bone. He was not Death, of course, and yet he was. He had the face, hadn't he? And one day, given decay's blessing, he'd show it. Such a pity that a scraping of flesh came between it and the naked eye.

Come away, the voices insisted. She knew they could not be fobbed off very much longer. Indeed there were some among them she thought she knew. A *moment*, she pleaded, *only a moment more*.

Kavanagh had finished his business at the murder scene. He checked his appearance in the wardrobe mirror, then went to the door. She went with him, intrigued by the utter banality of his expression. He slipped out onto the silent landing and then down the stairs, waiting for a moment when the night porter was otherwise engaged before stepping out into the street, and liberty.

Was it dawn that washed the sky, or the illuminations? Perhaps she had watched him from the corner of the room longer than she'd thought—hours passing as moments in the state she had so recently achieved.

Only at the last was she rewarded for her vigil, as a look she recognized crossed Kavanagh's face. Hunger! The man was hungry. He would not die of the plague, any more than she had. Its presence shone in him—gave a fresh luster to his skin, and a new insistence to his belly.

He had come to her a minor murderer, and was going from her as Death writ large. She laughed, seeing the self-fulfilling prophecy she had unwittingly engineered. For an instant his pace slowed, as if he might have heard her. But no; it was the drummer he was listening for, beating louder than ever in his ear and demanding, as he went, a new and deadly vigor in his every step.

HOW
SPOILERS
BLEED

L ocke raised his eyes to the trees. The wind was moving in them, and the commotion of their laden branches sounded like the river in full spate. One impersonation of many. When he had first come to the jungle he had been awed by the sheer multiplicity of beast and blossom, the relentless parade of life here. But he had learned better. This burgeoning diversity was a sham, the jungle pretending itself an artless garden. It was not. Where the untutored trespasser saw only a brilliant show of natural splendors, Locke now recognized a subtle conspiracy at work, in which each thing mirrored some other thing. The trees, the river; a blossom, a bird. In a moth's wing, a monkey's eye; on a lizard's back, sunlight on stones. Round and round in a dizzying circle of impersonations, a hall of mirrors which confounded the senses and would, given time, rot reason altogether. See us now, he thought drunkenly as they stood around Cherrick's grave, look at how we play the game too. We're living, but we impersonate the dead better than the dead themselves.

The corpse had been one scab by the time they'd hoisted it into a sack and carried it outside to this miserable plot behind Tetelman's house to bury. There were half a dozen other graves here. All Europeans, to judge by the names crudely burned into the wooden crosses: killed by snakes, or heat, or longing.

Tetelman attempted to say a brief prayer in Spanish, but the roar of the trees, and the din of birds making their way home to their roosts before night came down, all but drowned him out. He gave up eventually, and they made their way back into the cooler interior of the house, where Stumpf was sitting, drinking brandy and staring inanely at the darkening stain on the floorboards.

Outside, two of Tetelman's tamed Indians were shoveling the rank jungle earth on top of Cherrick's sack, eager to be done with the work and away before nightfall. Locke watched from the window. The gravediggers didn't talk as they labored, but filled up the shallow grave, then flattened the earth as best they could with the leather-tough soles of their feet. As they did so the stamping of the ground took on a rhythm. It occurred to Locke that the men were probably the worse for bad whisky; he knew few Indians who didn't drink like fishes. Now, staggering a little, they began to dance on Cherrick's grave.

"Locke?"

Locke woke. In the darkness, a cigarette glowed. As the smoker drew on it, and the tip burned more intensely, Stumpf's wasted features swam up out of the night.

"Locke? Are you awake?"

"What do you want?"

"I can't sleep," the mask replied. "I've been thinking. The supply plane comes in from Santarém the day after tomorrow. We could be back there in a few hours. Out of all this."

"Sure."

"I mean permanently," Stumpf said. "Away."

"Permanently?"

Stumpf lit another cigarette from the embers of his last before saying, "I don't believe in curses. Don't think I do."

"Who said anything about curses?"

"You saw Cherrick's body. What happened to him . . ."

"There's a disease," said Locke, "what's it called?—when the blood doesn't set properly?"

"Hemophilia," Stumpf replied. "He didn't have hemophilia and we both know it. I've seen him scratched and cut dozens of times. He mended like you or me."

Locke snatched at a mosquito that had alighted on his chest and ground it out between thumb and forefinger.

"All right. Then what killed him?"

"You saw the wounds better than I did, but it seemed to me his skin just broke open as soon as he was touched."

Locke nodded. "That's the way it looked."

"Maybe it's something he caught off the Indians."

Locke took the point. "*I* didn't touch any of them," he said.

"Neither did I. But he did, remember?"

Locke remembered; scenes like that weren't easy to forget, try as he might. "Christ," he said, his voice hushed, "what a fucking situation."

"I'm going back to Santarém. I don't want them coming looking for me."

"They're not going to."

"How do you know? We screwed up back there. We could have bribed them. Got them off the land some other way."

"I doubt it. You heard what Tetelman said. Ancestral territories."

"You can have my share of the land," Stumpf said. "I want no part of it."

"You mean it, then? You're getting out?"

"I feel dirty. We're spoilers, Locke."

"It's your funeral."

"I mean it. I'm not like you. Never really had the stomach for this kind of thing. Will you buy my third off me?"

"Depends on your price."

"Whatever you want to give. It's yours."

Confessional over, Stumpf returned to his bed, and lay down in the darkness to finish off his cigarette. It would soon be light. Another jungle dawn: a precious interval, all too short, before the world began to sweat. How he *hated* the place. At least he hadn't touched any of the Indians; hadn't even been within breathing distance of them. Whatever infection they'd passed on to Cherrick, he could surely not be tainted. In less than forty-eight hours he would be away to Santarém, and then on to some city, *any* city, where the tribe could never follow. He'd already done his penance, hadn't he? Paid for his greed and his arrogance with the rot in his abdomen and the terrors he knew he would never quite shake off again. Let that be punishment enough, he prayed, and slipped, before the monkeys began to call up the day, into a spoiler's sleep.

A gem-backed beetle, trapped beneath Stumpf's mosquito net, hummed around in diminishing circles, looking for some way out. It could find none. Eventually, exhausted by the search, it hovered over the sleeping man, then landed on his forehead. There it wandered, drinking at the pores. Beneath its imperceptible tread, Stumpf's skin opened and broke into a trail of tiny wounds.

They had come into the Indian hamlet at noon, the sun a basilisk's eye. At first they had thought the place deserted. Locke and Cherrick had advanced into the compound, leaving the dysentery-ridden Stumpf in the Jeep, out of the worst of the heat. It was Cherrick who first noticed the child. A potbellied boy of perhaps four or five, his face painted with thick bands of the scarlet vegetable dye *urucu*, had slipped out from his hiding place and come to peer at the trespassers, fearless in his curiosity. Cherrick stood still; Locke did the same. One by one, from the huts and from the shelter of the trees around the compound, the tribe appeared and stared, like the boy, at the newcomers. If there was a flicker of feeling on their broad, flat-nosed faces, Locke could not read it. These people—he thought of every Indian as part of one wretched tribe—were impossible to decipher; deceit was their only skill.

"What are you doing here?" he said. The sun was baking the back of his neck. "This is our land."

The boy still looked up at him. His almond eyes refused to fear.

"They don't understand you," Cherrick said.

"Get the Kraut out here. Let him explain it to them."

"He can't move."

"*Get him out here,*" Locke said. "I don't care if he's shat his pants."

Cherrick backed away down the track, leaving Locke standing in the ring of huts. He looked from doorway to doorway, from tree to tree, trying to estimate the numbers. There were at most three dozen Indians, two-thirds of them women and children, descendants of the great peoples that had once roamed the Amazon Basin in their tens of thousands. Now those tribes were all but decimated. The forest in which they had prospered for generations was being leveled and burned; eight-lane highways were speeding through their hunting grounds. All they held sacred—the wilderness and their place in its system—was being trampled and trespassed: they were exiles in their own land. But still they declined to pay homage to their new masters, despite the rifles they brought. Only death would convince them of defeat, Locke mused.

Cherrick found Stumpf slumped in the front seat of the Jeep, his pasty features more wretched than ever.

"Locke wants you," he said, shaking the German out of his doze. "The village is still occupied. You'll have to speak to them."

Stumpf groaned. "I can't move," he said, "I'm dying—"

"Locke wants you dead or alive," Cherrick said. Their fear of Locke, which went unspoken, was perhaps one of the two things they had in common, that and greed.

"I feel awful," Stumpf said.

"If I don't bring you, he'll only come himself," Cherrick pointed out. This was indisputable. Stumpf threw the other man a despairing glance, then nodded his jowly head. "All right," he said, "help me."

Cherrick had no wish to lay a hand on Stumpf. The man stank of his sickness; he seemed to be oozing the contents of his gut through his pores; his skin had the luster of rank meat. He took the outstretched hand nevertheless. Without aid, Stumpf would never make the hundred yards from Jeep to compound.

Ahead, Locke was shouting.

"Get moving," said Cherrick, hauling Stumpf down from the front seat and toward the bawling voice. "Let's get it over and done with."

When the two men returned into the circle of huts the scene had scarcely changed. Locke glanced around at Stumpf.

"We got trespassers," he said.

"So I see," Stumpf returned wearily.

"Tell them to get the fuck off our land," Locke said. "Tell them this is our territory; we bought it. Without sitting tenants."

Stumpf nodded, not meeting Locke's rabid eyes. Sometimes he hated the man almost as much as he hated himself.

"Go on . . ." Locke said, and gestured for Cherrick to relinquish his support of Stumpf. This he did. The German stumbled forward, head bowed. He took several seconds to work out his patter, then raised his head and spoke a few wilting words in bad Portuguese. The pronouncement was met with the same blank looks as Locke's performance. Stumpf tried again, rearranging his inadequate vocabulary to try and awake a flicker of understanding among these savages.

The boy who had been so entertained by Locke's cavortings now stood staring up at this third demon, his face wiped of smiles. This one was nowhere near as comical as the first. He was sick and haggard; he smelled of death. The boy held his nose to keep from inhaling the badness of the man.

Stumpf peered through greasy eyes at his audience. If they *did* understand, and were faking their blank incomprehension, it was a flawless performance. His limited skills defeated, he turned giddily to Locke.

"They don't understand me," he said.

"Tell them again."

"I don't think they speak Portuguese."

"Tell them anyway."

Cherrick cocked his rifle. "We don't have to talk with them," he said under his breath. "They're on our land. We're within our rights—"

"No," said Locke, "there's no need for shooting. Not if we can persuade them to go peacefully."

"They don't understand plain common sense," Cherrick said. "Look at them. They're animals. Living in filth."

Stumpf had begun to try and communicate again, this time accompanying his hesitant words with a pitiful mime.

"Tell them we've got work to do here," Locke prompted him.

"I'm trying my best," Stumpf replied testily.

"We've got papers."

"I don't think they'd be much impressed," Stumpf returned, with a cautious sarcasm that was lost on the other man.

"Just tell them to move on. Find some other piece of land to squat on."

Watching Stumpf put these sentiments into word and sign language, Locke was already running through the alternative options available. Either the Indians—the Txukahamei or the Achual or whatever damn family it was—accepted their demands and moved on, or else they would have to enforce the edict. As Cherrick had said, they were within their rights. They had papers from the development authorities; they had maps marking the division between one territory and the next; they had every sanction from signature to bullet. He had no active desire to shed blood. The world was still too full of bleeding-heart liberals and doe-eyed sentimentalists to make genocide the most convenient solution. But the gun had been used before, and would be used again, until every unwashed Indian had put on a pair of trousers and given up eating monkeys.

Indeed, the din of liberals notwithstanding, the gun had its appeal. It was swift, and absolute. Once it had had its short, sharp say, there was no danger of further debate, no chance that in ten years' time some mercenary Indian who'd found a copy of Marx in the gutter could come back claiming his tribal lands—oil, minerals, and all. Once gone, they were gone forever.

At the thought of these scarlet-faced savages laid low, Locke felt his trigger finger itch, physically *itch*. Stumpf had finished his encore; it had met with no response. Now he groaned, and turned to Locke.

"I'm going to be sick," he said. His face was bright white; the glamour of his skin made his small teeth look dingy.

"Be my guest," Locke replied.

"*Please*. I have to lie down. I don't want them watching me."

Locke shook his head. "You don't move till they listen. If we don't get any joy from them, you're going to see something to be sick about." Locke toyed with the stock of his rifle as he spoke, running a broken thumbnail along the nicks in it. There were perhaps a dozen, each one a human grave. The jungle concealed murder so easily; it almost seemed, in its cryptic fashion, to condone the crime.

Stumpf turned away from Locke and scanned the mute assembly. There were so many Indians here, he thought, and though he carried a pistol he was an inept marksman. Suppose they rushed Locke, Cherrick, and himself? He would not survive. And yet, looking at the Indians, he could see no sign of aggression among them. Once they had been warriors; now? Like beaten children, sullen and willfully stupid. There was some trace of beauty in one or two of the younger women; their skins, though grimy, were fine, their eyes black. Had he felt more healthy he might have been aroused by their nakedness, tempted to press his hands upon their shiny bodies. As it was their feigned incomprehension merely irritated him. They seemed, in their silence, like another species, as mysterious and unfathomable as mules or birds. Hadn't somebody in Uxituba told him that many of these people didn't even give their children proper names, that each was like a limb of the tribe, anonymous and therefore unfixable? He could believe that now, meeting the same dark stare in each pair of eyes, could believe that what they faced here was not three dozen individuals but a fluid system of hatred made flesh. It made him shudder to think of it.

Now, for the first time since their appearance, one of the assembly moved. He was an ancient, fully thirty years older than most of the tribe. He, like the rest, was all but naked. The sagging flesh of his limbs and breasts resembled tanned hide; his step, though the pale eyes suggested blindness, was perfectly confident. Once standing in front of the interlopers he opened his mouth—there were no teeth set in his rotted gums—and spoke. What emerged from his scraggy throat was a language made not of words but only of sound, a potpourri of jungle noises. There was no discernible pattern to the outpouring, it was simply a display—awesome in its way—of impersonations. The man could murmur like a jaguar, screech like a parrot; he could find in his throat the splash of rain on orchids, the howl of monkeys.

The sounds made Stumpf's gorge rise. The jungle had diseased him, dehydrated him and left him wrung out. Now this rheumy-eyed stickman was vomiting the whole odious place up at him. The raw heat in the circle of huts made Stumpf's head beat, and he was sure, as he stood listening to the sage's din, that the old man was measuring the rhythm of his nonsense to the thud at his temples and wrists.

"What's he saying?" Locke demanded.

"What does it sound like?" Stumpf replied, irritated by Locke's idiot questions. "It's all noises."

"The fucker's cursing us," Cherrick said.

Stumpf looked round at the third man. Cherrick's eyes were starting from his head.

"It's a curse," he said to Stumpf.

Locke laughed, unmoved by Cherrick's apprehension. He pushed Stumpf out of the way so as to face the old man, whose song-speech had now lowered in pitch; it was almost lilting. He was singing twilight, Stumpf thought: that brief ambiguity between the fierce day and the suffocating night. Yes, that was it. He could hear in the song the purr and the coo of a drowsy kingdom. It was so persuasive he wanted to lie down on the spot where he stood, and sleep.

Locke broke the spell. "What are you saying?" he spat in the tribesman's mazy face. "Talk sense!"

But the night noises only whispered on, an unbroken stream.

"This is our village," another voice now broke in; the man spoke as if translating the elder's words. Locke snapped round to locate the speaker. He was a thin youth, whose skin might once have been golden. "*Our* village. *Our* land."

"You speak English," Locke said.

"Some," the youth replied.

"Why didn't you answer me earlier?" Locke demanded, his fury exacerbated by the disinterest on the Indian's face.

"Not my place to speak," the man replied. "He is the elder."

"The Chief, you mean?"

"The Chief is dead. All his family is dead. This is the wisest of us—"

"Then you tell him—"

"No need to tell," the young man broke in. "He understands you."

"He speaks English too?"

"No," the other replied, "but he understands you. You are . . . transparent."

Locke half-grasped that the youth was implying an insult here, but wasn't quite certain. He gave Stumpf a puzzled look. The German shook his head. Locke returned his attention to the youth. "Tell him anyway," he said, "tell all of them. This is our land. We bought it."

"The tribe has always lived here," the reply came.

"Not any longer," Cherrick said.

"We've got papers," Stumpf said mildly, still hoping that the confrontation might end peacefully, "from the government."

"We were here before the government," the tribesman replied.

The old man had stopped talking the forest. Perhaps, Stumpf thought, he's coming to the beginning of another day, and stopped. He was turning away now, indifferent to the presence of these unwelcome guests.

"Call him back," Locke demanded, stabbing his rifle toward the young tribesman. The gesture was unambiguous. "Make him tell the rest of them they've got to go."

The young man seemed unimpressed by the threat of Locke's rifle, however, and clearly unwilling to give orders to his elder, whatever the imperative. He simply watched the old man walk back toward the hut from which he had emerged. Around the compound, others were also turning away. The old man's withdrawal apparently signaled that the show was over.

"*No!*" said Cherrick, "you're not *listening*." The color in his cheeks had risen a tone, his voice, an octave. He pushed forward, rifle raised. "*You fucking scum!*"

Despite his hysteria, he was rapidly losing his audience. The old man had reached the doorway of his hut, and now bent his back and disappeared into its recesses; the few members of the tribe who were still showing some interest in the proceedings were viewing the Europeans with a hint of pity for their lunacy. It only enraged Cherrick further.

"Listen to me!" he shrieked, sweat flicking off his brow as he jerked his head at one retreating figure and then at another. "*Listen*, you bastards."

"Easy . . ." said Stumpf.

The appeal triggered Cherrick. Without warning he raised his rifle to his shoulder, aimed at the open door of the hut into which the old man had vanished, and fired. Birds rose from the crowns of adjacent trees; dogs took to their heels. From within the hut came a tiny shriek, not like the old man's voice at all. As it sounded, Stumpf fell to his knees, hugging his belly, his gut in spasm. Face to the ground, he did not see the diminutive figure emerge from the hut and totter into the sunlight. Even when he did look up, and saw how the child with the scarlet face clutched his belly, he hoped his eyes lied. But they did not. It was blood that came from between the child's tiny fingers, and death that had stricken his face. He fell forward onto the impacted earth of the hut's threshold, twitched, and died.

Somewhere among the huts a woman began to sob quietly. For a moment the world spun on a pinhead, balanced exquisitely between silence and the cry that must break it, between a truce held and the coming atrocity.

"You stupid bastard," Locke murmured to Cherrick. Under his condemnation, his voice trembled. "Back off," he said. "Get up, Stumpf. We're not waiting. Get up and come now, or don't come at all."

Stumpf was still looking at the body of the child. Suppressing his moans, he got to his feet.

"Help me," he said. Locke lent him an arm. "Cover us," he said to Cherrick.

The man nodded, deathly pale. Some of the tribe had turned their gaze on the Europeans' retreat, their expressions, despite this tragedy, as inscrutable as ever. Only the sobbing woman, presumably the dead child's mother, wove between the silent figures, keening her grief.

Cherrick's rifle shook as he kept the bridgehead. He'd done the mathematics; if it came to a head-on collision they had little chance of survival. But even now, with the enemy making a getaway, there was no sign of movement among the Indians. Just the accusing facts: the dead boy, the warm rifle. Cherrick chanced a look over his shoulder. Locke and Stumpf were already within twenty yards of the Jeep, and there was still no move from the savages.

Then, as he looked back toward the compound, it seemed as though the tribe breathed together one solid breath, and hearing that sound Cherrick felt death wedge itself like a fish bone in his throat, too deep to be plucked out by his fingers, too big to be shat. It was just waiting there, lodged in his anatomy, beyond argument or appeal. He was distracted from its presence by a movement at the door of the hut. Quite ready to make the same mistake again, he took firmer hold of his rifle. The old man had reappeared at the door. He stepped over the corpse of the boy, which was lying where it had toppled. Again, Cherrick glanced behind him. Surely they were at the Jeep? But Stumpf had stumbled; Locke was even now dragging him to his feet. Cherrick, seeing the old man advancing toward him, took one cautious step backward, followed by another. But the old man was fearless. He walked swiftly across the compound, coming to stand so close to Cherrick, his body as vulnerable as ever, that the barrel of the rifle prodded his shrunken belly.

There was blood on both his hands, fresh enough to run down the man's arms when he displayed the palms for Cherrick's benefit. Had he touched the boy, Cherrick wondered, as he stepped out of the hut? If so, it had been an astonishing sleight of hand, for Cherrick had seen nothing. Trick or no trick, the significance of the display was perfectly apparent: he was being accused of murder. Cherrick wasn't about to be cowed, however. He stared back at the old man, matching defiance with defiance.

But the old bastard did nothing except show his bloody palms, his eyes full of tears. Cherrick could feel his anger growing again. He poked the man's flesh with his finger.

"You don't frighten me," he said, "you understand? I'm not a fool."

As he spoke he seemed to see a shifting in the old man's features. It was a trick of the sun, of course, or of bird shadow, but there was, beneath the corruption of age, a hint of the child now dead at the hut door: the tiny mouth even seemed to smile. Then, as subtly as it had appeared, the illusion faded again.

Cherrick withdrew his hand from the old man's chest, narrowing his eyes against further mirages. He then renewed his retreat. He had taken three steps only when something broke cover to his left. He swung round, raised his rifle, and fired. A piebald pig, one of several that had been grazing around the huts, was checked in its flight by the bullet, which struck it in the neck. It seemed to trip over itself, and collapsed headlong in the dust.

Cherrick swung his rifle back toward the old man. But he hadn't moved, except to open his mouth. His palate was making the sound of the dying pig. A choking squeal, pitiful and ridiculous, which followed Cherrick back up the path to the Jeep. Locke had the engine running. "Get in," he said. Cherrick needed no encouragement, but flung himself into the front seat. The interior of the vehicle was filthy hot, and stank of Stumpf's bodily functions, but it was as near safety as they'd been in the last hour.

"It was a pig," he said, "I shot a pig."

"I saw," said Locke.

"That old bastard . . ."

He didn't finish. He was looking down at the two fingers with which he had prodded the elder. "I touched him," he muttered, perplexed by what he saw. The fingertips were bloody, though the flesh he had laid his fingers upon had been clean.

Locke ignored Cherrick's confusion and backed the Jeep up to turn it around, then drove away from the hamlet, down a track that seemed to have become choked with foliage in the hour since they'd come up it. There was no discernible pursuit.

The tiny trading post to the south of Aveiro was scant of civilization, but it sufficed. There were white faces here, and clean water. Stumpf, whose condition had deteriorated on the return journey, was treated by Dancy, an Englishman who had the manner of a disenfranchised earl and a face like hammered steak. He claimed to have been a doctor once upon a sober time, and though he had no evidence of his qualifications, nobody contested his right to deal with Stumpf. The German was delirious, and on occasion violent, but Dancy, his small hands heavy with gold rings, seemed to take a positive delight in nursing his thrashing patient.

While Stumpf raved beneath his mosquito net, Locke and Cherrick sat in the lamplit gloom and drank, then told the story of their encounter with the tribe. It was Tetelman, the owner of the trading post's stores, who had most to say when the report was finished. He knew the Indians well.

"I've been here years," he said, feeding nuts to the mangy monkey that scampered on his lap. "I know the way these people think. They may act as though they're stupid, cowards even. Take it from me, they're neither."

Cherrick grunted. The quicksilver monkey fixed him with vacant eyes. "They didn't make a move on us," Cherrick said, "even though they outnumbered us ten to one. If that isn't cowardice, what is it?"

Tetelman settled back in his creaking chair, throwing the animal off his lap. His face was raddled and used. Only his lips, constantly rewetted from his glass, had any color; he looked, thought Locke, like an old whore. "Thirty years ago," Tetelman said, "this whole territory was their homeland. Nobody wanted it; they *went* where they liked, *did* what they liked. As far as we whites were concerned the jungle was filthy and disease-infected: we wanted no part of it. And, of course, in some ways we were right. It *is* filthy and disease-infected, but it's also got reserves we now want badly: minerals, oil maybe: power."

"We paid for that land," said Locke, his fingers jittery on the cracked rim of his glass. "It's all we've got now."

Tetelman sneered. "Paid?" he said. The monkey chattered at his feet, apparently as amused by this claim as its master. "No. You just paid for a blind eye so you could take it by force. You paid for the right to fuck up the Indians in any way you could. That's what your dollars bought, Mr. Locke. The government of this country is counting off the months until every tribe on the subcontinent is wiped out by you or your like. It's no use to play the outraged innocents. I've been here too long . . ."

Cherrick spat onto the bare floor. Tetelman's speech had heated his blood.

"And so why'd *you* come here, if you're so fucking clever?" he asked the trader.

"Same reason as you," Tetelman replied plainly, staring off into the trees beyond the plot of land behind the store. Their silhouettes shook against the sky; wind, or night birds.

"What reason's that?" Cherrick said, barely keeping his hostility in check.

"Greed," Tetelman replied mildly, still watching the trees. Something scampered across the low wooden roof. The monkey at Tetelman's feet listened, head cocked. "I thought I could make my fortune out here, the same way you do. I gave myself two years. Three at the most. That was the best part of two decades ago." He frowned; whatever thoughts passed behind his eyes, they were bitter. "The jungle eats you up and spits you out, sooner or later."

"Not me," said Locke.

Tetelman turned his eyes on the man. They were wet. "Oh yes," he said politely, "extinction's in the air, Mr. Locke. I can smell it." Then he turned back to looking at the window.

Whatever was on the roof now had companions.

"They won't come here, will they?" said Cherrick. "They won't follow us?"

The question, spoken almost in a whisper, begged for a reply in the negative. Try as he might Cherrick couldn't dislodge the sights of the previous day. It wasn't the boy's corpse that so haunted him: that he could soon learn to forget. But the elder—with his shifting, sunlit face and the palms raised as if to display some stigmata—he was not so forgettable.

"Don't fret," Tetelman said, with a trace of condescension. "Sometimes one or two of them will drift in here with a parrot to sell, or a few pots, but I've never seen them come here in any numbers. They don't like it. This is civilization as far as they're concerned, and it intimidates them. Besides, they wouldn't harm my guests. They need me."

"Need you?" said Locke. Who could need this wreck of a man?

"They use our medicines. Dancy supplies them. And blankets, once in a while. As I said, they're not so stupid."

Next door, Stumpf had begun to howl. Dancy's consoling voice could be heard, attempting to talk down the panic. He was plainly failing.

"Your friend's gone bad," said Tetelman.

"No friend," Cherrick replied.

"It rots," Tetelman murmured, half to himself.

"What does?"

"The soul." The word was utterly out of place from Tetelman's whisky-glossed lips. "It's like fruit, you see. It rots."

Somehow Stumpf's cries gave force to the observation. It was not the voice of a wholesome creature; there was putrescence in it.

More to direct his attention away from the German's din than out of any real interest, Cherrick said, "What do they give you for the medicine and the blankets? Women?"

The possibility clearly entertained Tetelman; he laughed, his gold teeth gleaming. "I've no use for women," he said. "I've had the syph for too many years." He clicked his fingers and the monkey clambered back up onto his lap. "The soul," he said, "isn't the only thing that rots."

"Well, what do you get from them, then?" Locke said. "For your supplies?"

"Artifacts," Tetelman replied. "Bowls, jugs, mats. The Americans buy them off me, and sell them again in Manhattan. Everybody wants something made by an extinct tribe these days. *Memento mori.*"

"Extinct?" said Locke. The word had a seductive ring; it sounded like life to him.

"Oh, certainly," said Tetelman. "They're as good as gone. If you don't wipe them out, they'll do it themselves."

"Suicide?" Locke said.

"In their fashion. They just lose heart. I've seen it happen half a dozen times. A tribe loses its land, and its appetite for life goes with it. They stop taking care of themselves. The women don't get pregnant anymore, the young men take to drink, the old men just starve themselves to death. In a year or two it's like they never existed."

Locke swallowed the rest of his drink, silently saluting the fatal wisdom of these people. They knew when to die, which was more than could be said for some he'd met. The thought of their death wish absolved him of any last vestiges of guilt. What was the gun in his hand, except an instrument of evolution?

On the fourth day after their arrival at the post, Stumpf's fever abated, much to Dancy's disappointment. "The worst of it's over," he announced. "Give him two more days' rest and you can get back to your labors."

"What are your plans?" Tetelman wanted to know.

Locke was watching the rain from the veranda. Sheets of water pouring from clouds so low they brushed the treetops. Then, just as suddenly as it had arrived, the downpour was gone, as though a tap had been turned off. Sun broke through; the jungle, new-washed, was steaming and sprouting and thriving again.

"I don't know what we'll do," said Locke. "Maybe get ourselves some help and go back in there."

"There are ways," Tetelman said.

Cherrick, sitting beside the door to get the benefit of what little breeze was available, picked up the glass that had scarcely been out of his hand in recent days, and filled it up again. "No more guns," he said. He hadn't touched his rifle since they'd arrived at the post; in fact he kept from contact with anything but a bottle and his bed. His skin seemed to crawl and creep perpetually.

"No need for guns," Tetelman murmured. The statement hung on the air like an unfulfilled promise.

"Get rid of them without guns?" said Locke. "If you mean waiting for them to die out naturally, I'm not that patient."

"No," said Tetelman, "we can be swifter than that."

"How?"

Tetelman gave the man a lazy look. "They're my livelihood," he said, "or part of it. You're asking me to help you make myself bankrupt."

He not only looks like an old whore, Locke thought, he thinks like one. "What's it worth? Your wisdom?" he asked.

"A cut of whatever you find on your land," Tetelman replied.

Locke nodded. "What have we got to lose? Cherrick? You agree to cut him in?" Cherrick's consent was a shrug. "All right," Locke said, "talk."

"They need medicines," Tetelman explained, "because they're so susceptible to our diseases. A decent plague can wipe them out practically overnight."

Locke thought about this, not looking at Tetelman. "One fell swoop," Tetelman continued. "They've got practically no defenses against certain bacteria. Never had to build up any resistance. The clap. Smallpox. Even measles."

"How?" said Locke.

Another silence. Down the steps of the veranda, where civilization finished, the jungle was swelling to meet the sun. In the liquid heat, plants blossomed and rotted and blossomed again.

"I asked *how*," Locke said.

"Blankets," Tetelman replied, "dead men's blankets."

A little before the dawn of the night after Stumpf's recovery, Cherrick woke suddenly, startled from his rest by bad dreams. Outside it was pitch-dark; neither moon nor stars relieved the depth of the night. But his body clock, which his life as a mercenary had trained to impressive accuracy, told him that first light was not far off, and he had no wish to lay his head down again and sleep. Not with the old man waiting to be dreamt. It wasn't just the raised palms, the blood glistening, that so distressed Cherrick. It was the words he'd dreamt coming from the old man's toothless mouth which had brought on the cold sweat that now encased his body.

What were the words? He couldn't recall them now, but wanted to, wanted the sentiments dragged into wakefulness, where they could be dissected and dismissed as ridiculous. They wouldn't come though. He lay on his wretched cot, the dark wrapping him up too tightly for him to move, and suddenly the bloody hands were there, in front of him, suspended in the pitch. There was no face, no sky, no tribe. Just the hands.

"Dreaming," Cherrick told himself, but he knew better.

And now, the voice. He was getting his wish; here were the words he had dreamt spoken. Few of them made sense. Cherrick lay like a newborn baby, listening to its parents talk but unable to make any significance of their exchanges. He was ignorant, wasn't he? He tasted the sourness of his stupidity for the first time since childhood. The voice made him fearful of ambiguities he had ridden roughshod over, of whispers his shouting life had rendered inaudible. He fumbled for comprehension, and was not entirely frustrated. The man was speaking of the world, and of exile from the world, of being broken always by what one seeks to possess. Cherrick struggled, wishing he could stop the voice and ask for explanation. But it was already fading, ushered away by the wild address of parrots in the trees, raucous and gaudy voices erupting suddenly on every side. Through the mesh of Cherrick's mosquito net he could see the sky flaring through the branches.

He sat up. Hands and voice had gone, and with them all but an irritating murmur of what he had almost understood. He had thrown off in sleep his single sheet; now he looked down at his body with distaste. His back and buttocks, and the underside of his thighs, felt sore. Too much sweating on coarse sheets, he thought. Not for the first time in recent days, he remembered a small house in Bristol which he had once known as home.

The noise of birds was filling his head. He hauled himself to the edge of the bed and pulled back the mosquito net. The crude weave of the net seemed to scour the palm of his hand as he gripped it. He disengaged his hold, and cursed to himself. There was again today an itch of tenderness in his skin that he'd suffered since coming to the post. Even the soles of his feet, pressed onto the floor by the weight of his body, seemed to suffer each knot and splinter. He wanted to be away from this place, and badly.

A warm trickle across his wrist caught his attention, and he was startled to see a rivulet of blood moving down his arm from his hand. There was a cut in the cushion of his thumb, where the mosquito net had apparently nicked his flesh. It was bleeding, though not copiously. He sucked at the cut, feeling again that peculiar sensitivity to touch that only drink, and that in abundance, dulled. Spitting out blood, he began to dress.

The clothes he put on were a scourge to his back. His sweat-stiffened shirt rubbed against his shoulders and neck; he seemed to feel every thread chafing his nerve endings. The shirt might have been sackcloth, the way it abraded him.

Next door, he heard Locke moving around. Gingerly finishing his dressing, Cherrick went through to join him. Locke was sitting at the table by the window. He was poring over a map of Tetelman's and drinking a cup of the bitter coffee Dancy was so fond of brewing, which he drank with a dollop of condensed milk. The two men had little to say to each other. Since the incident in the village all pretense of respect or friendship had disappeared. Locke now showed undisguised contempt for his sometime companion. The only fact that kept them together was the contract they and Stumpf had signed. Rather than breakfast on whisky, which he knew Locke would take as a further sign of his decay, Cherrick poured himself a slug of Dancy's emetic and went out to look at the morning.

He felt strange. There was something about this dawning day which made him profoundly uneasy. He knew the dangers of courting unfounded fears, and he tried to forbid them, but they were incontestable.

Was it simply exhaustion that made him so painfully conscious of his many discomforts this morning? Why else did he feel the pressure of his stinking clothes so acutely? The rasp of his boot collar against the jutting bone of his ankle, the rhythmical chafing of his trousers against his inside leg as he walked, even the grazing air that eddied around his exposed face and arms. The world was pressing on him—at least that was the sensation—pressing as though it wanted him out.

A large dragonfly, whining toward him on iridescent wings, collided with his arm. The pain of the collision caused him to drop his mug. It didn't break, but rolled off the veranda and was lost in the undergrowth. Angered, Cherrick slapped the insect off, leaving a smear of blood on his tattooed forearm to mark the dragonfly's demise. He wiped it off. It welled up again on the same spot, full and dark.

It wasn't the blood of the insect, he realized, but his own. The dragonfly had cut him somehow, though he had felt nothing. Irritated, he peered more closely at his punctured skin. The wound was not significant, but it *was* painful.

From inside he could hear Locke talking. He was loudly describing the inadequacy of his fellow adventurers to Tetelman.

"Stumpf's not fit for this kind of work," he was saying. "And Cherrick—"

"What about me?"

Cherrick stepped into the shabby interior, wiping a new flow of blood from his arm.

Locke didn't even bother to look up at him. "You're paranoid," he said plainly. "Paranoid and unreliable."

Cherrick was in no mood for taking Locke's foul-mouthing. "Just because I killed some Indian brat," he said. The more he brushed blood from his bitten arm, the more the place stung. "You just didn't have the balls to do it yourself."

Locke still didn't bother to look up from his perusal of the map. Cherrick moved across to the table.

"Are you listening to me?" he demanded, and added force to his question by slamming his fist down onto the table. On impact his hand simply burst open. Blood spurted out in every direction, spattering the map.

Cherrick howled, and reeled backward from the table with blood pouring from a yawning split in the side of his hand. The bone showed. Through the din of pain in his head he could hear a quiet voice. The words were inaudible, but he knew whose they were.

"I won't hear!" he said, shaking his head like a dog with a flea in its ear. He staggered back against the wall, but the briefest of contacts was another agony. *"I won't hear, damn you!"*

"What the hell's he talking about?" Dancy had appeared in the doorway, woken by the cries, still clutching the *Complete Works of Shelley* Tetelman had said he could not sleep without.

Locke readdressed the question to Cherrick, who was standing, wild-eyed, in the corner of the room, blood spitting from between his fingers as he attempted to stanch his wounded hand. "What are you saying?"

"He spoke to me," Cherrick replied, "the old man."

"What old man?" Tetelman asked.

"He means at the village," Locke said. Then, to Cherrick, "Is that what you mean?"

"He wants us out. Exiles. Like them. *Like them!*" Cherrick's panic was rapidly rising out of anyone's control, least of all his own.

"The man's got heat stroke," Dancy said, ever the diagnostician. Locke knew better.

"Your hand needs bandaging . . ." he said, slowly approaching Cherrick.

"I heard him . . ." Cherrick muttered.

"I believe you. Just slow down. We can sort it out."

"No," the other man replied, "it's pushing us out. Everything we touch. Everything we touch."

He looked as though he was about to topple over, and Locke reached for him. As his hands made contact with Cherrick's shoulders, the flesh beneath the shirt split, and Locke's hands were instantly soaked in scarlet. He withdrew them, appalled. Cherrick fell to his knees, which in their turn became new wounds. He stared down as his shirt and trousers darkened. "What's happening to me?" he wept.

Dancy moved toward him. "Let me help."

"No! Don't touch me!" Cherrick pleaded, but Dancy wasn't to be denied his nursing.

"It's all right," he said in his best bedside manner.

It wasn't. Dancy's grip, intended only to lift the man from his bleeding knees, opened new cuts wherever he took hold. Dancy felt the blood sprout beneath his hand, felt the flesh slip away from the bone. The sensation bested even his taste for agony. Like Locke, he forsook the lost man.

"He's rotting," he murmured.

Cherrick's body had split now in a dozen or more places. He tried to stand, half staggering to his feet only to collapse again, his flesh breaking open whenever he touched wall or chair or floor. There was no help for him. All the others could do was stand around like spectators at an execution, awaiting the final throes. Even Stumpf had roused himself from his bed and come through to see what all the shouting was about. He stood leaning against the door lintel, his disease-thinned face all disbelief.

Another minute, and blood loss defeated Cherrick. He keeled over and sprawled, facedown, across the floor. Dancy crossed back to him and crouched on his haunches beside his head.

"Is he dead?" Locke asked.

"Almost," Dancy replied.

"Rotted," said Tetelman, as though the word explained the atrocity they had just witnessed. He had a crucifix in his hand, large and crudely carved. It looked like Indian handiwork, Locke thought. The Messiah impaled on the tree was sloe-eyed and indecently naked. He smiled, despite nail and thorn.

Dancy touched Cherrick's body, letting the blood come with his touch, and turned the man over, then leaned in toward Cherrick's jittering face. The dying man's lips were moving oh so slightly.

"What are you saying?" Dancy asked; he leaned closer still to catch the man's words. Cherrick's mouth trailed bloody spittle, but no sound came.

Locke stepped in, pushing Dancy aside. Flies were already flitting around Cherrick's face. Locke thrust his bullnecked head into Cherrick's view. "You hear me?" he said.

The body grunted.

"You know me?"

Again, a grunt.

"You want to give me your share of the land?"

The grunt was lighter this time, almost a sigh.

"There's witnesses here," Locke said. "Just say yes. They'll hear you. Just say yes."

The body was trying its best. It opened its mouth a little wider.

"Dancy—" said Locke. "You hear what he said?"

Dancy could not disguise his horror at Locke's insistence, but he nodded.

"You're a witness."

"If you must," said the Englishman.

Deep in his body Cherrick felt the fish bone he'd first choked on in the village twist itself about one final time, and extinguish him.

"Did he say yes, Dancy?" Tetelman asked.

Dancy felt the physical proximity of the brute kneeling beside him. He didn't know what the dead man had said, but what did it matter? Locke would have the land anyway, wouldn't he?

"He said yes."

Locke stood up, and went in search of a fresh cup of coffee.

Without thinking, Dancy put his fingers on Cherrick's lids to seal his empty gaze. Under that lightest of touches the lid broke open and blood tainted the tears that had swelled where Cherrick's sight had been.

They had buried him toward evening. The corpse, though it had lain through the noon heat in the coolest part of the store, among the dried goods, had begun to putrefy by the time it was sewn up in canvas for the burial. The night following, Stumpf had come to Locke and offered him the last third of the territory to add to Cherrick's share, and Locke, ever the realist, had accepted. The terms, which were punitive, had been worked out the next day. In the evening of that day, as Stumpf had hoped, the supply plane came in. Locke, bored with Tetelman's contemptuous looks, had also elected to fly back to Santarém, there to drink the jungle out of his system for a few days, and return refreshed. He intended to buy up fresh supplies and, if possible, hire a reliable driver and gunman.

The flight was noisy, cramped and tedious; the two men exchanged no words for its full duration. Stumpf just kept his eyes on the tracts of unfelled wilderness they passed over, though from one hour to the next the scene scarcely changed. A panorama of sable green, broken on occasion by a glint of water, perhaps a column of blue smoke rising here and there, where land was being cleared; little else.

At Santarém they parted with a single handshake which left every nerve in Stumpf's hand scourged, and an open cut in the tender flesh between index finger and thumb.

Santarém wasn't Rio, Locke mused as he made his way down to a bar at the south end of the town, run by a veteran of Vietnam who had a taste for ad hoc animal shows. It was one of Locke's few certain pleasures, and one he never tired of, to watch a local woman, face dead as a cold manioc cake, submit to a dog or a donkey for a few grubby dollar bills. The women of Santarém were, on the whole, as unpalatable as the beer, but Locke had no eye for beauty in the opposite sex: it mattered only that their bodies be in reasonable working order, and not diseased. He found the bar and settled down for an evening of exchanging dirt with the American. When he tired of that—sometime after midnight—he bought a bottle of whisky and went out looking for a face to press his heat upon.

The woman with the squint was about to accede to a particular peccadillo of Locke's—one which she had resolutely refused until drunkenness persuaded her to abandon what little hope of dignity she had—when there came a rap on the door.

"Fuck," said Locke.

"Sí," said the woman. "Fook. Fook." It seemed to be the only word she knew in anything resembling English. Locke ignored her and crawled drunkenly to the edge of the stained mattress. Again, the rap on the door.

"Who is it?" he said.

"Senhor Locke?" The voice from the hallway was that of a young boy.

"Yes?" said Locke. His trousers had become lost in the tangle of sheets. "Yes? What do you want?"

"*Mensagem*," the boy said. "*Urgente. Urgente.*"

"For me?" He had found his trousers, and was pulling them on. The woman, not at all disgruntled by this desertion, watched him from the head of the bed, toying with an empty bottle. Buttoning up, Locke crossed from bed to door, a matter of three steps. He unlocked it. The boy in the darkened hallway was of Indian extraction to judge by the blackness of his eyes, and that peculiar luster his skin owned. He was dressed in a T-shirt bearing the Coca-Cola motif.

"*Mensagem*, Senhor Locke," he said again, ". . . *do hospital.*"

The boy was staring past Locke at the woman on the bed. He grinned from ear to ear at her cavortings.

"Hospital?" said Locke.

"*Sim.* Hospital Sacrado Coraçã de Maria."

It could only be Stumpf, Locke thought. Who else did he know in this corner of hell who'd call upon him? Nobody. He looked down at the leering child.

"*Vem comigo*," the boy said, "*vem comigo. Urgente.*"

"No," said Locke. "I'm not coming. Not now. You understand? Later. Later."

The boy shrugged. ". . . *Tá morrendo*," he said.

"Dying?" said Locke.

"*Sim. Tá morrendo.*"

"Well, let him. Understand me? You go back, and tell him. I won't come until I'm ready."

Again, the boy shrugged. "*E meu dinheiro?*" he said, as Locke went to close the door.

"You go to hell," Locke replied, and slammed it in the child's face.

When, two hours and one ungainly act of passionless sex later, Locke unlocked the door, he discovered that the child, by way of revenge, had defecated on the threshold.

The hospital Sacrado Coraçã de Maria was no place to fall ill; better, thought Locke, as he made his way down the dingy corridors, to die in your own bed with your own sweat for company than come here. The stench of disinfectant could not entirely mask the odor of human pain. The walls were ingrained with it; it formed a grease on the lamps, it slickened the unwashed floors. What had happened to Stumpf to bring him here? A barroom brawl, an argument with a pimp about the price of a woman? The German was just damn fool enough to get himself stuck in the gut over something so petty. "Senhor Stumpf?" he asked of a woman in white he accosted in the corridor. "I'm looking for Senhor Stumpf."

The woman shook her head, and pointed toward a harried-looking man farther down the corridor, who was taking a moment to light a small cigar. He let go the nurse's arm and approached the fellow. He was enveloped in a stinking cloud of smoke.

"I'm looking for Senhor Stumpf," he said.

The man peered at him quizzically.

"You are Locke?" he asked.

"Yes."

"Ah." He drew on the cigar. The pungency of the expelled smoke would surely have brought on a relapse in the hardiest patient. "I'm Dr. Edson Costa," the man said, offering his clammy hand to Locke. "Your friend has been waiting for you to come all night."

"What's wrong with him?"

"He's hurt his eye," Edson Costa replied, clearly indifferent to Stumpf's condition. "And he has some minor abrasions on his hands and face. But he won't have anyone go near him. He doctored himself."

"Why?" Locke asked.

The doctor looked flummoxed. "He pays to go in a clean room. Pays plenty. So I put him in. You want to see him? Maybe take him away?"

"Maybe," said Locke, unenthusiastically.

"His head . . ." said the doctor. "He has delusions."

Without offering further explanation, the man led off at a considerable rate, trailing tobacco smoke as he went. The route that wound out of the main building and across a small internal courtyard ended at a room with a glass partition in the door.

"Here," said the doctor. "Your friend. You tell him," he said as a parting snipe, "he pay more, or tomorrow he leaves."

Locke peered through the glass partition. The grubby-white room was empty but for a bed and a small table, lit by the same dingy light that cursed every wretched inch of this establishment. Stumpf was not on the bed, but squatting on the floor in the corner of the room. His left eye was covered with a bulbous padding, held in place by a bandage ineptly wrapped around his head.

Locke was looking at the man for a good time before Stumpf sensed that he was watched. He looked up slowly. His good eye, as if in compensation for the loss of its companion, seemed to have swelled to twice its natural size. It held enough fear for both it and its twin; indeed enough for a dozen eyes.

Cautiously, like a man whose bones are so brittle he fears an injudicious breath will shatter them, Stumpf edged up the wall and crossed to the door. He did not open it, but addressed Locke through the glass.

"Why didn't you come?" he said.

"I'm here."

"But *sooner*," said Stumpf. His face was raw, as if he'd been beaten. "Sooner."

"I had business," Locke returned. "What happened to you?"

"It's true, Locke," the German said, "everything is true."

"What are you talking about?"

"Tetelman told me. Cherrick's babblings. About being exiles. It's true. They mean to drive us out."

"We're not in the jungle now," Locke said. "You've got nothing to be afraid of here."

"Oh yes," said Stumpf, that wide eye wider than ever. "Oh yes! I saw him—"

"Who?"

"The elder. From the village. He was here."

"Ridiculous."

"*He was here*, damn you," Stumpf replied. "He was standing where you're standing. Looking at me through the glass."

"You've been drinking too much."

"It happened to Cherrick, and now it's happening to me. They're making it impossible to live—"

Locke snorted. "I'm not having any problem," he said.

"They won't let you escape," Stumpf said. "None of us'll escape. Not unless we make amends."

"You've got to vacate the room," Locke said, unwilling to countenance any more of this drivel. "I've been told you've got to get out by morning."

"No," said Stumpf, "I can't leave. I can't leave."

"There's nothing to fear."

"The dust," said the German. "The dust in the air. It'll cut me up. I got a speck in my eye—just a *speck*—and the next thing my eye's bleeding as though it'll never stop. I can't hardly lie down, the sheet's like a bed of nails. The soles of my feet feel as if they're going to split. You've got to help me."

"How?" said Locke.

"Pay them for the room. Pay them so I can stay till you can get a specialist from São Luís. Then go back to the village, Locke. Go back and tell them. I don't want the land. Tell them I don't own it any longer."

"I'll go back," said Locke, "but in my good time."

"You must go *quickly*," said Stumpf. "Tell them to let me be."

Suddenly, the expression on the partially masked face changed, and Stumpf looked past Locke at some spectacle down the corridor. From his mouth, slack with fear, came the small word, "Please."

Locke, mystified by the man's expression, turned. The corridor was empty except for the fat moths that were besetting the bulb. "There's nothing there," he said, turning back to the door of Stumpf's room. The wire-mesh glass of the window bore the distinct imprint of two bloody palms.

"He's here," the German was saying, staring fixedly at the miracle of the bleeding glass. Locke didn't need to ask who. He raised his hand to touch the marks. The handprints, still wet, were on *his* side of the glass, not on Stumpf's.

"My God," he breathed. How could anyone have slipped between him and the door and laid the prints there, sliding away again in the brief moment it had taken him to glance behind him? It defied reason. Again he looked back down the corridor. It was still bereft of visitors. Just the bulb—swinging slightly, as if a breeze of passage had caught it—and the moths' wings, whispering. "What's happening?" Locke breathed.

Stumpf, entranced by the handprints, touched his fingertips lightly to the glass. On contact, his fingers blossomed blood, trails of which idled down the glass. He didn't remove his fingers, but stared through at Locke with despair in his eye.

"See?" he said, very quietly.

"What are you playing at?" Locke said, his voice similarly hushed. "This is some kind of trick."

"No."

"You haven't got Cherrick's disease. You can't have. You didn't touch them. We *agreed*, damn you," he said, more heatedly. "Cherrick touched them, *we didn't*."

Stumpf looked back at Locke with something close to pity on his face.

"We were wrong," he said gently. His fingers, which he had now removed from the glass, continued to bleed, dribbling across the backs of his hands and down his arms. "This isn't something you can beat into submission, Locke. It's out of our hands." He raised his bloody fingers, smiling at his own wordplay: "See?" he said.

The German's sudden, fatalistic calm frightened Locke. He reached for the handle of the door and jiggled it. The room was locked. The key was on the inside, where Stumpf had paid for it to be.

"Keep out," Stumpf said. "Keep away from me."

His smile had vanished. Locke put his shoulder to the door.

"Keep out, I said," Stumpf shouted, his voice shrill. He backed away from the door as Locke took another lunge at it. Then, seeing that the lock must soon give, he raised a cry of alarm. Locke took no notice, but continued to throw himself at the door. There came the sound of wood beginning to splinter.

Somewhere nearby, Locke heard a woman's voice, raised in response to Stumpf's calls. No matter; he'd have his hands on the German before help could come, and then, by Christ, he'd wipe every last vestige of a smile from the bastard's lips. He threw himself against the door with increased fervor; again, and again. The door gave.

In the antiseptic cocoon of his room, Stumpf felt the first blast of unclean air from the outside world. It was no more than a light breeze that invaded his makeshift sanctuary, but it bore upon its back the debris of the world. Soot and seeds, flakes of skin itched off a thousand scalps, fluff and sand and twists of hair, the bright dust from a moth's wing. Motes so small the human eye only glimpsed them in a shaft of white sunlight, each a tiny, whirling speck quite harmless to most living organisms. But this cloud was lethal to Stumpf; in seconds his body became a field of tiny, seeping wounds.

He screeched, and ran toward the door to slam it closed again, flinging himself into a hail of minute razors, each lacerating him. Pressing against the door to prevent Locke from entering, his wounded hands erupted. He was too late to keep Locke out anyhow. The man had

pushed the door wide, and was now stepping through, his every movement setting up further currents of air to cut Stumpf down. He snatched
hold of the German's wrist. At his grip the skin opened as if beneath a
knife.

Behind him, a woman loosed a cry of horror. Locke, realizing that
Stumpf was past recanting his laughter, let the man go. Adorned with
cuts on every exposed part of his body, and gaining more by the moment,
Stumpf stumbled back, blind, and fell beside the bed. The killing air still
sliced him as he sank down; with each agonized shudder he woke new
eddies and whirlpools to open him up.

Ashen, Locke retreated from where the body lay, and staggered out
into the corridor. A gaggle of onlookers blocked it; they parted, however,
at his approach, too intimidated by his bulk and by the wild look on his
face to challenge him. He retraced his steps through the sickness-
perfumed maze, crossing the small courtyard and returning into the main
building. He briefly caught sight of Edson Costa hurrying in pursuit, but
did not linger for explanations.

In the vestibule, which despite the late hour was busy with victims of
one kind or another, his harried gaze alighted on a small boy perched on
his mother's lap. He had injured his belly, apparently. His shirt, which
was too large for him, was stained with blood, his face with tears. The
mother did not look up as Locke moved through the throng. The child
did, however. He raised his head as if knowing that Locke was about to
pass by, and smiled radiantly.

There was nobody Locke knew at Tetelman's store; and all the information he could bully from the hired hands, most of whom were drunk to
the point of being unable to stand, was that their masters had gone off
into the jungle the previous day. Locke chased the most sober of them
and persuaded him with threats to accompany him back to the village as
translator. He had no real idea of how he would make his peace with the
tribe. He was only certain that he had to argue his innocence. After all,
he would plead, it hadn't been *he* who had fired the killing shot. There
had been misunderstandings, to be certain, but he had not harmed the
people in any way. How could they, in all conscience, conspire to hurt
him? If they should require some penance of him he was not above
acceding to their demands. Indeed, might there not be some satisfaction
in the act? He had seen so much suffering of late. He wanted to be

cleansed of it. Anything they asked, within reason, he would comply with, anything to avoid dying like the others. He'd even give back the land.

It was a rough ride, and his morose companion complained often and incoherently. Locke turned a deaf ear. There was no time for loitering. Their noisy progress, the Jeep engine complaining at every new acrobatic required of it, brought the jungle alive on every side, a repertoire of wails, whoops, and screeches. It was an urgent, hungry place, Locke thought: and for the first time since setting foot on this subcontinent he loathed it with all his heart. There was no room here to make sense of events; the best that could be hoped was that one be allowed a niche to breathe awhile between one squalid flowering and the next.

Half an hour before nightfall, exhausted by the journey, they came to the outskirts of the village. The place had altered not at all in the meager days since he'd last been here, but the ring of huts was clearly deserted. The doors gaped; the communal fires, always alight, were ashes. There was neither child nor pig to turn an eye toward him as he moved across the compound. When he reached the center of the ring he stood still, looking about him for some clue as to what had happened there. He found none, however. Fatigue made him foolhardy. Mustering his fractured strength, he shouted into the hush:

"Where are you?"

Two brilliant red macaws, finger-winged, rose screeching from the trees on the far side of the village. A few moments after, a figure emerged from the thickest of balsa and jacaranda. It was not one of the tribe, but Dancy. He paused before stepping fully into sight, then, as he recognized Locke, a broad smile broke his face, and he advanced into the compound. Behind him the foliage shook as others made their way through it. Tetelman was there, as were several Norwegians, led by a man called Bjørnstrøm, whom Locke had encountered briefly at the trading post. His face, beneath a shock of sun-bleached hair, was like cooked lobster.

"My God," said Tetelman, "what are you doing here?"

"I might ask you the same question," Locke replied testily.

Bjørnstrøm waved down the raised rifles of his three companions and strode forward, bearing a placatory smile.

"Mr. Locke," the Norwegian said, extending a leather-gloved hand, "it is good we meet."

Locke looked down at the stained glove with disgust, and

Bjørnstrøm, flashing a self-admonishing look, pulled it off. The hand beneath was pristine.

"My apologies," he said. "We've been working."

"At what?" Locke asked, the acid in his stomach edging its way up into the back of his throat.

Tetelman spat. "Indians," he said.

"Where's the tribe?" Locke said.

Again, Tetelman: "Bjørnstrøm claims he's got rights to this territory ..."

"The tribe," Locke insisted, "where are they?"

The Norwegian toyed with his glove.

"Did you buy them out, or what?" Locke asked.

"Not exactly," Bjørnstrøm replied. His English, like his profile, was impeccable.

"Bring him along," Dancy suggested with some enthusiasm. "Let him see for himself."

Bjørnstrøm nodded. "Why not?" he said. "Don't touch anything, Mr. Locke. And tell your carrier to stay where he is."

Dancy had already about turned, and was heading into the thicket; now Bjørnstrøm did the same, escorting Locke across the compound toward a corridor hacked through the heavy foliage. Locke could scarcely keep pace; his limbs were more reluctant with every step he took. The ground had been heavily trodden along this track. A litter of leaves and orchid blossoms had been mashed into the sodden soil.

They had dug a pit in a small clearing no more than a hundred yards from the compound. It was not deep, this pit, nor was it very large. The mingled smells of lime and petrol canceled out any other scent.

Tetelman, who had reached the clearing ahead of Locke, hung back from approaching the lip of the earthworks, but Dancy was not so fastidious. He strode around the far side of the pit and beckoned to Locke to view the contents.

The tribe were putrefying already. They lay where they had been thrown, in a jumble of breasts and buttocks and faces and limbs, their bodies tinged here and there with purple and black. Flies built helter-skelters in the air above them.

"An education," Dancy commented.

Locke just looked on as Bjørnstrøm moved around the other side of the pit to join Dancy.

"All of them?" Locke asked.

The Norwegian nodded. "One fell swoop," he said, pronouncing each word with unsettling precision.

"Blankets," said Tetelman, naming the murder weapon.

"But so quickly . . ." Locke murmured.

"It's very efficient," said Dancy. "And difficult to prove. Even if anybody ever asks."

"Disease is natural," Bjørnstrøm observed. "Yes? Like the trees."

Locke slowly shook his head, his eyes pricking.

"I hear good things of you," Bjørnstrøm said to him. "Perhaps we can work together."

Locke didn't even attempt to reply. Others of the Norwegian party had laid down their rifles and were now getting back to work, moving the few bodies still to be pitched among their fellows from the forlorn heap beside the pit. Locke could see a child among the tangle, and an old man, whom even now the burial party was picking up. The corpse looked jointless as they swung it over the edge of the hole. It tumbled down the shallow incline and came to rest faceup, its arms flung up to either side of its head in a gesture of submission, or expulsion. It was the elder of course, whom Cherrick had faced. His palms were still red. There was a neat bullet-hole in his temple. Disease and hopelessness had not been entirely efficient, apparently.

Locke watched while the next of the bodies was thrown into the mass grave, and a third to follow that.

Bjørnstrøm, lingering on the far side of the pit, was lighting a cigarette. He caught Locke's eye.

"So it goes," he said.

From behind Locke, Tetelman spoke.

"We thought you wouldn't come back," he said, perhaps attempting to excuse his alliance with Bjørnstrøm.

"Stumpf is dead," said Locke.

"Well, even less to divide up," Tetelman said, approaching him and laying a hand on his shoulder. Locke didn't reply; he just stared down among the bodies, which were now being covered with lime, only slowly registering the warmth that was running down his body from the spot where Tetelman had touched him. Disgusted, the man had removed his hand, and was staring at the growing bloodstain on Locke's shirt.

TWILIGHT AT THE TOWERS

The photographs of Mironenko which Ballard had been shown in Munich had proved far from instructive. Only one or two pictured the KGB man full face; and of the others most were blurred and grainy, betraying their furtive origins. Ballard was not overmuch concerned. He knew from long and occasionally bitter experience that the eye was all too ready to be deceived; but there were other faculties—the remnants of senses modern life had rendered obsolete—which he had learned to call into play, enabling him to sniff out the least signs of betrayal. These were the talents he would use when he met with Mironenko. With them, he would root the truth from the man.

The truth? Therein lay the conundrum, of course, for in this context wasn't sincerity a movable feast? Sergei Zakharovich Mironenko had been a section leader in Directorate S of the KGB for eleven years, with access to the most privileged information on the dispersal of Soviet illegals in the West. In the recent weeks, however, he had made his disenchantment with his present masters, and his consequent desire to defect, known to the British Security Service. In return for the elaborate efforts which would have to be made on his behalf he had volunteered to act as an agent within the KGB for a period of three months, after which time he would be taken into the bosom of democracy and hidden where his vengeful overlords would never find him. It had fallen to Ballard to meet the Russian face-to-face, in the hope of establishing whether Mironenko's disaffection from his ideology was real or faked. The answer would not be found on Mironenko's lips, Ballard knew, but in some behavioral nuance which only instinct would comprehend.

Time was when Ballard would have found the puzzle fascinating, that his every waking thought would have circled on the unraveling ahead. But such commitment had belonged to a man convinced his actions had some significant effect upon the world. He was wiser now. The agents of East and West went about their secret works year in, year out. They plotted, they connived, occasionally (though rarely) they shed blood. There were debacles and trade-offs and minor tactical victories. But in the end things were much the same as ever.

This city, for instance. Ballard had first come to Berlin in April of 1969. He'd been twenty-nine, fresh from years of intensive training, and ready to live a little. But he had not felt easy here. He found the city charmless, often bleak. It had taken Odell, his colleague for those first two years, to prove that Berlin was worthy of his affections, and once Ballard fell he was lost for life. Now he felt more at home in this divided city than he ever had in London. Its unease, its failed idealism, and—perhaps most acutely of all—its terrible isolation, matched his. He and it, maintaining a presence in a wasteland of dead ambition.

He found Mironenko at the Gemäldegalerie, and yes, the photographs *had* lied. The Russian looked older than his forty-six years, and sicker than he'd appeared in those filched portraits. Neither man made any sign of acknowledgment. They idled through the collection for a full half hour, with Mironenko showing acute, and apparently genuine interest in the work on view. Only when both men were satisfied that they were not being watched did the Russian quit the building and lead Ballard into the polite suburbs of Dahlem to a mutually agreed safe house. There, in a small and unheated kitchen, they sat down and talked.

Mironenko's command of English was uncertain, or at least appeared so, though Ballard had the impression that his struggles for sense were as much tactical as grammatical. He might well have presented the same facade in the Russian's situation; it seldom hurt to appear less competent than one was. But despite the difficulties he had in expressing himself, Mironenko's avowals were unequivocal.

"I am no longer a Communist," he stated plainly. "I have not been a party member—not *here*"—he put his fist to his chest—"for many years."

He fetched an off-white handkerchief from his coat pocket, pulled off one of his gloves, and plucked a bottle of tablets from the folds of the handkerchief.

"Forgive me," he said as he shook tablets from the bottle, "I have pains. In my head, in my hands."

Ballard waited until he had swallowed the medication before asking him, "Why did you begin to doubt?"

The Russian pocketed the bottle and the handkerchief, his wide face devoid of expression.

"How does a man lose his . . . his faith?" he said. "Is it that I saw too much, or too little, perhaps?"

He looked at Ballard's face to see if his hesitant words had made sense. Finding no comprehension there he tried again.

"I think the man who does not believe he is lost, is lost."

The paradox was elegantly put; Ballard's suspicion as to Mironenko's true command of English was confirmed.

"Are you lost *now*?" Ballard inquired.

Mironenko didn't reply. He was pulling his other glove off and staring at his hands. The pills he had swallowed did not seem to be easing the ache he had complained of. He fisted and unfisted his hands like an arthritis sufferer testing the advance of his condition. Not looking up, he said:

"I was taught that the Party had solutions to everything. That made me free from fear."

"And now?"

"Now?" he said. "Now I have strange thoughts. They come to me from nowhere . . ."

"Go on," said Ballard.

Mironenko made a tight smile. "You must know me inside out, yes? Even what I dream?"

"Yes," said Ballard.

Mironenko nodded. "It would be the same with us," he said. Then, after a pause: "I've thought sometimes I would break open. Do you understand what I say? I would crack, because there is such rage inside me. And that makes me afraid, Ballard. I think they will see how much I hate them." He looked up at his interrogator. "You must be quick," he said, "or they will discover me. I try not to think of what they will do." Again, he paused. All trace of the smile, however humorless, had gone. "The Directorate has sections even I don't have knowledge of. Special hospitals, where nobody can go. They have ways to break a man's soul in pieces."

Ballard, ever the pragmatist, wondered if Mironenko's vocabulary wasn't rather high-flown. In the hands of the KGB he doubted if he would be thinking of his *soul's* contentment. After all, it was the body that had the nerve endings.

They talked for an hour or more, the conversation moving back and forth between politics and personal reminiscence, between trivia and confessional. At the end of the meeting Ballard was in no doubt as to Mironenko's antipathy to his masters. He was, as he had said, a man without faith.

The following day Ballard met with Cripps in the restaurant at the Schweizerhof Hotel, and made his verbal report on Mironenko.

"He's ready and waiting. But he insists we be quick about making up our minds."

"I'm sure he does," Cripps said. His glass eye was troubling him today; the chilly air, he explained, made it sluggish. It moved fractionally more slowly than his real eye, and on occasion Cripps had to nudge it with his fingertip to get it moving.

"We're not going to be rushed into any decision," Cripps said.

"Where's the problem? I don't have any doubt about his commitment, or his desperation."

"So you said," Cripps replied. "Would you like something for dessert?"

"Do you doubt my appraisal? Is that what it is?"

"Have something sweet to finish off, so that I don't feel an utter reprobate."

"You think I'm wrong about him, don't you?" Ballard pressed. When Cripps didn't reply, Ballard leaned across the table. "You do, don't you?"

"I'm just saying there's reason for caution," Cripps said. "If we finally choose to take him on board the Russians are going to be very distressed. We have to be sure the deal's worth the bad weather that comes with it. Things are so dicey at the moment."

"When aren't they?" Ballard replied. "Tell me a time when there wasn't some crisis in the offing?" He settled back in the chair and tried to read Cripps's face. His glass eye was, if anything, more candid than the real one.

"I'm sick of this damn game," Ballard muttered.

The glass eye roved. "Because of the Russian?"

"Maybe."

"Believe me," said Cripps, "I've got good reason to be careful with this man."

"Name one."

"There's nothing verified."

"What have you got on him?" Ballard insisted.

"As I say, rumor," Cripps replied.

"Why wasn't I briefed about it?"

Cripps made a tiny shake of his head. "It's academic now," he said. "You've provided a good report. I just want you to understand that if things don't go the way you think they should it's not because your appraisals aren't trusted."

"I see."

"No you don't," said Cripps. "You're feeling martyred, and I don't altogether blame you."

"So what happens now? I'm supposed to forget I ever met the man?"

"Wouldn't do any harm," said Cripps. "Out of sight, out of mind."

Clearly Cripps didn't trust Ballard to take his own advice. Though Ballard made several discreet inquiries about the Mironenko case in the following week, it was plain that his usual circle of contacts had been warned to keep their lips sealed.

As it was , the next news about the case reached Ballard via the pages of the morning papers, in an article about a body found in a house near the station on Kaiser Damm. At the time of reading he had no way of knowing how the account tied up with Mironenko, but there was enough detail in the story to arouse his interest. For one, he had the suspicion that the house named in the article had been used by the Service on occasion; for another, the article described how two unidentified men had almost been caught in the act of removing the body, further suggesting that this was no crime of passion.

About noon, he went to see Cripps at his offices in the hope of coaxing him with some explanation, but Cripps was not available, nor would he be, his secretary explained, until further notice; matters arising had taken him back to Munich. Ballard left a message that he wished to speak with him when he returned.

As he stepped into the cold air again, he realized that he'd gained an admirer, a thin-faced individual whose hair had retreated from his brow, leaving a ludicrous forelock at the high-water mark. Ballard knew him in passing from Cripps's entourage but couldn't put a name to the face. It was swiftly provided.

"Suckling," the man said.

"Of course," said Ballard. "Hello."

"I think maybe we should talk, if you have a moment," the man said. His voice was as pinched as his features; Ballard wanted none of his gossip. He was about to refuse the offer when Suckling said, "I suppose you heard what happened to Cripps."

Ballard shook his head. Suckling, delighted to possess this nugget, said again, "We should talk."

They walked along the Kantstrasse toward the zoo. The street was busy with lunchtime pedestrians, but Ballard scarcely noticed them. The story that Suckling unfolded as they walked demanded his full and absolute attention.

It was simply told. Cripps, it appeared, had made an arrangement to meet with Mironenko in order to make his own assessment of the Russian's integrity. The house in Schönberg chosen for the meeting had been used on several previous occasions, and had long been considered one of the safest locations in the city. It had not proved so the previous evening, however. KGB men had apparently followed Mironenko to the house, and then attempted to break the party up. There was nobody to testify to what had happened subsequently—both the men who had accompanied Cripps, one of them Ballard's old colleague Odell—were dead; Cripps himself was in a coma.

"And Mironenko?" Ballard inquired.

Suckling shrugged. "They took him home to the Motherland, presumably," he said.

Ballard caught a whiff of deceit off the man.

"I'm touched that you're keeping me up to date," he said to Suckling. "But *why*?"

"You and Odell were friends, weren't you?" came the reply. "With Cripps out of the picture you don't have many of those left."

"Is that so?"

"No offense intended," Suckling said hurriedly, "but you've got a reputation as a maverick."

"Get to the point," Suckling protested. "I just thought you ought to know what had happened. I'm putting my neck on the line here."

"Nice try," said Ballard. He stopped walking. Suckling wandered on a pace or two before turning to find Ballard grinning at him.

"Who sent you?"

"Nobody sent me," Suckling said.

"Clever to send the court gossip. I almost fell for it. You're very plausible."

There wasn't enough fat on Suckling's face to hide the tic in his cheek.

"What do they suspect me of? Do they think I'm conniving with Mironenko, is that it? No, I don't think they're that stupid."

Suckling shook his head, like a doctor in the presence of some incurable disease. "You like making enemies?" he said.

"Occupational hazard. I wouldn't lose any sleep over it. I don't."

"There's changes in the air," Suckling said. "I'd make sure you have your answers ready."

"Fuck the answers," Ballard said courteously. "I think it's about time I worked out the right questions."

Sending Suckling to sound him out smacked of desperation. They wanted inside information, but about what? Could they seriously believe he had some involvement with Mironenko, or worse, with the KGB itself? He let his resentment subside; it was stirring up too much mud, and he needed clear water if he was to find his way free of this confusion. In one regard, Suckling was perfectly correct: he *did* have enemies, and with Cripps indisposed he was vulnerable. In such circumstances there were two courses of action. He could return to London, and there lie low, or wait around in Berlin to see what maneuver they tried next. He decided on the latter. The charm of hide-and-seek was rapidly wearing thin.

As he turned north onto Leibnizstrasse he caught the reflection of a gray-coated man in a shop window. It was a glimpse, no more, but he had the feeling that he knew the fellow's face. Had they put a watchdog onto him? he wondered. He turned, and caught the man's eye, holding it. The suspect seemed embarrassed, and looked away. A performance perhaps, and then again, perhaps not. It mattered little, Ballard thought. Let them watch him all they liked. He was guiltless. If indeed there was such a condition this side of insanity.

A strange happiness had found Sergei Mironenko, happiness that came without rhyme or reason, and filled his heart up to overflowing.

Only the previous day circumstances had seemed unendurable. The aching in his hands and head and spine had steadily worsened, and was now accompanied by an itch so demanding he'd had to snip his nails to the flesh to prevent himself doing serious damage. His body, he had concluded, was in revolt against him. It was that thought which he had tried to explain to Ballard: that he was divided from himself, and feared that he would soon be torn apart. But today the fear had gone.

Not so the pains. They were, if anything, worse than they'd been yesterday. His sinews and ligaments ached as if they'd been exercised beyond the limits of their design; there were bruises at all his joints, where blood had broken its banks beneath the skin. But that sense of imminent rebellion had disappeared, to be replaced with a dreamy peacefulness. And at its heart, such happiness.

When he tried to think back over recent events, to work out what had cued this transformation, his memory played tricks. He had been called to meet with Ballard's superior; *that* he remembered. Whether he had gone to the meeting, he did not. The night was a blank.

Ballard would know how things stood, he reasoned. He had liked and trusted the Englishman from the beginning, sensing that despite the many differences between them they were more alike than not. If he let his instinct lead, he would find Ballard, of that he was certain. No doubt the Englishman would be surprised to see him, even angered at first. But when he told Ballard of this newfound happiness surely his trespasses would be forgiven?

Ballard dined late, and drank until later still in The Ring, a small transvestite bar he had been first taken to by Odell almost two decades ago. No doubt his guide's intention had been to prove his sophistication by showing his raw colleague the decadence of Berlin, but Ballard, though he never felt any sexual frisson in the company of The Ring's clientele, had immediately felt at home here. His neutrality was respected; no attempts were made to solicit him. He was simply left to drink and watch the passing parade of genders.

Coming here tonight raised the ghost of Odell, whose name would now be scrubbed from conversation because of his involvement with the Mironenko affair. Ballard had seen this process at work before. History did not forgive failure, unless it was so profound as to achieve a kind of grandeur. For the Odells of the world—ambitious men who had found themselves through little fault of their own in a cul-de-sac from which all retreat was barred—for such men there would be no fine words spoken nor medals struck. There would only be oblivion.

It made him melancholy to think of this, and he drank heavily to keep his thoughts mellow, but when—at two in the morning—he stepped out onto the street, his depression was only marginally dulled. The good burghers of Berlin were well abed; tomorrow was another working day. Only the sound of traffic from the Kurfürstendamm offered sign of life somewhere near. He made his way toward it, his thoughts fleecy.

Behind him, laughter. A young man—glamorously dressed as a starlet—tottered along the pavement arm in arm with his unsmiling escort. Ballard recognized the transvestite as a regular at the bar; the client, to judge by his sober suit, was an out-of-towner slaking his thirst for boys dressed as girls behind his wife's back. Ballard picked up his pace. The young man's laughter, its musicality patently forced, set his teeth on edge.

He heard somebody running nearby, caught a shadow moving out of the corner of his eye. His watchdog, most likely. Though alcohol had blurred his instincts, he felt some anxiety surface, the root of which he couldn't fix. He walked on. Featherlight tremors ran in his scalp.

A few yards on, he realized that the laughter from the street behind him had ceased. He glanced over his shoulder, half-expecting to see the boy and his customer embracing. But both had disappeared, slipped off down one of the alleyways, no doubt, to conclude their contract in darkness. Somewhere near, a dog had begun to bark wildly. Ballard turned round to look back the way he'd come, daring the deserted street to display its secrets to him. Whatever was arousing the buzz in his head and the itch on his palms, it was no commonplace anxiety. There was something wrong with the street, despite its show of innocence; it hid terrors.

The bright lights of the Kurfürstendamm were no more than three minutes' walk away, but he didn't want to turn his back on this mystery and take refuge there. Instead he proceeded to walk back the way he'd come, slowly. The dog had now ceased its alarm, and settled into silence; he had only his footsteps for company.

He reached the corner of the first alleyway and peered down it. No light burned at window or doorway. He could sense no living presence in the gloom. He crossed over the alley and walked on to the next. A luxurious stench had crept into the air, which became more lavish yet as he approached the corner. As he breathed it in, the buzz in his head deepened to a threat of thunder.

A single light flickered in the throat of the alley, a meager wash from an upper window. By it, he saw the body of the out-of-towner lying sprawled on the ground. He had been so traumatically mutilated it seemed an attempt might have been made to turn him inside out. From the spilled innards, that ripe smell rose in all its complexity.

Ballard had seen violent death before, and thought himself indifferent to the spectacle. But something here in the alley threw his calm into disarray. He felt his limbs begin to shake. And then, from beyond the throw of light, the boy spoke.

"In God's name . . ." he said. His voice had lost all pretension to femininity; it was a murmur of undisguised terror.

Ballard took a step down the alley. Neither the boy, nor the reason for his whispered prayer, became visible until he had advanced ten yards. The boy was half-slumped against the wall among the refuse. His sequins and taffeta had been ripped from him; the body was pale and sexless. He seemed not to notice Ballard: his eyes were fixed on the deepest shadows.

The shaking in Ballard's limbs worsened as he followed the boy's gaze; it was all he could do to prevent his teeth from chattering. Nevertheless he continued his advance, not for the boy's sake (heroism had little merit, he'd always been taught) but because he was curious, more than curious, *eager,* to see what manner of man was capable of such casual violence. To look into the eyes of such ferocity seemed at that moment the most important thing in all the world.

Now the boy saw him, and muttered a pitiful appeal, but Ballard scarcely heard it. He felt other eyes upon him, and their touch was like a blow. The din in his head took on a sickening rhythm, like the sound of helicopter rotors. In mere seconds it mounted to a blinding roar.

Ballard pressed his hands to his eyes, and stumbled back against the wall, dimly aware that the killer was moving out of hiding (refuse was overturned) and making his escape. He felt something brush against him, and opened his eyes in time to glimpse the man slipping away down the passageway. He seemed somehow misshapen, his back crooked, his head too large. Ballard loosed a shout after him, but the berserker ran on, pausing only to look down at the body before racing toward the street.

Ballard heaved himself from the wall and stood upright. The noise in his head was diminishing somewhat; the attendant giddiness was passing.

Behind him, the boy had begun sobbing. "Did you see?" he said. "Did you *see?*"

"Who was it? Somebody you knew?"

The boy stared at Ballard like a frightened doe, his mascaraed eyes huge.

"Somebody . . . ?" he said.

Ballard was about to repeat the question when there came a shriek of brakes, swiftly followed by the sound of the impact. Leaving the boy to pull his tattered trousseau about him, Ballard went back into the street. Voices were raised nearby; he hurried to their source. A large car was straddling the pavement, its headlights blazing. The driver was being helped from his seat, while his passengers—partygoers, to judge by their dress and drink-flushed faces—stood and debated furiously as to how the accident had happened. One of the women was talking about an animal in the road, but another of the passengers corrected her. The body that lay in the gutter where it had been thrown was not that of an animal.

Ballard had seen little of the killer in the alleyway but he knew instinctively that this was he. There was no sign of the malformation he thought he'd glimpsed, however, just a man dressed in a suit that had seen better days, lying facedown in a patch of blood. The police had already arrived, and an officer shouted to him to stand away from the body, but Ballard ignored the instruction and went to steal a look at the dead man's face. There was nothing there of the ferocity he had hoped so much to see. But there was much he recognized nevertheless.

The man was Odell.

He told the officers that he had seen nothing of the accident, which was essentially true, and made his escape from the scene before events in the adjacent alley were discovered.

It seemed every corner turned on his route back to his rooms brought a fresh question. Chief among them: why had he been lied to about Odell's death, and what psychosis had seized the man that made him capable of the slaughter Ballard had witnessed? He would not get the answers to these questions from his sometime colleagues, that he knew. The only man whom he might have beguiled an answer from was Cripps. He remembered the debate they'd had about Mironenko, and Cripps's talk of "reasons for caution" when dealing with the Russian. The Glass Eye had known then that there was something in the wind, though surely even he had not envisaged the scale of the present disaster. Two highly valued agents murdered, Mironenko missing, presumed dead, he himself—if Suckling was to be believed—at death's door. And all this begun with Sergei Zakharovich Mironenko, the lost man of Berlin. It seemed his tragedy was infectious.

Tomorrow, Ballard decided, he would find Suckling and squeeze some answers from him. In the meantime, his head and his hands ached, and he wanted sleep. Fatigue compromised sound judgment, and if ever he needed that faculty it was now. But despite his exhaustion, sleep eluded him for an hour or more, and when it came it was no comfort. He dreamt whispers, and hard upon them, rising as if to drown them out, the roar of the helicopters. Twice he surfaced from sleep with his head pounding; twice a hunger to understand what the whispers were telling him drove him to the pillow again. When he woke for the third time, the noise between his temples had become crippling, a thought-canceling assault which made him fear for his sanity. Barely able to see the room through the pain, he crawled from his bed.

"Please . . ." he murmured, as if there were somebody to help him from his misery.

A cool voice answered him out of the darkness:

"What do you want?"

He didn't question the questioner, merely said:

"Take the pain away."

"You can do that for yourself," the voice told him.

He leaned against the wall, nursing his splitting head, tears of agony coming and coming. "I don't know *how,*" he said.

"Your dreams give you pain," the voice replied, *"so you must forget them. Do you understand? Forget them, and the pain will go."*

He understood the instruction, but not how to realize it. He had no powers of government in sleep. He was the object of these whispers, not they his. But the voice insisted.

"The dream means you harm, Ballard. You must bury it. Bury it deep."

"Bury it?"

"Make an image of it, Ballard. Picture it in detail."

He did as he was told. He imagined a burial party, and a box, and in the box, this dream. He made them dig deep, as the voice instructed him, so that he would never be able to disinter this hurtful thing again. But even as he imagined the box lowered into the pit, he heard its boards creak. The dream would not lie down. It beat against confinement. The boards began to break.

"Quickly!" the voice said.

The din of the rotors had risen to a terrifying pitch. Blood had begun to pour from his nostrils; he tasted salt at the back of his throat.

"Finish it!" the voice yelled above the tumult. *"Cover it up!"*

Ballard looked into the grave. The box was thrashing from side to side.

"Cover it, damn you!"

He tried to make the burial party obey, tried to will them to pick up their shovels and bury the offending thing alive, but they would not. Instead they gazed into the grave as he did and watched as the contents of the box fought for light.

"No!" the voice demanded, its fury mounting. *"You must not look!"*

The box danced in the hole. The lid splintered. Briefly, Ballard glimpsed something shining up between the boards.

"It will kill you!" the voice said, and as if to prove its point the volume of the sound rose beyond the point of endurance, washing out burial party, box and all in a blaze of pain. Suddenly it seemed that what the voice said was true, that he was near to death. But it wasn't the dream that was conspiring to kill him, but the sentinel they had posted between him and it: this skull-splintering cacophony.

Only now did he realize that he'd fallen on the floor, prostrate beneath this assault. Reaching out blindly he found the wall, and hauled himself toward it, the machines still thundering behind his eyes, the blood hot on his face.

He stood up as best he could and began to move toward the bathroom. Behind him the voice, its tantrum controlled, began its exhortation afresh. It sounded so intimate that he looked round, fully expecting to see the speaker, and he was not disappointed. For a few flickering moments he seemed to be standing in a small, windowless room, its walls painted a uniform white. The light here was bright and dead, and in the center of the room stood the face behind the voice, smiling.

"Your dreams give you pain," he said. This was the first commandment again. *"Bury them, Ballard, and the pain will pass."*

Ballard wept like a child; this scrutiny shamed him. He looked away from his tutor to bury his tears.

"Trust us," another voice said, close by. *"We're your friends."*

He didn't trust their fine words. The very pain they claimed to want to save him from was of their making; it was a stick to beat him with if the dreams came calling.

"We want to help you," one or other of them said.

"No . . ." he murmured. "No damn you . . . I don't . . . I don't believe . . ."

The room flickered out, and he was in the bedroom again, clinging to the wall like a climber to a cliff face. Before they could come for him with more words, more pain, he edged his way to the bathroom door, and stumbled blindly toward the shower. There was a moment of panic while he located the taps, and then the water came on at a rush. It was bitterly cold, but he put his head beneath it, while the onslaught of rotor blades tried to shake the plates of his skull apart. Icy water trekked down his back, but he let the rain come down on him in a torrent, and by degrees, the helicopters took their leave. He didn't move, though his body juddered with cold, until the last of them had gone; then he sat on the edge of the bath, mopping water from his neck and face and body, and eventually, when his legs felt courageous enough, made his way back into the bedroom.

He lay down on the same crumpled sheets in much the same position as he'd lain in before, yet nothing *was* the same. He didn't know what had changed in him, or how. But he lay there without sleep disturbing his serenity through the remaining hours of the night, trying to puzzle it out, and a little before dawn he remembered the words he had muttered in the face of the delusion. Simple words, but oh, their power.

"I don't believe . . ." he said, and the commandments trembled.

It was half an hour before noon when he arrived at the small book-exporting firm which served Suckling for cover. He felt quick-witted, despite the disturbance of the night, and rapidly charmed his way past the receptionist and entered Suckling's office unannounced. When Suckling's eyes settled on his visitor he started from his desk as if fired upon.

"Good morning," said Ballard. "I thought it was time we talked."

Suckling's eyes fled to the office door, which Ballard had left ajar.

"Sorry, is there a draft?" Ballard closed the door gently. "I want to see Cripps," he said.

Suckling waded through the sea of books and manuscripts that threatened to engulf his desk. "Are you out of your mind, coming back here?"

"Tell them I'm a friend of the family," Ballard offered.

"I can't believe you'd be so stupid."

"Just point me to Cripps, and I'll be away."

Suckling ignored him in favor of his tirade. "It's taken two years to establish my credentials here."

Ballard laughed.

"I'm going to report this, damn you!"

"I think you should," said Ballard, turning up the volume. "In the meanwhile: *where's Cripps?*"

Suckling, apparently convinced that he was faced with a lunatic, controlled his apoplexy. "All right," he said. "I'll have somebody call on you, take you to him."

"Not good enough," Ballard replied. He crossed to Suckling in two short strides and took hold of him by his lapel. He'd spent at most three hours with Suckling in ten years, but he'd scarcely passed a moment in his presence without itching to do what he was doing now. Knocking the man's hands away, he pushed Suckling against the book-lined wall. A stack of volumes, caught by Suckling's heel, toppled.

"Once more," Ballard said. "The old man."

"Take your fucking hands off me," Suckling said, his fury redoubled at being touched.

"Again," said Ballard. *"Cripps."*

"I'll have you carpeted for this. I'll have you *out!*"

Ballad leaned toward the reddening face, and smiled.

"I'm out anyway. People have died, remember? London needs a sacrificial lamb, and I think I'm it." Suckling's face dropped. "So I've got nothing to lose, have I?" There was no reply. Ballard pressed closer to Suckling, tightening his grip on the man. *"Have I?"*

Suckling's courage failed him. "Cripps is dead," he said.

Ballard didn't release his hold. "You said the same about Odell—" he remarked. At the name, Suckling's eyes widened. "—And I saw him only last night," Ballard said, "out on the town."

"You saw Odell?"

"Oh yes."

Mention of the dead man brought the scene in the alleyway back to mind. The smell of the body, the boy's sobs. There were other faiths, thought Ballard, beyond the one he'd once shared with the creature beneath him. Faiths whose devotions were made in heat and blood, whose dogmas were dreams. Where better to baptize himself into that new faith than here, in the blood of the enemy?

Somewhere, at the very back of his head, he could hear the helicopters, but he wouldn't let them take to the air. He was strong today, his head, his hands, all *strong*. When he drew his nails toward Suckling's eyes the blood came easily. He had a sudden vision of the face beneath the flesh, of Suckling's features stripped to the esssence.

"Sir?"

Ballard glanced over his shoulder. The receptionist was standing at the open door.

"Oh. I'm sorry," she said, preparing to withdraw. To judge by her blushes she assumed this was a lovers' tryst she'd walked in upon.

"*Stay,*" said Suckling. "Mr. Ballard . . . was just leaving."

Ballard released his prey. There would be other opportunities to have Suckling's life.

"I'll see you again," he said.

Suckling drew a handkerchief from his top pocket and pressed it to his face.

"Depend upon it," he replied.

Now they would come for him, he could have no doubt of that. He was a rogue element, and they would strive to silence him as quickly as possible. The thought did not distress him. Whatever they had tried to make him forget with their brainwashing was more ambitious than they had anticipated; however deeply they had taught him to bury it, it was digging its way back to the surface. He couldn't see it yet, but he knew it was near. More than once on his way back to his rooms he imagined eyes at his back. Maybe he was still being tailed, but his instincts informed him otherwise. The presence he felt close by—so near that it was sometimes at his shoulder—was perhaps simply another part of him. He felt protected by it, as by a local god.

He had half expected there to be a reception committee awaiting him at his rooms, but there was nobody. Either Suckling had been obliged to delay his alarm call, or else the upper echelons were still debating their tactics. He pocketed those few keepsakes that he wanted to preserve from their calculating eyes, and left the building again without anyone making a move to stop him.

It felt good to be alive, despite the chill that rendered the grim streets grimmer still. He decided, for no particular reason, to go to the zoo, which, though he had been visiting the city for two decades, he had never done. As he walked, it occurred to him that he'd never been as free as he was now, that he had shed mastery like an old coat. No wonder they feared him. They had good reason.

Kantstrasse was busy, but he cut his way through the pedestrians easily, almost as if they sensed a rare certainty in him and gave him a wide berth. As he approached the entrance to the zoo, however, somebody jostled him. He looked round to upbraid the fellow, but caught only the back of the man's head as he was submerged in the crowd heading onto Hardenbergstrasse. Suspecting an attempted theft, he checked his pockets, to find that a scrap of paper had been slipped into one. He knew better than to examine it on the spot, but casually glanced round again to see if he recognized the courier. The man had already slipped away.

He delayed his visit to the zoo and went instead to the Tiergarten, and there—in the wilds of the great park—found a place to read the message. It was from Mironenko, and it requested a meeting to talk of a matter of considerable urgency, naming a house in Marienfelde as a venue. Ballard memorized the details, then shredded the note.

It was perfectly possible that the invitation was a trap, of course, set either by his own faction or by the opposition. Perhaps a way to test his allegiance, or to manipulate him into a situation in which he could be easily dispatched. Despite such doubts he had no choice but to go, however, in the hope that this blind date was indeed with Mironenko. Whatever dangers this rendezvous brought, they were not so new. Indeed, given his long-held doubts of the efficacy of sight, hadn't every date he'd ever made been in some sense *blind*?

By early evening the damp air was thickening toward a fog, and by the time he stepped off the bus on Hildburghauserstrasse it had a good hold on the city, lending the chill new powers to discomfort.

Ballard went quickly through the quiet streets. He scarcely knew the

district at all, but its proximity to the Wall bled it of what little charm it
might once have possessed. Many of the houses were unoccupied; of
those that were not most were sealed off against the night and the cold
and the lights that glared from the watchtowers. It was only with the aid
of a map that he located the tiny street Mironenko's note had named.

No lights burned in the house. Ballard knocked hard, but there was
no answering footstep in the hall. He had anticipated several possible
scenarios, but an absence of response at the house had not been among
them. He knocked again and again. It was only then that he heard sounds
from within, and finally the door was opened to him. The hallway was
painted gray and brown, and lit only by a bare bulb. The man silhouetted
against this drab interior was not Mironenko.

"Yes?" he said. "What do you want?" His German was spoken with a
distinct Muscovite inflection.

"I'm looking for a friend of mine," Ballard said.

The man, who was almost as broad as the doorway he stood in, shook
his head.

"There's nobody here," he said. "Only me."

"I was told—"

"You must have the wrong house."

No sooner had the doorkeeper made the remark than noise erupted
from down the dreary hallway. Furniture was being overturned; somebody had begun to shout.

The Russian looked over his shoulder and went to slam the door in
Ballard's face, but Ballard's foot was there to stop him. Taking advantage
of the man's divided attention, Ballard put his shoulder to the door, and
pushed. He was in the hallway—indeed he was halfway down it—before
the Russian took a step in pursuit. The sound of demolition had escalated, and was now drowned out by the sound of a man squealing. Ballard
followed the sound past the sovereignty of the lone bulb and into gloom
at the back of the house. He might well have lost his way at that point but
that a door was flung open ahead of him.

The room beyond had scarlet floorboards; they glistened as if freshly
painted. And now the decorator appeared in person. His torso had been
ripped open from neck to navel. He pressed his hands to the breached
dam, but they were useless to stem the flood; his blood came in spurts,
and with it, his innards. He met Ballard's gaze, his eyes full to overflowing with death, but his body had not yet received the instruction to lie

down and die; it juddered on in a pitiful attempt to escape the scene of execution behind him.

The spectacle had brought Ballard to a halt, and the Russian from the door now took hold of him, and pulled him back into the hallway, shouting into his face. The outburst, in panicked Russian, was beyond Ballard, but he needed no translation of the hands that encircled his throat. The Russian was half his weight again, and had the grip of an expert strangler, but Ballard felt effortlessly the man's superior. He wrenched the attacker's hands from his neck, and struck him across the face. It was a fortuitous blow. The Russian fell back against the staircase, his shouts silenced.

Ballard looked back toward the scarlet room. The dead man had gone, though scraps of flesh had been left on the threshold.

From within, laughter.

Ballard turned to the Russian.

"What in God's name's going on?" he demanded, but the other man simply stared through the open door.

Even as he spoke, the laughter stopped. A shadow moved across the blood-splattered wall of the interior, and a voice said:

"Ballard?"

There was a roughness there, as if the speaker had been shouting all day and night, but it was the voice of Mironenko.

"Don't stand out in the cold," he said, "come on in. And bring Solomonov."

The other man made a bid for the front door, but Ballard had hold of him before he could take two steps.

"There's nothing to be afraid of, Comrade," said Mironenko. "The dog's gone." Despite the reassurance, Solomonov began to sob as Ballard pressed him toward the open door.

Mironenko was right: it *was* warmer inside. And there was no sign of a dog. There was blood in abundance, however. The man Ballard had last seen teetering in the doorway had been dragged back into this abattoir while he and Solomonov had struggled. The body had been treated with astonishing barbarity. The head had been smashed open; the innards were a grim litter underfoot.

Squatting in the shadowy corner of this terrible room, Mironenko. He had been mercilessly beaten, to judge by the swelling about his head and upper torso, but his unshaven face bore a smile for his savior.

"I knew you'd come," he said. His gaze fell upon Solomonov. "They followed me," he said. "They meant to kill me, I suppose. Is that what you intended, Comrade?"

Solomonov shook with fear—his eyes flitting from the bruised moon of Mironenko's face to the pieces of gut that lay everywhere about—finding nowhere a place of refuge.

"What stopped them?" Ballard asked.

Mironenko stood up. Even this slow movement caused Solomonov to flinch.

"Tell Mr. Ballard," Mironenko prompted, "tell him what happened." Solomonov was too terrified to speak. "He's KGB, of course," Mironenko explained. "Both trusted men. But not trusted enough to be warned, poor idiots. So they were sent to murder me with just a gun and a prayer." He laughed at the thought. "Neither of which were much use in the circumstances."

"I beg you . . ." Solomonov murmured, ". . . let me go. I'll say nothing."

"You'll say what they want you to say, Comrade, the way we all must," Mironenko replied. "Isn't that right, Ballard? All slaves of our faith?"

Ballard watched Mironenko's face closely; there was a fullness there that could not be entirely explained by the bruising. The skin almost seemed to crawl.

"They have made us forgetful," Mironenko said.

"Of what?" Ballard inquired.

"Of ourselves," came the reply, and with it Mironenko moved from his murky corner and into the light.

What had Solomonov and his dead companion done to him? His flesh was a mass of tiny contusions, and there were bloodied lumps at his neck and temples which Ballard might have taken for bruises but that they palpitated, as if something nested beneath the skin. Mironenko made no sign of discomfort, however, as he reached out to Solomonov. At his touch the failed assassin lost control of his bladder, but Mironenko's intentions were not murderous. With eerie tenderness he stroked a tear from Solomonov's cheek. "Go back to them," he advised the trembling man. "Tell them what you've seen."

Solomonov seemed scarcely to believe his ears, or else suspected— as did Ballard—that this forgiveness was a sham, and that any attempt to leave would invite fatal consequences.

But Mironenko pressed his point. "Go on," he said, "leave us please. Or would you prefer to stay and eat?"

Solomonov took a single, faltering step toward the door. When no blow came he took a second step, and a third, and now he was out of the door and away.

"Tell them!" Mironenko shouted after him. The front door slammed.

"Tell them what?" said Ballard.

"That I've remembered," Mironenko said. "That I've found the skin they stole from me."

For the first time since entering this house, Ballard began to feel queasy. It was not the blood or the bones underfoot, but a look in Mironenko's eyes. He'd seen eyes as bright once before. But where?

"You—" he said quietly, "you did this."

"Certainly," Mironenko replied.

"How?" Ballard said. There was a familiar thunder climbing from the back of his head. He tried to ignore it, and press some explanation from the Russian. "How, damn you?"

"We are the same," Mironenko replied. "I smell it in you."

"No," said Ballard. The clamor was rising.

"The doctrines are just words. It's not what we're taught but what we *know* that matters. In our marrow, in our souls."

He had talked of souls once before, of places his masters had built in which a man could be broken apart. At the time Ballard had thought such talk mere extravagance; now he wasn't so sure. What was the burial party all about, if not the subjugation of some secret part of him? The marrow part, the soul part.

Before Ballard could find the words to express himself, Mironenko froze, his eyes gleaming more brightly than ever.

"They're outside," he said.

"Who are?"

The Russian shrugged. "Does it matter?" he said. "Your side or mine. Either one will silence us if they can."

That much was true.

"We must be quick," he said, and headed for the hallway. The front door stood ajar. Mironenko was there in moments. Ballard followed. Together they slipped out onto the street.

The fog had thickened. It idled around the streetlamps, muddying their light, making every doorway a hiding place. Ballard didn't wait to tempt the pursuers out into the open, but followed Mironenko, who was already well ahead, swift despite his bulk. Ballard had to pick up his pace to keep the man in sight. One moment he was visible, the next the fog closed around him.

The residential property they moved through now gave way to more anonymous buildings, warehouses perhaps, whose walls stretched up into the murky darkness unbroken by windows. Ballard called after him to slow his crippling pace. The Russian halted and turned back to Ballard, his outline wavering in the besieged light. Was it a trick of the fog, or had Mironenko's condition deteriorated in the minutes since they'd left the house? His face seemed to be seeping; the lumps on his neck had swelled further.

"We don't have to run," Ballard said, "they're not following."

"They're always following," Mironenko replied, and as if to give weight to the observation Ballard heard fog-deadened footsteps in a nearby street.

"No time to debate," Mironenko murmured, and turning on his heel, he ran. In seconds, the fog had spirited him away again.

Ballard hesitated another moment. Incautious as it was, he wanted to catch a glimpse of his pursuers so as to know them for the future. But now, as the soft pad of Mironenko's step diminished into silence, he realized that the other footsteps had also ceased. Did they know he was waiting for them? He held his breath, but there was neither sound nor sign of them. The delinquent fog idled on. He seemed to be alone in it. Reluctantly, he gave up waiting and went after the Russian at a run.

A few yards on, the road divided. There was no sign of Mironenko in either direction. Cursing his stupidity in lingering behind, Ballard followed the route which was most heavily shrouded in fog. The street was short, and ended at a wall lined with spikes, beyond which there was a park of some kind. The fog clung more tenaciously to this space of damp earth than it did to the street, and Ballard could see no more than four or five yards across the grass from where he stood. But he knew intuitively that he had chosen the right road, that Mironenko had scaled this wall and was waiting for him somewhere close by. Behind him, the fog kept its counsel. Either their pursuers had lost him, or their way, or both. He hoisted himself up onto the wall, avoiding the spikes by a whisper, and dropped down on the opposite side.

The street had seemed pin-drop quiet, but it clearly wasn't, for it was quieter still inside the park. The fog was chillier here, and pressed more insistently upon him as he advanced across the wet grass. The wall behind him—his only point of anchorage in this wasteland—became a ghost of itself, then faded entirely. Committed now, he walked on a few more steps, not certain that he was even taking a straight route. Suddenly the fog curtain was drawn aside and he saw a figure waiting for him a few yards ahead. The bruises now twisted his face so badly Ballard would not have known it to be Mironenko, but that his eyes still burned so brightly.

The man did not wait for Ballard, but turned again and loped off into insolidity, leaving the Englishman to follow, cursing both the chase and the quarry. As he did so, he felt a movement close by. His senses were useless in the clammy embrace of fog and night, but he saw with that other eye, heard with that other ear, and he knew he was not alone. Had Mironenko given up the race and come back to escort him? He spoke the man's name, knowing that in doing so he made his position apparent to any and all, but equally certain that whoever stalked him already knew precisely where he stood.

"Speak," he said.

There was no reply out of the fog.

Then, movement. The fog curled upon itself and Ballard glimpsed a form dividing the veils. Mironenko! He called after the man again, taking several steps through the murk in pursuit, and suddenly something was stepping out to meet him. He saw the phantom for a moment only, long enough to glimpse incandescent eyes and teeth grown so vast they wrenched the mouth into a permanent grimace. Of those facts—eyes and teeth—he was certain. Of the other bizarreries—the bristling flesh, the monstrous limbs—he was less sure. Maybe his mind, exhausted with so much noise and pain, was finally losing its grip on the real world, inventing terrors to frighten him back into ignorance.

"Damn you," he said, defying both the thunder that was coming to blind him again and the phantoms he would be blinded to. Almost as if to test his defiance, the fog up ahead shimmered and parted and something that he might have taken for human, but that it had its belly to the ground, slunk into view and out. To his right he heard growls; to his left, another indeterminate form came and went. He was surrounded, it seemed, by mad men and wild dogs.

And Mironenko, where was he? Part of this assembly, or prey to it?

Hearing a half-word spoken behind him, he swung round to see a figure that was plausibly that of the Russian backing into the fog. This time he didn't walk in pursuit, he *ran*, and his speed was rewarded. The figure reappeared ahead of him, and Ballard stretched to snatch at the man's jacket. His fingers found purchase, and all at once Mironenko was reeling round, a growl in his throat, and Ballard was staring into a face that almost made him cry out. His mouth was a raw wound, the teeth vast, the eyes slits of molten gold; the lumps at his neck had swelled and spread, so that the Russian's head was no longer raised above his body but part of one undivided energy, head becoming torso without an axis intervening.

"Ballard," the beast smiled.

Its voice clung to coherence only with the greatest difficulty, but Ballard heard the remnants of Mironenko there. The more he scanned the simmering flesh, the more appalled he became.

"Don't be afraid," Mironenko said.

"What disease is this?"

"The only disease I ever suffered was forgetfulness, and I'm cured of that—" He grimaced as he spoke, as if each word was shaped in contradiction to the instincts of his throat.

Ballard touched his hand to his head. Despite his revolt against the pain, the noise was rising and rising.

". . . You remember too, don't you? You're the same."

"No," Ballard muttered.

Mironenko reached a spine-haired palm to touch him. "Don't be afraid," he said. "You're not alone. There are many of us. Brothers and sisters."

"I'm not your brother," Ballard said. The noise was bad, but the face of Mironenko was worse. Revolted, he turned his back on it, but the Russian only followed him.

"Don't you taste freedom, Ballard? And life. Just a breath away." Ballard walked on, the blood beginning to creep from his nostrils. He let it come. "It only hurts for a while," Mironenko said. "Then the pain goes . . ."

Ballard kept his head down, eyes to the earth. Mironenko, seeing that he was making little impression, dropped behind.

"They won't take you back!" he said. "You've seen too much."

The roar of helicopters did not entirely blot out these words. Ballard knew there was truth in them. His step faltered, and through the cacophony he heard Mironenko murmur:

"Look . . ."

Ahead, the fog had thinned somewhat, and the park wall was visible through rags of mist. Behind him, Mironenko's voice had descended to a snarl.

"Look at what you are."

The rotors roared; Ballard's legs felt as though they would fold up beneath him. But he kept up his advance toward the wall. Within yards of it, Mironenko called after him again, but this time the words had fled altogether. There was only a low growl. Ballard could not resist looking, just once. He glanced over his shoulder.

Again the fog confounded him, but not entirely. For moments that were both an age and yet too brief, Ballard saw the thing that had been Mironenko in all its glory, and at the sight the rotors grew to screaming pitch. He clamped his hands to his face. As he did so a shot rang out, then another, then a volley of shots. He fell to the ground, as much in weakness as in self-defense, and uncovered his eyes to see several human figures moving in the fog. Though he had forgotten their pursuers, they had not forgotten him. They had traced him to the park, and stepped into the midst of this lunacy, and now men and half men and things not men were lost in the fog, and there was bloody confusion on every side. He saw a gunman firing at a shadow, only to have an ally appear from the fog with a bullet in his belly; saw a thing appear on four legs and flit from sight again on two; saw another run by carrying a human head by the hair, and laughing from its snouted face.

The turmoil spilled toward him. Fearing for his life, he stood up and staggered back toward the wall. The cries and shots and snarls went on; he expected either bullet or beast to find him with every step. But he reached the wall alive, and attempted to scale it. His coordination had deserted him, however. He had no choice but to follow the wall along its length until he reached the gate.

Behind him the scenes of unmasking and transformation and mistaken identity went on. His enfeebled thoughts turned briefly to Mironenko. Would he, or any of his tribe, survive this massacre?

"Ballard," said a voice in the fog. He couldn't see the speaker, although he recognized the voice. He'd heard it in his delusion, and it had told him lies.

He felt a pinprick at his neck. The man had come from behind, and was pressing a needle into him.

"Sleep," the voice said. And with the words came oblivion.

At first he couldn't remember the man's name. His mind wandered like a lost child, although his interrogator would time and again demand his attention, speaking to him as though they were old friends. And there was indeed something familiar about his errant eye that went on its way so much more slowly than its companion. At last, the name came to him.

"You're Cripps," he said.

"Of course I'm Cripps," the man replied. "Is your memory playing tricks? Don't concern yourself. I've given you some suppressants, to keep you from losing your balance. Not that I think that's very likely. You've fought the good fight, Ballard, in spite of considerable provocation. When I think of the way Odell snapped . . ." He sighed. "Do you remember last night at all?"

At first his mind's eye was blind. But then the memories began to come. Vague forms moving in a fog.

"The park," he said at last.

"I only just got you out. God knows how many are dead."

"The other . . . . the Russian . . . ?"

"Mironenko?" Cripps prompted. "I don't know. I'm not in charge any longer, you see; I just stepped in to salvage something if I could. London will need us again, sooner or later. Especially now they know the Russians have a special corps like us. We'd heard rumors, of course; and then, after you'd met with him, began to wonder about Mironenko. That's why I set up the meeting. And of course when I saw him, face-to-face, I *knew*. There's something in the eyes. Something hungry."

"I saw him change—"

"Yes, it's quite a sight, isn't it? The power it unleashes. That's why we developed the program, you see, to harness that power, to have it work for us. But it's difficult to control. It took years of suppression therapy, slowly burying the desire for transformation, so that what we had left was a man with a beast's faculties. A wolf in sheep's clothing. We thought we had the problem beaten, that if the belief systems didn't keep you subdued, the pain response would. But we were wrong." He stood up and crossed to the window. "Now we have to start again."

"Suckling said you'd been wounded."

"No. Merely demoted. Ordered back to London."

"But you're not going."

"I will now, now that I've found you." He looked round at Ballard. "You're my vindication, Ballard. You're living proof that my techniques are viable. You have full knowledge of your condition, yet the therapy holds the leash." He turned back to the window. Rain lashed the glass. Ballard could almost feel it upon his head, upon his back. Cool, sweet rain. For a blissful moment he seemed to be running in it, close to the ground, and the air was full of the scents the downpour had released from the pavements.

"Mironenko said—"

"Forget Mironenko," Cripps told hm. "He's dead. You're the last of the old order, Ballard. And the first of the new."

Downstairs, a bell rang. Cripps peered out of the window at the streets below.

"Well, well," he said, "a delegation, come to beg us to return. I hope you're flattered." He went to the door. "Stay here. We needn't show you off tonight. You're weary. Let them wait, eh? Let them sweat." He left the stale room, closing the door behind him. Ballard heard his footsteps on the stairs. The bell was being rung a second time. He got up and crossed to the window. The weariness of the late afternoon light matched his weariness; he and his city were still of one accord, despite the curse that was upon him. Below, a man emerged from the back of the car and crossed to the front door. Even at this acute angle Ballard recognized Suckling.

There were voices in the hallway, and with Suckling's appearance the debate seemed to become more heated. Ballard went to the door and listened, but his drug-dulled mind could make little sense of the argument. He prayed that Cripps would keep to his word, and not allow them to peer at him. He didn't want to be a beast like Mironenko. It wasn't freedom, was it, to be so terrible? It was merely a different kind of tyranny. But then he didn't want to be the first of Cripps's heroic new order either. He belonged to nobody, he realized, not even himself. He was hopelessly lost. And yet hadn't Mironenko said at that first meeting that the man who did not believe himself lost, *was* lost? Perhaps better that—better to exist in the twilight between one state and another, to prosper as best he could by doubt and ambiguity—than to suffer the certainties of the tower.

The debate below was gaining in momentum. Ballard opened the door so as to hear better. It was Suckling's voice that met him. The tone was waspish, but no less threatening for that.

"It's over . . ." he was telling Cripps, ". . . don't you understand plain English?" Cripps made an attempt to protest, but Suckling cut him short. "Either you come in a gentlemanly fashion or Gideon and Sheppard carry you out. Which is it to be?"

"What is this?" Cripps demanded. "You're nobody, Suckling. You're comic relief."

"That was yesterday," the man replied. "There've been some changes made. Every dog has his day, isn't that right? You should know that better than anybody. I'd get a coat if I were you. It's raining."

There was a short silence, then Cripps said:

"All right. I'll come."

"Good man," said Suckling sweetly. "Gideon, go check upstairs."

"I'm alone," said Cripps.

"I believe you," said Suckling. Then to Gideon. "Do it anyway."

Ballard heard some body move across the hallway, and then a sudden flurry of movement. Cripps was either making an escape bid or attacking Suckling, one of the two. Suckling shouted out; there was a scuffle. Then, cutting through the confusion, a single shot.

Cripps cried out; then came the sound of him falling.

Now Suckling's voice, thick with fury. "Stupid," he said. "Stupid."

Cripps groaned something which Ballard didn't catch. Had he asked to be dispatched, perhaps, for Suckling told him: "No. You're going back to London. Sheppard, stop him bleeding. Gideon, upstairs."

Ballard backed away from the head of the stairs as Gideon began his ascent. He felt sluggish and inept. There was no way out of this trap. They would corner him and exterminate him. He was a beast, a mad dog in a maze. If he'd only killed Suckling when he'd had the strength to do so. But then what good would that have done? The world was full of men like Suckling, men biding their time until they could show their true colors: vile, soft, secret men. And suddenly the beast seemed to move in Ballard, and he thought of the park and the fog and the smile on the face of Mironenko, and he felt a surge of grief for something he'd never had: the life of a monster.

Gideon was almost at the top of the stairs. Though it could only delay the inevitable by moments, Ballard slipped along the landing and opened the first door he found. It was the bathroom. There was a bolt on the door, which he slipped into place.

The sound of running water filled the room. A piece of gutter had broken, and was delivering a torrent of rainwater onto the windowsill. The sound, and the chill of the bathroom, brought the night of delusions back. He remembered the pain and blood, remembered the shower— water beating on his skull, cleansing him of the taming pain. At the thought, four words came to his lips unbidden.

"I do not believe."

He had been heard.

"There's somebody up here," Gideon called. The man approached the door, and beat on it. "Open up!"

Ballard heard him quite clearly, but didn't reply. His throat was burning, and the roar of rotors was growing louder again. He put his back to the door and despaired.

Suckling was up the stairs and at the door in seconds. "Who's in there?" he demanded to know. "Answer me! Who's in *there?*" Getting no response, he ordered that Cripps be brought upstairs. There was more commotion as the order was obeyed.

"For the last time—" Suckling said.

The pressure was building in Ballard's skull. This time it seemed the din had lethal intentions; his eyes ached, as if about to be blown from their sockets. He caught sight of something in the mirror above the sink, something with gleaming eyes, and again, the words came—"I do not believe"—but this time his throat, hot with other business, could barely pronounce them.

"*Ballard,*" said Suckling. There was triumph in the word. "My God, we've got Ballard as well. This is our lucky day."

No, thought the man in the mirror. There was nobody of that name here. Nobody of any name at all, in fact, for weren't names the first act of faith, the first board in the box you buried freedom in? The thing he was becoming would not be named, nor boxed, nor buried. Never again.

For a moment he lost sight of the bathroom, and found himself hovering above the grave they had made him dig, and in the depths the box danced as its contents fought its premature burial. He could hear the wood splintering—or was it the sound of the door being broken down?

The box lid flew off. A rain of nails fell on the heads of the burial party. The noise in his head, as if knowing that its torments had proved fruitless, suddenly fled, and with it the delusion. He was back in the bathroom, facing the open door. The men who stared through at him had the faces of fools. Slack, and stupefied with shock—seeing the way he was wrought. Seeing the snout of him, the hair of him, the golden eye and the yellow tooth of him. Their horror elated him.

"Kill it!" said Suckling, and pushed Gideon into the breach. The man already had his gun from his pocket and was leveling it, but his trigger finger was too slow. The beast snatched his hand and pulped the flesh around the steel. Gideon screamed, and stumbled away down the stairs, ignoring Suckling's shouts.

As the beast raised his hand to sniff the blood on his palm, there was a flash of fire, and he felt the blow to his shoulder. Sheppard had no chance to fire a second shot, however, before his prey was through the door and upon him. Forsaking his gun, he made a futile bid for the stairs, but the beast's hand unsealed the back of his head in one easy stroke. The gunman toppled forward, the narrow landing filling with the smell of him. Forgetting his other enemies, the beast fell upon the offal and ate.

Somebody said: "Ballard."

The beast swallowed down the dead man's eyes in one gulp, like prime oysters.

Again, those syllables. "Ballard." He would have gone on with his meal, but the sound of weeping pricked his ears. Dead to himself he was, but not to grief. He dropped the meat from his fingers and looked back along the landing.

The man who was crying only wept from one eye; the other gazed on, oddly untouched. But the pain in the living eye was profound indeed. It was despair, the beast knew; such suffering was too close to him for the sweetness of transformation to have erased it entirely. The weeping man was locked in the arms of another man, who had his gun placed against the side of his prisoner's head.

"If you make another move," the captor said, "I'll blow his head off. Do you understand me?"

The beast wiped his mouth.

"Tell him, Cripps! He's your baby. Make him understand."

The one-eyed man tried to speak, but words defeated him. Blood from the wound in his abdomen seeped between his fingers.

"Neither of you need die," the captor said. The beast didn't like the music of his voice; it was shrill and deceitful. "London would much prefer to have you alive. So why don't you tell him, Cripps? Tell him I mean him no harm."

The weeping man nodded.

"Ballard . . ." he murmured. His voice was softer than the other. The beast listened.

"Tell me, Ballard," he said, "how does it feel?"

The beast couldn't quite make sense of the question.

"Please tell me. For curiosity's sake—"

"Damn you," said Suckling, pressing the gun into Cripps's flesh. "This isn't a debating society."

"Is it good?" Cripps asked, ignoring both man and gun.

"Shut up!"

"Answer me, Ballard. *How does it feel?*"

As he stared into Cripps's despairing eyes, the meaning of the sounds he'd uttered came clear, the words falling into place like the pieces of a mosaic. "Is it good?" the man was asking.

Ballard heard laughter in his throat, and found the syllables there to reply.

"Yes," he told the weeping man. "Yes. It's good."

He had not finished his reply before Cripps's hand sped to snatch at Suckling's. Whether he intended suicide or escape nobody would ever know. The trigger finger twitched, and a bullet flew up through Cripps's head and spread his despair across the ceiling. Suckling threw the body off, and went to level the gun, but the beast was already upon him.

Had he been more of a man, Ballard might have thought to make Suckling suffer, but he had no such perverse ambition. His only thought was to render the enemy extinct as efficiently as possible. Two sharp and lethal blows did it. Once the man was dispatched, Ballard crossed over to where Cripps was lying. His glass eye had escaped destruction. It gazed on fixedly, untouched by the holocaust all around them. Unseating it from the maimed head, Ballard put it in his pocket, then he went out into the rain.

It was dusk. He did not know which district of Berlin he'd been brought to, but his impulses, freed of reason, led him via the back streets and shadows to a wasteland on the outskirts of the city, in the middle of which stood a solitary ruin. It was anybody's guess as to what the building might once have been (an abattoir? an opera house?), but by some freak of fate it had escaped demolition, though every other building had been leveled for several hundred yards in each direction. As he made his way across the weed-clogged rubble, the wind changed direction by a few degrees and carried the scent of his tribe to him. There were many there, together in the shelter of the ruin. Some leaned their backs against the wall and shared a cigarette; some were perfect wolves, and haunted the darkness like ghosts with golden eyes; yet others might have passed for human entirely, but for their trails.

Though he feared that names would be forbidden among this clan, he asked two lovers who were rutting in the shelter of the wall if they knew of a man called Mironenko. The bitch had a smooth and hairless back, and a dozen full teats hanging from her belly.

"Listen," she said.

Ballard listened, and heard somebody talking in a corner of the ruin. The voice ebbed and flowed. He followed the sound across the roofless interior to where a wolf was standing, surrounded by an attentive audience, an open book in its front paws. At Ballard's approach one or two of the audience turned their luminous eyes up to him. The reader halted.

"Ssh!" said one, "the Comrade is reading to us."

It was Mironenko who spoke. Ballard slipped into the ring of listeners beside him, as the reader took up the story afresh.

"And God blessed them, and God said unto them, Be fruitful, and multiply, and replenish the earth . . ."

Ballard had heard the words before, but tonight they were new.

". . . and subdue it: and have dominion over the fish of the sea, and over the fowl of the air . . ."

He looked around the circle of listeners as the words described their familiar pattern.

". . . and over every living thing that moveth upon the earth."

Somewhere near, a beast was crying.

THE LAST
ILLUSION

What happened then—when the magician, having mesmerized the caged tiger, pulled the tasseled cord that released a dozen swords upon its head—was the subject of heated argument both in the bar of the theater and later, when Swann's performance was over, on the sidewalk of Fifty-first Street. Some claimed to have glimpsed the bottom of the cage opening in the split second that all other eyes were on the descending blades, and seen the tiger swiftly spirited away as the woman in the red dress took its place behind the lacquered bars. Others were just as adamant that the animal had never been in the cage to begin with, its presence merely a projection which had been extinguished as a mechanism propelled the woman from beneath the stage; this, of course, at such a speed that it deceived the eye of all but those swift and suspicious enough to catch it. And the swords? The nature of the trick which had transformed them in the mere seconds of their gleaming descent from steel to rose petals was yet further fuel for debate. The explanations ranged from the prosaic to the elaborate, but few of the throng that left the theater lacked some theory. Nor did the arguments finish there, on the sidewalk. They raged on, no doubt, in the apartments and restaurants of New York.

The pleasure to be had from Swann's illusions was, it seemed, twofold. First: the spectacle of the trick itself—in the breathless moment when disbelief was, if not suspended, at least taken on tiptoe. And second, when the moment was over and logic restored, in the debate as to how the trick had been achieved.

"How do you do it, Mr. Swann?" Barbara Bernstein was eager to know.

"It's magic," Swann replied. He had invited her backstage to examine the tiger's cage for any sign of fakery in its construction; she had found none. She had examined the swords: they were lethal. And the petals, fragrant. Still she insisted:

"Yes, but *really* . . ." She leaned close to him. "You can tell me," she said, "I promise I won't breathe a word to a soul."

He returned her a slow smile in place of a reply.

"Oh, I know . . ." she said, "you're going to tell me that you've signed some kind of oath."

"That's right," Swann said.

"—And you're forbidden to give away any trade secrets."

"The intention is to give you pleasure," he told her. "Have I failed in that?"

"Oh no," she replied, without a moment's hesitation. "Everybody's talking about the show. You're the toast of New York."

"No," he protested.

"Truly," she said. "I know people who would give their eyeteeth to get into this theater. And to have a guided tour backstage . . . well, I'll be the envy of everybody."

"I'm pleased," he said, and touched her face. She had clearly been anticipating such a move on his part. It would be something else for her to boast of: her seduction by the man critics had dubbed the Magus of Manhattan.

"I'd like to make love to you," he whispered to her.

"Here?" she said.

"No," he told her. "Not within earshot of the tigers."

She laughed. She preferred her lovers twenty years Swann's junior—he looked, someone had observed, like a man in mourning for his profile, but his touch promised wit no boy could offer. She liked the tang of dissolution she sensed beneath his gentlemanly facade. Swann was a dangerous man. If she turned him down she might never find another.

"We could go to a hotel," she suggested.

"A hotel," he said, "is a good idea."

A look of doubt had crossed her face.

"What about your wife . . . ?" she said. "We might be seen."

He took her hand. "Shall we be invisible, then?"

"I'm serious."

"So am I," he insisted. "Take it from me; seeing is not believing. I should know. It's the cornerstone of my profession." She did not look much reassured. "If anyone recognizes us," he told her, "I'll simply tell them their eyes are playing tricks."

She smiled at this, and he kissed her. She returned the kiss with unquestionable fervor.

"Miraculous," he said, when their mouths parted. "Shall we go before the tigers gossip?"

He led her across the stage. The cleaners had not yet got about their business, and there, lying on the boards, was a litter of rosebuds. Some had been trampled, a few had not. Swann took his hand from hers, and walked across to where the flowers lay.

She watched him stoop to pluck a rose from the ground, enchanted by the gesture, but before he could stand upright again something in the air above him caught her eye. She looked up and her gaze met a slice of silver that was even now plunging toward him. She made to warn him, but the sword was quicker than her tongue. At the last possible moment he seemed to sense the danger he was in and looked round, the bud in his hand, as the point met his back. The sword's momentum carried it through his body to the hilt. Blood fled from his chest and splashed the floor. He made no sound, but fell forward, forcing two-thirds of the sword's length out of his body again as he hit the stage.

She would have screamed, but her attention was claimed by a sound from the clutter of magical apparatus arrayed in the wings behind her, a muttered growl which was indisputably the voice of the tiger. She froze. There were probably instructions on how best to stare down rogue tigers, but they were techniques she, as a Manhattanite born and bred, wasn't acquainted with.

"Swann?" she said, hoping this yet might be some baroque illusion staged purely for her benefit. "Swann. Please get up."

But the magician only lay where he had fallen, the pool spreading from beneath him.

"If this is a joke," she said testily, "I'm not amused." When he didn't rise to her remark she tried a sweeter tactic. "Swann, my sweet, I'd like to go now, if you don't mind."

The growl came again. She didn't want to turn and seek out its source, but equally she didn't want to be sprung upon from behind.

Cautiously she looked round. The wings were in darkness. The clutter of properties kept her from working out the precise location of the beast. She could hear it still, however: its tread, its growl. Step by step, she retreated toward the apron of the stage. The closed curtains sealed her off from the auditorium, but she hoped she might scramble under them before the tiger reached her.

As she backed against the heavy fabric, one of the shadows in the wings forsook its ambiguity, and the animal appeared. It was not beautiful, as she had thought it when behind bars. It was vast and lethal and hungry. She went down on her haunches and reached for the hem of the curtain. The fabric was heavily weighted, and she had more difficulty lifting it than she'd expected, but she had managed to slide halfway under the drape when, head and hands pressed to the boards, she sensed the thump of the tiger's advance. An instant later she felt the splash of its breath on her bare back, and screamed as it hooked its talons into her body and hauled her from the sight of safety toward its steaming jaws.

Even then, she refused to give up her life. She kicked at it and tore out its fur in handfuls, and delivered a hail of punches to its snout. But her resistance was negligible in the face of such authority; her assault, for all its ferocity, did not slow the beast a jot. It ripped open her body with one casual clout. Mercifully, with that first wound her senses gave up all claim to verisimilitude, and took instead to preposterous invention. It seemed to her that she heard applause from somewhere, and the roar of an approving audience, and that in place of the blood that was surely springing from her body there came fountains of sparkling light. The agony her nerve endings were suffering didn't touch her at all. Even when the animal had divided her into three or four parts her head lay on its side at the edge of the stage and watched as her torso was mauled and her limbs devoured.

And all the while, when she wondered how all this could be possible—that her eyes could live to witness this last supper—the only reply she could think of was Swann's:

"*It's magic*," he'd said.

Indeed, she was thinking that very thing, that this must *be* magic, when the tiger ambled across to her head, and swallowed it down in one bite.

Among a certain set Harry D'Amour liked to believe he had some small reputation—a coterie which did not, alas, include his ex-wife, his creditors, or those anonymous critics who regularly posted dog excrement through his office mailbox. But the woman who was on the phone now, her voice so full of grief she might have been crying for half a year, and was about to begin again, *she* knew him for the paragon he was.

"—I need your help, Mr. D'Amour, very badly."

"I'm busy on several cases at the moment," he told her. "Maybe you could come to the office?"

"I can't leave the house," the woman informed him. "I'll explain everything. Please come."

He was sorely tempted. But there *were* several outstanding cases, one of which, if not solved soon, might end in fratricide. He suggested she try elsewhere.

"I can't go to just anybody," the woman insisted.

"Why me?"

"I read about you. About what happened in Brooklyn."

Making mention of his most conspicuous failure was not the surest method of securing his services, Harry thought, but it certainly got his attention. What had happened in Wyckoff Street had begun innocently enough, with a husband who'd employed him to spy on his adulterous wife, and had ended on the top story of the Lomax house with the world he thought he'd known turning inside out. When the body count was done, and the surviving priests dispatched, he was left with fear of stairs, and more questions than he'd ever answer this side of the family plot. He took no pleasure in being reminded of those terrors.

"I don't like to talk about Brooklyn," he said.

"Forgive me," the woman replied, "but I need somebody who has experience with . . . with the occult." She stopped speaking for a moment. He could still hear her breath down the line: soft, but erratic.

"I need you," she said. He had already decided, in that pause when only her fear had been audible, what reply he would make.

"I'll come."

"I'm grateful to you," she said. "The house is on East Sixty-first Street—"

He scribbled down the details. Her last words were, "Please hurry." Then she put down the phone.

He made some calls, in the vain hope of placating two of his more excitable clients, then pulled on his jacket, locked the office, and started downstairs. The landing and the lobby smelled pungent. As he reached the front door he caught Chaplin, the janitor, emerging from the basement.

"This place stinks," he told the man.

"It's disinfectant."

"It's cat piss," Harry said. "Get something done about it, will you? I've got a reputation to protect."

He left the man laughing.

The brownstone on East Sixty-first Street was in pristine condition. He stood on the scrubbed step, sweaty and sour-breathed, and felt like a slob. The expression on the face that met him when the door opened did nothing to dissuade him of that opinion.

"Yes?" it wanted to know.

"I'm Harry D'Amour," he said. "I got a call."

The man nodded. "You'd better come in," he said, without enthusiasm.

It was cooler in than out, and sweeter. The place reeked of perfume. Harry followed the disapproving face down the hallway and into a large room, on the other side of which—across an Oriental carpet that had everything woven into its pattern but the price—sat a widow. She didn't suit black, or tears. She stood up and offered her hand.

"Mr. D'Amour?"

"Yes."

"Valentin will get you something to drink if you'd like."

"Please. Milk, if you have it." His belly had been jittering for the last hour, since her talk of Wyckoff Street, in fact.

Valentin retired from the room, not taking his beady eyes off Harry until the last possible moment.

"Somebody died," said Harry, once the man had gone.

"That's right," the widow said, sitting down again. At her invitation he sat opposite her, among enough cushions to furnish a harem. "My husband."

"I'm sorry."

"There's no time to be sorry," she said, her every look and gesture betraying her words. He was glad of her grief; the tearstains and the fatigue blemished a beauty which, had he seen it unimpaired, might have rendered him dumb with admiration.

"They say that my husband's death was an accident," she was saying. "I know it wasn't."

"May I ask . . . your name?"

"I'm sorry. My name is Swann, Mr. D'Amour. Dorothea Swann. You may have heard of my husband?"

"The magician?"

"*Illusionist*," she said.

"I read about it. Tragic."

"Did you ever see his performance?"

Harry shook his head. "I can't afford Broadway, Mrs. Swann."

"We were only over for three months, while his show ran. We were going back in September . . ."

"Back?"

"To Hamburg," she said. "I don't like this city. It's too hot. And too cruel."

"Don't blame New York," he said. "It can't help itself."

"Maybe," she replied, nodding. "Perhaps what happened to Swann would have happened anyway, wherever we'd been. People keep telling me: it was an accident. That's all. Just an accident."

"But you don't believe it?"

Valentin had appeared with a glass of milk. He set it down on the table in front of Harry. As he made to leave, she said, "Valentin. The letter?"

He looked at her strangely, almost as though she'd said something obscene.

"*The letter*," she repeated.

He exited.

"You were saying—"

She frowned. "What?"

"About it being an accident."

"Oh yes. I lived with Swann seven and a half years, and I got to understand him as well as anybody ever could. I learned to sense when he wanted me around, and when he didn't. When he didn't, I'd take myself off somewhere and let him have his privacy. Genius needs privacy. And he *was* a genius, you know. The greatest illusionist since Houdini."

"Is that so?"

"I'd think sometimes—it was a kind of miracle that he let me into his life . . ."

Harry wanted to say Swann would have been mad not to have done so, but the comment was inappropriate. She didn't want blandishments, didn't need them. Didn't need anything, perhaps, but her husband alive again.

"Now I think I didn't know him at all," she went on, "didn't *understand* him. I think maybe it was another trick. Another part of his magic."

"I called him a magician a while back," Harry said. "You corrected me."

"So I did," she said, conceding his point with an apologetic look. "Forgive me. That was Swann talking. He *hated* to be called a magician. He said that was a word that had to be kept for miracle workers."

"And he was no miracle worker?"

"He used to call himself the Great Pretender," she said. The thought made her smile.

Valentin had reappeared, his lugubrious features rife with suspicion. He carried an envelope, which he clearly had no desire to give up. Dorothea had to cross the carpet and take it from his hands.

"Is this wise?" he said.

"Yes," she told him.

He turned on his heel and made a smart withdrawal.

"He's grief-stricken," she said. "Forgive him his behavior. He was with Swann from the beginning of his career. I think he loved my husband as much as I did."

She ran her finger down into the envelope and pulled the letter out. The paper was pale yellow, and gossamer-thin.

"A few hours after he died, this letter was delivered here by hand," she said. "It was addressed to him. I opened it. I think you ought to read it."

She passed it to him. The hand it was written in was solid and unaffected.

Dorothea, he had written, *if you are reading this, then I am dead.*

> *You know how little store I set by dreams and premonitions and such, but for the last few days strange thoughts have just crept into my head, and I have the suspicion that death is very close to me. If so, so. There's no help for it. Don't waste time trying to puzzle out the whys and wherefores; they're old news*

now. Just know that I love you, and that I have always loved you in my way. I'm sorry for whatever unhappiness I've caused, or am causing now, but it was out of my hands.

I have some instructions regarding the disposal of my body. Please adhere to them to the letter. Don't let anybody try to persuade you out of doing as I ask.

I want you to have my body watched night and day until I'm cremated. Don't try and take my remains back to Europe. Have me cremated here, as soon as possible, then throw the ashes in the East River.

My sweet darling, I'm afraid. Not of bad dreams, or of what might happen to me in this life, but of what my enemies may try to do once I'm dead. You know how critics can be: they wait until you can't fight them back, then they start the character assassinations. It's too long a business to try and explain all of this, so I must simply trust you to do as I say.

Again, I love you, and I hope you never have to read this letter.

Your adoring
Swann.

"Some farewell note," Harry commented when he'd read it through twice. He folded it up and passed it back to the widow.

"I'd like you to stay with him," she said. "Corpse-sit, if you will. Just until all the legal formalities are dealt with and I can make arrangements for his cremation. It shouldn't take them long. I've got a lawyer working on it now."

"Again: why me?"

She avoided his gaze. "As he says in the letter, he was never superstitious. But I am. I believe in omens. And there was an odd atmosphere about the place in the days before he died. As if we were watched."

"You think he was murdered?"

She mused on this, then said, "I don't believe it was an accident."

"These enemies he talks about . . ."

"He was a great man. Much envied."

"Professional jealousy? Is that a motive for murder?"

"Anything can be a motive, can't it?" she said. "People get killed for the color of their eyes, don't they?"

Harry was impressed. It had taken him twenty years to learn how arbitrary things were. She spoke it as conventional wisdom.

"Where is your husband?" he asked her.

"Upstairs," she said. "I had the body brought back here, where I could look after him. I can't pretend I understand what's going on, but I'm not going to risk ignoring his instructions."

Harry nodded.

"Swann was my life," she added softly, apropos of nothing, and everything.

She took him upstairs. The perfume that had met him at the door intensified. The master bedroom had been turned into a Chapel of Rest, knee-deep in sprays and wreaths of every shape and variety; their mingled scents verged on the hallucinogenic. In the midst of this abundance, the casket—an elaborate affair in black and silver—was mounted on trestles. The upper half of the lid stood open, the plush overlay folded back. At Dorothea's invitation he waded through the tributes to view the deceased. He liked Swann's face; it had humor, and a certain guile; it was even handsome in its weary way. More: it had inspired the love of Dorothea; a face could have few better recommendations. Harry stood waist-high in flowers and, absurd as it was, felt a twinge of envy for the love this man must have enjoyed.

"Will you help me, Mr. D'Amour?"

What could he say but, "Yes, of course I'll help." That, and, "Call me Harry."

He would be missed at Wing's Pavilion tonight. He had occupied the best table there every Friday night for the past six and a half years, eating at one sitting enough to compensate for what his diet lacked in excellence and variety the other six days of the week. This feast—the best Chinese cuisine to be had south of Canal Street—came *gratis*, thanks to services he had once rendered the owner. Tonight the table would go empty.

Not that his stomach suffered. He had only been sitting with Swann an hour or so when Valentin came up and said:

"How do you like your steak?"

"Just shy of burned," Harry replied.

Valentin was none too pleased by the response. "I hate to overcook good steak," he said.

"And I hate the sight of blood," Harry said, "even if it isn't my own."

The chef clearly despaired of his guest's palate, and turned to go.

"Valentin?"

The man looked round.

"Is that your Christian name?" Harry asked.

"Christian names are for Christians," came the reply.

Harry nodded. "You don't like my being here, am I right?"

Valentin made no reply. His eyes had drifted past Harry to the open coffin.

"I'm not going to be here for long," Harry said, "but while I am, can't we be friends?"

Valentin's gaze found him once more.

"I don't have any friends," he said without enmity or self-pity. "Not now."

"OK. I'm sorry."

"What's to be sorry for?" Valentin wanted to know. "Swann's dead. It's all over, bar the shouting."

The doleful face stoically refused tears. A stone would weep sooner, Harry guessed. But there was grief there, and all the more acute for being dumb.

"One question."

"Only one?"

"Why didn't you want me to read his letter?"

Valentin raised his eyebrows slightly; they were fine enough to have been penciled on. "He wasn't insane," he said. "I didn't want you thinking he was a crazy man, because of what he wrote. What you read you keep to yourself. Swann was a legend. I don't want his memory besmirched."

"You should write a book," Harry said. "Tell the whole story once and for all. You were with him a long time, I hear."

"Oh yes," said Valentin, "long enough to know better than to tell the truth."

So saying he made an exit, leaving the flowers to wilt, and Harry with more puzzles on his hands than he'd begun with.

Twenty minutes later, Valentin brought up a tray of food: a large salad, bread, wine, and the steak. It was one degree short of charcoal.

"Just the way I like it," Harry said, and set to guzzling.

He didn't see Dorothea Swann, though God knows he thought about her often enough. Every time he heard a whisper on the stairs, or footsteps along the carpeted landing, he hoped her face would appear at the door, an invitation on her lips. Not perhaps the most appropriate of thoughts, given the proximity of her husband's corpse, but what would the illusionist care now? He was dead and gone. If he had any generosity of spirit he wouldn't want to see his widow drown in her grief.

Harry drank the half-carafe of wine Valentin had brought, and when—three-quarters of an hour later—the man reappeared with coffee and Calvados, he told him to leave the bottle.

Nightfall was near. The traffic was noisy on Lexington and Third. Out of boredom he took to watching the street from the window. Two lovers feuded loudly on the sidewalk, and only stopped when a brunette with a harelip and a Pekingese stood watching them shamelessly. There were preparations for a party in the brownstone opposite: he watched a table lovingly laid, and candles lit. After a time the spying began to depress him, so he called Valentin and asked if there was a portable television he could have access to. No sooner said than provided, and for the next two hours he sat with the small black-and-white monitor on the floor among the orchids and the lilies, watching whatever mindless entertainment it offered, the silver luminescence flickering on the blooms like excitable moonlight.

A quarter after midnight, with the party across the street in full swing. Valentin came up. "You want a nightcap?" he asked.

"Sure."

"Milk, or something stronger?"

"Something stronger."

He produced a bottle of fine cognac and two glasses. Together they toasted the dead man.

"Mr. Swann."

"Mr. Swann."

"If you need anything more tonight," Valentin said, "I'm in the room directly above. Mrs. Swann is downstairs, so if you hear somebody moving about, don't worry. She doesn't sleep well these nights."

"Who does?" Harry replied.

Valentin left him to his vigil. Harry heard the man's tread on the stairs, and then the creaking of floorboards on the level above. He returned his attention to the television, but he'd lost the thread of the movie he'd been watching. It was a long stretch till dawn; meanwhile New York would be having itself a fine Friday night: dancing, fighting, fooling around.

The picture on the television set began to flicker. He stood up and started to walk across to the set, but he never got there. Two steps from the chair where he'd been sitting, the picture folded up and went out altogether, plunging the room into total darkness. Harry briefly had time to register that no light was finding its way through the windows from the street. Then the insanity began.

Something moved in the blackness: vague forms rose and fell. It took him a moment to recognize them. The flowers! Invisible hands were tearing the wreaths and tributes apart, and tossing the blossoms up into the air. He followed their descent, but they didn't hit the ground. It seemed the floorboards had lost all faith in themselves, and disappeared, so the blossoms just kept falling—*down, down*—through the floor of the room below, and through the basement floor, away to God alone knew what destination. Fear gripped Harry, like some old dope pusher promising a terrible high. Even those few boards that remained beneath his feet were becoming insubstantial. In seconds he would go the way of the blossoms.

He reeled around to locate the chair he'd got up from—some fixed point in this vertiginous nightmare. The chair was still there; he could just discern its form in the gloom. With torn blossoms raining down upon him he reached for it, but even as his hand took hold of the arm, the floor beneath the chair gave up the ghost, and now, by a ghastly light that was thrown up from the pit that yawned beneath his feet, Harry saw it tumble away into hell, turning over and over till it was pinprick small.

Then it was gone; and the flowers were gone, and the walls and the windows and every damn thing was gone but *him.*

Not quite everything. Swann's casket remained, its lid still standing open, its overlay neatly turned back like the sheet on a child's bed. The trestle had gone, as had the floor beneath the trestle. But the casket floated in the dark air for all the world like some morbid illusion, while from the depths a rumbling sound accompanied the trick like the roll of a snare drum.

Harry felt the last solidity failing beneath him, felt the pit call. Even as his feet left the ground, that ground faded to nothing, and for a terrifying moment he hung over the Gulfs, his hands seeking the lip of the casket. His right hand caught hold of one of the handles, and closed thankfully around it. His arm was almost jerked from its socket as it took his body weight, but he flung his other arm up and found the casket

edge. Using it as purchase, he hauled himself up like a half-drowned
sailor. It was a strange lifeboat, but then this was a strange sea. Infinitely
deep, infinitely terrible.

Even as he labored to secure himself a better handhold, the casket
shook, and Harry looked up to discover that the dead man was sitting
upright. Swann's eyes opened wide. He turned them on Harry; they were
far from benign. The next moment the dead illusionist was scrambling to
his feet—the floating casket rocking ever more violently with each movement. Once vertical, Swann proceeded to dislodge his guest by grinding
his heel in Harry's knuckles. Harry looked up at Swann, begging for him
to stop.

The Great Pretender was a sight to see. His eyes were starting from
his sockets; his shirt was torn open to display the exit wound in his chest.
It was bleeding afresh. A rain of cold blood fell upon Harry's upturned
face. And still the heel ground at his hands. Harry felt his grip slipping.
Swann, sensing his approaching triumph, began to smile.

"Fall, boy!" he said. "Fall!"

Harry could take no more. In a frenzied effort to save himself he let
go of the handle in his right hand, and reached up to snatch at Swann's
trouser leg. His fingers found the hem, and he pulled. The smile vanished from the illusionist's face as he felt his balance go. He reached
behind him to take hold of the casket lid for support, but the gesture only
tipped the casket farther over. The plush cushion tumbled past Harry's
head; blossoms followed.

Swann howled in his fury and delivered a vicious kick to Harry's
hand. It was an error. The casket tipped over entirely and pitched the
man out. Harry had time to glimpse Swann's appalled face as the illusionist fell past him. Then he too lost his grip and tumbled after him.

The dark air whined past his ears. Beneath him, the Gulfs spread
their empty arms. And then, behind the rushing in his head, another
sound: a human voice.

"Is he dead?" it inquired.

"No," another voice replied, "no, I don't think so. What's his name,
Dorothea?"

"D'Amour."

"Mr. D'Amour? Mr. D'Amour."

Harry's descent slowed somewhat. Beneath him, the Gulfs roared
their rage.

The voice came again, cultivated but unmelodious. "Mr. D'Amour."

"Harry," said Dorothea.

At that word, from that voice, he stopped falling, felt himself borne up. He opened his eyes. He was lying on a solid floor, his head inches from the blank television screen. The flowers were all in place around the room, Swann in his casket, and God—if the rumors were to be believed—in his heaven.

"I'm alive," he said.

He had quite an audience for his resurrection. Dorothea, of course, and two strangers. One, the owner of the voice he'd first heard, stood close to the door. His features were unremarkable, except for his brows and lashes, which were pale to the point of invisibility. His female companion stood nearby. She shared with him this distressing banality, stripped bare of any feature that offered a clue to their natures.

"Help him up, angel," the man said, and the woman bent to comply. She was stronger than she looked, readily hauling Harry to his feet. He had vomited in his strange sleep. He felt dirty and ridiculous.

"What the hell happened?" he asked, as the woman escorted him to the chair. He sat down.

"He tried to poison you," the man said.

"Who did?"

"Valentin, of course."

"Valentin?"

"He's gone," Dorothea said. "Just disappeared." She was shaking. "I heard you call out, and came in here to find you on the floor. I thought you were going to choke."

"It's all right," said the man, "everything is in order now."

"Yes," said Dorothea, clearly reassured by his bland smile. "This is the lawyer I was telling you about, Harry. Mr. Butterfield."

Harry wiped his mouth. "Pleased to meet you," he said.

"Why don't we all go downstairs?" Butterfield said. "And I can pay Mr. D'Amour what he's due."

"It's all right," Harry said, "I never take my fee until the job's done."

"But it is done," Butterfield said. "Your services are no longer required here."

Harry threw a glance at Dorothea. She was plucking a withered anthurium from an otherwise healthy spray.

"I was contracted to stay with the body—"

"The arrangements for the disposal of Swann's body have been made," Butterfield returned. His courtesy was only just intact. "Isn't that right, Dorothea?"

"It's the middle of the night," Harry protested. "You won't get a cremation until tomorrow morning at the earliest."

"Thank you for your help," Dorothea said. "But I'm sure everything will be fine now that Mr. Butterfield has arrived. Just fine."

Butterfield turned to his companion.

"Why don't you go out and find a cab for Mr. D'Amour?" he said. Then, looking at Harry: "We don't want you walking the streets, do we?"

All the way downstairs, and in the hallway as Butterfield paid him off, Harry was willing Dorothea to contradict the lawyer and tell him she wanted Harry to stay. But she didn't even offer him a word of farewell as he was ushered out of the house. The two hundred dollars he'd been given were, of course, more than adequate recompense for the few hours of idleness he'd spent there, but he would happily have burned all the bills for one sign that Dorothea gave a damn that they were parting. Quite clearly she did not. On past experience it would take his bruised ego a full twenty-four hours to recover from such indifference.

He got out of the cab on Third around Eighty-third Street, and walked through to a bar on Lexington where he knew he could put half a bottle of bourbon between himself and the dreams he'd had.

It was well after one. The street was deserted, except for him and for the echo his footsteps had recently acquired. He turned the corner onto Lexington, and waited. A few beats later, Valentin rounded the same corner. Harry took hold of him by his tie.

"Not a bad noose," he said, hauling the man off his heels.

Valentin made no attempt to free himself. "Thank God you're alive," he said.

"No thanks to you," Harry said. "What did you put in the drink?"

"Nothing," Valentin insisted. "Why should I?"

"So how come I found myself on the floor? How come the bad dreams?"

"Butterfield," Valentin said. "Whatever you dreamt, he brought with him, believe me. I panicked as soon as I heard him in the house, I admit it. I know I should have warned you, but I knew if I didn't get out quickly I wouldn't get out at all."

"Are you telling me he would have killed you?"

"Not personally, but yes." Harry looked incredulous. "We go way back, him and me."

"He's welcome to you," Harry said, letting go of the tie. "I'm too damn tired to take any more of this shit." He turned from Valentin and began to walk away.

"Wait," said the other man, "I know I wasn't too sweet with you back at the house, but you've got to understand, things are going to get bad. For both of us."

"I thought you said it was all over but the shouting?"

"I thought it was. I thought we had it all sewn up. Then Butterfield arrived and I realized how naive I was being. They're not going to let Swann rest in peace. Not now, not ever. We have to save him, D'Amour."

Harry stopped walking and studied the man's face. To pass him in the street, he mused, you wouldn't have taken him for a lunatic.

"Did Butterfield go upstairs?" Valentin inquired.

"Yes, he did. Why?"

"Do you remember if he approached the casket?"

Harry shook his head.

"Good," said Valentin. "Then the defenses are holding, which gives us a little time. Swann was a fine tactician, you know. But he could be careless. That was how they caught him. Sheer carelessness. He knew they were coming for him. I told him outright. I said we should cancel the remaining performances and go home. At least he had some sanctuary there."

"You think he was murdered?"

"Jesus Christ," said Valentin, almost despairing of Harry, "of course he was murdered."

"So he's past saving, right? The man's dead."

"Dead, yes. Past saving? No."

"Do you talk gibberish to everyone?"

Valentin put his hand on Harry's shoulder. "Oh no," he said, with unfeigned sincerity. "I don't trust anyone the way I trust you."

"This is very sudden," said Harry. "May I ask why?"

"Because you're in this up to your neck, the way I am," Valentin replied.

"No, I'm not," said Harry, but Valentin ignored the denial, and went on with his talk. "At the moment we don't know how many of them there are, of course. They might simply have sent Butterfield, but I think that's unlikely."

"Who's Butterfield with? The Mafia?"

"We should be so lucky," said Valentin. He reached in his pocket and pulled out a piece of paper. "This is the woman Swann was with," he said, "the night at the theater. It's possible she knows something of their strength."

"There was a witness?"

"She didn't come forward, but yes, there was. I was his procurer, you see. I helped arrange his several adulteries, so that none ever embarrassed him. See if you can get to her—" He stopped abruptly. Somewhere close by, music was being played. It sounded like a drunken jazz band extemporizing on bagpipes, a wheezing, rambling cacophony. Valentin's face instantly became a portrait of distress. "God help us . . ." he said softly, and began to back away from Harry.

"What's the problem?"

"Do you know how to pray?" Valentin asked him as he retreated down Eighty-third Street. The volume of the music was rising with every interval.

"I haven't prayed in twenty years," Harry replied.

"Then *learn*," came the response, and Valentin turned to run.

As he did so a ripple of darkness moved down the street from the north, dimming the luster of bar signs and streetlamps as it came. Neon announcements suddenly guttered and died; there were protests out of upstairs windows as the lights failed and, as if encouraged by the curses, the music took on a fresh and yet more hectic rhythm. Above his head Harry heard a wailing sound, and looked up to see a ragged silhouette against the clouds which trailed tendrils like a man-o'-war as it descended upon the street, leaving the stench of rotting fish in its wake. Its target was clearly Valentin. Harry shouted above the wail and the music and the panic from the blackout, but no sooner had he yelled than he heard Valentin shout out from the darkness, a pleading cry that was rudely cut short.

He stood in the murk, his feet unwilling to carry him a step nearer the place from which the plea had come. The smell still stung his nostrils; nosing it, his nausea returned. And then, so did the lights, a wave of power igniting the lamps and the bar signs as it washed back down the street. It reached Harry, and moved on to the spot where he had last seen

Valentin. It was deserted; indeed the sidewalk was empty all the way down to the next intersection.

The driveling jazz had stopped.

Eyes peeled for man, beast, or the remnants of either, Harry wandered down the sidewalk. Twenty yards from where he had been standing, the concrete was wet. Not with blood, he was pleased to see; the fluid was the color of bile, and stank to high heaven. Among the splashes were several slivers of what might have been human tissue. Evidently Valentin had fought, and succeeded in opening a wound in his attacker. There were more traces of the blood farther down the sidewalk, as if the injured thing had crawled some way before taking flight again. With Valentin, presumably. In the face of such strength Harry knew his meager powers would have availed him not at all, but he felt guilty nevertheless. He'd heard the cry—seen the assailant swoop—and yet fear had sealed his soles to the ground.

He'd last felt fear the equal of this in Wyckoff Street, when Mimi Lomax's demon-lover had finally thrown off any pretense to humanity. The room had filled with the stink of ether and human dirt, and the demon had stood there in its appalling nakedness and shown him scenes that had turned his bowels to water. They were with him now, those scenes. They would be with him forever.

He looked down at the scrap of paper Valentin had given him: the name and address had been rapidly scrawled, but they were just decipherable.

A wise man, Harry reminded himself, would tear this note up and throw it down into the gutter. But if the events in Wyckoff Street had taught him anything, it was that once touched by such malignancy as he had seen and dreamt in the last few hours, there could be no casual disposal of it. He had to follow it to its source, however repugnant that thought was, and make with it whatever bargains the strength of his hand allowed.

There was no good time to do business like this: the present would have to suffice. He walked back to Lexington and caught a cab to the address on the paper. He got no response from the bell marked Bernstein, but roused the doorman and engaged in a frustrating debate with him through the glass door. The man was angry to have been raised at such an hour; Miss Bernstein was not in her apartment, he insisted, and remained untouched even when Harry intimated that there might be some life-or-death urgency in the matter. It was only when he produced his wallet that the fellow displayed the least flicker of concern. Finally, he let Harry in.

"She's not up there," he said, pocketing the bills. "She's not been in for days."

Harry took the elevator: his shins were aching, and his back too. He wanted sleep, bourbon, then sleep. There was no reply at the apartment as the doorman had predicted, but he kept knocking and calling her.

"Miss Bernstein? Are you there?"

There was no sign of life from within, not, at least, until he said:

"I want to talk about Swann."

He heard an intake of breath, close to the door.

"Is somebody there?" he asked. "Please answer. There's nothing to be afraid of."

After several seconds a slurred and melancholy voice murmured: "Swann's dead."

At least *she* wasn't, Harry thought. Whatever forces had snatched Valentin away, they had not yet reached this corner of Manhattan. "May I talk to you?" he requested.

"No," she replied. Her voice was a candle flame on the verge of extinction.

"Just a few questions, Barbara."

"I'm in the tiger's belly," the slow reply came, "and it doesn't want me to let you in."

Perhaps they *had* got here before him.

"Can't you reach the door?" he coaxed her. "It's not so far . . ."

"But it's eaten me," she said.

"*Try*, Barbara. The tiger won't mind. *Reach.*"

There was silence from the other side of the door, then a snuffling sound. Was she doing as he had requested? It seemed so. He heard her fingers fumbling with the catch.

"That's it," he encouraged her. "Can you turn it? Try to turn it."

At the last instant he thought: suppose she's telling the truth, and there *is* a tiger in there with her? It was too late for retreat, the door was opening. There was no animal in the hallway. Just a woman, and the smell of dirt. She had clearly neither washed nor changed her clothes since fleeing from the theater. The evening gown she wore was soiled and torn, her skin was gray with grime. He stepped into the apartment.

She moved down the hallway away from him, desperate to avoid his touch.

"It's all right," he said, "there's no tiger here."

Her wide eyes were almost empty; what presence roved there was lost to sanity.

"Oh there is," she said, "I'm in the tiger. I'm in it forever."

As he had neither the time nor the skill required to dissuade her from this madness, he decided it was wiser to go with it.

"How did you get there?" he asked her. "Into the tiger? Was it when you were with Swann?"

She nodded.

"You remember that, do you?"

"Oh yes."

"What do you remember?"

"There was a sword; it fell. He was picking up—" She stopped and frowned.

"Picking up what?"

She seemed suddenly more distracted than ever. "How can you hear me," she wondered, "when I'm in the tiger? Are you in the tiger too?"

"Maybe I am," he said, not wanting to analyze the metaphor too closely.

"We're here forever, you know," she informed him. "We'll never be let out."

"Who told you that?"

She didn't reply, but cocked her head a little.

"Can you hear?" she said.

"Hear?"

She took another step back down the hallway. Harry listened, but he could hear nothing. The growing agitation on Barbara's face was sufficient to send him back to the front door and open it, however. The elevator was in operation. He could hear its soft hum across the landing. Worse: the lights in the hallway and on the stairs were deteriorating, the bulbs losing power with every foot the elevator ascended.

He turned back into the apartment and went to take hold of Barbara's wrist. She made no protest. Her eyes were fixed on the doorway through which she seemed to know her judgment would come.

"We'll take the stairs," he told her, and led her out onto the landing. The lights were within an ace of failing. He glanced up at the floor numbers being ticked off above the elevator doors. Was this the top floor they were on, or one shy of it? He couldn't remember, and there was no time to think before the lights went out entirely.

He stumbled across the unfamiliar territory of the landing with the girl in tow, hoping to God he'd find the stairs before the elevator reached this floor. Barbara wanted to loiter, but he bullied her to pick up her pace. As his foot found the top stair the elevator finished its ascent.

The doors hissed open, and a cold fluorescence washed the landing. He couldn't see its source, nor did he wish to, but its effect was to reveal to the naked eye every stain and blemish, every sign of decay and creeping rot, that the paintwork sought to camouflage. The show stole Harry's attention for a moment only, then he took a firmer hold of the woman's hand and they began their descent. Barbara was not interested in escape, however, but in events on the landing. Thus occupied she tripped and fell heavily against Harry. The two would have toppled if he hadn't caught hold of the banister. Angered, he turned to her. They were out of sight of the landing, but the light crept down the stairs and washed over Barbara's face. Beneath its uncharitable scrutiny Harry saw decay busy in her. Saw rot in her teeth, and the death in her skin and hair and nails. No doubt he would have appeared much the same to her, were she to have looked, but she was still staring back over her shoulder and up the stairs. The light source was on the move. Voices accompanied it.

"The door's open," a woman said.

"What are you waiting for?" a voice replied. It was Butterfield.

Harry held both breath and wrist as the light source moved again, toward the door presumably, and then was partially eclipsed as it disappeared into the apartment.

"We have to be quick," he told Barbara. She went with him down three or four steps and then, without warning, her hand leapt for his face, nails opening his cheek. He let go of her hand to protect himself, and in that instant she was away—back up the stairs.

He cursed and stumbled in pursuit of her, but her former sluggishness had lifted; she was startlingly nimble. By the dregs of light from the landing he watched her reach the top of the stairs and disappear from sight.

"Here I am," she called out as she went.

He stood immobile on the stairway, unable to decide whether to go or stay, and so unable to move at all. Ever since Wyckoff Street he'd hated stairs. Momentarily the light from above flared up, throwing the shadows of the banisters across him, then it died again. He put his hand to his face. She had raised weals, but there was little blood. What could he hope from her if he went to her aid? Only more of the same. She was a lost cause.

Even as he despaired of her he heard a sound from round the corner at the head of the stairs, a soft sound that might have been either a foot-step or a sigh. Had she escaped their influence after all? Or perhaps not even reached the apartment door, but thought better of it and about-turned? Even as he was weighing up the odds he heard her say:

"Help me . . ." The voice was a ghost of a ghost, but it was indis-putably hers, and she was in terror.

He reached for his .38 and started up the stairs again. Even before he had turned the corner he felt the nape of his neck itch as his hackles rose.

She was there. But so was the tiger. It stood on the landing, mere feet from Harry, its body humming with latent power. Its eyes were molten, its open maw impossibly large. And there, already in its vast throat, was Barbara. He met her eyes out of the tiger's mouth, and saw a flicker of comprehension in them that was worse than any madness. Then the beast threw its head back and forth to settle its prey in its gut. She had been swallowed whole, apparently. There was no blood on the landing, nor about the tiger's muzzle, only the appalling sight of the girl's face disappearing down the tunnel of the animal's throat.

She loosed a final cry from the belly of the thing, and as it rose it seemed to Harry that the beast attempted a grin. Its face crinkled up grotesquely, the eyes narrowing like those of a laughing Buddha, the lips peeling back to expose a sickle of brilliant teeth. Behind this display the cry was finally hushed. In that instant the tiger leaped.

Harry fired into its devouring bulk, and as the shot met its flesh, the leer and the maw and the whole striped mass of it unwove in a single beat. Suddenly it was gone, and there was only a drizzle of pastel confetti spiraling down around him. The shot had aroused interest. There were raised voices in one or two of the apartments, and the light that had accompanied Butterfield from the elevator was brightening through the open door of the Bernstein residence. He was almost tempted to stay and see the light bringer, but discretion bettered his curiosity, and he turned and made his descent, taking the stairs two and three at a time. The confetti tumbled after him, as if it had a life of its own. Barbara's life, perhaps, transformed into paper pieces and tossed away.

He reached the lobby breathless. The doorman was standing there, staring up the stairs vacantly.

"Somebody get shot?" he inquired.

"No," said Harry, "eaten."

As he headed for the door he heard the elevator start to hum as it descended. Perhaps merely a tenant, coming down for a predawn stroll. Perhaps not.

He left the doorman as he had found him, sullen and confused, and made his escape into the street, putting two block lengths between him and the apartment building before he stopped running. They did not bother to come after him. He was beneath their concern, most likely.

So what was he to do now? Valentin was dead. Barbara Bernstein too. He was none the wiser now than he'd been at the outset, except that he'd learned again the lesson he'd been taught in Wyckoff Street: that when dealing with the Gulfs it was wiser never to believe your eyes. The moment you trusted your senses, the moment you believed a tiger to *be* a tiger, you were half theirs.

Not a complicated lesson, but it seemed he had forgotten it, like a fool, and it had taken two deaths to teach it to him afresh. Maybe it would be simpler to have the rule tattooed on the back of his hand, so that he couldn't check the time without being reminded: *never believe your eyes*.

The principle was still fresh in his mind as he walked back toward his apartment and a man stepped out of the doorway and said:

"Harry."

It *looked* like Valentin, a wounded Valentin, a Valentin who'd been dismembered and sewn together again by a committee of blind surgeons, but the same man in essence. But then the tiger had looked like a tiger, hadn't it?

"It's me," he said.

"Oh no," Harry said, "not this time."

"What are you talking about? *It's Valentin.*"

"So prove it."

The other man looked puzzled. "This is no time for games," he said, "we're in desperate straits."

Harry took his .38 from his pocket and pointed at Valentin's chest. "Prove it or I shoot you," he said.

"Are you out of your mind?"

"I saw you torn apart."

"Not quite," said Valentin. His left arm was swathed in makeshift bandaging from fingertip to midbicep. "It was touch and go," he said, "but everything has its Achilles' heel. It's just a question of finding the right spot."

Harry peered at the man. He wanted to believe that this was indeed Valentin, but it was too incredible to believe that the frail form in front of him could have survived the monstrosity he'd seen on Eighty-third Street. No, this was another illusion. Like the tiger: paper and malice.

The man broke Harry's train of thought. "Your steak . . ." he said.

"My steak?"

"You like it almost burned," Valentin said. "I protested, remember?"

Harry remembered. "Go on," he said.

"And you said you hated the sight of blood. Even if it wasn't your own."

"Yes," said Harry. His doubts were lifting. "That's right."

"You asked me to prove I'm Valentin. That's the best I can do." Harry was almost persuaded. "In God's name," Valentin said, "do we have to debate this standing on the street?"

"You'd better come in."

The apartment was small, but tonight it felt more stifling than ever. Valentin sat himself down with a good view of the door. He refused spirits or first aid. Harry helped himself to bourbon. He was on his third shot when Valentin finally said:

"We have to go back to the house, Harry."

"What?"

"We have to claim Swann's body before Butterfield."

"I did my best already. It's not my business anymore."

"So you leave Swann to the Pit?" Valentin said.

"She doesn't care, why should I?"

"You mean Dorothea? She doesn't know what Swann was involved with. That's why she's so trusting. She has suspicions maybe, but insofar as it is possible to be guiltless in all of this, she is." He paused to adjust the position of his injured arm. "She was a prostitute, you know. I don't suppose she told you that. Swann once said to me he married her because only prostitutes know the value of love."

Harry let this apparent paradox go.

"Why did she stay with him?" he asked. "He wasn't exactly faithful, was he?"

"She loved him," Valentin replied. "It's not unheard of."

"And you?"

"Oh, I loved him too, in spite of his stupidities. That's why we have to help him. If Butterfield and his associates get their hands on Swann's mortal remains, there'll be all hell to pay."

"I know. I got a glimpse at the Bernstein place."

"What did you see?"

"Something and nothing," said Harry. "A tiger, I thought; only it wasn't."

"The old paraphernalia," Valentin commented.

"And there was something else with Butterfield. Something that shed light: I didn't see what."

"The Castrato," Valentin muttered to himself, clearly discomfited. "We'll have to be careful."

He stood up, the movement causing him to wince. "I think we should be on our way, Harry."

"Are you paying me for this?" Harry inquired, "or am I doing it all for love?"

"You're doing it because of what happened at Wyckoff Street," came the softly spoken reply. "Because you lost poor Mimi Lomax to the Gulfs, and you don't want to lose Swann. That is, if you've not already done so."

They caught a cab on Madison Avenue and headed back uptown to Sixty-first Street, keeping their silence as they rode. Harry had half a hundred questions to ask of Valentin. Who was Butterfield, for one, and what was Swann's crime that he be pursued to death and beyond? So many puzzles. But Valentin looked sick and unfit for plying with questions. Besides, Harry sensed that the more he knew the less enthusiastic he would be about the journey they were now taking.

"We have perhaps one advantage," Valentin said as they approached Sixty-first Street. "They can't be expecting this frontal attack. Butterfield presumes I'm dead, and probably thinks you're hiding your head in mortal terror."

"I'm working on it."

"You're not in danger," Valentin replied, "at least not the way Swann is. If they were to take you apart limb by limb it would be nothing beside the torments they have waiting for the magician."

"Illusionist," Harry corrected him, but Valentin shook his head.

"Magician he was, magician he will always be."

The driver interrupted before Harry could quote Dorothea on the subject.

"What number you people want?" he said.

"Just drop us here on the right," Valentin instructed him. "And wait for us, understand?"

"Sure."

Valentin turned to Harry. "Give the man fifty dollars."

"*Fifty?*"

"Do you want him to wait or not?"

Harry counted four tens and ten singles into the driver's hand.

"You'd better keep the engine running," he said.

"Anything to oblige," the driver grinned.

Harry joined Valentin on the sidewalk and they walked the twenty-five yards to the house. The street was still noisy, despite the hour: the party that Harry had seen in preparation half a night ago was at its height. There was no sign of life at the Swann residence, however.

Perhaps they *don't* expect us, Harry thought. Certainly this head-on assault was about the most foolhardy tactic imaginable, and as such might catch the enemy off-guard. But were such forces ever off-guard? Was there ever a minute in their maggoty lives when their eyelids drooped and sleep tamed them for a space? No. In Harry's experience it was only the good who needed sleep; iniquity and its practitioners were awake every eager moment, planning fresh felonies.

"How do we get in?" he asked as they stood outside the house.

"I have the key," Valentin replied, and went to the door.

There was no retreat now. The key was turned, the door was open, and they were stepping out of the comparative safety of the street. The house was as dark within as it had appeared from without. There was no sound of human presence on any of the floors. Was it possible that the defenses Swann had laid around his corpse had indeed rebuffed Butterfield, and that he and his cohorts had retreated? Valentin quashed such misplaced optimism almost immediately, taking hold of Harry's arm and leaning close to whisper:

"*They're here.*"

This was not the time to ask Valentin how he knew, but Harry made a mental note to inquire when, or rather *if,* they got out of the house with their tongues still in their heads.

Valentin was already on the stairs. Harry, his eyes still accustoming themselves to the vestigial light that crept in from the street, crossed the hallway after him. The other man moved confidently in the gloom, and Harry was glad of it. Without Valentin plucking at his sleeve, and guiding him around the half-landing, he might well have crippled himself.

Despite what Valentin had said, there was no more sound or sight of occupancy up here than there had been below, but as they advanced toward the master bedroom where Swann lay, a rotten tooth in Harry's lower jaw that had lately been quiescent began to throb afresh, and his bowels ached to break wind. The anticipation was crucifying. He felt a barely suppressible urge to yell out, and to oblige the enemy to show its hand, if indeed it had hands to show.

Valentin had reached the door. He turned his head in Harry's direction, and even in the murk it was apparent that fear was taking its toll on him too. His skin glistened, he stank of fresh sweat.

He pointed toward the door. Harry nodded. He was as ready as he was ever going to be. Valentin reached for the door handle. The sound of the lock mechanism seemed deafeningly loud, but it brought no response from anywhere in the house. The door swung open, and the heady scent of flowers met them. They had begun to decay in the forced heat of the house; there was a rankness beneath the perfume. More welcome than the scent was the light. The curtains in the room had not been entirely drawn, and the streetlamps described the interior: the flowers massed like clouds around the casket; the chair where Harry had sat, the Calvados bottle beside it; the mirror above the fireplace showing the room its secret self.

Valentin was already moving across to the casket, and Harry heard him sigh as he set eyes on his old master. He wasted little time, but immediately set to lifting the lower half of the casket lid. It defeated his single arm, however, and Harry went to his assistance, eager to get the job done and be away. Touching the solid wood of the casket brought his nightmare back with breath-snatching force: the Pit opening beneath him, the illusionist rising from his bed like a sleeper unwillingly woken. There was no such spectacle now, however. Indeed a little life in the corpse might have made the job easier. Swann was a big man, and his limp body was uncooperative to a fault. The simple act of lifting him from his casket took all their breath and attention. He came at last, though reluctantly, his long limbs flopping about.

"Now . . ." said Valentin, ". . . downstairs."

As they moved to the door something in the street ignited, or so it seemed, for the interior suddenly brightened. The light was not kind to their burden. It revealed the crudity of the cosmetics applied to Swann's face, and the burgeoning putrescence beneath. Harry had an instant only to appreciate these felicities, and then the light brightened again, and he realized that it wasn't *out*side, but *in*.

He looked up at Valentin, and almost despaired. The luminescence was even less charitable to servant than to master; it seemed to strip the flesh from Valentin's face. Harry caught only a glimpse of what it revealed beneath—events stole his attention an instant later—but he saw enough to know that had Valentin not been his accomplice in this venture he might well have run from him.

"*Get him out of here!*" Valentin yelled.

He let go of Swann's legs, leaving Harry to steer Swann single-handed. The corpse proved recalcitrant, however. Harry had only made two cursing steps toward the exit when things took a turn for the cata-clysmic.

He heard Valentin unloose an oath, and looked up to see that the mirror had given up all pretense to reflection, and that something was moving up from its liquid depths, bringing the light with it.

"What is it?" Harry breathed.

"The Castrato," same the reply. "Will you *go?*"

There was no time to obey Valentin's panicked instruction, however, before the hidden thing broke the plane of the mirror and invaded the room. Harry had been wrong. It did not carry the light with it as it came: it *was* the light. Or rather, some holocaust blazed in its bowels, the glare of which escaped through the creature's body by whatever route it could. It had once been human, a mountain of a man with the belly and the breasts of a Neolithic Venus. But the fire in its body had twisted it out of true, breaking out through its palms and its navel, burning its mouth and nostrils into one ragged hole. It had, as its name implied, been unsexed; from that hole too, light spilled. By it, the decay of the flowers speeded into seconds. The blossoms withered and died. The room was filled in moments with the stench of rotting vegetable matter.

Harry heard Valentin call his name, once, and again. Only then did he remember the body in his arms. He dragged his eyes from the hovering Castrato, and carried Swann another yard. The door was at his back, and open. He dragged his burden out into the landing as the Castrato kicked over the casket. He heard the din, and then shouts from Valentin. There followed another terrible commotion, and the high-pitched voice of the Castrato, talking through that hole in its face.

"Die and be happy," it said, and a hail of furniture was flung against the wall with such force chairs embedded themselves in the plaster. Valentin had escaped the assault, however, or so it seemed, for an instant later Harry heard the Castrato shriek. It was an appalling sound: pitiful and revolting. He would have stopped his ears but that he had his hands full.

He had almost reached the top of the stairs. Dragging Swann a few steps farther, he laid the body down. The Castrato's light was not dimmed, despite its complaints; it still flickered on the bedroom wall like a midsummer thunderstorm. For the third time tonight—once on Eighty-third Street, and again on the stairs of the Bernstein place—Harry hesitated. If he went back to help Valentin perhaps there would be worse sights to see than ever Wyckoff Street had offered. But there could be no retreat this time. Without Valentin he was lost. He raced back down the landing and flung open the door. The air was thick, the lamps rocking. In the middle of the room hung the Castrato, still defying gravity. It had hold of Valentin by his hair. Its other hand was poised, first and middle fingers spread like twin horns, about to stab out its captive's eyes.

Harry pulled his .38 from his pocket, aimed, and fired. He had always been a bad shot when given more than a moment to take aim, but in extremis, when instinct governed rational thought, he was not half bad. This was such an occasion. The bullet found the Castrato's neck and opened another wound. More in surprise than pain, perhaps, it let Valentin go. There was a leakage of light from the hole in its neck, and it put its hand to the place.

Valentin was quickly on his feet.

"Again," he called to Harry. "*Fire again!*"

Harry obeyed the instruction. His second bullet pierced the creature's chest, his third its belly. This last wound seemed particularly traumatic; the distended flesh, ripe for bursting, broke—and the trickle of light that spilled from the wound rapidly became a flood as the abdomen split.

Again the Castrato howled, this time in panic, and lost all control of its flight. It reeled like a pricked balloon toward the ceiling, its fat hands desperately attempting to stem the mutiny in its substance. But it had reached critical mass; there was no making good the damage done. Lumps of its flesh began to break from it. Valentin, either too stunned or too fascinated, stood staring up at the disintegration while rains of cooked meat fell around him. Harry took hold of him and hauled him back toward the door.

The Castrato was finally earning its name, unloosing a desolate ear-piercing note. Harry didn't wait to watch its demise, but slammed the bedroom door as the voice reached an awesome pitch, and the windows smashed.

Valentin was grinning.

"Do you know what we did?" he said.

"Never mind. Let's just get the fuck out of here."

The sight of Swann's corpse at the top of the stairs seemed to chasten Valentin. Harry instructed him to assist, and he did so as efficiently as his dazed condition allowed. Together they began to escort the illusionist down the stairs. As they reached the front door there was a final shriek from above, as the Castrato came apart at the seams. Then silence.

The commotion had not gone unnoticed. Revelers had appeared from the house opposite; a crowd of late-night pedestrians had assembled on the sidewalk. "Some party," one of them said as the trio emerged.

Harry had half expected the cab to have deserted them, but he had reckoned without the driver's curiosity. The man was out of his vehicle and staring up at the second-floor window.

"Does he need a hospital?" he asked as they bundled Swann into the back of the cab.

"No." Harry returned, "he's about as good as he's going to get."

"Will you *drive?*" said Valentin.

"Sure. Just tell me where to."

"Anywhere," came the weary reply. "Just get out of here."

"Hold it a minute," the driver said. "I don't want any trouble."

"Then you'd better *move,*" said Valentin. The driver met his passenger's gaze. Whatever he saw there, his next words were:

"I'm driving," and they took off along East Sixty-first like the proverbial bat out of hell.

"We did it, Harry," Valentin said when they'd been traveling for a few minutes. "We got him back."

"And that *thing?* Tell me about it."

"The Castrato? What's to tell? Butterfield must have left it as a watchdog, until he could bring in a technician to decode Swann's defense mechanisms. We were lucky. It was in need of milking. That makes them unstable."

"How do you know so much about all of this?"

"It's a long story," said Valentin, "and not for a cab ride."

"So what now? We can't drive round in circles all night."

Valentin looked across at the body that sat between them, prey to every whim of the cab's suspension and road-menders' craft. Gently, he put Swann's hands on his lap.

"You're right, of course," he said. "We have to make arrangements for the cremation as swiftly as possible."

The cab bounced across a pothole. Valentin's face tightened.

"Are you in pain?" Harry asked him.

"I've been in worse."

"We could go back to my apartment, and rest there."

Valentin shook his head. "Not very clever," he said, "it's the first place they'll look."

"My office, then—"

"The second place."

"Well, Jesus, this cab's going to run out of gas, eventually."

At this point the driver intervened.

"Say, did you people mention cremation?"

"Maybe," Valentin replied.

"My brother-in-law's got a funeral business out in Queens."

"Is that so?" said Harry.

"Very reasonable rates. I can recommend him. No shit."

"Could you contact him *now?*" Valentin said.

"It's two in the morning."

"We're in a hurry."

The driver reached up and adjusted his mirror; he was looking at Swann.

"You don't mind me asking, do you," he said, "but is that a body you got back there?"

"It is," said Harry, "and he's getting impatient."

The driver made a whooping sound. "Shit!" he said. "I've had a woman drop twins in that seat; I've had whores do business; I even had an alligator back there one time. But this beats them all!" He pondered for a moment, then said, "You kill him, did you?"

"No," said Harry.

"Guess we'd be heading for the East River if you had, eh?"

"That's right. We just want a decent cremation. And *quickly*."

"That's understandable."

"What's your name?" Harry asked him.

"Winston Jowitt. But everybody calls me Byron. I'm a poet, see? Leastways, I am on weekends."

"Byron."

"See, any other driver would be freaked out, right? Finding two guys with a body in the backseat. But the way I see it, it's all material."

"For the poems."

"Right," said Byron. "The Muse is a fickle mistress. You have to take it where you find it, you know? Speaking of which, you gentlemen got any idea where you want to go?"

"Make it your offices," Valentin told Harry. "And he can call his brother-in-law."

"Good," said Harry. Then, to Byron:

"Head west along Forty-fifth Street to Eighth."

"You got it," said Byron, and the cab's speed doubled in the space of twenty yards. "Say," he said, "you guys fancy a poem?"

"Now?" said Harry.

"I like to improvise," Byron replied. "Pick a subject. Any subject."

Valentin hugged his wounded arm close. Quietly, he said, "How about the end of the world?"

"Good subject," the poet replied, "just give me a minute or two."

"So soon?" said Valentin.

They took a circuitous route to the office while Byron Jowitt tried a selection of rhymes for Apocalypse. The sleepwalkers were out on Forty-fifth Street, in search of one high or another; some sat in the doorways, one lay sprawled across the sidewalk. None of them gave the cab or its occupants more than the briefest perusal. Harry unlocked the front door and he and Byron carried Swann up to the third floor.

The office was home away from home: cramped and chaotic. They put Swann in the swivel chair behind the furred coffee cups and the alimony demands heaped on the desk. He looked easily the healthiest of

the quartet. Byron was sweating like a bull after the climb; Harry felt—
and surely looked—as though he hadn't slept in sixty days; Valentin sat
slumped in the clients' chair, so drained of vitality he might have been at
death's door.

"You look terrible," Harry told him.

"No matter," he said, "it'll all be done soon."

Harry turned to Byron. "How about calling this brother-in-law of
yours?"

While Byron set to doing so, Harry returned his attention to
Valentin.

"I've got a first-aid box somewhere about," he said. "Shall I bandage
up that arm?"

"Thank you, but no. Like you, I hate the sight of blood. Especially
my own."

Byron was on the phone, chastising his brother-in-law for his ingrat-
itude. "What's your beef? I got you a client! I *know* the time, for Christ's
sake, but business is business . . ."

"Tell him we'll pay double his normal rate," Valentin said.

"You hear that, Mel? *Twice* your usual fee. So get over here, will
you?" He gave the address to his brother-in-law and put down the
receiver. "He's coming over," he announced.

"Now?" said Harry.

"Now." Byron glanced at his watch. "My belly thinks my throat's cut.
How about we eat? You got an all-night place near here?"

"There's one a block down from here."

"You want food?" Byron asked Valentin.

"I don't think so," he said. He was looking worse by the moment.

"OK," Byron said to Harry, "just you and me then. You got ten I
could borrow?"

Harry gave him a bill, the keys to the street door, and an order for
doughnuts and coffee, and Byron went on his way. Only when he'd gone
did Harry wish he'd convinced the poet to stave off his hunger pangs
awhile. The office was distressingly quiet without him: Swann in residence behind the desk, Valentin succumbing to sleep in the other chair.
The hush brought to mind another such silence, during that last, awesome night at the Lomax house when Mimi's demon-lover, wounded by
Father Hesse, had slipped away into the walls for a while and left them
waiting and waiting, knowing it would come back but not certain of when

or how. Six hours they'd sat—Mimi occasionally breaking the silence with laughter or gibberish—and the first Harry had known of its return was the smell of cooking excrement, and Mimi's cry of "Sodomite!" as Hesse surrendered to an act his faith had too long forbidden him. There had been no more silence then, not for a long space: only Hesse's cries, and Harry's pleas for forgetfulness. They had all gone unanswered.

It seemed he could hear the demon's voice now, its demands, its invitations. But no, it was only Valentin. The man was tossing his head back and forth in sleep, his face knotted up. Suddenly he started from his chair, one word on his lips:

"Swann!"

His eyes opened, and as they alighted on the illusionist's body, which was propped in the chair opposite, tears came uncontrollably, wracking him.

"He's dead," he said, as though in his dream he had forgotten that bitter fact. "I failed him, D'Amour. That's why he's dead. Because of my negligence."

"You're doing your best for him now," Harry said, though he knew the words were poor compensation. "Nobody could ask for a better friend."

"I was never his friend," Valentin said, staring at the corpse with brimming eyes. "I always hoped he'd one day trust me entirely. But he never did."

"Why not?"

"He couldn't afford to trust anybody. Not in his situation." He wiped his cheeks with the back of his hand.

"Maybe," Harry said, "it's about time you told me what all this is about."

"If you want to hear."

"I want to hear."

"Very well," said Valentin. "Thirty-two years ago, Swann made a bargain with the Gulfs. He agreed to be an ambassador for them if they, in return, gave him magic."

"Magic?"

"The ability to perform miracles. To transform matter. To bewitch souls. Even to drive out God."

"That's a miracle?"

"It's more difficult than you think," Valentin replied.

"So Swann *was* a genuine magician?"

"Indeed he was."

"Then why didn't he use his powers?"

"He did," Valentin replied. "He used them every night, at every performance."

Harry was baffled. "I don't follow."

"Nothing the Prince of Lies offers to humankind is of the least value," Valentin said, "or it wouldn't be offered. Swann didn't know that when he first made his Covenant. But he soon learned. Miracles are useless. Magic is a distraction from the real concerns. It's rhetoric. Melodrama."

"So what exactly are the real concerns?"

"You should know better than I," Valentin replied. "Fellowship, maybe? Curiosity? Certainly it matters not in the least if water can be made into wine, or Lazarus to live another year."

Harry saw the wisdom of this, but not how it had brought the magician to Broadway. As it was, he didn't need to ask. Valentin had taken up the story afresh. His tears had cleared with the telling; some trace of animation had crept back into his features.

"It didn't take Swann long to realize he'd sold his soul for a mess of pottage," he explained. "And when he did he was inconsolable. At least he was for a while. Then he began to contrive a revenge."

"How?"

"By taking hell's name in vain. By using the magic which it boasted of as a trivial entertainment, degrading the power of the Gulfs by passing off their wonder-working as mere illusion. It was, you see, an act of heroic perversity. Every time a trick of Swann's was explained away as sleight of hand, the Gulfs squirmed."

"Why didn't they kill him?" Harry said.

"Oh, they tried. Many times. But he had allies. Agents in their camp who warned him of their plots against him. He escaped their retribution for years that way."

"Until now?"

"Until now," Valentin sighed. "He was careless, and so was I. Now he's dead, and the Gulfs are itching for him."

"I see."

"But we were not entirely unprepared for this eventuality. He had made his apologies to heaven, and I dare to hope he's been forgiven his trespasses. Pray that he has. There's more than *his* salvation at stake tonight."

"Yours too?"

"All of us who loved him are tainted," Valentin replied, "but if we can destroy his physical remains before the Gulfs claim them we may yet avoid the consequences of his Covenant."

"Why did you wait so long? Why didn't you just cremate him the day he died?"

"Their lawyers are not fools. The Covenant specifically prescribes a period of lying-in-state. If we had attempted to ignore that clause his soul would have been forfeited automatically."

"So when is this period up?"

"Three hours ago, at midnight," Valentin replied. "That's why they're so desperate, you see. And so dangerous."

Another poem came to Byron Jowitt as he ambled back up Eighth Avenue, working his way through a tuna salad sandwich. His Muse was not to be rushed. Poems could take as long as five minutes to be finalized, longer if they involved a double rhyme. He didn't hurry on his journey back to the offices, therefore, but wandered in a dreamy sort of mood, turning the lines every which way to make them fit. That way he hoped to arrive back with another finished poem. Two in one night was damn good going.

He had not perfected the final couplet, however, by the time he reached the door. Operating on automatic pilot, he fumbled in his pocket for the keys D'Amour had loaned him and let himself in. He was about to close the door again when a woman stepped through the gap, smiling at him. She was a beauty, and Byron, being a poet, was a fool for beauty.

"Please," she said to him, "I need your help."

"What can I do for you?" said Byron through a mouthful of food.

"Do you know a man by the name of D'Amour? Harry D'Amour?"

"Indeed I do. I'm going up to his place right now."

"Perhaps you could show me the way?" the woman asked him, as Byron closed the door.

"Be my pleasure," he replied, and led her across the lobby to the bottom of the stairs.

"You know, you're very sweet," she told him, and Byron melted.

Valentin stood at the window.

"Something wrong?" Harry asked.

"Just a feeling," Valentin commented. "I have a suspicion maybe the Devil's in Manhattan."

"So what's new?"

"That maybe he's coming for us." As if on cue there was a knock at the door. Harry jumped. "It's all right," Valentin said, "he never knocks."

Harry went to the door, feeling like a fool.

"Is that you, Byron?" he asked before unlocking it.

"Please," said a voice he thought he'd never hear again. "Help me . . ."

He opened the door. It was Dorothea, of course. She was colorless as water, and as unpredictable. Even before Harry had invited her across the office threshold, a dozen expressions, or hints of such, had crossed her face; anguish, suspicion, terror. And now, as her eyes alighted upon the body of her beloved Swann, relief and gratitude.

"You *do* have him," she said, stepping into the office.

Harry closed the door. There was a chill from up the stairs.

"Thank God. Thank God." She took Harry's face in her hands and kissed him lightly on the lips. Only then did she notice Valentin.

She dropped her hands.

"What's *he* doing here?" she asked.

"He's with me. With us."

She looked doubtful. "No," she said.

"We can trust him."

"I said *no!* Get him out, Harry." There was a cold fury in her; she shook with it. *"Get him out!"*

Valentin stared at her, glassy-eyed. "The lady doth protest too much," he murmured.

Dorothea put her fingers to her lips as if to stifle any further outburst. "I'm sorry," she said, turning back to Harry, "but you must be told what this man is capable of—"

"Without him your husband would still be at the house, Mrs. Swann," Harry pointed out. "*He's* the one you should be grateful to, not me."

At this, Dorothea's expression softened, through bafflement to a new gentility.

"Oh?" she said. Now she looked back at Valentin. "I'm sorry. When you ran from the house I assumed some complicity . . ."

"With whom?" Valentin inquired.

She made a tiny shake of her head, then said, "Your arm. Are you hurt?"

"A minor injury," he returned.

"I've already tried to get it rebandaged," Harry said. "But the bastard's too stubborn."

"Stubborn I am," Valentin replied, without inflection.

"But we'll be finished here soon—" said Harry.

Valentin broke in. "Don't tell her anything," he snapped.

"I'm just going to explain about the brother-in-law—" Harry said.

"The brother-in-law?" Dorothea said, sitting down. The sigh of her legs crossing was the most enchanting sound Harry had heard in twenty-four hours. "Oh please tell me about the brother-in-law . . ."

Before Harry could open his mouth to speak, Valentin said, "It's not her, Harry."

The words, spoken without a trace of drama, took a few seconds to make sense. Even when they did, their lunacy was self-evident. Here she was in the flesh, perfect in every detail.

"What are you talking about?" Harry said.

"How much more plainly can I say it?" Valentin replied. "*It's not her.* It's a trick. An illusion. They know where we are, and they sent *this* up to spy out our defenses."

Harry would have laughed but that these accusations were bringing tears to Dorothea's eyes.

"Stop it," he told Valentin.

"No, Harry. You *think* for a moment. All the traps they've laid, all the beasts they've mustered. You suppose she could have escaped that?" he moved away from the window toward Dorothea. "Where's Butterfield?" he spat. "Down the hall, waiting for your signal?"

"Shut up," said Harry.

"He's scared to come up here himself, isn't he?" Valentin went on. "Scared of Swann, scared of us, probably, after what we did to his gelding."

Dorothea looked at Harry. "Make him stop," she said.

Harry halted Valentin's advance with a hand on his bony chest.

"You heard the lady," he said.

"That's no lady," Valentin replied, his eyes blazing. "I don't know what it is, but it's no lady."

Dorothea stood up. "I came here because I hoped I'd be safe," she said.

"You *are* safe," Harry said.

"Not with him around, I'm not," she replied, looking back at Valentin. "I think I'd be wiser going."

Harry touched her arm.

"No," he told her.

"Mr. D'Amour," she said sweetly, "you've already earned your fee ten times over. Now I think it's time *I* took responsibility for my husband."

Harry scanned that mercurial face. There wasn't a trace of deception in it.

"I have a car downstairs," she said. "I wonder . . . could you carry him downstairs for me?"

Harry heard a noise like a cornered dog behind him and turned to see Valentin standing beside Swann's corpse. He had picked up the heavy-duty cigarette lighter from the desk and was flicking it. Sparks came, but no flame.

"What the hell are you doing?" Harry demanded.

Valentin didn't look at the speaker, but at Dorothea.

"She knows," he said.

He got the knack of the lighter; the flame flared up.

Dorothea made a small, desperate sound.

"Please don't," she said.

"We'll all burn with him if necessary," Valentin said.

"He's insane." Dorothea's tears had suddenly gone.

"She's right," Harry told Valentin, "you're acting like a madman."

"And you're a fool to fall for a few tears!" came the reply. "Can't you see that if she takes him we've lost everything we've fought for?"

"Don't listen," she murmured. "You know me, Harry. You trust me."

"What's under that face of yours?" Valentin said. "What are you? A Coprolite? Homunculus?"

The names meant nothing to Harry. All he knew was the proximity of the woman at his side, her hand laid upon his arm.

"And what about you?" she said to Valentin. Then, more softly, "Why don't you show us your wound?"

She forsook the shelter of Harry's side and crossed to the desk. The lighter flame guttered at her approach.

"Go on," she said, her voice no louder than a breath, ". . . I *dare* you."

She glanced round at Harry. "Ask him, D'Amour," she said. "Ask him to show you what he's got hidden under the bandages."

"What's she talking about?" Harry asked. The glimmer of trepidation in Valentin's eyes was enough to convince Harry there was merit in Dorothea's request. "Explain," he said.

Valentin didn't get the chance, however. Distracted by Harry's demand, he was easy prey when Dorothea reached across the desk and knocked the lighter from his hand. He bent to retrieve it, but she seized on the ad hoc bundle of bandaging and pulled. It tore, and fell away.

She stepped back. "See?" she said.

Valentin stood revealed. The creature on Eighty-third Street had torn the sham of humanity from his arm; the limb beneath was a mass of blue-black scales. Each digit of the blistered hand ended in a nail that opened and closed like a parrot's beak. He made no attempt to conceal the truth. Shame eclipsed every other response.

"I warned you," she said, "I warned you he wasn't to be trusted."

Valentin stared at Harry. "I have no excuses," he said. "I only ask you to believe that I want what's best for Swann."

"How can you?" Dorothea said. "You're a demon."

"More than that," Valentin replied, "I'm Swann's Tempter. His familiar, his creature. But I belong to him more than I ever belonged to the Gulfs. And I will defy them"—he looked at Dorothea—"and their agents."

She turned to Harry. "You have a gun," she said. "Shoot the filth. You mustn't suffer a thing like that to live."

Harry looked at the pustulant arm, at the clacking fingernails: what further repugnance was there in wait behind the flesh facade?

"Shoot it," the woman said.

He took his gun from his pocket. Valentin seemed to have shrunk in the moments since the revelation of his true nature. Now he leaned against the wall, his face slimy with despair.

"Kill me, then," he said to Harry, "kill me if I revolt you so much. But, Harry, I *beg* you, don't give Swann to her. Promise me that. Wait for the driver to come back, and dispose of the body by whatever means you can. Just don't give it to her!"

"Don't listen," Dorothea said. "He doesn't care about Swann the way I do."

Harry raised the gun. Even looking straight at death, Valentin did not flinch.

"You've failed, Judas," she said to Valentin. "The magician's mine."

"What magician?" said Harry.

"Why Swann, of course!" she replied lightly. "How many magicians have you got up here?"

Harry dropped his bead on Valentin.

"He's an illusionist," he said, "you told me that at the very beginning. Never call him a magician, you said."

"Don't be pedantic," she replied, trying to laugh off her faux pas.

He leveled the gun at her. She threw back her head suddenly, her face contracting, and unloosed a sound of which, had Harry not heard it from a human throat, he would not have believed the larynx capable. It rang down the corridor and the stairs, in search of some waiting ear.

"Butterfield is here," said Valentin flatly.

Harry nodded. In the same moment she came toward him, her features grotesquely contorted. She was strong and quick, a blur of venom that took him off-guard. He heard Valentin tell him to kill her, before she transformed. It took him a moment to grasp the significance of this, by which time she had her teeth at his throat. One of her hands was a cold vise around his wrist; he sensed strength in her sufficient to powder his bones. His fingers were already numbed by her grip; he had no time to do more than depress the trigger. The gun went off. Her breath on his throat seemed to gush from her. Then she loosed her hold on him, and staggered back. The shot had blown open her abdomen.

He shook to see what he had done. The creature, for all its shriek, still resembled a woman he might have loved.

"Good," said Valentin, as the blood hit the office floor in gouts. "Now it must show itself."

Hearing him, she shook her head. "This is all there is to show," she said.

Harry threw the gun down. "My God," he said softly, "it's her . . ."

Dorothea grimaced. The blood continued to come. "Some *part* of her," she replied.

"Have you always been with them, then?" Valentin asked.

"Of course not."

"Why, then?"

"Nowhere to go . . ." she said, her voice fading by the syllable. "Nothing to believe in. All lies. Everything: *lies.*"

"So you sided with Butterfield?"

"Better hell," she said, "than a false heaven."

"Who taught you that?" Harry murmured.

"Who do you think?" she replied, turning her gaze on him. Though her strength was going out of her with the blood, her eyes still blazed. "You're finished, D'Amour," she said. "You, and the demon, and Swann. There's nobody left to help you now."

Despite the contempt in her words he couldn't stand and watch her bleed to death. Ignoring Valentin's imperative that he keep clear, he went across to her. As he stepped within range she lashed out at him with astonishing force. The blow blinded him a moment; he fell against the tall filing cabinet, which toppled sideways. He and it hit the ground together. *It* spilled papers, he, curses. He was vaguely aware that the woman was moving past him to escape, but he was too busy keeping his head from spinning to prevent her. When equilibrium returned she had gone, leaving her bloody handprints on wall and door.

Chaplin, the janitor, was protective of his territory. The basement of the building was a private domain in which he sorted through office trash and fed his beloved furnace, and read aloud his favorite passages from the Good Book, all without fear of interruption. His bowels—which were far from healthy—allowed him little slumber. A couple of hours a night, no more, which he supplemented with dozing through the day. It was not so bad. He had the seclusion of the basement to retire to whenever life upstairs became too demanding, and the forced heat would sometimes bring strange waking dreams.

Was this such a dream: this insipid fellow in his fine suit? If not, how had he gained access to the basement, when the door was locked and bolted? He asked no questions of the intruder. Something about the way the man stared at him baffled his tongue. "Chaplin," the fellow said, his thin lips barely moving, "I'd like you to open the furnace."

In other circumstances he might well have picked up his shovel and clouted the stranger across the head. The furnace was his baby. He knew, as no one else knew, its quirks and occasional petulance; he loved, as no one else loved, the roar it gave when it was content; he did not take kindly to the proprietorial tone the man used. But he'd lost the will to resist. He picked up a rag and opened the peeling door, offering its hot heart to this man as Lot had offered his daughters to the stranger in Sodom.

Butterfield smiled at the smell of heat from the furnace. From three floors above he heard the woman crying out for help, and then, a few moments later, a shot. She had failed. He had thought she would. But her life was forfeit anyway. There was no loss in sending her into the breach, in the slim chance that she might have coaxed the body from its keepers. It would have saved the inconvenience of a full-scale attack, but no matter. To have Swann's soul was worth any effort. He had defiled the good name of the Prince of Lies. For that he would suffer as no other miscreant magician ever had. Beside Swann's punishment, Faust's would be an inconvenience, and Napoleon's a pleasure cruise.

As the echoes of the shot died above, he took the black lacquer box from his jacket pocket. The janitor's eyes were turned heavenward. He too had heard the shot.

"It was nothing," Butterfield told him. "Stoke the fire."

Chaplin obeyed. The heat in the cramped basement rapidly grew. The janitor began to sweat; his visitor did not. He stood mere feet from the open furnace door and gazed into the brightness with impassive features. At last, he seemed satisfied.

"Enough," he said, and opened the lacquer box. Chaplin thought he glimpsed movement in the box, as though it were full to the lid with maggots, but before he had a chance to look more closely both the box and contents were pitched into the flames.

"Close the door," Butterfield said. Chaplin obeyed. "You may watch over them awhile, if it pleases you. They need the heat. It makes them mighty."

He left the janitor to keep his vigil beside the furnace and went back up to the hallway. He had left the street door open, and a pusher had come in out of the cold to do business with a client. They bartered in the shadows, until the pusher caught sight of the lawyer.

"Don't mind me," Butterfield said, and started up the stairs. He found the widow Swann on the first landing. She was not quite dead, but he quickly finished the job D'Amour had started.

"We're in trouble," said Valentin. "I hear noises downstairs. Is there any other way out of here?"

Harry sat on the floor, leaning against the toppled cabinet, and tried not to think of Dorothea's face as the bullet found her, or of the creature he was now reduced to needing.

"There's a fire escape," he said; "it runs down to the back of the building."

"Show me," said Valentin, attempting to haul him to his feet.

"Keep your hands off me!"

Valentin withdrew, bruised by the rebuff. "I'm sorry," he said. "Maybe I shouldn't hope for your acceptance. But I do."

Harry said nothing, just got to his feet among the litter of reports and photographs. He'd had a dirty life: spying on adulteries for vengeful spouses, dredging gutters for lost children, keeping company with scum because it rose to the top and the rest just drowned. Could Valentin's soul be much grimier?

"The fire escape's down the hall," he said.

"We can still get Swann out," Valentin said. "Still give him a decent cremation—" The demon's obsession with his master's dignity was chastening in its way. "But you have to help me, Harry."

"I'll help you," he said, avoiding sight of the creature. "Just don't expect love and affection."

If it were possible to hear a smile, that's what he heard.

"They want this over and done with before dawn," the demon said.

"It can't be far from that now."

"An hour, maybe," Valentin replied. "But it's enough. Either way, it's enough."

The sound of the furnace soothed Chaplin; its rumbles and rattlings were as familiar as the complaint of his own intestines. But there was another sound growing behind the door, the like of which he'd never heard before. His mind made foolish pictures to go with it. Of pigs laughing, of glass and barbed wire being ground between the teeth, of hoofed feet dancing on the door. As the noises grew, so did his trepidation, but when he went to the basement door to summon help it was locked; the key had gone. And now, as if matters weren't bad enough, the light went out.

He began to fumble for a prayer—"Holy Mary, Mother of God, pray for us sinners now and at the hour—"

But he stopped when a voice addressed him, quite clearly.

"Michelmas," it said.

It was unmistakably his mother. And there could be no doubt of its source either. It came from the furnace.

"*Michelmas*," she demanded, "are you going to let me cook in here?"

It wasn't possible, of course, that she was there in the flesh: she'd been dead thirteen long years. But some phantom, perhaps? He believed in phantoms. Indeed he'd seen them on occasion, coming and going from the cinemas on Forty-second Street, arm in arm.

"Open up, Michelmas," his mother told him, in that special voice she used when she had some treat for him. Like a good child, he approached the door. He had never felt such heat off the furnace as he felt now; he could smell the hairs on his arms wither.

"*Open the door*," Mother said again. There was no denying her. Despite the searing air, he reached to comply.

"That fucking janitor," said Harry, giving the sealed fire-escape door a vengeful kick. "This door's supposed to be left unlocked at all times." He pulled at the chains that were wrapped around the handles. "We'll have to take the stairs."

There was a noise from the back down the corridor, a roar in the heating system which made the antiquated radiators rattle. At that moment, down in the basement, Michelmas Chaplin was obeying his mother and opening the furnace door. A scream climbed from below as his face was blasted off, then, the sound of the basement door being smashed open.

Harry looked at Valentin, his repugnance momentarily forgotten.

"We shan't be taking the stairs," the demon said.

Bellowings and chatterings and screechings were already on the rise. Whatever had found birth in the basement, it was precocious.

"We have to find something to break down the door," Valentin said, "*anything*."

Harry tried to think his way through the adjacent offices, his mind's eye peeled for some tool that would make an impression on either the fire door or the substantial chains which kept it closed. But there was nothing useful; only typewriters and filing cabinets.

"*Think*, man," said Valentin.

He ransacked his memory. Some heavy-duty instrument was required. A crowbar, a hammer. An ax! There was an agent called Shapiro on the floor below, who exclusively represented porno performers, one of whom had attempted to blow his balls off the month before. She'd failed, but he'd boasted one day on the stairs that he had now purchased the biggest ax he could find, and would happily take the head of any client who attempted an attack upon his person.

The commotion from below was simmering down. The hush was, in its way, more distressing than the din that had preceded it.

"We haven't got much time," the demon said.

Harry left him at the chained door. "Can you get Swann?" he said, as he ran.

"I'll do my best."

By the time Harry reached the top of the stairs, the last chatterings were dying away; as he began down the flight they ceased altogether. There was no way now to judge how close the enemy were. On the next floor? Round the next corner? He tried not to think of them, but his feverish imagination populated every dirty shadow.

He reached the bottom of the flight without incident, however, and slunk along the darkened second-floor corridor to Shapiro's office. Halfway to his destination, he heard a low hiss behind him. He looked over his shoulder, his body itching to run. One of the radiators, heated beyond its limits, had sprung a leak. Steam was escaping from its pipes, and hissing as it went. He let his heart climb down out of his mouth, and then hurried on to the door of Shapiro's office, praying that the man hadn't simply been shooting the breeze with his talk of axes. If so, they were done for. The office was locked, of course, but he elbowed the frosted glass out, and reached through to let himself in, fumbling for the light switch. The walls were plastered with photographs of sex goddesses. They scarcely claimed Harry's attention; his panic fed upon itself with every heartbeat he spent here. Clumsily he scoured the office, turning furniture over in his impatience. But there was no sign of Shapiro's ax.

Now, another noise from below. It crept up the staircase and along the corridor in search of him—an unearthly cacophony like the one he'd heard on Eighty-third Street. It set his teeth on edge; the nerve of his rotting molar began to throb afresh. What did the music signal? Their advance?

In desperation he crossed to Shapiro's desk to see if the man had any other item that might be pressed into service, and there tucked out of sight between desk and wall, he found the ax. He pulled it from hiding. As Shapiro had boasted, it was hefty, its weight the first reassurance

Harry had felt in too long. He returned to the corridor. The steam from the fractured pipe had thickened. Through its veils it was apparent that the concert had taken on new fervor. The doleful wailing rose and fell, punctuated by some flaccid percussion.

He braved the cloud of steam and hurried to the stairs. As he put his foot on the bottom step the music seemed to catch him by the back of the neck, and whisper *"Listen"* in his ear. He had no desire to listen; the music was vile. But somehow—while he was distracted by finding the ax—it had wormed its way into his skull. It drained his limbs of strength. In moments the ax began to seem an impossible burden.

"Come on down," the music coaxed him, *"come on down and join the band."*

Though he tried to form the simple word "No," the music was gaining influence upon him with every note played. He began to hear melodies in the caterwauling, long circuitous themes that made his blood sluggish and his thoughts idiot. He knew there was no pleasure to be had at the music's source—that it tempted him only to pain and desolation—yet he could not shake off its delirium. His feet began to move to the call of the pipers. He forgot Valentin, Swann, and all ambition for escape, and instead began to descend the stairs. The melody became more intricate. He could hear voices now, singing some charmless accompaniment in a language he didn't comprehend. From somewhere above, he heard his name called, but he ignored the summons. The music clutched him close, and now—as he descended the next flight of stairs—the musicians came into view.

They were brighter than he had anticipated, and more various. More baroque in their configurations (the manes, the multiple heads); more particular in their decoration (the suit of flayed faces, the rouged anus); and, his drugged eyes now stung to see, more atrocious in their choice of instruments. Such instruments! Byron was there, his bones sucked clean and drilled with stops, his bladder and lungs teased through slashes in his body as reservoirs for the piper's breath. He was draped, inverted, across the musician's lap, and even now was played upon—the sacs ballooning, the tongueless head giving out a wheezing note. Dorothea was slumped beside him, no less transformed, the strings of her gut made taut between her splinted legs like an obscene lyre, her breasts drummed upon. There were other instruments too, men who had come off the street and fallen prey to the band. Even

Chaplin was there, much of his flesh burned away, his rib cage played upon indifferently well.

"I didn't take you for a music lover," Butterfield said, drawing upon a cigarette and smiling in welcome. "Put down your ax and join us."

The word *ax* reminded Harry of the weight in his hands, though he couldn't find his way through the bars of music to remember what it signified.

"Don't be afraid," Butterfield said, "you're an innocent in this. We hold no grudge against you."

"Dorothea . . ." he said.

"She was an innocent too," said the lawyer, "until we showed her some sights."

Harry looked at the woman's body, at the terrible changes that they had wrought upon her. Seeing them, a tremor began in him, and something came between him and the music; the imminence of tears blotted it out.

"Put down the ax," Butterfield told him.

But the sound of the concert could not compete with the grief that was mounting in him. Butterfield seemed to see the change in his eyes, the disgust and anger growing there. He dropped his half-smoked cigarette and signaled for the music making to stop.

"Must it be death, then?" Butterfield said, but the inquiry was scarcely voiced before Harry started down the last few stairs toward him. He raised the ax and swung it at the lawyer but the blow was misplaced. The blade plowed the plaster of the wall, missing its target by a foot.

At this eruption of violence the musicians threw down their instruments and began across the lobby, trailing their coats and tails in blood and grease. Harry caught their advance from the corner of his eye. Behind the horde, still rooted in the shadows, was another form, larger than the largest of the mustered demons, from which there now came a thump that might have been that of a vast jackhammer. He tried to make sense of sound or sight, but could do neither. There was no time for curiosity; the demons were almost upon him.

Butterfield glanced round to encourage their advance, and Harry—catching the moment—swung the ax a second time. The blow caught Butterfield's shoulder; the arm was instantly severed. The lawyer shrieked; blood sprayed the wall. There was no time for a third blow, however. The demons were reaching for him, smiles lethal.

He turned on the stairs and began up them, taking the steps two, three, and four at a time. Butterfield was still shrieking below; from the flight above he heard Valentin calling his name. He had neither time nor breath to answer.

They were on his heels, their ascent a din of grunts and shouts and beating wings. And behind it all, the jackhammer thumped its way to the bottom of the flight, its noise more intimidating by far than the chatterings of the berserkers at his back. It was in his belly, that thump, in his bowels. Like death's heartbeat, steady and irrevocable.

On the second landing he heard a whirring sound behind him, and half turned to see a human-headed moth the size of a vulture climbing the air toward him. He met it with the ax blade and hacked it down. There was a cry of excitement from below as the body flapped down the stairs, its wings working like paddles. Harry sped up the remaining flight to where Valentin was standing, listening. It wasn't the clatter he was attending to, or the cries of the lawyer; it was the jackhammer.

"They brought the Raparee," he said.

"I wounded Butterfield—"

"I heard. But that won't stop them."

"We can still try the door."

"I think we're too late, my friend."

"No!" said Harry, pushing past Valentin. The demon had given up trying to drag Swann's body to the door, and had laid the magician out in the middle of the corridor, his hands crossed on his chest. In some last mysterious act of reverence he had set folded paper bowls at Swann's head and feet, and laid a tiny origami flower at his lips. Harry lingered only long enough to reacquaint himself with the sweetness of Swann's expression, and then ran to the door and proceeded to hack at the chains. It would be a long job. The assault did more damage to the ax than to the steel links. He didn't dare give up, however. This was their only escape route now, other than flinging themselves to their deaths from one of the windows. That he would do, he decided, if the worst came to the worst. Jump and die, rather than be their plaything.

His arms soon became numb with the repeated blows. It was a lost cause; the chain was unimpaired. His despair was further fueled by a cry from Valentin—a high, weeping call that he could not leave unanswered. He left the fire door and returned past the body of Swann to the head of the stairs.

The demons had Valentin. They swarmed on him like wasps on a sugar stick, tearing him apart. For the briefest of moments he struggled free of their rage, and Harry saw the mask of humanity in rags and the truth glistening bloodily beneath. He was as vile as those besetting him, but Harry went to his aid anyway, as much to wound the demons as to save their prey.

The wielded ax did damage this way and that, sending Valentin's tormentors reeling back down the stairs, limbs lopped, faces opened. They did not all bleed. One sliced belly spilled eggs in thousands, one wounded head gave birth to tiny eels, which fled to the ceiling and hung there by their lips. In the melee he lost sight of Valentin. Forgot about him, indeed, until he heard the jackhammer again, and remembered the broken look on Valentin's face when he'd named the thing. He'd called it the *Raparee*, or something like that.

And now, as his memory shaped the word, it came into sight. It shared no trait with its fellows; it had neither wings nor mane nor vanity. It seemed scarcely even to be flesh, but *forged*, an engine that needed only malice to keep its wheels turning.

At its appearance, the rest retreated, leaving Harry at the top of the stairs in a litter of spawn. Its progress was slow, its half-dozen limbs moving in oiled and elaborate configurations to pierce the walls of the staircase and so haul itself up. It brought to mind a man on crutches, throwing the sticks ahead of him and levering his weight after, but there was nothing invalid in the thunder of its body, no pain in the white eye that burned in its sickle head.

Harry thought he had known despair, but he had not. Only now did he taste its ash in his throat. There was only the window left for him. That, and the welcoming ground. He backed away from the top of the stairs, forsaking the ax.

Valentin was in the corridor. He was not dead, as Harry had presumed, but kneeling beside the corpse of Swann, his own body drooling from a hundred wounds. Now he bent close to the magician. Offering his apologies to his dead master, no doubt. But no. There was more to it than that. He had the cigarette lighter in his hand, and was lighting a taper. Then, murmuring some prayer to himself as he went, he lowered the taper to the mouth of the magician. The origami flower caught and flared up. Its flame was oddly bright, and spread with supernatural efficiency across Swann's face and down his body. Valentin hauled himself to his feet, the firelight burnishing his scales. He found enough strength to incline his head to the body as its cremation began, and then his wounds overcame him. He fell backward, and lay still. Harry watched as the flames mounted. Clearly the body had been sprinkled with gasoline or something similar, for the fire raged up in moments, gold and green.

Suddenly, something took hold of his leg. He looked down to see that a demon, with flesh like ripe raspberries, still had an appetite for him. Its tongue was coiled around Harry's shin, its claws reached for his groin. The assault made him forget the cremation or the Raparee. He bent to tear at the tongue with his bare hands, but its slickness confounded his attempts. He staggered back as the demon climbed his body, its limbs embracing him.

The struggle took them to the ground, and they rolled away from the stairs, along the other arm of the corridor. The struggle was far from uneven; Harry's repugnance was at least the match of the demon's ardor. His torso pressed to the ground, he suddenly remembered the Raparee. Its advance reverberated in every board and wall.

Now it came into sight at the top of the stairs, and turned its slow head toward Swann's funeral pyre. Even from this distance Harry could see that Valentin's last-ditch attempts to destroy his master's body had failed. The fire had scarcely begun to devour the magician. They would have him still.

Eyes on the Raparee, Harry neglected his more intimate enemy, and it thrust a piece of flesh into his mouth. His throat filled up with pungent fluid; he felt himself choking. Opening his mouth, he bit down hard upon the organ, severing it. The demon did not cry out, but released sprays of scalding excrement from pores along its back, and disengaged itself. Harry spat its muscle out as the demon crawled away. Then he looked back toward the fire.

All other concerns were forgotten in the face of what he saw.

Swann had stood up.

He was burning from head to foot. His hair, his clothes, his skin. There was no part of him that was not alight. But he was standing, nevertheless, and raising his hands to his audience in welcome.

The Raparee had ceased its advance. It stood a yard or two from Swann, its limbs absolutely still, as if it were mesmerized by this astonishing trick.

Harry saw another figure emerge from the head of the stairs. It was Butterfield. His stump was roughly tied off, a demon supported his lopsided body.

"Put out the fire," demanded the lawyer of the Raparee, "it's not so difficult."

The creature did not move.

"*Go on,*" said Butterfield. "It's just a trick of his. He's dead, damn you. It's just conjuring."

"No," said Harry.

Butterfield looked his way. The lawyer had always been insipid. Now he was so pale his existence was surely in question.

"What do you know?" he said.

"It's not conjuring," said Harry. "It's *magic.*"

Swann seemed to hear the word. His eyelids fluttered open, and he slowly reached into his jacket and with a flourish produced a handkerchief. It too was on fire. It too was unconsumed. As he shook it out tiny bright birds leaped from its folds on humming wings. The Raparee was entranced by this sleight of hand. Its gaze followed the illusory birds as they rose and were dispersed, and in that moment the magician stepped forward and embraced the engine.

It caught Swann's fire immediately, the flames spreading over its flailing limbs. Though it fought to work itself free of the magician's hold, Swann was not to be denied. He clasped it closer than a long-lost brother, and would not leave it be until the creature began to wither in the heat. Once the decay began, it seemed the Raparee was devoured in seconds, but it was difficult to be certain. The moment—as in the best performances—was held suspended. Did it last a minute? Two minutes? Five? Harry would never know. Nor did he care to analyze. Disbelief was for cowards, and doubt a fashion that crippled the spine. He was content to watch—not knowing if Swann lived or died, if birds, fire, corridor, or if he himself—Harry D'Amour—were real or illusory.

Finally, the Raparee was gone. Harry got to his feet. Swann was also standing, but his farewell performance was clearly over.

The defeat of the Raparee had bested the courage of the horde. They had fled, leaving Butterfield alone at the top of the stairs.

"This won't be forgotten, or forgiven," he said to Harry. "There's no rest for you. Ever. I am your enemy."

"I hope so," said Harry.

He looked back toward Swann, leaving Butterfield to his retreat. The magician had laid himself down again. His eyes were closed, his hands replaced on his chest. It was as if he had never moved. But now the fire was showing its true teeth. Swann's flesh began to bubble, his clothes to peel off in smuts and smoke. It took a long while to do the job, but eventually the fire reduced the man to ash.

By that time it was after dawn, but today was Sunday, and Harry knew there would be no visitors to interrupt his labors. He would have time to gather up the remains, to pound the bone shards and put them with the ashes in a duffel bag. Then he would go out and find himself a bridge or a dock, and put Swann into the river.

There was precious little of the magician left once the fire had done its work, and nothing that vaguely resembled a man.

Things came and went away; that was a kind of magic. And in between? Pursuits and conjurings, horrors, guises. The occasional joy.

That there was room for joy, ah! that was magic too.